Nobody Said It'd be Easy

Nobody Said
It'd be Easy

Patty Blount

TULE
PUBLISHING

Chapter One

G ABRIEL IVERS SCRUBBED a hand down his face and prayed for patience. Five, four, three, two...

"Daddy!"

Right on cue. His six-year-old charged into the kitchen where he'd been catching up on some paperwork, followed by his nine-year-old.

"Daddy, Livvie says I can't twirl, but I can so. Right, Daddy? Right?" Maddie lisped slightly thanks to two missing teeth. *Crap.* He'd totally forgotten about the Tooth Fairy's visit tonight. He hoped he had cash in his wallet to put under her pillow.

"Dad, my ears are tired and really want Maddie to shut up," Olivia countered.

He chuckled even as he groaned. "Maddie. We've talked about this."

"But, Daddy—"

Gabe held up a palm. "Madison. It's getting late. I know how much you love to dance but this close to bedtime is quiet time. No twirling. No dancing. No singing. Right now, it's time for books."

"Aw." She stomped a little foot and crossed her arms. "Books are so boring."

"Dad, can I read in *your* room?" Olivia asked.

"Sure."

As Olivia hurried down the hall to his bedroom and shut the door, Maddie whined some more. "That's not fair! I want to read in your room, too."

"Your sisters are allowed in my room because I can trust them not to break anything. Since you just told me how boring books are, I don't think you'll be reading in there. I think you'll be jumping on my bed."

Madison was, by far, his most impulsive child, which—because she was also his most energetic—unnerved him.

"I'll be good, Daddy. I will, I promise. Please, can I?"

Gabe glanced at the clock on the stove and winced. Time had gotten past him. "Not tonight. It's already too late. Right now, bath time and then, bed."

It was actually past time. Baby Emerson was already down for the night. At two, she didn't last long past seven-thirty so as soon as dinner was done, it was bath and bed for her while the other girls watched TV or played quietly. It was now almost eight-thirty but he still hadn't given Maddie a bath. He permitted Kimberly and Olivia to stay up until ten or so. Staggering his daughters' bedtimes was extra work but often the only way he got one-on-one time with them.

He closed his laptop and the notes he was jotting down in a small notebook, slid both carefully to the top shelf in the bookcase in his living room. "Come on, Ducky. Fast bath tonight. I already let you stay up later than usual."

To his shock, Maddie didn't fight him. "Okay, Daddy." And then she let out one of her trademarked gasps. "I know! I can play with the finger paints in the bathtub."

He didn't answer because sometimes, you had to pick your battles. He took her hand, led her to the bathroom opposite the bedroom and started the water running. "Strip, but don't get in that tub yet, okay?"

"Okay, Daddy."

He went into the girls' bedroom where Emmy breathed deeply in her crib. He was ridiculously grateful that she could sleep through the chaos the rest of the girls could create. He grabbed pajamas for Maddie and returned to the bathroom.

"Ooo, unicorn jammies. Yay! I really like unicorns, Daddy. Can we get one?"

He lifted her into the tub, held her while she settled. "No, honey. They're not real."

"Aw." She found a way to extend that sound into three different syllables. "They're so cute."

"What would you do with a unicorn?" he asked, hoping to distract her from wanting to play. He grabbed the small bucket he kept on the tub ledge, filled it, then poured it out over her long dark hair.

"I'd feed it and comb its pretty white hair and put ribbons in it and it would be my best friend."

He shampooed her hair, cursing mentally when he noticed another snarl. "Where would it sleep?"

"In my bed."

He laughed. "Where would you sleep?"

"I could sleep with Livvie."

Yeah, *that* would go over well.

He got her hair rinsed and her body washed before his back started to scream—which he considered a major victory.

"Okay, out you go." He pulled the stopper before she could protest and held out his hands. When she stood up, he lifted her out of the tub and into a fluffy towel. "Do you have any more loose teeth?"

He watched while Maddie stuck her tongue in the space where her front teeth used to be.

"Nah. Not yet." Another gasp. "We have to put my tooth under my pillow."

"We will. Right now, let's comb out your hair." He helped her put on fresh underwear and pajamas, and then sat on the toilet with her on his lap to begin the long, often torturous process of hair detangling.

Of the four girls, Maddie most resembled her mother. She had the same huge brown eyes, the same thick dark hair that had caught Gabe's eye back when he was fifteen years old. He'd married Janey right after college, popped out a kid or four...and then, Bam!

She was gone.

Been gone for two years now. Two years and two months, to be exact. Not that he was counting or anything.

Okay, so maybe he was counting.

It was just something he did to see how long it took to get over the love of your life dying. One year? Two?

Nope. Not yet.

Mike said it was time for Gabe to get off the bench. *Get back on the field, man! Get some skin in the game. Get some, get some!* High five, shoulder slap, bro hug. Mike was all about variety. He may have been his oldest and closest friend, but Mike had no idea that Gabe's flesh crawled at the thought of touching another woman, no idea that he stopped caring if he woke up every morning. Mike never understood that Gabe was a one-woman kind of guy so Gabe never told Mike that the only reason he *did* get out of bed every day was because of the four pieces of his heart that still beat.

Kimberly.

Olivia.

Madison.

Emerson.

"Ow, Daddy!"

"Sorry, honey." Gabe drew the brush slowly through Maddie's hair, working on the smaller tangles until her hair lay smooth against her back.

"Daddy, I don't want a new mom."

His hand froze. "Um. Okay. How come?"

She lifted a narrow shoulder. "Livvie said stepmoms are mean."

He swallowed the stream of curses begging to cut loose. She was six years old, six *frigging* years old and shouldn't be thinking about stepmoms, shouldn't be thinking about *new* moms because her mom should still be alive. The injustice of it grabbed him around the throat and threatened to choke him until he shoved it back down and chained it there. When he was sure, when he knew he could speak, he slung an arm over Maddie's shoulders and said, "Well, as it happens, I don't want a new mom either."

That was pure truth. He had no interest in giving the girls a new mom.

But God, he wished he could get the old one back.

"Daddy, can we watch TV a little tonight?" Olivia asked

from the door, pulling him out of his thoughts. "There's a biography on LeeAnne Walters I want to see."

"Who's that?" He smiled with pride. Olivia was more interested in biographies than fiction. Of all the girls, she was his most logical, most curious.

"She's one of the first people who noticed something was wrong with Flint, Michigan's water supply."

"No kidding?" It didn't surprise him that his nine-year-old knew all about Flint's water issues.

"Yep. The show starts at ten."

Gabe frowned. "Liv, that's way past bedtime. I'll record the show for you instead, okay?"

She sighed, but nodded without argument.

"We're done in here if you want to take your shower."

He found an outfit for Maddie to wear to school in the morning, sat with her in the living room while she amused him with more ideas for the care and feeding of a unicorn and tucked her in bed by nine-thirty. Liv was right behind her.

By ten o'clock, Gabe's eyes were drooping and he could barely remember his name but he looked for Kimberly.

"Hey, Cocoa-Pop."

She looked up from the tablet.

"What are you reading?" He glanced at the screen. She angled it so he could see the latest title by a popular young adult author she enjoyed.

"You all set for school in the morning?"

"Yeah. Homework's done."

Amen to that, he thought. He sat on the bed next to her. "You're quiet today. You okay?"

Shrugging, she shifted to make more room for him. "I guess."

"School's okay?"

Another shrug. "It's school. It pretty much sucks."

He huffed out a laugh. "I just wondered if you made any new friends."

She shook her head. "Not really. I have a couple, but I really miss Brenna and Kaylie."

Gabe pressed his lips together. When he took this job and moved to this apartment, he'd thought it would be good for them. After Janey died and all the babysitting arrangements he made fell apart, Janey's parents invited him to move in with them. They adored the girls and he loved them. They were great people. But they had their own ideas on how to raise girls. They didn't support Olivia's curiosity and they could barely tolerate Maddie's exuberance. Because he frequently disagreed with them, he thought it best to find his own arrangement or risk a rift as big as the one between him and *his* mom.

He hardly talked to her. She had her own life and remembered them usually at the holidays. Otherwise, she essentially ignored her granddaughters and he'd decided to stop making excuses for her. He hated to deny the girls their only other relatives so taking this job and this apartment had been his only option.

He wished he'd thought about things like being the new kids in town and sharing one bedroom and one bathroom. At the time, he'd thought being home for the girls when they got out of school instead of out scaling tall structures was all that mattered.

Gabe sighed. "Maybe we could invite them over one day?"

Kimberly shook her head, lowered the blue eyes she'd gotten from him. "And do what? Watch Maddie twirl? No way."

That was a point, he conceded with another sigh. The apartment wasn't big enough for hanging out.

"Skype?"

That put a light in her eyes. "Could I?"

"Sure. But not now. It's bedtime."

"Okay. Can I text them now to ask when it's okay?"

"Sure."

She handed him the tablet so he could log in to the message app. He was hyper-vigilant about the internet. Kim didn't have a cell phone or social media accounts. When she needed Skype or text messaging, she used his accounts and only when he supervised. She didn't have the passwords. He let her text her best friends for a few minutes and then called it.

"They said Saturday, Daddy." She powered down the tablet, left it on his bed.

"That's great. Night."

She pecked him on the cheek. "Night."

Gabe didn't remember changing into pajamas or getting into bed. But he must have gone to bed because suddenly, the baby woke him.

"Dad-dee."

He wrenched an eye open, focused it on the alarm clock blazing the time. Three-twenty-seven—a.m.

Aw, hell.

He forced the other eye open, trying to focus on the slight form of his youngest child standing in the band of light cast by the bulb he always left on in the hall, her lower lip stuck out about a mile and huge tears dripping down her face.

He reached out and lifted his daughter into his arms. "Hey, hey, hey, what's the matter, E-Rex?" he murmured. She put her head right on his chest, sniffling back tears. He cuddled her there for a minute or...or five. At twelve and nine, Kimberly and Olivia were too big to be held against his heart like this. They grumbled and complained about sharp whiskers. But baby Emerson?

He was holding on to this one as long as she'd let him.

She stuffed a thumb in her mouth and wriggled her butt trying to burrow closer, a sign that she was sleepy. That butt was clad in a very soggy diaper, which explained why she was awake at this unholy hour.

Still holding her, he got out of bed and took her back to her room. He grabbed a fresh diaper from the package on top of a chest he'd refinished in antique white back when Kimberly was born, and made a fast job of changing Emmy's bottom. Job done, he tried to tuck her back into her crib, but she threw a leg over the rail before he'd taken one step.

"Dad-dee!"

"Shh, shh, shh!" He did *not* want the entire house awake. First thing tomorrow, he was installing a roof on her crib. With locks. And an alarm system. A silent one, of course.

"Put your little head down. Want Daddy to rub your back?"

She gave him a solemn heart-breaking nod and obediently rolled over. He adjusted her blanket, put a large hand on that small back and rubbed in slow circles. She was just about asleep when Madison's head lifted.

"Daddy, is it morning time?"

Silently spelling out another curse, Gabe shook his head. "No, Maddie. Go back to sleep."

"But why are you up?"

"I don't *want* to be up. Emmy had a bad dream."

"Oh."

Gabe could see the wheels spinning in Maddie's little head. When she gasped and thrust her hand under her pillow, he almost cursed out loud.

He'd forgotten about the Tooth Fairy.

"Aw." She whined. "The Tooth Fairy didn't come!"

"Maddie, it's not morning. You have to go to sleep and stay asleep. Tomorrow, you'll see the Tooth Fairy will be here."

"I was asleep but I'm not tired anymore."

Gabe wasn't buying a word of this for a minute.

"You hafta rub my back, too."

"I don't think so, Maddie."

"But, Daddy, that's not fair! Rub my back, too. Pleeeeeeease?"

A groan from the bottom bunk of the beds on the other wall made Gabe sigh.

"Will you shut up, Maddie?" Olivia said. "I have a test in the morning."

Gabe prayed for patience. "Go back to sleep, all of you."

"I was asleep until everybody started crying," Olivia protested.

"Rub my back," Maddie cried, which woke Emmy up again, which got Olivia huffing and complaining.

"Oh my God, just shut up for five freakin' minutes, Maddie!" Olivia jumped out of her bunk in an explosion of blankets, grabbed her pillow, and stalked out of the room.

"Where are you going?" he demanded.

"I'm sleeping in your bed," she announced and got her sisters riled up all over again.

"That's not fair!" Maddie scrambled up but Gabe was too fast for her. Gently, but firmly, he tucked her back into her own bed.

"Dad-dee bed," Emmy cried.

What little patience he still had finally snapped. "Madison Elise, what's not fair is Daddy being too tired to work. Now, you are going to stay in this bed for the rest of the night or there will be no movie for you tomorrow. Is that clear?"

All the girls knew when Dad whipped out their middle names, he wasn't happy. Still, he knew she was just being six. Forcing his temper down, he smiled when she nodded and settled back onto her pillow.

He resettled Emmy back into her bed, rubbed her back for a few more minutes while Madison sniffled back tears. Feeling like the world's biggest ass, he pressed a noisy kiss to Maddie's cheek. "See you in the morning, sweetheart."

"Ow, Daddy. Stabby beard."

"I don't have a beard, silly goose. My face is tired and needs to sleep. Tomorrow, it'll be smooth again."

Intrigued, Madison rolled over. "It will?"

"Sure will." He drew a hand over his face, the whiskers

rasping under his fingers. The girls hated the whiskers. He probably should shave twice a day, but who had the time? "Better go to sleep so my face can wake up soft later, okay?"

"Okay, Daddy. Night!"

"Good night."

He closed the door to the girls' room with a sigh. Three out of four asleep. He'd give Liv a few minutes and move her back to her own bed. On bare feet, he padded to the small galley kitchen off the apartment's living room, grabbed the notebook off its shelf and a couple of pain relief tablets from the bottle high up in a kitchen cabinet for the headache forming behind his eyeballs.

His family needed a bigger place before they killed each other...or him. The only reason he'd taken this unit was because it was one of the perks of being the building superintendent—no rent. But four girls in one bedroom was a disaster. One of the building's three-bedroom duplexes had just been vacated. Its rent was high. Higher than the mortgage on the upstate house he and Janey had owned before her death. But maybe he could talk Mike's uncle, the building's owner, into letting him pay the difference between the rent on this apartment and that one. He wasn't sure how he was going to swing that amount, though.

Twenty minutes later, he collapsed on the sofa and dropped his head into his hands with a loud sigh. He had a plan now, a plan that would take a lot of juggling, but could work. All he had to do was find some part-time engineering or inspecting work, pick up some extra cash. He could still manage the building.

He needed to square it with Mike first, but he wasn't

worried.

Mike Kinsella had been Gabe's friend since they were Maddie's age. They'd been through it all…school, football, broken hearts, first cars and first loves. Mike had been Gabe's best man and was godfather to all four of his girls. And when he'd lost Janey, Mike was the first call Gabe had made.

Gabe had a difficult time facing Janey's parents after her death. Oh, they'd welcomed him into their family, but Janey died on his watch. How the hell do you apologize for that? How do you ever make that right? They never said it. They didn't need to.

He blamed himself.

Mike helped him care for the girls. He called his uncle, who owned several buildings in the New York borough of Queens, including a garden apartment building in Bayside. Styled like an old Tudor, it took up most of a city block, featured twenty ground-floor and second-floor apartments arranged around a central courtyard. It needed a new superintendent to live on-site in exchange for a small salary and two-bedroom apartment, rent-free.

They'd headed to Bayside just over a year ago. For the most part, it worked well. But the girls were really getting on each other's nerves, and by extension, his. If he didn't find a way to separate Kimberly and Olivia from Madison soon, blood might be drawn. Chatty Maddie could talk the ears off a dead body and he was close to slitting his own throat.

He lifted his eyes to the picture the kids had put on the refrigerator door. Janey's beautiful brown eyes looked back at him, full of humor and love. It had been taken the day they'd brought Emerson home from the hospital, baby number four and the absolute last, he'd sworn. Janey had merely laughed and said, "We'll see." Exactly what she'd said after each of the previous children. Only this time, it had been true. She'd died barely four months later.

Now, it was up to him to figure out how to manage things like braids and feeding schedules and homework and after-school activities and mean girls and teething, and a host of other childhood issues he'd been utterly unprepared to tackle alone.

"God, Janey. I miss you," he whispered to the photograph. Gabe swore he heard her giggle and figured it was time to grab some sleep. He stood, collected his paperwork into a pile and put it all on top of the refrigerator. His spine popped and cracked in blessed relief. He made sure the stove was off—it was, and the door locked—it was. He walked back to his bedroom, stopping at the door just across from the bathroom where a sign said *Girlz Rule* in pink glitter paint. He quietly opened it, walked inside, aiming his cell phone's flashlight app to avoid tripping over discarded clothes, toys, and once—a tiny figure who'd fallen out of bed.

Emerson slept with her thumb in her mouth, clutching her Teddy bear. Madison was curled up in a cat shape in her twin bed. Across the room in the top bunk, Kimberly slept soundly. He shut the door, hit the bathroom across the hall, and in his bedroom, watched Olivia breathe for a minute or two. He was too tired to carry her back to her bed so he shuffled back to the couch and stretched out.

He'd sleep here for what was left of the night.

Ah, hell. Maddie's tooth.

He dragged himself upright, found his wallet, and carefully slid a buck under Maddie's pillow, then spent fifteen aggravating minutes trying to find the tooth that had found its way under the bed.

He returned to the sofa, stretched out on his back and finally, fell asleep.

∾

FOUR SECONDS LATER, giggles woke him.

No, no, no, no. It could not be morning.

"Shh, he's waking up!"

That was Kimberly.

More giggles.

"But his face didn't get soft!"

Madison.

"That's because he didn't shave yet, dopey." Olivia. Always the voice of logic.

"I'm not dopey, you are!" Maddie shot back.

More giggles. "Pwetty Dad-dee." Emmy was up, too? Awesome. The gang's all here. He hoped to God he wasn't sporting morning wood because there was no way in hell he wanted to explain *that* to four little girls when he'd had maybe an hour of sound sleep that night. They were already far too fascinated with the concept of peeing while standing up.

Madison had walked in on him when she was about four years old and with wide eyes asked, "What is that big thing, Daddy?" He'd immediately shooed her out of the bathroom so he could finish his business, only to find the group of them having a conference in the hall. Kimberly had put both hands on her narrow hips, cocked her head to the side and said, "Maddie says you can pee standing up. That's not true, is it?" He'd had to mop the bathroom when Olivia had taken that news as a challenge and then, Maddie told everyone they met from the mail carrier to the waiting room at Janey's obstetrics appointment about his *big thing* that lets him pee while standing up.

Janey had laughed herself silly about that but he'd been afraid he'd have to enroll the lot of them in therapy. Fixing the lock on the bathroom door had immediately climbed to the top of his to-do list.

Several small hands were in his hair. The giggles continued. He let out a snore every few minutes, hating to ruin their fun. They'd had precious little of that in their young lives, especially Kimberly. She was the oldest. She remembered. Emerson wouldn't remember at all.

He never could decide which was worse.

Somebody crawled over his prostrate form, putting a small foot right on top of that *big thing* and his eyes popped open whether he wanted them to or not.

"Hi, Dad-dee!" Emmy slapped both chubby hands to his face and grinned down at him.

"Mmm."

"Morning, Daddy!" Maddie was at his feet.

"Hi, Daddy." Olivia. She was sitting on the arm of the couch.

"Hey, Dad." Kimberly, leaning against the wall.

All four of them had wide, wide smiles.

"What? What's funny?"

Giggles.

He glanced at the oven clock, saw that it was past seven. Damn it. He had to get everybody dressed, fed, and off to school by eight and be back here by nine for the inspector.

"Okay, okay, 'nuff laughing at the old man. Everybody get dressed. Breakfast in ten." He flung aside the blanket and swung his legs to the floor, stretching his arms over his still-tired body. The girls ran back to their room, the giggles and shrieks going through him like drill bits. Gabe stood up, staggered to the bathroom—made damn sure the door was locked—and lifted the toilet seat. When he'd finished and glanced at his reflection in the mirror, he let out a laugh. There were at least two dozen clips and barrettes in his too-long hair—pink ones, purple ones, blue ones, yellow ones. He looked like a deranged unicorn.

He began pulling them from his hair but the phone rang.

"Daddy, it's Mrs. Morgan!" Kimberly called.

He forgot about the clips and took the phone from her. "Well," Gabe smiled down at her, tugging on a lock of his hair. "I guess it could have been worse. They could have given me a makeover while I slept." He shivered dramatically, earning a big smile from his eldest daughter. "Why don't you grab a spatula while I crack these eggs?" Into the phone, he said, "Hey, Mrs. M. What can I do for you?"

"It's my toilet, Gabe. It won't flush."

"Did it overflow?"

"No, thank goodness. But nothing happens at all when I jiggle the handle."

"Okay. I'll be over later. Meanwhile, you come on over here and use mine."

"Thank you, I'll do that."

He ended the call, tossed the phone to the table. Kimberly fed some bread into the toaster while he brewed a single cup of coffee.

A large one.

"Maddie! Livvie! Get moving."

"Coming, Daddy!"

It didn't take long to scramble the eggs, butter the toast. By the time all his daughters joined them at the table, he had the juice poured and a handful of Cheerios and banana slices on Emmy's tray.

"Hair?" he asked.

Olivia spoke up first. "A braid, Daddy."

Madison was next. "Ponytail!"

Kimberly didn't answer him.

"Kim?"

She only shrugged. "I'll do it."

He grabbed the basket where he usually kept the girls' hair accessories from its home on the kitchen counter and started pulling out elastics and clips and a brush. Maddie's hair was snarled again and she began to scream he was hurting her. "Maddie, maybe we should get your hair cut short."

"No! I want my hair like Mommy's."

"But you've got a giant knot in your hair."

She stuck her lip out and crossed her arms, so he grabbed the bottle of detangler and tried again. He managed to pull it up into a messy ponytail, finishing it off with a pair of rainbow barrettes. Olivia's braid took a bit longer, but soon he had her hair secured, too. The baby was easy. Emerson didn't have much hair yet, so he scooped the top up and added a fabric Velcro holder.

His cell phone rang next. Gabe checked the ID and took the call. "Jim! Long time." Jim was a coworker from his time at Paradigm Construction.

"Hi, Gabe. I'm sorry for calling so early, but I've got an opportunity for you, if you're interested. Remember that fire escape project? It's turning out to be a real beast. I need someone like you to help manage it."

Gabe did a mental fist-pump of victory. Here was that extra money he needed. "Sounds great, but can I call you later? I've gotta get my kids to school."

A knock on the door added more chaos to his morning.

"It's Mrs. Morgan, Daddy," Olivia announced from the sofa she'd jumped on to look out the window.

He unfastened the deadbolt, opened the door and revealed the elderly tenant from Apartment B, still wearing her bathrobe.

"Just down the hall, Mrs. M."

She shot him a look of pure mortification, but nodded. He turned back to the phone in his hand. "Sorry, Jim. You were saying?"

"Look, can we just discuss this idea in person? I want you to return as a consultant. Part-time. Set your own schedule and name your rate."

"Yeah, but not today. I don't have babysitting lined up." Gabe snagged a pen and notepad from the drawer in the kitchen, calculating how much compensation to request so he could finally afford that duplex, as well as babysitters to cover the time he'd be away.

"Jim, I'll get back to you this afternoon. I'm sorry, it's nuts here right now." He hung up just as Mrs. Morgan walked out of his bathroom and Emmy hurled her cup to the floor.

"Sorry, Daddy." Kimberly dove under the table to retrieve the baby's cup, hurried to the sink to rinse it off before giving it back to a crying Emerson.

"You need help." Mrs. Morgan surveyed the kitchen with her hands on her hips just as the phone rang again.

"I got this," Gabe assured her while Olivia slid out of her chair to bring him the magnetic clipboard hanging on the refrigerator. He jotted down Mrs. Morgan's toilet and then answered the next call.

"Gabe, it's Mike."

"Hey, Mike," he said, grinning. "Glad you called. I need to run something by you."

"Hold that thought. I'll be by Friday night, but just got off the phone with my uncle. That vacant duplex? He's renting it to some friend of a friend's daughter. Bad marriage, worse divorce. She needs a new address fast. She's moving in this morning and she'll need the keys."

Gabe's stomach fell. He shut his eyes and tamped down on the disappointment as his entire plan for that same duplex went up in a finger snap. The same plan he'd sketched out through eyes so tired, he was sure they'd bled. "Oh. Right. The duplex. Okay. No worries, Mike." His voice had gone up an entire octave.

"Name's Amelia. She's had some bad luck lately. Besides the divorce, there was some kind of a surgery. She needs a place and—well…"

"It's okay, Mike. Don't sweat it," Gabe played it easy while inside, he felt like a failure. The girls needed more space. He *had* to find a way to make that happen.

"I'll make you a deal. I'll babysit. For the whole weekend. You can head east and fish for two entire days."

"Deal," Gabe said instantly.

Mike laughed. "I knew that would work. Now put the girls on the phone."

While the girls talked to "Uncle" Mike, Gabe let go of his dream to give the girls more space. Maybe he could build some organizers or something for this apartment.

It wasn't ideal. But he'd make it work.

He had to.

Chapter Two

A MELIA BLAKE SAT beside the window that overlooked 7th Avenue. New York hummed as traffic idled and pedestrians clogged the intersection but she wasn't looking at them. She was looking for *him*.

She glanced at the watch on her wrist. Just going on seven AM. She had to get the timing just right. Jared was a creature of habit...as was she. He always left at 6:55. Always. It was now 6:57. From the window of the apartment she'd once shared with him, she watched and waited. At 7:02, she finally spotted him, walking with Candi.

With an I.

Lia sneered. *How old do you have to be to stop dotting that I with a cutesy heart?* That's what Jared wondered when they'd met their new upstairs neighbor three years earlier. It hadn't taken Candi long, Lia noted. Three years to steal her husband.

Her life.

Then again, Lia had no real idea exactly when Jared had first hooked up with Candi-with-an-I. She'd been too busy juggling temperature charts and infertility specialists, not to mention her clients. She'd had no clue he was unhappy, no clue he'd been cheating on her, no clue her own marriage

22

was anything but an illusion, just like her parents'.

That's the word Jared used when he asked her for a divorce. *Illusion*.

She'd been in the hospital, recovering from a miscarriage and emergency hysterectomy.

He'd walked in, sat down, told her what was up, and then, just to rub salt into her freshly stapled incision, told her he'd never meant for any of this to happen, that he was sorry. He'd wanted to leave sooner, but when she'd gotten pregnant—finally—he'd felt that he had to stay. For the baby's sake.

A cliché. He ended their marriage and her dreams with a stupid cliché.

She hated him in that moment. He should have left the minute he'd developed feelings for Candi-with-an-I. If he had, she'd never have gotten pregnant. And if she'd never gotten pregnant, she'd still have that dream of motherhood to sustain her.

In a gesture no doubt intended to be magnanimous, Jared told her she was welcome to their apartment. He'd already moved upstairs. Ridiculously, she *had*. She had no idea what she'd been thinking.

She managed half a laugh. Thinking was obviously not so high on her to-do list. She'd been too busy mourning.

She remembered sitting alone in her hospital room with the bouquet of flowers in her arms, plucking off every last petal and leaf, imagining they were Jared's balls. She was still plucking when Roseann and Vivian arrived and by the time her mother showed up, her anger had given way to grief...grief not just for the child she'd lost and the husband she'd loved, but for something that went way deeper.

"Where's Dad?" she'd asked her mother, her voice thick from crying, but Victoria had lifted her shoulders the way she always did when Lia asked that question.

"Oh, he wanted to be here, *amie*, but he had that golf thing."

Golf. Right.

Lia was about ten years old when she'd guessed the truth about Santa Claus. She was only slightly older when she'd figured out Greg Blake was a man who'd never wanted kids or a wife and after he'd found himself chained by both, enjoyed pretending he had neither. Evidently, not even his daughter's miscarriage and emergency hysterectomy could compel him to skip a date with his latest good-time girl. When she was thirteen, she asked Victoria why she put up with it but her mother shushed her. She asked again when she was seventeen and Victoria said she knew who Gregory Blake was when she married him.

Which was no answer at all if you asked Lia.

When she was a child, she'd questioned and wondered and cried alone in her bed at night, and promised herself that when she grew up, she'd make the family she wished she'd had. She'd find a husband who respected her, who loved her, and together, they'd have children who'd never question or wonder or cry alone.

While she'd curled in a ball in that hospital bed, she mourned that child as much as the one she'd lost...maybe even more.

"Amelia, I told you from the beginning that men don't appreciate women with lofty goals but you insisted on starting that business and now look what happened," Victoria told her. "Your husband is playing house with someone else." Victoria seemed incapable of seeing her own hypocrisy and Lia was too full of grief to deal with her.

That business had been another dream of hers. Oh, sure, it had never held a place of prominence like her dream of a loving family. But it was important. It gave her a sense of pride.

It was *hers*.

Jared encouraged her and spent countless hours talking over ideas and strategies with her...well, she talked and he just mm-hmm'd in the right places. She knew he never really believed she'd succeed so she'd been determined to prove she could. Lia provided remote administrative help to a variety of clients—things like specialized subject matter research for authors of novels and textbooks, social network monitoring for other small business owners, invoicing and bookkeeping, newsletter management, blogging, and essential marketing activities. She had no staff. It was just her, which was okay because she was damn good at this work. She loved that her days were never routine. BVS—*Blake Virtual Services*—took off.

When Lia felt ready to expand operations, hire on staff, find office space, that's when Jared said he wanted to start a family. She put those plans on hold and...and on hold again. When it was clear there was a problem, she began treatment. Fourteen months of it.

For...nothing. No baby. No husband. No family.

But she still had BVS. And she had Roseann Paneduro.

It had been Roseann who'd sent her mother away,

Roseann who'd sat with her while she sobbed for all that she'd lost, and Roseann who'd taken her home with her to recover from surgery. After talking things through with her best friend, Lia decided not to fight Jared on the divorce. What would have been the point? But Lia argued about staying in the apartment she and Jared found and decorated together because yeah, there was some perverse part of her that needed to force him to deal with her.

"Lia, even if he does feel sorry for you—and I truly doubt he's capable of that—he's still going home with Candi. Is that what you want to see every day?"

Yes. Yes, damn it, it was. She wanted, needed Jared to face her, to see the hollows he'd put under her eyes, see the pain he'd etched on her face.

She watched him now, walking down the street to catch the subway he'd already missed, surprised to find no spark of feeling, no pang of pain. Maybe it was because he wasn't the only reason she was lurking behind the curtains they'd hung together.

Candi was.

Lia glanced at her watch again. 7:07 now. At 7:10 every morning, Candi rode the elevator up from the lobby, carrying the to-go cup of coffee she bought after walking Jared to the train station.

It was impossible to hide it now.

Candi had stolen her husband and would soon give birth to his child…the child that should have been *hers*.

Absently, Lia rubbed at one of the scars on her belly. Though they were long since healed, they seemed to ache when she saw Candi's baby bump. As soon as she'd noticed that bump, she'd called Roseann and said, "Help."

Roseann got her a lead on a place in Queens. Bayside, to be exact. A nice duplex in a garden apartment building.

Her phone buzzed. Without pulling her eyes from the window, she answered. "Hello?"

"Lia, get your face away from that window and drive away."

Lia managed a small smile. The jury was out on her parents but she trusted that her friends loved her. "I told them seven-thirty."

Roseann cursed. "Okay, look. As soon as they get there, I want you to leave. Just get in the car and go. Don't look back. The movers know what to do."

"Yeah." Her voice held no interest and Roseann instantly noticed.

"You're making the right decision."

At this, Lia huffed out a laugh. She'd thought Jared was the right decision once. Look where that got her. "It doesn't matter."

"Lia, this new place is perfect. It's far enough away that you won't keep bumping into Jared and Candi every time you turn a corner, yet still close enough for us to hang whenever we want. The train station is like four or five blocks. It's ideal."

Lia shivered at the word. *Ideal.* God, was there ever a more stupid word than *ideal?* Nothing was *ideal* and when it was, it was almost certainly another illusion, like her marriage, like her family.

"...three bedrooms means you can store a lot of your stuff plus set up dedicated office space. That's a write-off, you know." Roseann had been singing the praises of this phantom apartment for days now. And because Roseann thought it was *ideal,* Lia went along. She didn't care that much one way or the other where she lived as long as it wasn't here.

"Okay, the truck just pulled up. I'll call you later."

"Call me when you get there. I'll head out tonight, after work, help you settle in."

"Sure."

Roseann sighed. "Lia. This is a good move. I feel it."

Lia bit her lip. "Yeah. Maybe." She hadn't even seen this apartment. She was trusting someone else to make an important decision because it was so painfully clear her own judgment was faulty.

They ended the call. Lia scooped her planner, her maps, and her notes into a large bag, grabbed her keys and left the apartment without looking back. Down at the curb, she greeted the movers, directed them to her unit. Everything was boxed and labeled. Sorted. She had a grid of the new apartment and knew which boxes were to go in which rooms.

Lists, maps, plans…they were all the tools of her trade. Ruthlessly organized, she shined when hard work turned easy, when things were exactly where they were supposed to be. She relied on working smart, efficiently, and now that she was free of Jared, she could expand her business as she'd always planned and do it all from her new place.

The movers assured her they had the new address and she left them to their business.

As she drove to the tunnel and left Manhattan, Lia decided Roseann was right. Making this move as quickly as she could arrange it meant she'd never have to think of Jared, Candi-with-an-I, or their baby again.

BY THE TIME she'd arrived in Queens, she was starving and decided breakfast should be her first order of business. She traded the Long Island Expressway for the Cross Island Parkway, enjoying the way the September sun glittered on the water to her right. There was a pedestrian path there, full of people jogging, bike riding, and walking dogs. She'd studied the maps and knew the Northern Boulevard exit would get her closest to her destination but elected to drive a few miles further north, to Bell Boulevard.

Lia wanted to explore.

The Bell Boulevard exit took her near a large shopping center. She ducked inside, found a place to park her Hyundai, and treated herself to a bagel and coffee. Bagels were a guilty pleasure and she'd decided finding a great bagel shop had to be her first priority. She sat facing the window and scanned the shopping center. Movie theater, groceries, dry cleaners, restaurants…well, she wouldn't go without a thing.

Twenty minutes later, she was back behind the wheel, traveling south on Bell. She liked the way it felt here. Busy, though not as busy as Manhattan. Tree-lined streets, plenty of shopping. Within minutes, she'd located her new neighborhood and driven by the building…a grand Tudor that took up most of the block it sat on, solid brick construction, sloping roofs, turrets and gables. It reminded her of something out of Austen. There were several restaurant options just up the street, and since she didn't cook, not even a little, this made her happy, especially the fun pizza place on the corner about one block south of her new address. Laundromat next door, which was handy since she hadn't inquired yet if the apartment had facilities on the premises. Her bank had a branch not even ten minutes away.

Ideal, Roseann had said. Okay, maybe...

Her phone buzzed. Rolling her eyes, Lia hit the steering wheel button to answer the call.

"So? Was I right?"

Lia laughed. Speak of the devil herself. "Liking the neighborhood so far. Haven't seen inside yet."

"Well, what are you waiting for?"

"I decided to explore. I just had the most amazing bagel. Now, I'm trying to find a place to park so I can scope out my dinner options."

"Okay. Call me later. Better yet, send me pictures!"

Lia ended the call and pulled to the curb. She needed to get out and walk for a while. See if this neighborhood could feel like home. She watched children walking to school. She gathered her bag and her notes and her phone and her coffee and hit the pavement with a little grin.

So far so good. She'd found the library, introduced herself to a librarian, and loved the friendly welcome she received at a coffee shop that had the most delicious pastries in their case. Lia decided that would be one of her first stops after she got settled. She glanced at the time, decided she should meet the superintendent and collect the keys because the moving van should be arriving soon.

Her car was parked on the corner just ahead. The blare of horns and a few raised voices caught her attention.

"Get the hell out of the way, you faggot!" The driver of the van shouted at a man in the street whose SUV was apparently stalled.

Lia's step faltered.

The man was utterly captivating. Lean and tall, probably a foot taller than her own five feet, four inches, what he did to the faded blue jeans and black T-shirt he wore should be illegal. He had an unruly mop of dark blond hair held by a trio of plastic rainbow barrettes. He flipped up a finger at the shouting driver and lifted the hood on his SUV. With a few angry words, he stalked to the rear of his vehicle and began directing the line of cars around it.

He moved like a cat. Oh, no. Not like Jingles, the cat her grandmother had had when she was a little girl. No. He moved like a panther, all sleek muscle and grace.

She stood and watched him for a minute or two because, why not? And then she sighed. It was so unfair. A man this beautiful, this outrageously sexy, and he was gay.

Just as well, she concluded.

Thanks to Jared, she no longer had any interest in men and hoped she never did again.

Chapter Three

HORNS BLEW BEHIND him. Gabe tried to activate the emergency flashers, but the car was dead. He'd just gotten the girls to school when his SUV stalled at a stop sign.

"F-u-c—"

"Dad-dee?"

"It's okay, E-Rex. Car's broken. Daddy will fix it." Just like he fixed every other damn thing. He grabbed his keys, popped the hood, and locked Emmy inside the vehicle while he stepped out to wave traffic around him. The street was narrow—one lane of traffic in either direction, separated by a double-yellow line. Parked cars edged both sides of the street. There was nowhere to push the SUV—assuming he could even move it by himself. The inspector was due by nine and damn it, he had a whole clipboard of things to do today. Damn it all the way to hell and back again.

A woman walked toward him and he forgot all about his annoyance. She didn't walk so much as…flow, he decided. She wore jeans and a soft, flowy T-shirt under a light jacket, but that wasn't why he noticed her. He'd been caught by her hair. Dark auburn and long, it bounced all around her shoulders, and glowed like fire where the sun hit it. She walked toward him, lips curved in a smile that sucked him in like a vortex. Jeez, she was beautiful.

And jeez, what the hell was wrong with him? He was married—

The pain shot through him like a bullet.

"Car trouble?" she asked.

"Dead battery."

Her eyebrows popped up from behind the oversized sunglasses she wore and he frowned. Why did that shock her? Did she really presume he couldn't diagnose car trouble?

"Ah," she said. That was it. Just *ah*. And continued to look him up and down, the smile on her lips.

Annoyance flared. "What?" he demanded.

She shook her head and held up her hands, one of which clutched a pile of papers and a book. A map, he noticed. And a notebook.

"You're blocking traffic," she finally said.

"I'm aware. As I said, dead battery."

Her lips twitched and Gabe wondered just what the hell she found so funny.

Temper blazed and he bit his tongue, deciding to take the high road. "I don't suppose you have a car nearby and could give me a jump start?"

"Yes, actually, I do," she responded. "Mine is the car you're currently blocking."

She pointed to an aging Hyundai parked right beside his, at the corner. If Gabe hadn't been pissed off, he might have appreciated the serendipity. "This is yours? This is perfect."

"Uh, sorry?"

"I've got jumper cables. Give me a jump and I can move mine right into your spot. Then I won't have to have it towed. I can walk back here and repair it myself—" When? When in the actual hell was he going to do that? "Tonight." He waved a hand. He'd figure it out.

She smiled. "I like your nails."

He glanced down at his cotton candy pink nail polish and tried not to blush. His daughters enjoyed their Friday night manicure parties. They'd been disappointed enough. He wasn't about to tell them real men didn't wear nail polish. "So do my kids."

He strode around to the rear of the truck, snatched the jumper cables and Emmy wriggled around in her car seat. "Dad-dee!"

"It's okay, Emmy. Daddy's fixing the car."

"Dad-dee!" She started to wail and he sighed. Okay. He moved to her door, sprung her free from the car seat. With his daughter in one hand and cables in the other, he returned to the woman who owned the Hyundai.

"Pop your hood."

"What's that?" she asked, a horrified expression on her face.

Gabe looked around. And when he realized she'd been referring to *his daughter*, his jaw clenched. "*That* is commonly known as a baby."

The woman's face went red and she looked down for a moment. "I'm sorry. I didn't mean—I just wondered—well, how are you going to jump-start a car with a baby in your arms? She could get hurt."

Gabe would die before he let that happen. "Fine. You hold her."

The woman literally jumped back a step. "No! I can't do

that."

Through gritted teeth, Gabe asked, "Any particular reason why not?"

"Because!" She waved a hand. "I'm...I'm a stranger. I'll make her cry."

Emmy was already screaming so Gabe figured it couldn't get much worse. "I'll risk it. Here." He leaned over, handed Emmy to her before either of them knew what was happening.

Emmy balked and tried to cling to him like a sock on a towel fresh from the dryer but he peeled her off. "It's okay, baby. Daddy's gonna fix the car. You watch, okay?"

The woman held Emmy like she was a bomb about to detonate, which—Gabe had to admit—wasn't far from the truth. Emmy's wails were climbing the decibel chart.

That's when the most extraordinary transformation happened.

It was almost as if Emmy had cast a spell over this woman. Or maybe, the woman cast a spell over Emmy. Their eyes met. The woman shook her head, as if to clear it. She smiled and cooed at his daughter, bounced her and talked nonsense about the pizza slice on her T-shirt. Emmy soon stopped screaming. She even spoke to the woman, told her that Daddy was going to fix the car.

She may have more confidence in his abilities than he did.

The woman followed Emmy's every syllable, trying to decipher what was often gibberish. Fear gave way to intrigue to...to pure, naked emotion. He figured they were good now, so he made quick work of the job, talking to the baby the whole time.

"Look at the cables, sweetheart. What color is this?"

She blinked tear-filled eyes at him. "Wed."

"Red, good girl. The red one goes here. What color is this one?"

"Back."

"Black, yes! High five." He held up a palm and Emmy slapped it. "Okay, the black one goes here." He hooked up the cables and said, "Hey, go rev your engine a bit, will you?"

"You—um—you want me to rev my engine," she echoed, the words sounding almost dirty the way she said them. She had a soft, sort of smoky voice.

Praying for patience, he slowly nodded. "Please."

Still holding Emmy, the woman slipped behind the wheel, the baby now on her lap.

"Dad-dee! I dwive." Emmy gripped the Hyundai's steering wheel and pulled a face of such intensity, he realized, after a second, that it was probably the one he wore while trying to get the girls to school on time.

Yeah. He'd work on that.

When he heard her engine rev, he tried cranking his ignition. It was slow at first and then, the engine caught. He let it run for a few minutes, his eyes pinned to the dashboard, where an indicator light glowed steady. "Hell." The rest of the curses, he spelled.

He walked back to her. "You can stop revving it now."

"Oh. Good." She took her foot off the accelerator and stuck Emmy out the door like a sack of groceries. He grabbed his daughter and Emmy curled into him like they'd been cruelly parted for centuries.

"Okay, baby girl, okay."

"Car fix, Dad-dee?"

"No, E-Rex. It's not."

The woman lifted her dark glasses, revealing an arresting pair of brown eyes. "It's not? What do you mean, it's not?"

"It's the alternator, not the battery."

"But it's running."

"Yes and it's going to drain again because the alternator isn't charging."

"Great. Are you telling me I'm trapped here?"

"No. It'll hold for a few minutes. As soon as you move your car, I'll slide into your spot, get it out of traffic. Thanks for the jump. And for holding my daughter."

Those amazing dark eyes warmed as they slid to Emmy and the woman nodded. "You're welcome. Are we, um, finished?"

"Yeah. Gimme a minute. I'll get her buckled back into her seat and disconnect the cables."

Gabe soothed Emerson, rocking and bouncing her as he walked back to his SUV. She put her head on his shoulder, one chubby hand wrapped around the longest part of his hair. "Okay, baby girl. We're going to walk home in your stroller, but first, Daddy has to park the car. You sit in your seat for a few minutes. Be right back."

"No! Dad-dee!" She screamed and arched her back, but he got her buckled in. He shut the rear door, disconnected the cables, dropped the hoods on both cars.

"Okay. That's it. You can pull out now. Thanks again."

"You're welcome." She replaced her sunglasses. "Your daughter..." she began and trailed off, biting her lip. "You're very lucky."

"I know it." He grinned.

She said nothing else.

He watched her slide back into her own car, her butt in those jeans hypnotizing him. Then he climbed back into his own vehicle, tossed the cables on the passenger seat. As soon as she pulled out, he maneuvered into her spot, rushing because he knew he had only minutes before the battery drained again, since the alternator wasn't charging it.

The gorgeous redhead was long gone by the time he'd pulled Emmy's stroller from the rear, unfolded it and got her transferred from car seat to stroller. They were only a few blocks from home where the inspector from the city was likely already waiting for him. But he had to make a stop first. He steered Emmy's stroller into the auto parts store on Bell Boulevard, strode to the desk and asked the clerk if they had any alternators in stock for his particular SUV.

Two hundred dollars later, he, his daughter, and his alternator were on their way back to the apartment.

Pete, the city inspector, was a decent guy, and smiled wide at Emmy and wider at him. "Nice hair, man."

Gabe rolled his eyes. "One of these years, I'll find time to get it cut." He pushed Emmy's stroller into the apartment, cut her loose, and grabbed his master key ring. Gabe and Emmy took Pete through each unit, making sure no fire or building codes had been violated by unsuspecting—or uncaring—tenants. Mrs. Morgan complained, loudly, when he knocked on B.

"I'll be back for the toilet as soon as the inspection is done."

"That was hours ago!" she protested.

"I know. I'm sorry. I had car trouble." He fished his key from his pocket. "Here. Take this. Go settle at my place. Make yourself some tea or coffee, watch TV. Take a nap if you want. The bathroom's just down the hall. My place is your place, okay?"

She took his key with a grateful nod.

Gabe adjusted Emmy on his hip and followed Pete to the next unit. Nobody was home in the next several apartments they visited. He'd given all the tenants ample notice about today's inspection, including the time window. They'd had the option of remaining home to observe or leaving their deadbolts unfastened so he could gain access with his master. Unit by unit, they went and an hour later, Pete shook Gabe's hand. "Okay, that's it for this inspection. Thanks, Gabe."

Emmy offered him one chubby hand. "Bye-bye, Miss Emerson." Pete shook the little hand and laughed. "She sure is a cutie, Gabe."

"Takes after her mother," Gabe said, pride in his voice.

"She's a good baby. Never let out a peep, the whole time I was here."

"That's because she's spoiled rotten, aren't you?" Gabe kissed the baby's cheek with a loud smack, making her squeal and giggle. "Okay, we've got a toilet to fix in B. See you soon, Pete."

Fifteen minutes later, Gabe was once again in Mrs. Morgan's unit, holding Emmy with one hand and his toolbox with the other. Mrs. Morgan had followed them. He set baby and tools down on the spotless black and white tile floor all the units had and opened the clasps on the toolbox.

"Okay, Emmy, the toilet is broken. Let's fix it, okay?"

"Potty bwoke?" She shot it a look of concern like it was a puppy. "Car?"

"Yes, sweetheart. We'll fix the car later. Right now, it's the potty's turn."

Gabe saw the water level was higher than normal, so didn't risk a test flush. He removed the tank lid, set it carefully down inside the tub. He reached into the tank, making what Madison called a stinky face, and tugged the chain. The toilet emptied.

"Yay!" Emmy clapped.

"Yay is right," Gabe agreed. "Okay. No clogs."

"No cogs!" Emmy echoed.

Mrs. Morgan put in her two cents. "You're not going to allow that baby to put her hands in the toilet, are you?"

He shook his head. "No, ma'am. But I need her where I can keep an eye on her."

"Well, why didn't you say so? I'll watch her while you work."

That was fine by him. He rubbed his face against his upper arm and nodded. "Okay. Appreciate it."

"Emerson, would you like a cookie?"

Emmy let out a very Maddie-like gasp and nodded. "Cookie!" She happily took off with Mrs. Morgan and Gabe quickly changed out the parts inside the toilet tank in half the time it would have taken him if Emmy had 'helped'.

The parts in this toilet were ancient. He marveled that Mrs. Morgan had not had any issues with it before. He'd better check *all* the toilets. The last thing he needed was one breaking and flooding the unit beneath it. He'd send the tenants an email tonight and set up that inspection.

He scrubbed his hands in the sink, grabbed his toolbox and found Emerson sitting in the living room with Mrs. Morgan, sharing a plate of cookies. The room was tidy, though a bit cluttered. Mrs. Morgan had a fondness for lace doilies. They covered every surface of the room. There was a sofa on the wall, a thickly cushioned chair with an ottoman facing the ancient TV set that sat on a wheeled stand on another wall. A stack of magazines waited on a side table with a pair of glasses on top. The whole place smelled of Lemon Pledge.

"Cookie, Dad-dee."

"I see. And how many have you had?"

"Dis many." She held out all the fingers on both hands and he groaned.

"She's had two." Mrs. Morgan stood up.

"Oh, I guess we'd better work on her counting. The toilet's working fine now. And thanks for minding her." He couldn't help but smile at his daughter as he took her hand.

"Just what sort of name is Emerson for a girl?" she demanded, holding out his key.

Gabe pressed his lips together to hold back the sharp retort that dangled there.

When he didn't say anything, Mrs. Morgan coughed once. "If I'd had a daughter, I'd have named her Diane. That's a good name."

"Have any children yourself?" Gabe asked.

Mrs. Morgan's face brightened. "Three sons. All grown up. One's in California. Another's in Ohio. And the last one's in the service. Got me six grandchildren." She hurried to a table, picked up a framed photo and brought it back to him. "This was my Mother's Day gift."

Dutifully, Gabe examined the smiling faces in the picture. Blinding smiles, dark hair cropped close to their heads, it was easy to see their family resemblance. "That's a beautiful family."

Mrs. Morgan beamed. "She's very well behaved," she offered as she followed them to the door and Gabe recognized that as reparation for her earlier crack at Emerson's name.

"She does me proud. They all do."

"You're doing a good job with them. And for us."

Gabe inclined his head.

"You need a haircut. I'll mind her for you while you do that."

He frowned. Another thing to add to his list. "Have to fix my car first. Say bye-bye, Emmy."

"Bye!" The baby waved, half-eaten cookie clutched in her hand.

Slowly, they walked back to his unit, Apartment F, Emmy stopping to look at flowers and the birds and a squirrel. He had to get the car fixed so he scooped Emmy up in his free arm.

"Does Daddy get a bite of your cookie?"

She held it up to his face and then snatched it away with a squeal. Gabe feigned outrage, as he walked up the steps that led to a central courtyard and froze.

"You," the woman who owned the Hyundai said.

Chapter Four

L IA LIFTED HER sunglasses, watched the man with the pretty baby move.

His gait devoured the pavement and with hardly three strides, he'd reached her. "So you're Amelia? I'm the super. Gabe."

Super Gabe. The ridiculous urge to giggle struck her. Not so super since she'd had to rescue *him*. But then again, the clips in his hair and pink polish on his fingers meant he was some kind of Super Dad.

And that meant everything in Lia's book.

He carried his pretty baby on his hip and a heavy toolbox in his hand. What a picture he made. A tall man, easily six-three or six-four, with broad shoulders, large hands, and all that toasted almond hair that looked as if it had been professionally highlighted—and still held up by the same three shiny clips she'd spotted earlier, one of which was adorned with a rainbow heart. His nail polish was chipped and, strangely, that made it somehow sweeter. His black T-shirt had a pizza pie on the front, missing one slice and she grinned. She'd caught him giving her a good long look earlier, which confused her because this beautiful baby whose bright blue eyes broke her heart wore a coordinating T-shirt with the missing slice. It branded them as a unit, a family.

Her heart gave one traitorous beat before pounding at top speed and she willed it to behave itself. Yes, so he was the hottest guy she'd seen in—well, ever—and that included her ex, but that wasn't what had sent her heart tripping. It was knowing with one glance that this was a man who'd do anything for his family. There was simply nothing sexier than that. Not for Lia.

But he had a family, which made him off-limits. She would never do to this man's wife what Candi-with-an-I had done to her.

She cleared her throat, waved a hand. "I'm told you'll have the keys to my unit, some paperwork to sign, and can give me a receipt for the rent check I'll write you."

His gaze stayed locked on her, goofy smile on his face. Lia felt her face heat up under his scrutiny.

"Oh. Right. Come on in. I'll get them for you."

He put the toolbox down next to the door in front of which she'd been standing for at least thirty minutes now. He shoved a hand into his pocket, came out with some keys.

Lia waited and noticed the baby studying her like she was a brand-new toy. She waved at the little girl.

The baby smiled and burrowed against her father's neck as he opened the door and stepped inside.

"Okay, Emmy. Down you go."

Lia froze with one foot in the apartment. *Emma*. The name she'd chosen for her own baby. No. No, the universe just couldn't be that cruel. When he turned to retrieve the toolbox, his eyebrows lifted.

"What?"

She couldn't answer him. She'd been punished enough. She wasn't even sure what crime, what mortal sin she'd committed to suffer like this.

Large hands grasped her arms, jolting her from her self-flagellation. "You okay? You're going a little green. Are you sick or something?"

Lia swallowed hard, shook her head. "Her name is Emma?"

"No." A frown creased his forehead. "I call her Emmy. It's short for Emerson."

Relief so profound washed over. "Oh, that's beautiful."

He angled his head and then gave her a nod. "Okay. Come on in, then."

He let her go and she shivered, abruptly cold. On legs that shook, she stepped into his apartment, waited while he shut the door, put the toolbox beside it. Then, he and the baby disappeared down the hall, leaving her alone.

She found herself standing in a large living room. To her right was a galley kitchen. She took in the breakfast mess on his table, the pink plastic play set erected in the corner of his living room, the dolls, clothes, and books scattered around the room. The refrigerator held crayon art, photographs, and a calendar. There were more tools on the counter, and a large basket of—of what looked like hair accessories on the table.

"Emmy, how's your diaper?"

"Yuck, Dad-dee."

"Be right out," he called to her. She managed a strangled response.

Not Emma. Not Emma. Lia squeezed her eyes shut, willed the tears back as the child's peals of laughter were answered with deeper chuckles from her father. Then, she took a good look around. She slipped off her jacket, eyeing the breakfast mess. And then she shrugged, briskly stacked plates, took them to the sink she filled with hot water and a squirt of the soap she'd found beside it. She grabbed a sponge and began scrubbing at the bits of scrambled egg stuck to plates. In minutes, she had the dishes scrubbed clean. The kitchen, aside from the breakfast dishes, was sparse. He had no appliances cluttering the counters except for one—a coffee maker.

She noticed an open space on the refrigerator door and decided that must be where the magnetic clipboard she spotted on the table hung. She replaced it and stopped to admire the photo of a beautiful smiling brunette. This must be his wife. Brown hair, brown eyes, she looked like a model. Where was she? Was theirs a reverse parenting arrangement where she went to work and he stayed home?

The patter of tiny feet running toward her had her looking over her shoulder and down into the baby's happy face.

"Hi!"

"Hi, yourself." She crouched down to the toddler's level. "My name is Lia. Can you say that?"

The baby scrunched up her face and tried repeating it. "Eee-uh."

Lia applauded. "Oh, good girl. Is your name Emmy?"

The baby gave her a single nod, huge blue eyes glued to Lia's face.

And then she noticed the large boots behind the baby. Lia shot back to her feet.

"Any particular reason you did my dishes?" He waved a

big hand over the sink.

"Um, well, I saw the mess—"

"I'd have gotten to it when Emmy took her afternoon nap. Like I always do."

She registered the insult in his voice and understood. She wasn't passing judgment…or not trying to, at least, though it was hard especially after the way he'd eyeballed her while his poor wife was out trying to smash through glass ceilings.

Lia met his gaze without flinching. "I was trying to help. It's a compulsion with me. If you fill your sink with soapy water while you eat breakfast and soak the dishes until you get around to them, they'll wash in no time." That was a tip from one of her clients, who wrote life hack books. Lia loved it because it fit her motto. *Work smart, not hard.* It's what she did. Organized. Pitched in. Revamped.

Like her life, she thought with a start.

But he didn't thank her, just stared at her. "I don't need help."

The resentment in his tone got her own dander up. "Yes. You did. With the car," she reminded him. And then she blurted out, "I could cut your hair, if you want. You wouldn't need the clips."

He only stared at her, face inscrutable, while the baby babbled at their feet. There was an energy between them, rippling and sizzling. She damn well didn't like it but she couldn't deny it. Could he? She held her ground, challenging him.

Daring him.

When his eyes dipped to her mouth, she knew he'd felt it, too. And still, she didn't move.

"Dad-dee! Cup." The toddler took the cup from her father's hand and held it up to him. He turned, took milk from the refrigerator, and poured some for her, carefully fastening the lid.

Then he spelled out a curse, lifted a hand to his head like he'd only just then heard what she'd said about the hair clips. He removed all three of them, tossed them with the rest.

"I forgot about these. My kids like to ambush me when I'm asleep." He laughed and shook his head.

He had a great laugh.

"Sure explains a lot of strange things today." He raked his hands through all that toasted almond hair and her tongue peeked out to lick her lips. He whipped around and said over his shoulder, "Come on. I'll let you into the unit. We'll do the paperwork later. It's time for her lunch and then a nap."

The spell was broken. Lia took a breath. "Lunch time already? Wow. Time sure flew by me today."

"Yeah, sorry about the delay. The car and then…" He waved a hand toward the toolbox still near the door.

"Not a problem." She followed him to the door, enchanted when he scooped little Emmy into his arms to press a kiss to her head. Things moved in her.

Things she swore she'd never feel again.

Chapter Five

GABE STRODE OUT of the courtyard and up the three steps of the stone stoop to the front door of what would now be Amelia's apartment. She practically jogged to keep up with him. His heart was galloping behind his ribs and his palms were sweaty. The more time he spent with her, the more nervous he grew.

That she was beautiful wasn't the issue. He'd been around dozens of beautiful women in his life.

It was that he'd *noticed*.

He hadn't noticed another woman since the day he'd met Janey, when they were in high school. Unfortunately for him, Janey hadn't noticed *him* until a few years later. But Janey was gone and so was that part of his life. He never fooled around with tenants or the single mothers in the PTA. He didn't want his girls hearing gossip or anything else that might make them believe he'd disrespected their mother but more than that…he just wasn't interested.

Until now.

What was it about her that kept turning him back into that teenage guy without a clue?

Must be those eyes, he decided. Those huge, dark, expressive, hypnotic eyes. They reminded him so much of

Janey's. They were like mood rings. He'd taken one look at her, standing at his sink, and immediately assumed she'd been passive-aggressively criticizing his housekeeping. When he called her out on it, her eyes immediately told him he'd been wrong.

Her eyes *spoke* to him.

They told him he'd insulted her. They'd also told him something else.

She wanted him. There was interest there.

And the thought *appealed* to him.

Janey was gone and he had no *right* to think about anybody else in those terms. And dammit, he *was* thinking.

Retreat, retreat, retreat!

He climbed up the steps that led to the front door of Unit D, opened the door and handed them to her. "Here." He stepped aside so she could enter the space that he'd hoped to make his own.

"Wait, Mr. Ivers."

Cursing again, he turned and waited, impatient, for her to say what she had to say. Instead, she stepped closer and he almost swayed.

Lilacs.

She smelled like the lilacs that bloomed around Mike's upstate house. It was all he could do not to bury his face in all that hair.

"I really am sorry about your dishes. I was trying to help, not insult you."

He stared at her for a minute or two, until Emmy squirmed in his arms. Those amazing dark eyes were full of honesty. "No problem. I…well, I'm sorry for over-reacting."

She smiled, a fast curve of full, peach-colored lips. He stepped closer, pulled by the magic of those dark chocolate eyes. God, she smelled nice. If he closed his eyes, he'd believe he was actually in Mike's yard where all those lilacs bloomed.

"Dad-dee, down." Emmy commanded and absently, he obeyed. She took off like a shot, her little canvas shoes squeaking on the hardwood floors and Gabe jolted back to reality.

"F-u-c-k me," he muttered, running after her. "Emmy! Get back here." He needed to retreat. *Now.*

He heard Amelia close the door and that warning bell changed to a klaxon as he chased his daughter into the kitchen, snagging her before she put fingerprints on the fixtures.

"Oh, wow! This is beautiful." Amelia's eyes scanned the rich cherry cabinets and she ran a hand slowly over the pale gray granite counter. Unlike his kitchen, which was part of his living room, this one was a separate room with an L-shaped counter and room for a small table.

"Appliances included but no dishwasher."

"What about washer and dryer?"

He strode to the door at one end of the long room, showed her the stackable units.

"What's this door?" She straightened up and peered through the small window.

"Rear entry. It leads to the courtyard." He flipped the locks, opened the door and showed her the view.

"Is there a bathroom on this level?"

He shook his head, refastening the rear door. "One bath. But it's large. Mike didn't tell you anything about this place?"

"Mike who?"

"Kinsella. The owner. Well, his uncle is technically the owner, but he does most of the property management."

"No, I'm not especially close to the Kinsellas. I needed a place—fast. A friend of a friend knows Vince Kinsella."

Gabe nodded. "Mike's uncle."

He led her to the stairs. "Upstairs, there's a master, two small bedrooms, and bathroom."

They climbed the stairs, Lia leading and Gabe trying heroically not to stare at her ass.

"The two small bedrooms are the same size. This is the master." He opened a door and stepped inside. "This switch controls the overhead light and that outlet," he explained, pointing to an outlet in the corner of the large room. "Make sure you don't plug in your alarm clock there."

"Got it." She stepped inside, looked around. The unit had no carpeting so her tennis shoes squeaked on the hardwood floors. She opened the closet, peered inside. "So bed goes here." She spread both arms in front of the long wall that faced two narrow windows. "Dresser there."

Bed. Gabe's mind went blank. Her bed. Emmy squirmed in his arms so he put her down again. She promptly ran to the closet and tried to hide. Lia moved to the windows, glanced down. "How do these open?"

"They've got cranks." He stepped toward her, reached for the lock and rotated the handle to demonstrate.

She opened the other side. "Oh. Heavy."

"Yeah," he agreed, eyes pinned to her mouth. It was a really great mouth. Wide, soft lips that made him wonder what it would be like to kiss her, feel all that blazing hair spill over them and just sink into all that softness.

They'd taste...sweet, he decided. He'd start at the corner, the one where the dimple was, and then he'd cover her entire mouth and it would be amazing. He'd fill up on her scent, take his hands on a cruise over the satin expanse of her skin.

"Dad-dee!" Emmy smacked his legs and suddenly, he was sucked out of his fantasy, crashing back down to earth with an audible gasp.

Amelia stared back at him, lips parted and damn him, it physically hurt to tear his eyes away.

"Dad-dee!"

He cursed viciously and silently because he'd just fantasized about kissing a tenant, about kissing a woman he'd just met.

About kissing a woman who wasn't Janey.

"What, sweetheart?"

"Dad-dee, wanna bath." Emmy ran toward the bathtub. He was right behind her, scooped her up.

"No. You'll take a bath tonight. Right now, you need lunch."

He headed for the door, calling out behind him. "We'll do the paperwork later. Key's on your kitchen counter."

"Thank you!" she called back.

OUTSIDE IN THE clean fall air, he drew a deep breath and walked back through the courtyard to his own apartment.

"That was close, Emmy."

"Cose, Dad-dee," she agreed.

He unlocked his door, let the baby loose, and let out a low whistle. Amelia Blake was hot, no doubt. But—

No.

He was not going there. He jerked open the refrigerator door, pulled out an apple, a carton of yogurt, and a plastic container of chicken he'd grilled for last night's dinner. He cut up the chicken and the apple, grabbed a spoon and—and—

Emmy was gone.

"Hey, where'd you go, E-Rex?"

A muffled giggle was his only response. Grinning, he followed the sound and found Emmy tangled up in his unmade bed. "Gotcha!"

She squealed in delight and he tossed her up and into his arms so he could strap her into her high chair. "Lunch time, Emmy."

He strode back to the kitchen while his daughter clapped her chubby hands together. "Yay!"

"Here you go. You got yogurt and chicken and apples."

"Ooo. Apples."

She gobbled up her lunch and soon started her cranky dance. He unfastened her from the high chair, took her to the bedroom where he stripped off her pink jacket, her white shoes, found her blanket and favorite stuffed toy, and put her in her crib. She cried bitterly, as she always did, but he knew she'd be zonked in about five minutes.

He shut the door and returned to the kitchen to make himself a chicken sandwich to go with the extra-large cup of coffee he planned to inject directly into a vein. He took coffee and sandwich to the sofa, spotted the note he'd jotted that morning.

Call Jim re: part-time work.

He grabbed his phone, called Jim at Paradigm.

"Jim. It's Gabe. Can you tell me more about what you'd need me to do? I'm interested."

He and Jim talked for fifteen minutes. By the time Gabe began his household chores, the basic form of a new plan started to take shape. He could return to engineering work part-time, maybe once a week. It would give him a nice infusion of cash, allowing him the flexibility to scoop up a larger unit as soon as one became available. He'd have to talk to the girls, of course. But it could work.

Amelia had already done the dishes, which he should have thanked her for, instead of, well, instead of jumping to conclusions. He made his bed, picked up clothes, dusted furniture, and dumped the laundry basket outside the door to the girls' room.

Emmy was quiet now.

He poked his head in. She was sound asleep, her bear and blanket clutched tightly in her arms and tear tracks still fresh on her face. He leaned on the doorframe and just watched her. His own mini-me. Maddie was completely Janey's. That punch in the gut hurt bad, but he breathed through it and heard Amelia Blake's words.

You're very lucky.

Somehow, it didn't seem to hurt as deep.

Laundry going, dusting done, he'd been about to plan that night's dinner when a soft knock sounded on the door.

He strode to the window, glanced out and froze.

Amelia Blake was on his front steps.

Damn it, damn it, damn it.

For about five seconds, he considered not answering the door. But that was chicken-shit and he knew it. He opened the door with a cautious, "Hi."

Amelia frowned at his tone. "Your sippy cup." She held it up by one of its bright pink plastic handles.

Manners demanded he acknowledge her courtesy with gratitude. "Thanks." He tried to close the door fast, but she slapped a hand to it.

The eyebrows arching over those fascinating eyes slammed together. "Did I do something or say something wrong? I'm sorry if I did. I just…"

He'd upset her. Good. Maybe she'd leave. *Please, please, please, leave.* "No, nothing. It's…it's fine."

Dark eyes softening, she cocked her head and studied him. "Look, Mr. Ivers. I said I was sorry about the dishes. I didn't mean to upset you. I thought I was helping."

"Yeah, no, it's fine."

She gave him the *yeah, right* look and changed the subject. "The movers arrived and are hauling in my stuff right now. Meanwhile, I have questions." From the leather bag strapped to her shoulder, she removed a thick spiral-bound notebook whose cover said MY JOURNAL in fancy script. She opened the book and ran an index finger down a list. "Am I allowed to decorate and if so, to what extent? Can I remove a cabinet and have a dishwasher installed at my own expense? And what about security? I would like a security system installed. Also, you didn't tell me anything about parking or storage. Is there a garage? If so, is it included in the rent? Finally, what services do you provide? If I needed a shelf hung, would you do that?"

His mind blanked when she asked about *his services*.

Christ, he was thirty-seven years old and one question from this woman had him thinking like an adolescent boy again. Furious with himself, he took a deep breath, and opened the door to her. "Come in." He headed for the kitchen area, held out a chair.

She stepped into his living room again, closing the door behind her. He watched her eyes scan the apartment, taking in the vacuum he hadn't put away yet, and his face burned. "Oh, um. Let me just put that away." He busied himself wrapping the cord around the vacuum, grabbed it and hid it in his bedroom.

"You've done a ton of work since we parted. Do you do windows? I'll hire you to clean my place."

He gaped at her. *Parted?* Who spoke like this? "You talk like a Jane Austen novel."

She lifted her eyebrows. "Well, that's good, since I once wanted to become a literary editor." And then she narrowed her eyes. "You've read Austen?"

He hadn't read Austen since he and Janey were dating and he'd wanted to impress her but the question as well as the incredulous tone insulted him anyway. "Yeah, I have." he snapped.

He froze when she jerked at his tone. Enough was enough. He wasn't a love-sick fifteen-year-old anymore. He raked his hands through his hair and indicated the chair. "I'm sorry again. I'd tell you it's not you, it's me, but that's such a stupid—"

"Cliché."

"Exactly."

She walked over, took the chair he'd held out for her.

The way she moved…he could watch her for hours. If not for the squeak of shoes on the wood floor, he'd never have heard her move.

Ballet.

She reminded him of ballet.

God, it had been thirty years since he'd seen a ballet. He must have been four—no, six. That's right. It had been a first grade field trip. They'd taken a fancy bus with a bathroom in it all the way to Manhattan to see *Swan Lake*. He'd thought it was dumb until a dancer lifted one leg high over her head. He'd tried it as soon as he got home and had to contend with pain for nearly a week after he'd pulled a groin muscle. He should take the girls, he suddenly thought. They'd love it. Why hadn't he ever thought to take his daughters to a ballet?

"I'm sorry," she said quietly.

Blinking, he lifted his eyebrows. "What for?"

She bit her lip and then shrugged. "Something about me makes you sad, which you try to cover up with mad."

He didn't bother denying it. Their eyes met and something inside him went *click.*

He spelled out another curse as Lia stood and left his apartment.

As soon as Lia had seen the apartment, she doubled down on her promise to make this move work. Her first step toward that goal?

Expanding Blake Virtual Services.

Her clients had been patient while she'd recovered. It was time to repay them.

The movers hadn't taken very long to haul Lia's boxes and furniture inside. As soon as they'd left, she found her tools and assembled her bed frame, muscled the mattress into place, and spent a satisfying hour spreading out her new bedding. She'd been told the apartment would be all neutral walls, so she'd chosen dramatic gray bedding with a bold print.

Now, she wanted food and decided that would provide the perfect opportunity to check in with her clients. Okay, two birds, one stone. She grabbed her bag and headed for the pizza place that she'd noticed nearby.

The September weather was perfect so Lia decided to walk, taking her time, smiling at a group of people standing on a corner.

Oh, right. It was almost three o'clock. That must be the school bus stop. She walked by, turned in to the pizza store and ordered a slice and a Coke, took it to the high counter by the window and watched the neighborhood go by. She took out her journal and her phone, checked email, checked texts, made some notes.

One of her authors needed her to do some chocolate history research for a cookbook project. Another client, a mathematics professor, needed her to look up everything she could find on some obscure mathematical theory for an article she was writing for the *New York Times*. She added to her notes, then shifted gears. She needed supplies. Groceries. And she needed a desk, maybe some shelves. She'd have to unpack her kitchen first, then toiletries.

A movement from the corner of her eye snagged her attention.

Gabriel.

He was pushing Emmy in her stroller, carrying a heavy pack on one shoulder. His pretty hair clips were gone now and wasn't that too bad? He didn't care who thought it was strange; he wore hair clips and nail polish to make his daughter smile. As he approached, Lia watched three women exchange grins. When one fanned her face, Lia bit back a smile of her own. Yep. Gabriel Ivers was hot; there was no doubt about that.

She watched him closely as he stopped to chat with the bus stop crowd, crouched down to Emmy's level when one of the women tickled her belly. He waited for a few minutes, adjusting his heavy pack, then disappeared behind the large yellow bus that stopped to drop off children.

Oh. Right. He still had to repair his car.

When the bus pulled away, Gabriel was gone. Lia found herself angling her head to see down the side street where his car had stalled. That's where he'd be.

Should she offer to help him? She could mind little Emmy while he worked.

Which made her no better than Candi-with-an-I.

Abruptly, she dropped her napkin and collected her trash. She needed to stay well away from Gabriel Ivers and his daughter.

Well away.

Chapter Six

G ABE STARED AT the lease document, signed by Amelia
Blake.

A year. A whole year. Oh, boy. He was in trouble.

He filed the lease in the desk tucked into the corner of
his bedroom and tried not to think about her. Tried not to
think of that mane of auburn hair that smelled like lilacs, or
the soft husky voice that made him think of silk and satin.

The timer went off in the kitchen. He hurried to the oven, pulled out the meatloaf.

"Stop it, Maddie!" Olivia shouted from the living room.

He glanced up. Maddie, dressed in her princess outfit,
was twirling around in circles.

She liked to make the skirt flare out.

Emmy giggled but Olivia was trying to watching TV,
and growing more annoyed by the second. He grabbed plates
from a cabinet, put a slab of meat on each, put them on the
table and before any more tempers flared, called, "Girls.
Dinner time."

"Meatloaf, again?" Maddie complained, as she took her
seat.

Gabe lifted a brow. "Maybe you'd like to cook instead?"

She bit her lip and shook her head. "What else are we

having?"

"Potatoes, gravy, and green beans."

"Yay! I love gravy, right, Daddy? Right?"

"Yes, Maddie. I'll give you a bit extra, okay?"

"Okay."

"Kim, could you buckle Emmy in her chair?"

She did, but with considerable attitude. He tossed utensils and napkins into the center of the table. From the refrigerator, he took the carton of milk out. He sat down, cut up a slice of meatloaf for Emmy's tray, and tried to ignore Kimberly's bad mood, Olivia's frustration, and Maddie's chatter.

"Daddy, what's in meatloaf?"

"Uh, meat, breadcrumbs, eggs, and some spices."

"What's in meat?" She continued to dance in her chair.

Battling the urge to sigh, he said, "Well, this meat is beef. Some meat is chicken and other meat is pork."

"What's beef?"

"Maddie, please eat."

"But what kind of meat is beef?"

"It's cow, dummy." Olivia grabbed the carton of milk.

"Olivia," he snapped. "Stop using that word."

Maddie's lip quivered. "Cow?" She put down her fork. "Daddy, I can't eat a cow! Cows are nice and it's not nice to…to cook them!" She burst into tears and Gabe's patience shattered.

"Eat your dinner or go to bed."

"But, Daddy! It's a poor little animal."

"Fine. Don't eat the meat. Here. Eat extra vegetables." He scooped another helping of green beans onto her plate, watched her lip quiver some more.

"Mmmm, this cow is yummy," Olivia taunted.

"Olivia. Would you like to go to bed now, too?"

She instantly settled down.

"Ooo, I know! Let's have chocolate milk, Daddy, okay? Huh, can we, please?"

"No, Maddie."

"Pleeeeeease?"

"No." His voice rose and everybody magically went silent. He cleared his throat. "We need to have a family meeting."

Kimberly's fork froze halfway to her mouth and her eyes snapped to his. "Why? What's wrong?"

Gabe opened his mouth only to shut it again. Where the hell did he start? "Um."

"Are you gonna die, Daddy?" Maddie asked quietly.

He could only gape at his daughter.

"Dad?" Olivia, this time.

Gabe jerked. "No. No, sweetheart, I'm fine. I'm not sick. Everything's fine."

"Then why, Daddy? We do we have to have a meeting?" Maddie asked.

He dropped his fork, sucked in a deep breath. "Okay. So, I've been thinking about a lot of things. Like living here." He didn't miss the look his two eldest daughters shared. "It's been two years since Mommy died, a bit over a year since we moved here."

"I really miss her, Daddy." Maddie's lower lip quivered.

"Me too, Ducky." He coughed once. "I took this job so I could stay home with you guys but...I don't know if it's working out. All of you sharing a bedroom, getting on each other's nerves. I have an idea for giving us all some privacy. So I wanted to talk to you about maybe moving again. Getting a bigger place. More room. But I'd have to go back to work to make that happen and that means…"

"You won't be here. And we'd be alone." Olivia slouched in her seat, her meatloaf untouched.

From her high chair, Emmy quietly watched everybody, sensing their tension.

"No. No, Newton, you wouldn't be all alone. I was thinking maybe part-time. I'd have to find a babysitter for Emmy, but if I did most of the work while you all are in school, you won't even know I'm gone."

"And we could move to a house with a backyard and lots of rooms?" Olivia asked.

"Eventually. But I was thinking we might be able to get a bigger apartment here so I could still be the super. For a while." He waited a beat. "Well? Does anybody have anything to say?" He looked from Kimberly to Olivia to Maddie to Emmy and back to Maddie. She'd have something to say.

"Don't you love us anymore?"

Her words were a lance straight through Gabe's heart. He dropped to his knees next to Maddie's chair. "I love you all to the moon and back, Maddie. Nothing will ever change that."

"Then how come you wanna leave us?"

He cupped her cheek, hoping she didn't notice how much his hand shook. "I'm not leaving you. But I need to go back to work so I can make more money and find us a bigger place to live."

"But—"

"Maddie." Kimberly took her sister's hand. "Stop. Daddy misses his work, you know?"

"Yeah," his little chatterbox nodded solemnly. "I miss my work, too."

That made him laugh. "What work is that, Ducky?"

She thought about it for a moment, her face screwed up in concentration. "I can't remember. But it was 'portant."

"Oh, work is always important," he agreed. "So, do we agree?"

"Wait," Kimberly said. "What about more privacy?"

"Oh, right." Gabe stood up, retrieved the notes he'd kept safe from little hands. "If I move my bed out here, in the living room, you and Olivia can share my room. Maddie and Emmy can keep your room."

"Awwww." Maddie pouted. "But I'll miss them. Will you miss me, too? Will you?" When her sisters said nothing, Maddie turned to Gabe. "Daddy, Kimby and Livvie aren't gonna miss me!"

"Maddie. Stop." Gabe held up his hand while Kim and Liv exchanged excited glances.

"We can have your whole room?" Olivia asked.

"Yeah. I've been thinking of some things I can build you, like desks for homework."

"But, Daddy." Maddie patted his arm. "Where's your big bed gonna go?"

"Right there." Gabe pointed to the living room wall that held their sofa. "There are sofas that fold out into beds."

Kimberly put down her fork and looked at Olivia. "That doesn't seem very fair."

"Hey, if it means peace settles across the Ivers land, I'm okay with it. So." Gabe folded his hands. "Time to vote. Everybody okay with me working part-time?"

Kimberly nodded. "Yeah."

"Liv?"

She shrugged. "I guess."

"Maddie?"

"Okay, Daddy."

"Emmy?"

"Cup!"

"Close enough," Gabe said with a laugh and handed his youngest daughter her cup.

ᕔ

THE NEXT MORNING, he stepped off the train at 10:25 and made his way up the stairs and through Penn Station to find the subway that would take him to the job site. He'd forgotten to get his hair cut. Again. But there were no plastic rainbow clips in it today.

He'd checked twice.

Another wave of anxiety coursed through him and he had to remind himself that he used to do this work every day. No reason he couldn't handle it for a few hours.

At five minutes to eleven, he found Jim, hard hat under his arm, cup of coffee in his hand, reviewing the plans for the project with a few workers.

"Hey, Jim."

"Gabe! You made it." He put the hat on, switched the coffee to his left hand and gave Gabe a hearty handshake.

"This is Lou and this is Ramon. Lou's the foreman and Ramon is the plumbing contractor doing the sprinkler systems."

The original goal of this project was to replace all the fire escapes on the exterior of a residential building. But Gabe had explained that the codes had changed. He'd recommended removing the fire escapes and reconstructing all interior stairwells to make them fireproof with self-closing doors, sprinkler systems, and connections to neighboring stairwells. It was an ambitious and expensive proposal, but the client accepted it because it was an investment that would pay for itself when he wanted to sell. The first few phases of the project had gone on without Gabe, like getting the designs drafted and approved, and then applying for the necessary permits, selecting and scheduling the various crews. He knew Ramon and Lou by reputation and was happy to be working with them.

Gabe shook each man's hand.

"Nice nails." Lou shot a smirk toward Ramon as he shook Gabe's hand.

Gabe shrugged. So much for reputations. He'd completely forgotten about the bright color. "Like it? My daughters picked it out. They'll be happy to hear you like it, too."

"Oh, sure. *Daughters*. Got it." Ramon laughed.

"All right, let's get to work," Jim said, shaking his head. "Gabe's job is to assist me with site supervision," Jim told the other men. "You'll keep him apprised of anything that knocks us off schedule, even for a minute—got it?"

Gabe asked for copies of the SSP—the site safety plan—

and asked clarifying questions about some of its content like materials safety and where first aid kits were located, should the need arise. He also asked to review the JHAs for each of the trades. Lou promised to get him those Job Hazard Assessments as soon as possible.

The hours passed quickly. Gabe examined the job site and was satisfied the work performed so far met requirements. They walked through the site several times, making notes and marking the places where demo had already been done. He'd asked for more signs on a top-floor barricade, making sure it was clearly marked as a danger zone.

At three o'clock, he left the other men with his cell number and instructions to call him if anything changed, and caught the subway back to Penn Station, anxious to see his girls.

He'd missed them, of course. He'd expected that. What he hadn't expected was to feel like he'd had a limb amputated. He couldn't wait to get home and hug the whole lot of them. But on the train ride home, it was thoughts of Amelia Blake that kept filling his head.

Chapter Seven

I N HER SHINY new kitchen, Lia happily made herself some coffee and breakfast—cold cereal—grabbed her laptop and posted this week's blog about taking good notes when you didn't know shorthand. She called her blog *Work Smart Not Hard* and firmly believed note-taking was a dying art. She sipped her coffee and checked her email, where a message from one of her clients gave her an idea for another blog post—recipes for people who didn't cook.

And that sparked an even better idea...she'd start a newsletter for her new neighbors. Her mind fired off a bunch of ideas and she filled pages with notes on how to monetize it. When her cell rang, she nearly didn't answer it.

"Hi, Ro."

"She lives! Let me guess. You've been working every waking moment?"

Lia laughed. "Yep."

"So the new place is working for you?"

"Yes. You were right."

"I usually am," Roseann said, making Lia laugh. "Now tell me why you haven't been in touch."

Lia hesitated. Roseann had a way of cutting through all the bullshit, zeroing in to the heart of a matter, but she didn't want to talk about what she already knew. Gabriel Ivers was off-limits. "I'm expanding my business, Ro. I wanted to do this over a year go. Hire staff, take on more clients, offer more services. Since the second I walked in the door here, I've been getting idea after idea." All of this was true so Lia didn't feel too bad about omitting Gabriel. "I'm launching a building-wide newsletter focusing on small spaces and time savers. I'm on my way to the neighborhood shops to sell ads so I can monetize it. Last night, I developed an online portfolio of other projects I've done. With luck, I may be able to secure advertising and new work at the same time."

"Whoa, you have been busy," Roseann said. "Now tell me how you're really doing."

"I think I'm in love with my super's baby," Lia blurted and then bit her lip. She hadn't meant to say that. Why, why did she say it?

"Your super's baby," Roseann repeated. "Oh, Lia. Honey."

"It's okay, Ro. I met them the day I moved in. He had car trouble so I held the baby while he tried to fix the car."

"You held the baby."

"Oh, you should see her, Roseann. She's completely adorable. Spitting image of her father. Big blue eyes, blonde curls just beginning to come in. I think she's about two. She said I had pretty hair." *Pwetty*, Emmy had said. And then she'd touched Lia's hair.

"Just like her father, huh? I've never met Gabriel Ivers. What's he like?"

Lia's face grew warm while she tried to think of the right

words. "He's like, the most perfect father you can imagine. Ro, he had pink nail polish on and barrettes in his hair because his daughter likes to play dress-up or something."

"Wow."

"You should have seen it. The car is dead in the middle of the street. He's standing there with the hair clips and the nail polish, wearing jeans, work boots and a T-shirt that's got this picture of a pizza pie with a slice missing. Drivers are honking and cursing at him but he just opens the back door to the truck, takes out this baby and she's wearing a T-shirt just like his, only hers is the single slice missing from his. They were just so...so..."

"Lia."

"I know, I know! I'm not getting attached, really."

"You already are and you need to be careful. Ivers is off the market."

"I know," Lia snapped. "I'm not Candi."

There was a long silence and then Roseann said, "Of course you're not. I didn't mean to imply anything by that. I don't want to see you hurt more, Lia. You can understand my concern, right? You just told me you fell in love with this baby."

And this would be exactly why she'd been avoiding Roseann's calls for the last week. She didn't want to be psychoanalyzed.

"Yeah. Sure. Can we talk later? I'm starving and need to head up to the shops."

Roseann didn't bother to point out she'd called Lia's cell. They both knew that was an excuse to end this conversation.

"Lia, you don't have to love someone else's baby. I get

that nothing I can do can fix your marriage or your body. But I *can* do something to help you become the mom you wanted to be. When you're ready, when you're *sure*, I'll carry your baby for you. So would Viv."

Lia stopped breathing. A wave of pure love swamped over her. "God, Ro. Oh my God." She squeezed her eyes shut. When she could speak again, she whispered, "You talked about this with Vivian?"

"Yes," Roseann said. "We know you. We'll make sure you'll be who you want to be. If that's being a mother, you'll have the option, I promise you."

The first tear fell then. "I…I love you."

"No, no, no! No crying! I told you this to cheer you up, not make you sadder."

"I'm not sad," Lia objected. And she wasn't. Not a bit.

Not anymore.

After she ended the call, Lia dried her tears, washed her face, repaired her makeup, and let her mind wander with all manner of possibilities. If Roseann and Vivian were truly serious, she could have a baby right now. There was no reason to wait. No need for a father. She could do this on her own. For the first time in more than a year, she felt…whole. With a huge happy smile, she grabbed her bag and left the apartment.

Outside in the bright autumn sun, the air was blue with curses. She looked, found a woman pounding on the front door to one of the other units in her building.

"Um, can I help you?" Lia asked.

The woman whipped around. "Not unless you have a master key, no."

"Did you try the super?"

Brown eyes rolled toward heaven. "Yeah. Not home. Neither are my roommates and I've been up for thirty-six hours straight now."

Lia took in the hospital scrubs and ID clipped to a pocket. "I'm Lia Blake. I live there." She indicated her unit.

"Oh, you took the vacant duplex. Great space. I'm Mei. I think. I'm not entirely sure I'm not dreaming this entire conversation."

Lia laughed. "Come on." She took out her keys, led Mei to her own door. "You can use my guest room."

The woman's brown eyes popped wide. "Seriously?"

"We're neighbors, aren't we? Neighbors help each other."

"Honey, this is Bayside. Most neighbors never even meet each other."

"I'm working on that," Lia revealed, leading Mei upstairs to one of the small bedrooms. "I'm sorry there's no bed yet. But the sofa's pretty comfortable and it's yours for however long you need. We'll hang something on the doorknob so I know you're in here. When you leave, just leave the door open."

Mei stared at her, brown eyes wide with shock. "I think I'm gonna like you, Lia."

"You're in healthcare, I see. Doctor? Nurse?" Lia found a sheet and pillow, arranged both on the sofa.

"I'm a surgical intern at Flushing Hospital. How about you? What do you do?"

"I've got my own business. I'm a virtual assistant. I juggle a bunch of clients, provide support services for them."

"That's pretty cool. So how do you like our building so

far?"

"I really love it. It was a spur-of-the-moment move for me so I had some qualms."

"Uh-oh. Bad break-up?" Mei sat on the sofa, gave it a bounce, and leaned over to take off her Crocs.

"Yes. Divorce. The ex decided to move upstairs with his mistress and new baby and I refused to let them rub my face in their happiness and that is probably way too much information for someone who's been up for thirty-six hours. Sorry." Lia flashed a sheepish grin.

"Nope. It's the perfect amount of information." Mei stretched out on the couch. "That single sentence tells me you're a take-no-shit kind of person and I like that."

Amused, Lia smiled. "How about you? How long have you lived here?"

"Uh, let's see," Mei pursed her lips. "I moved in after one of the other roommates didn't work out. I have two. Alyssa and Demaris. They both work in the city. Alyssa's in finance and Demaris is an event planner at the Javitz Center." She curled her legs under her and regarded Lia thoughtfully. "You know, since you're divorced and all, we have something in common. I've sworn off men now."

Laughing, Lia leaned on the doorframe. "Completely?"

Considering, Mei admitted, "I wouldn't say no if Thor or Captain America knocked on my door. Maybe."

"Wow. Sounds like you may be more jaded than I am."

"We'll have to trade war stories sometime."

"I'd like that. Maybe one night, we can hang with pizza and a nice bottle of wine. A girls' night. I'd love to meet your roommates, too."

At that, Mei rolled her eyes. "That's gonna be tough. We're rarely all home at the same time."

Lia stood up, headed for the door. "It was really nice meeting you. I'm heading out but I'll be super quiet when I get back."

"Thanks for letting me crash here. Oh, one thing?"

Lia stopped and turned to face Mei. "What's that?"

She ran a hand over her tousled hair. "The super. Have you met him yet?"

"Mr. Ivers? Sure. He seems very nice. And such a good father."

"Oh, he is. Can you keep an eye out for him? Ask him for the key to my place so I can get in later? I have to be back at the hospital tonight." Mei shut her eyes, turned onto her side.

"Sure thing." Lia hovered by the door, dying to ask the question. "Um, have you met his family?"

"Family? I've met his kids, sure. But his wife's gone. She died a few months after the baby was born. That's why he moved here. So he could take care of his kids himself." She cracked open one eye. "If you're looking in that direction, you should know it's futile. He never looks back."

"Got it. Okay. Sleep well."

Lia shut the door with a hand to her mouth. Dead. That beautiful smiling face on the refrigerator door in Gabriel's apartment was gone?

No wonder he always seemed so sad.

She headed back downstairs, made some more notes for the building newsletter idea before heading out. In less than an hour of going door-to-door on Bell Boulevard, she'd secured advertising from four businesses including the bakery where she'd indulged in a bag of brownies.

They were still warm.

She was a block away from her unit when she stepped up behind three little girls.

"Oh my God, Maddie, will you just shut up?" one of the girls ordered. She had dark eyes and dark hair pulled up in a ponytail and her round face wore that expression of profound annoyance Lia remembered well from her own youth.

"No, Livvie, and you can't make me!" the child she'd called Maddie shouted. That child also had dark eyes but her dark hair was tumbling loose and hung in her eyes. "I'm telling Daddy!" She started to run ahead, but the tallest girl caught her, held her back.

"Maddie. Stop. Daddy went to work today and said I'm in charge and I'm telling you to listen."

"But, Kimberly, that's not fair!" Maddie whined. "Olivia's always telling me to shut up and I can't. I had to be quiet all day in school and now I get to talk as much as I want. Daddy said so."

"Daddy's working today, dummy," Olivia shot back. "He can't hear you, but I can and I said shut up."

"Oh." Maddie stamped a foot, drew the syllable out into one long whine.

Lia studied the trio. These had to be the rest of the Ivers girls. Kimberly, the oldest, looked just like Emmy, Gabe's baby. Before Olivia could hurt the smallest girl, Lia stepped forward. "Girls. Don't be mean."

Kimberly gave her a look of wariness. Maddie, the littlest, gave her sister a look of triumph. And Olivia, the one with the ponytail, glared at her with annoyance.

"You're a stranger. I don't listen to strangers," she said with a sniff. But, Lia noted with interest, she tugged her little sister closer to her side.

"You're quite right about that. You shouldn't talk to strangers. But I'm your neighbor. I live right there." She pointed to her front door. "I just moved in. And because I already met your dad and baby sister, I'm going to guess you're Kimberly, Olivia, and Maddie Ivers."

Maddie clapped her hands. "Yay! You got us all right."

Lia gave her a little bow.

"Do you have any kids I can play with? I'm a real good friend, right, Kimby? Right? Right?"

That bitter pang of grief arrowed through her heart and Lia shook her head. "No. I don't have any kids of my own. And I'm sure you're a very nice friend."

Olivia rolled her dark eyes skyward and shot Lia a dirty look. She plopped down on one of the steps that led up to the courtyard, where their front door was. Maddie and Kimberly walked toward that door, not noticing Olivia's absence.

Lia was fairly sure a girl this young shouldn't be outside without supervision so she plopped down beside her. "So how old are you, Olivia?"

"Nine. How old are you?"

"Um, thirty. That's a lot more than nine."

Sneering, Olivia said, "Duh. I can do math, you know."

"Right. So Maddie must drive you crazy?"

Another eye-roll. "You have no idea. She's so annoying. Talk, talk, talk. If my ears could talk, they'd tell her to shut up, too."

A laugh burst from Lia's lips. "That bad?"

"My dad says Maddie talks a lot because it's how she processes things. I disagree. She talks a lot because she's an extrovert. Kimberly and me, we're introverts. Plus, she just loves to annoy us. I also think she has attention deficit disorder but my dad always gets super-mad when I say that, so...I don't anymore."

Impressed with the little girl's vocabulary, not to mention her insight, Lia asked, "Don't you do things that annoy her?"

"No. I just like to read. That can't possibly annoy anybody."

"I love to read. What books do you like?"

"Books about women in science are my favorite."

"Oh, like Marie Curie?"

Another look of disgust. "That is so annoying." The child huffed out a sigh. "Everybody always says Marie Curie when I say women in science. She's not the only one, you know. How come nobody ever mentions Caroline Herschel or Ruth Graves Wakefield? Did you know that Rosalind Franklin discovered DNA before Watson and Crick did, but they got the credit? They based their research off her work!"

Whoa! Lia raised her hands. "I know a lot of things about a lot of things but I did *not* know that. So what is Wakefield famous for discovering?"

The girl giggled, a sound so incongruous with the outrage a second ago, Lia giggled, too. "She invented the chocolate chip cookie. Toll house."

"No kidding? Wow."

"I know, right? So cool."

"I have lots of books at my place. As long as your dad says it's okay, you can come over whenever you need quiet time. Speaking of your dad, could you ask him to come see me when he gets home?"

Olivia angled her head and studied Lia through narrow eyes. "It's not gonna work, you know."

Confused, Lia shook her head. "What?"

"My dad won't marry you. You're not the first tenant we've had who was nice to me just so she could impress my dad."

"I'm not—that's not—I don't even like your dad!" Lia lied.

"Yeah, right," Olivia said with a sneer. "I used to be friends with this girl at school but she didn't really like me. Her mom just wanted to marry my dad. My dad's smart. He knows some people are nice just because they want to impress him. But he's never impressed. So don't be nice to me just for that."

"I wasn't." Lia held up her hands.

"So...I can still come over when I want to be by myself?"

No! "Um. Sure. If it's okay with your dad."

Olivia studied her, narrowing her dark eyes like she was trying to X-ray Lia, then ran up the stairs into the courtyard without another word.

❧

THAT EVENING, LIA indulged in a gooey brownie and a glass of wine to celebrate the four new advertisers for her first newsletter. She'd already finished several design mock-ups for the ads the Bell Boulevard businesses had ordered—the bakery who'd supplied her gooey brownie being her first. They'd be small squares that would run along the right side of the newsletter.

A quiet knock on the back door made her heart skip a beat. She peered through the window, found Gabriel standing there. He wore a sport jacket over a button-down shirt tucked into his jeans and had that day-old scruff darkening his jawline. He looked hot and male and...tired.

"Hi," she said, pulling open the door.

"Hey, my daughter said you needed help with something?"

"Yes. I met Mei, one of our neighbors. She's locked out of her unit and hoped you had a spare key."

Frowning, he nodded. "Sure, I've got a master, but why are you—"

"She's upstairs, asleep in my guest room."

"Oh. Yeah. Sure. I think I have a spare key, too. I'll go look. Be back in a few."

Lia watched him stride away, long legs flexing in his jeans. Five minutes later, he was back with a key. "If this doesn't work, I'm home for the rest of the night. She can just call or knock on my door. Tell her if I don't answer right away, to knock louder. It's probably bath time and Maddie's screams can get loud."

She took the key from him, and damn it, that stupid little tingle was still there when she touched his hand. "I'll tell her. I don't know what time she plans on getting up. I do know she has to be back at the hospital tonight."

Gabriel nodded, shoved his hands in his pockets. "I didn't know you knew Mei."

"Oh, I don't. We met today when she got locked out."

Cue awkward silence.

"So your daughter doesn't like baths?"

Gabriel blinked. "She likes baths fine. It's brushing the knots out of her hair that she hates. I like this table," he said, changing subjects so quickly, Lia frowned. "It's well-made art. Where'd you get it?" He ran his hand over the gleaming wood surface.

"A shop in SoHo."

Nodding, he took a look around. "So, is the apartment okay? No issues with any of the plumbing or whatever?"

Slowly, Lia shook her head. "No. It's great."

"Um, so what do you do? For a living, I mean?" he asked and then his eyes went round. "Sorry! That sounds really nosy. I just noticed you hardly leave the apartment so…"

"You wondered." She smiled.

"Yeah," Gabriel admitted with a smile, forming those sexy crinkles around his eyes. They were a blue she'd never seen before…kind of the color the sky turns before the sun starts to set.

"I'm self-employed. I work from home mostly. I'm a virtual assistant. I provide various types of administrative support to other professionals who can't afford full-time staff but don't have the time to do the work themselves."

Gabriel lifted a brow and leaned against her door. "Yeah? Like what?"

"It depends on the client. A lot of my work comes from staffing agencies. Some of my clients are authors who ask for help doing research or running promotions for their books. I also have a number of teachers on my list, college professors mostly, and some PhD candidates doing dissertations—Oh! I have a comedian as a client, too. He hired me to help run his social networks."

"Sounds like you juggle a lot of priorities."

"I do. That's what makes the work fun. Every day is different. What about you? What do you do?"

"Besides the building you mean? I'm an engineer. Large structures, mostly. Bridges, monuments, stuff like that. I just went back to work after—" Abruptly, he stopped and pressed his lips together and Lia's heart twisted.

Yes, there was so much pain there. "Oh, right. Your daughter mentioned that. Olivia? Is that your second-born?"

The smile returned. Bloomed large, in fact. "Yeah. Liv's a force of nature. Very smart. Independent." And then, he frowned, shaking his head. "Something's up with her. Haven't been able to wiggle it free yet."

Lia bit her lip. Should she tell him what the little girl had told her?

"What?"

"Well, she mentioned something about a friend's mom wanting to marry you?"

At Gabriel's look of total shock, Lia raised both hands. "She never mentioned names. All she said was a friend she used to have was her friend only because her mother wanted to get close to you."

He stared at the ground, rubbed a hand over his neck and cleared his throat. "Well, that explains some things. Shit. I… Wow. I don't even know how to… Jeez." He shook his head, laughed once, looked everywhere but directly at her.

"I'm sorry about that. Of all the girls, she tends to be the most, I don't know—direct, I guess."

When those sad blue eyes wandered to the brownie on her kitchen table, Lia knew they both needed a subject change.

Fast.

"Want one? They're from the bakery on Bell."

He smiled halfway. "I'd love one but the girls are alone and—"

"Oh, right! Of course." Lia hadn't even wondered who was watching them while he was finding that key. Yet more proof, as if she needed it, that she wasn't meant to be a mom. "I could wrap one up for you," she offered with a nervous smile.

She heard his quick intake of breath, watched his eyes drop to her mouth, but he shook his head. "No, better not. If I have one, they'll all cry for one, too."

"You could always save it for after they go to bed."

His face lit up and then he angled his head, studying her. "That's...that's a good idea. Devious, but really good. Okay. I'll take it."

"Great!" She left him still leaning against her door, reached for the bag of brownies on her kitchen counter, and wrapped one up in a new bag for him. "Here. Enjoy."

"I will. Thanks."

"Well." She waved a hand, laughed once.

"Yeah. Right. I should go. I have to get dinner going."

"Oh. Yeah. So do I."

With a grin, he took his brownie and strode off. Lia shut her back door and leaned against it, fanning her face.

Wow. Just...wow.

Chapter Eight

B Y THE END of October, Lia's first newsletter issue was ready for distribution. She printed out copies and woke early to put them through mail slots across the building. The newsletter had turned into the first phase of her what was now a multi-phase business expansion plan. Next, she hoped to create a vlog for which she'd record interviews with various local businesses along a theme of some sort. In keeping with her *small spaces, time savers* idea, she'd decided her first video would be her new desk. She'd planned to put it in one of the small bedrooms but changed her mind. She'd put it in the living room, near her front window. Her business was now the center of her life. It should be the center of her home, too. The room was large enough for the desk and for her sofa.

She'd spent hours organizing the L-shaped unit, polishing its smooth wood surface. It had places for paper and pads, pens and other office supplies. It hid most of the unsightly wires her equipment still had. Best of all, it had shelving behind doors. She'd papered the inside of those doors with sticky notes, but most of her to-do list was stored in an online app she could access from phone or laptop. She loved how well the desk embodied her business motto: work smart, not hard. It fit into her home like a piece of furniture should. And it fit into her work as a piece of equipment should. Yes, she decided with a happy smile. This apartment had been a good decision.

Roseann and Vivian were coming over tonight. Roseann hadn't been here since she'd moved in and Vivian hadn't seen the place at all yet. With the furniture now in place, Lia couldn't wait to see their reactions. She called in an order to what had become her favorite pizza place and knew her friends would bring the wine and chocolate and pajamas, should things get rowdy.

It was Friday night. They could get rowdy if they wanted to.

She stepped out her front door, breathed in the air that was still fairly warm for October, and trotted down the steps to the sidewalk. She'd just passed the courtyard when an anxious voice reached her.

"...I can't take him out but I also need to pick up that prescription. No, they don't deliver."

It was her neighbor in Unit Q, which appeared to be a mirror image of her own duplex.

"...Well, when can you leave?"

Her voice held frustration and exhaustion and that bitter tone born from years of irritation. Lia stopped, looked around, found the woman sitting on the bottom step of her front stoop, smoking a cigarette. Messy hair tied back in a ponytail matched Lia's assessment of the situation. This woman had gone without sleep for quite some time.

The woman's blue eyes narrowed as she spotted Lia.

"Do you mind? This is a private conversation."

"Not at all. I thought I might be able to help?"

The woman's lips tightened. "I don't need help."

"It's really no bother. I'm walking up the street to pick up my dinner. I can easily pop into the pharmacy. It's right across the street."

Desperation had taken over the annoyed gleam in the neighbor's eyes. "I gotta go." She ended her call, stubbed out her cigarette in a small pail filled with sand. "Who the hell are you?"

"Lia. Amelia Blake. Unit D. Who the hell are you?" She matched tone for tone and the woman laughed.

"I'm Jessica Vella. I've got a sick kid in there and haven't slept for two days now. My husband doesn't seem to grasp the gravity of the situation." She waved a hand over the phone sitting on the step next to a pack of cigarettes and a lighter. "Oh! You're newsletter Lia?"

"Yep, newsletter Lia." She laughed. "Sorry to hear about your son. But the offer stands. I'm picking up some dinner. The pharmacy's directly across the street."

"That would be amazing. His name is Mason Vella and his date of birth is July 7th, 2014. There are two prescriptions. One's an antibiotic, the other is—hopefully—a powerful decongestant so he can sleep through a night."

"Where is he now?"

"He's been asleep for the last ten minutes. I had to toss a coin to decide between shower or smoke break before he wakes up coughing." She ran a hand over dirty hair, winced.

"Okay, be back in fifteen minutes."

"Thanks."

With a warm smile, Jessica jogged up the stairs to her

door. Lia started walking, enjoying the crunch of autumn leaves under her feet. The sun was low in the sky but she left her sunglasses off, enjoying its warmth. In the pharmacy, it took less than five minutes to retrieve little Mason's prescriptions. She lingered a bit longer to find a treat for him. Little boys liked cars, didn't they? She bought him a toy car and on a whim, added freezer pops.

Next up, the pizza store.

As soon as she stepped into the restaurant, she spotted Gabriel at the counter.

"EEEEEE-AAH!" Emmy clapped her chubby hands from the stroller he kept one hand on.

Gabriel spun around.

So did the three older girls.

Lia's belly clenched. The entire Ivers family was out and about today. Another punch to her gut. Did he have any idea how lucky he was, she wondered? Four little lives to adore, to raise, to love? Kimberly's blue eyes were so like her father's right down to that little hint of sadness. Maddie's brown eyes lit up like a Broadway theater, while she tapped her father's arm relentlessly.

"Daddy, it's Lia! She's our new friend, right? Hi! Hi!" The child waved with such enthusiasm, Lia was reminded of a tail wagging the dog. "I'm Madison! Do you remember me? Will you be my friend, too?"

"Maddie, be quiet." Kimberly held her back.

Gabriel smiled at Lia when she crouched to greet the baby.

"Hi, Emmy. How are you today?" Emmy wore a T-shirt with a picture of a fully charged battery on it. She glanced at her father and bit back a smile. His shirt had the same image, except the battery had only one bar. "Really loving the shirts. Do you have a whole collection of them?"

Gabriel's grin widened.

"I have one, too! See?" Maddie tugged on her shirt.

"Yes, it's awesome."

"Eee-ah. I got dis!" Emmy thrust a small stuffed animal at her.

"Oh, you have a puppy." Lia took the small toy and admired it. "What's his name?"

"Puppy!"

"That's a great name." She gave Emmy back her dog, met the curious looks from Gabriel's other daughters.

"I'm Lia," she reminded them.

The girls didn't say anything until Gabriel cleared his throat.

"You remember our neighbor, Lia?"

"Hi," Kimberly said, shyly.

Olivia scowled at Lia and she had to swallow a grin.

"Are you gonna kiss my dad?" she demanded.

"Olivia!"

Both Gabriel and Kimberly spun on the younger girl. She shoved her hands into the kangaroo pocket of her hoodie, but didn't apologize. Lia felt her face warm.

Madison was still chattering. "We got new nail polish to try tonight. Wanna see it?" And then she gasped. "I know! You can come over and paint nails, too. Can she, Daddy? Huh, huh?"

"Maddie, Lia has her own things to do. Go sit down at that table and stop being annoying."

"I'm not annoying, am I, Lia? Am I?"

"No, not a bit," Lia assured her as Kimberly ushered the two smaller girls to a table in the corner of the shop.

"Hi, Lia. Back so soon?"

"Dinner," she replied as Gabriel stepped to the side, still waiting for his own order.

"Right. You got a large pie, a salad, and a baked ziti dinner."

"That's right."

"Lot of food," Gabriel remarked.

"I hope so. I've got company coming."

His eyebrows went up and then slammed together. "Oh." He said it so softly, she could almost convince herself he'd said nothing at all.

How odd. Why would he care if she had friends over? As soon as her order was boxed and paid for, she grabbed it and turned to the door.

"Bye, everybody."

"Bye-bye!" The baby waved.

She left, juggling a plastic bag from each wrist and holding the pizza box in her hands.

Outside, she blew out a long breath. That was seriously strange. He wasn't angry. But he was *bothered*. But the question remained...why?

Her heart beat faster and her skin tingled. She'd seen the way he'd looked her over when she'd jump-started his car. There was interest there, she was certain of it. So why hadn't he acted on it?

Why hadn't she?

A little girl's shriek answered the question for her: because he has four children. He had no room for her in his life.

Lia walked fast, determined to leave Gabriel Ivers alone no matter how attracted she was, and have a great time with Roseann and Vivian. She'd just crossed the street when a shrill whistle pierced the air. She whipped around to find Gabriel's third child, Maddie, streaking toward her.

"Lia! Lia! It's me! It's Maddie, your new friend!"

Behind the child, she saw Gabriel break into a full run and knew Maddie was going to be in serious trouble. So she took matters into her own hands. She dropped her food, dropped the pharmacy bags, and ran back across the street, causing one car to stop short and blare its horn. She caught the little girl, stopped her from dashing directly into traffic. Crouching down so they were eye level, she said, "Madison, we are not friends. Not yet. You are not to leave your father's side unless he says it's okay. Is that clear?"

The bright and sunny smile on the little girl's face evaporated. "But…but…I thought…"

Gabriel skidded to a stop at Lia's feet, grabbed his daughter's arms. "Madison Elise Ivers, what's the rule about running away when I have my hands full with Emmy?" His face had gone pale.

Maddie turned sad brown eyes to her father. "Not to."

He made a sound of frustration. "Not to. So you remember the rule but you broke it anyway."

"I just wanted to see—"

"Stop talking right now," Gabriel ordered. Blotches from anger reddened his face.

Maddie began to cry and Lia felt terrible.

"When I have your sister in her stroller, where are you supposed to be?"

"But Daddy, I—"

"Answer my question, Madison. Where are you supposed to be?"

She lowered her head and hiccuped as the tears fell. "Right next to you."

"Did you stay right next to me?"

"N...no."

"No. You did not. So that means, when we get home, you'll go straight to your room after supper."

"But we have new nail polish—"

"Straight to your room."

"But, Daddy—"

In a lightning-fast move, Gabriel scooped Madison into his arms. "I said straight to your room."

Gabriel's patience had clearly reached its limit and Lia was almost sure she heard it snap. His voice had risen an entire octave. Feeling enormously guilty, she put a hand on his arm, found it rock solid. "Gabriel, I'm sorry. This was my fault. I'm—"

He spun on her. "It was *not* your fault. She knows not to take off without me, especially not near a busy street and she knows when I'm at the end of my patience. Madison is six years old. Not a baby anymore. She knows what the consequences are for breaking my rules."

Lia nodded, still holding his arm. "It's just that she was so excited about your new nail polish. I'd hate for her to miss manicure night because of me."

A muscle ticked in Gabe's jaw. "Amelia, I get you're trying to help but *I'm* the parent. I got this."

Whoa. Full name. Because she felt about six years old herself, she held up both hands. "Right. Of course."

He carefully crossed the street, making sure Olivia and Kimberly, pushing Emmy's stroller, were beside him. Lia recrossed the street with him, surprised when he kneeled down to retrieve the food and the pharmacy bag she'd dropped to the ground. Little Mason's prescription had fallen out. Gabriel picked it up with his free hand, handed it to her with a raised eyebrow.

Lia did not offer any explanation. She took her belongings and began walking, believing it best to just stay out of his way. Maddie's sobs broke her heart. Gabriel stalked in stony silence with Maddie in his arms, forcing Kimberly and Olivia to half-jog just to keep pace.

"There you are!" a familiar voice called out.

"Roseann!" Lia rushed to hug her dearest friend as best as she could manage with her hands full. "I hope you weren't waiting long?"

"Nope, just pulled up." She turned with a smile to greet Gabriel. "I'm Roseann and you are—"

"Busy." He walked right by without even slowing down.

Lia and Roseann watched Gabriel put Maddie down at the top of the courtyard steps, then turn to carry Emmy's stroller up. He never even looked back.

"Wow. Rude," Roseann announced. "Where's Vivian?"

"Running late," Lia said, balancing bags and the pizza box on her hip so she could fish her keys from her bag. "Take this on in. I have to drop this next door first." Lia handed Roseann the food and jogged up the stairs to Jessica

Vella's unit with the pharmacy bag, gave the door a light knock.

Jessica opened the door with a look of such relief, Lia grinned.

"Thank you so much. What do I owe you?"

"Receipt for the medicine's in the bag. The rest is a gift. I'm right next door whenever you're ready. Hope Mason feels better."

"You're an angel. A savior. Quite possibly my new best friend."

Laughing, Lia waved a hand toward her own front door. "Well, you know where I live if you want a glass of wine one night."

"I will totally take you up on that." When a child's cry sounded, Jessica sighed. "Duty calls. Thanks again, Lia."

Lia headed for her own front door, found Roseann checking out the living room.

"This is a great space, Lia. Bigger than I expected." Roseann turned, gave Lia a hug and a kiss on her cheek. "So...what's up with Chuckles?" She jerked a thumb over her shoulder.

Lia laughed. "That was Gabriel Ivers, my super. His daughter scared a few years off his life. Took off running, trying to catch up to me and nearly ran into traffic."

"Oh, so he's gonna chain her up in the dungeon?"

Lia laughed and headed for the kitchen. "No. He's sending her to her room while her sisters have their manicure night."

Roseann followed and ran a hand down a counter. "Hey, this is like an actual kitchen, not just a corner of a room."

"Yeah, it is pretty awesome." Lia fetched plates and utensils and began spreading things out on one of those pretty granite counters. She loved the gray streaks that ran through the surface, thought it was a nice contrast to the dark wood of the cabinetry.

"So what's his story?" Roseann asked, jerking her head toward the rear door that was just steps away from Gabriel's front door.

"Well, all I know is he lost his wife. Four daughters he's raising by himself."

"Wow. Okay." Roseann shrugged. "I suppose a bit of slack for his earlier rudeness is called for here."

Lia smiled and held up her hand, thumb and index finger touching. "Little bit."

"Show me the rest of the place?"

Lia gave her hands a quick rinse. "I've got a washer and dryer there. Upstairs, there are three bedrooms plus the bathroom. Wait until you see it. It's huge!"

Once upstairs, Roseann nodded. "Wow, you weren't kidding. And a real claw-foot tub?"

"I know, right?" Proudly, Lia opened the door to the linen closet. "And lots of closet space."

"Which bedroom is yours?"

Lia opened the door to her room. "This one."

"Oh, this is beautiful." Roseann poked her head inside. "Love that artwork."

Pleased, Lia turned and glanced at the array of baskets hanging on one wall. Inside, the baskets held a number of small items like jewelry or scarves. "One of my small spaces newsletter tips. Decorating that does double duty." She cocked her head and studied the arrangement with a critical eye. "They look okay? I had some trouble hanging them."

"You didn't ask Mr. Personality next door?"

To her great embarrassment, Lia blushed. "No. I try not to bother him."

"Lia, it's part of his job!"

She hid her face in her hands. "It's not a good idea, Ro. I'm already too attached to that baby."

Roseann held up her hands in surrender. "Okay. Let's go have some of the amazing wine I brought."

Once again downstairs, Lia got out glasses and found her corkscrew.

"So, Super Man across the way...I think you two could—"

"No! Absolutely not." Lia scooped some hot and melty baked ziti onto plates, handed one to Roseann. "Weren't you listening? I can't be trusted around that man."

"Well, why not? He's incredibly attractive. I can't decide if I like those pretty blue eyes or that full, sexy sneer better."

Lia rolled her eyes. "I'm not looking for anybody right now, and most especially not looking for an instant family."

"Whoa, whoa, whoa!" Roseann held up two hands in a *stop* gesture. "I never said anything about attaching yourself to him. I was thinking more of a fling. You know...to get you back in the saddle again."

"Oh my God, Ro." Lia hid her face in her hands. "He's not a horse."

Roseann laughed, sipped her wine and scooped up a bite of ziti. "You know how the song goes? Save a horse, ride a cowboy."

Lia fanned her hot face and tried not to let her best friend see just how much that suggestion interested her.

∾

GABE REMEMBERED NOT to slam the door just in the nick of time. "Wash your hands."

All the girls ran for the bathroom like soldiers heeding the call of reveille. Guilt began to worm its way through him but he squashed it like a bug. He had a right to his anger. Madison knew better than to go off running down a busy street. If Kim and Liv hadn't been there to mind Emmy, he would have had *to choose*—

When the wave of panic threatened to drown him again, he sucked in a deep breath and began pulling out paper plates, napkins, utensils. He filled Emmy's sippy cup, began dicing up a slice of pizza into bite-sized squares, put it all on her high chair tray. One by one, the girls returned to the table, took their seats, eyes pinned to him.

"Is nobody hungry?" he asked.

Still quiet, the girls slowly began to eat. The sounds of chewing were interrupted by an occasional hiccup from Maddie, whose face was red and her eyes still full of tears.

"Kim, Liv. You have any major homework assignments we need to plan this weekend?"

Kim shook her head. Liv shrugged. "I have to write a term paper. I wanted to do a project, but Mr. Kress said no. He hates me."

A term paper? Jeez, she was in fourth grade.

"It's like a long essay," Kimberly offered. "You pick a

topic, do a ton of research about it, then write the research."

Gabe swallowed some water. "Um, not exactly. You pick a topic. But the research you do is supposed to answer a question, convince people that your answer to the question is correct."

Olivia frowned. "How do you do that when you're not sure?"

"That's the point of the term paper. To teach you how to be sure." Gabe took another bite of pizza. "So what topics do you have to choose from?" When Kimberly had these assignments, there was always a list.

"Um, there's like twenty on the list. I don't remember them."

"Okay, show me the list as soon as you're done."

"But, Daddy, it's—"

"I know what day it is, Liv. Show me the list when you've finished eating."

Three sets of shoulders drooped another inch...four if he counted Emmy's. He tried not to sigh. He was still pissed.

Why was he pissed? Yes, so Maddie had run off. Madison was an impulsive child and he often had to keep a closer eye on her than on the baby. So why had this time made him so furious?

Lia.

She'd been here for barely a couple of months and already, she'd made his life harder than it already was...taking the apartment that would have solved his sibling rivalry squabbles, enticing his daughter into taking off like a rocket. Jesus, his heart was still racing. Maddie hadn't done something like that since she was in diapers. As rambunctious as

Emmy could be at times, even *she* knew not to run off. Bell Boulevard was a busy street. If Lia hadn't been there...

If Lia hadn't been there, damn it, his daughter would have had no reason to take off.

"Dad?"

"What?"

Jeez, whose voice was that coming out of his mouth? He looked up just in time to see all of his kids recoiling from him like he'd taken out a whip.

"I'm sorry, girls. I'm sorry. Really."

They stared at him like he'd spoken in tongues.

"What did you want to ask, Cocoa-Pop?"

She lifted a shoulder, picked a glop of cheese from her half-eaten slice of pizza. "Nothing."

"Kim, I'm sorry. Really. Go ahead. Ask."

Kim looked at Liv and then carefully back at her plate. "That lady. Lia. It's okay if you...you know...*like* her."

The emphasis she placed on the word seemed to suck all of the oxygen out of the room. "Like her?" he echoed.

"You were pretty mean to her. Boys are always mean to the girls they like," Kimberly said and Olivia nodded her agreement.

"I don't know her," he finally replied and it was true. He didn't.

"But if you do like her and want to, um...you know...go out with her or something...we wouldn't mind—"

"Yes, we would," Olivia put in, glaring at her sister, which was apparently the only thing Maddie needed to start talking again.

"I wouldn't mind, Daddy. I like her 'cause she's nice and

pretty and smells really good and—"

"Shut up, Maddie." Olivia turned. "This is all your fault anyway."

"Is not!" Maddie leaned forward, spilling a glass of water.

Gabe resisted the urge to just get up and walk out. He loved his daughters. He loved them with every cell in his body, but sometimes, like right now, he'd gladly trade the pack of them for a fishing rod and bucket of bait.

"Enough," he said with enough of his earlier anger still lacing the words that everyone immediately cowered again. He tossed a pile of napkins on the spill. "I already told you, I don't know her. She is not our friend," he added for Maddie's benefit. "She's our neighbor. If we become friends and I decide I *do* like her, then we'll talk."

"But, Daddy, I don't want a stepmother." Olivia shoved back from the table with a huff.

"Sit down and finish your dinner," Gabe ordered through clenched teeth. "If I do decide I like her, that's our business, not yours. Liking somebody is a far cry from asking her to marry me and become your stepmother."

"That's not fair!"

"Olivia, what's not fair is a nine-year-old dictating my life to me. Are you finished with your pizza?"

"Yeah."

"Good. You can go to your room now."

Olivia's mouth opened to spew more outrage but Gabe held up a hand. "Maddie, you go, too. No manicures tonight. I've had more than enough from the whole bunch of you and just want to be by myself. Get ready for bed. No TV, no games, no talking."

"I hate you!" Olivia shrieked and stormed off.

"Me, too!" Maddie followed, slamming the bedroom door after her.

Gabe might have laughed at their performances if he didn't feel so utterly worthless. Even his little E-Rex was uncharacteristically quiet during her bath tonight. By the time he'd finished bathing the baby and reading Emmy a story, Maddie had already fallen asleep, tears marking tracks down her cheeks. Olivia was still awake, aiming brown laser glares through his back while he put Emmy in her crib.

"Good night, Olivia," he said softly.

She didn't respond and that was okay. Tomorrow was another day. Tomorrow, he'd apologize to Amelia Blake. He'd taken a chunk out of her—and her friend, he remembered with a wince. He'd seen the hurt in her eyes when he'd snapped at her—and hated that he'd caused it. She was...

Hell. He wasn't sure exactly what she was. Sure was pretty, though. All that auburn hair that turned to fire in the sunlight...the curves he couldn't help but notice in her jeans...huge brown eyes that instantly turned hot when she was pissed...full lips that reminded him of peaches, of all things.

He left the girls' bedroom and collapsed next to Kim on the sofa. She was watching some sitcom he'd never seen before. "Should we see if there's a decent movie on?"

She shrugged, but said nothing.

He grabbed the remote, scrolled through the channel guide. "See anything you want to watch?"

Another shrug.

"Kimmy, conversation works best when more than one

person does all the talking."

"I'm allowed to talk now?"

Gabe opened his mouth, then shut it. He tried again. "Okay. I guess I deserved that. Yes, you're allowed to talk."

"Livvie thinks all stepmothers are evil."

"And where did she get this from?"

"From Zoe at school. Her mom got married again and Zoe got a stepbrother and stepsister. They take Zoe's stuff without asking and her mom always takes *their* side instead of Zoe's. She wants to go live with her dad now."

Gabe stared at his daughter in shock. "And you think I'd do that, too? Thanks a lot."

Kimberly made a sound of frustration. "That's just it, Daddy! Zoe didn't think her mom would do it either, but she is."

"And how do you know all this? You don't even go to that school."

Kimberly lifted one shoulder again. "Liv and I talk. After Maddie falls asleep. You know…"

Yeah. He did know. Sighing heavily, he scratched the back of his neck. "Kimmy, Cocoa-Pop, listen to me. I'm not looking to get married again. I don't even want to date anybody. So it's kind of silly to get this mad over stuff that's not a problem. What *is* a problem is one of my daughters ran down a busy street, forcing me to go after her and leave my other daughters by themselves. That's why I'm so mad."

Kimberly thought that over but shook her head. "No, Daddy. You got mad as soon as Maddie said she wanted to be Lia's friend. Actually, you've been mad since Lia moved in and it's not fair."

She went to her room, softly shut the door, leaving him alone with nothing but the echo of her words.

He got up, moved to the living room window and cranked it open, the fresh night air doing nothing to calm him. It's not that he was mad. He was...frustrated. He...well, damn it, he was attracted to Amelia Blake and just what the hell was wrong with that, anyway? He was a grown-ass man. He was allowed to look at attractive people, wasn't he? Jeez, he hadn't even glanced at a member of the opposite sex since he met Janey and now one lived right next door and—

Holy hell.

She lived right next door.

He scrubbed a hand over his face and ground his teeth together. There was no harm looking at Lia or flirting with her, especially since she looked and flirted right back. If things...took off from there, then he'd talk to the girls.

～

"THERE. THAT'S THAT." Lia lifted her hair off her neck and rubbed where a single tight knot had formed.

"I'm spent," Vivian announced and flopped down to the sofa the three women had just muscled into place. "Is there any more wine?"

"Yes, there's another bottle." Roseann extended a hand to help her up.

Lia cranked open a window and fanned her face, then retrieved the last of the wine. "You guys are the best."

"Damn right we are." Viv thrust a fist in the air. "Fill me

up." She held out her glass.

"Wine's not gonna help. We need massages," Lia grumbled.

"Wait, I think there's a delivery service for that," Roseann said and Vivian perked up.

"Massages? Really?"

"No, not really."

"Cruel, Roseann. Bitchy and cruel." Vivian lifted her head to glare at Roseann. "As soon as I can move, I'm going to kick your ass."

Lia laughed. It was awesome having both of her best friends here to help. They'd repositioned her sofa, the one piece of furniture Jared hadn't fought over.

"You know, I've always hated these lamps," Lia admitted.

"You do?" Roseann asked, lifting her head from the back of the sofa.

"Yeah. I don't know why I wanted them."

"Because Jared picked them out. Obviously." Viv sneered at them. "They are pretty hideous."

"How much do you hate them, Lia?"

Carefully, Lia studied the tall white porcelain monstrosities that featured a bunch of naked and dancing cherubim.

"Um, all the way."

With her eyes pinned on Lia's, Roseann slowly extended a hand and pushed the lamp to the floor, grinning savagely when it shattered.

"Oh my God, Ro!" Vivian jumped while Lia merely sat there, gaping.

"What? She said she hates them." Roseann angled her head at Lia. "Why don't you kill its mate?"

"Kill the—For heaven's sake." Lia pressed her lips together.

"Come on. You know you want to. You can buy new ones. I'll buy them, in fact."

She could, couldn't she? Smiling slowly, Lia considered that. She slowly extended a hand and shoved the other lamp to the floor where it too shattered into a few hundred pieces.

"Oh my God, you're right. That felt ah-mazing." Lia shut her eyes and enjoyed the sensation of having murdered something Jared picked out. "Is this what cats feel like?"

"Told ya."

She gave it a minute. "So...who's cleaning this up?"

The sound of a heavy fist on her back door quieted all three of them.

"Lia!" *Bang, bang, bang.* "Lia! Are you okay?"

Lia rushed to the back door, flung it open to reveal a wild Gabriel holding a—a hammer?

He stood there, eyes scanning the room for threats while all three of them gaped at him.

"Well. Hello, again, Super Man."

He ignored Roseann, locked eyes with Lia. "You okay? I heard glass shatter."

Heard the—Oh. She slapped a hand to her mouth. She'd forgotten the windows were open. "Oh my God, I am so sorry. We were just—Oh, Gabriel. I am really, really sorry. We had a small mishap."

He was still gripping the hammer like it was Thor's. With his jaw clenched and chest heaving, he said, "Uh-huh."

"It's okay, Gabriel. Everything's okay. I'll tape it all up in cardboard and mark *glass* on it so you won't cut yourself when you put the trash out."

After a minute, he lowered the hammer, dragged a hand through his hair and sighed. He suddenly noticed Roseann and Vivian. "Oh. Company. Right."

"I'm Roseann. We met before. And this is Vivian."

He winced and managed a small smile. "I'm sorry about before. I was in the middle of a tantrum." He shifted the hammer to his left hand so he could extend his right.

"Your daughter did seem upset," Roseann remarked, shaking his hand.

"Not her. Me." He flashed that awkward smile that seemed to make Lia's pulse skip.

"Um, how about a glass of wine? You might need it more than we do." Vivian took the bottle from the coffee table but Gabe waved her off.

"No. Thanks. I left my girls alone."

"We're sorry for scaring you," Lia said.

"Okay, then. Good night."

Gabriel went out the back door and Lia shut and locked it after him. Then, she closed the living room windows, too.

"Well. That was, er, interesting." Roseann sipped her wine.

"Interesting? Not the word I'd use." Vivian shook her head. "The way he charged in here, hammer swinging? That was freaking hot."

"Hammer...swinging?" Roseann burst into gut-busting laughter but Lia ignored them both.

She felt absolutely horrible, indulging in childish stunts like breaking lamps. She'd never even considered how the sound of smashing glass might frighten the other tenants.

She could almost hear her mother's voice, scolding her. "Of course you didn't, Lia. You never think before you act."

She'd seen Gabriel's face earlier when Maddie had scared him, seen the pure terror in his eyes and known she was responsible for it. And now, she'd done it again. She fetched the broom and dustpan from their closet in the kitchen and began sweeping up the mess, listening to Vivian and Roseann giggle about Gabriel's hammer. More than once, Roseann teased her about Superintendent/Tenant games, but Lia refused to play along. She would never do anything to put that look of pure helpless terror in Gabriel's eyes again.

Chapter Nine

ON SATURDAY MORNING, Gabe awoke before the girls and thought about mixing up pancakes. He'd had a restless night, dreaming of Madison running straight into an oncoming car and dreaming of Amelia Blake holding him, moving underneath him only to shift to her holding his daughter on her lap.

It was extremely unsettling and he kept jolting awake over and over again and refused, just flat-out refused to admit it was lust more than fear that disturbed his dreams. By three in the morning, he'd finally gotten out of bed to watch Maddie sleep for a few minutes, just to prove to himself it was fear.

Today would be a bagel morning instead of pancakes. He took his coffee to the sofa, flipped on the TV.

"Good morning, Ducky." He grinned as Madison joined him.

"Morning, Daddy." She peered up at him through a mess of tangled brown hair. "How come your face didn't get soft today?"

Gabe's lips twitched. "Uh, well, I guess it's because I didn't sleep enough. It's okay. When I shave later, I'll put some lotion on it. Go get dressed. We're going to the bagel store for breakfast today."

"Ooo. Can I get a rainbow bagel?"

"Sure, if they have any."

"Daddy," Maddie said, jumping on the sofa. "The bagel store's right near the pizza store and I promise I won't run away this time. I'll hold on to Emmy's stroller and Kimby's hand and Olivia's, too."

"You'd need three hands for that, dummy." Olivia wandered in, yawning.

"Liv. Stop calling your sister a dummy," Gabe snapped. Jeez, it wasn't even eight a.m. yet and already, the bickering had begun.

"Sorry," Olivia said without any conviction.

Gabe took a sip of coffee, padded on bare feet to the girls' room to liberate Emmy from her crib. Kimberly was still sound asleep.

"Dad-dee! Morning time, Dad-dee."

"Morning, E-Rex. Let's do that diaper, okay?"

"'Kay, Dad-dee."

Emmy dropped like a log to Maddie's bed. "You're getting too big for diapers, Emmy. It's almost time for the potty."

She looked at him with wide blue eyes. "I go on potty?"

"Sure."

"'Kay!"

And she took off like a bullet. He caught up to her in time to prevent her from falling in. "Easy, E-Rex. Hold on. Look what I got for you." He sifted through the toilet paper rolls, tissue boxes, and soap bars stored under the sink, found the potty ring they'd used for Madison, fitted it onto the toilet and lifted her on top. "How's that?"

Giggling, Emmy kicked her legs. "I on da potty."

"Yes, you are. Can you do pee-pee here instead of in your diaper?"

She pushed and strained and a second later, gasped when the sound of tinkling reached her ears.

"Yay!" Gabe applauded. "High five."

"Yay!" Emmy clapped, too, and then slapped his palm. "I tell Maddie."

He caught her when she leaped off the toilet. "First, wash your hands. Then tell Maddie." She did and took off, squealing.

"Dad! Emmy's naked!"

Gabe dropped his head into his hands for a moment then hurried to the living room, whistling for everyone's attention. "Okay, everybody get dressed. We're leaving in fifteen minutes." He went to his own room to do just that, closing the door firmly behind him. He tugged on jeans, a dark blue shirt that boasted *I make cute kids* and rooted through his drawers for a pair of socks. In the next room, he heard raised voices again and decided against breaking it up.

Instead, he busied himself making his bed, straightening up his bedroom. He threw his pajamas into the laundry basket, headed for the girls' room to find three angry faces at the bottom of the bunk beds.

He'd designed and made those beds himself.

Instead of a ladder, he'd fashioned a staircase that opened into drawers. On the opposite end, he'd built in a small desk. Olivia's bed jutted out from beneath Kim's at a right angle. The bunk beds took up one entire corner of the girls' room.

On the other wall, he'd squished in Emmy's crib and Maddie's single bed plus the dresser he'd refinished. He'd put up shelves all over the room and there still wasn't enough space for everything. The desk was never used for homework. It had become an extension of the dresser, holding clothes.

His thoughts wandered back to his plans for creating space where there wasn't any, his engineer's brain looking for opportunities to utilize every wasted inch. It was time to stop planning and start building.

Kim was still asleep. He stepped up on the bed. "Kim. We're going for bagels."

"Daddy, please let me sleep. I'm really tired."

"What about breakfast?"

"Just bring me back a plain bagel, okay?" She rolled over, shut her eyes.

"Sure thing, Cocoa-Pop. Okay, Maddie. Find clothes." He pulled a shirt over Emmy's head that matched his. Hers said *Cute Kid.* Just to be safe, he added extra clothes to the backpack and the toilet seat ring. He turned to hair next. Olivia's ponytail, Emmy's Velcro clip and Maddie...well, Maddie had another huge snarl. Gabe pulled hers into a ponytail, too.

When Maddie saw Emmy's shirt, she had to find hers, as well. Olivia didn't care one way or the other and soon, they were ready to leave.

Outside, the weather was gorgeous. There was a crisp breeze, but it was still bright and sunny. He put on sunglasses and as they passed Lia's kitchen door, he stopped and knocked twice.

It took a minute, but Lia unfastened the deadbolt and

opened the door. All that fiery hair was scraped back in a bun and he thought that was a crime. She was dressed in those jeans that raised his heart rate, and a flowy T-shirt that rippled in the breeze.

She took his breath away.

He cleared his throat. "We're doing bagels for breakfast today. Would you like to join us? I think all of us, but especially me, owe you an apology for yesterday."

Maddie nodded once. "I'm very sorry I didn't listen to my daddy, Lia."

Lia's smile spread wide and then faded when Olivia rolled her eyes. Gabe opened his mouth to scold her and then shut it. He'd get to the bottom of Liv's behavior later.

Lia flashed another smile at his shirt. "Can't argue with that. You do make cute kids."

"I got one too! See?" Maddie showed Lia her coordinating shirt.

"I see. How about you, Olivia?"

The girl shrugged. "I'm done being cute."

Okay, then. "Where's Kimberly?"

"Still sleeping," Gabe replied as Lia stepped out and locked her door. They started walking. Gabe lifted Emmy's stroller down the courtyard steps and smiled as Maddie kept her word, walking calmly with one hand holding the stroller. Olivia walked on the other side, shuffling through leaves. Lia walked beside Maddie and Gabe found himself sneaking glances at her.

"Daddy, can we do nail polish tonight if I'm really good?"

"Sure, Ducky. We can."

"Can Lia do nail polish, too? Please?"

"If she wants."

"Dad-dee, bird!" Emmy pointed at a pigeon that swooped down in front of them to snatch a muffin paper that had fallen from a trash can on the corner where they waited for the green light.

"Yes, Emmy. That's a pigeon."

The light turned green and Gabe shifted his hand to Maddie's. Just in case.

"Daddy, is it okay if I skip soccer today?" Olivia asked when they reached the opposite curb.

He glanced at her, found her looking down at her feet, a tiny frown marring her forehead. "Well, first tell me why."

She shrugged. "Just don't feel like it."

"I got that. But why? Did you not sleep well?"

Olivia sighed. "I…well…I just don't want to."

"Livvie, your team might be upset if you don't show up. They might be tired and just don't want to play, either, but they'll show up. If you don't, how do you think it'll make them feel?"

Maddie gasped. "Oh, I know! They'll feel really sad. Right, Daddy? Right, right?"

"Exactly, Maddie."

But Olivia only rolled her eyes. "Fine. I'll play. But can you just leave Emmy home with Kim?"

Gabe stopped walking. All the girls turned to look at him. He studied his second-born child for a long moment and then crouched down so he was at eye level. "Olivia Grace, I love you." He waited a beat until her dark eyes lifted to his, told him all that he needed to know. "I love you and if it feels like I don't, then I'm sorry for it and I'll do better. If you want to spend time with me, just the two of us, we can do that. But maybe not during your game time, because Maddie's right. It wouldn't be fair to your teammates."

She looked down, twirled the end of her ponytail and bit her lip, but then, she nodded. "Okay. I'll play."

He gave that ponytail a playful tug and was about to stand up when she shocked him by flinging herself at him in a hug so strong, it took his breath away. Over her head, he saw Lia bite her lip and look away, and figured this was awkward, but there was no way he was letting go. Olivia was not a hug-and-kiss fan. Of the four girls, she was the one most often embarrassed by his antics, like the pink polish on his nails, or hugs in public places—like the middle of Bell Boulevard on a Saturday morning. She was the quietest, the most curious of the quartet, too. He should have known something was up with her after last night's outburst.

But he hadn't paid attention.

He tightened his arms around her and vowed to do better.

"Me, too! Me, too!" Maddie cried and piled on. That got Emmy started so he leaned into her stroller to give her a loud kiss and a hug, too. "And Lia! Don't forget Lia, Daddy."

Oh, boy. He wasn't going to take advantage of the situation.

But Lia, it seemed, had other ideas. She wrapped her arms around him and laughed. "Yay, I get hugs and kisses, too?"

Playing along, he pressed a loud smack to her cheek, which made Maddie giggle and Olivia pout, and him...well, it made him aware.

Very aware.

When they started walking again, Lia looked at him. "Gabriel, I'm happy to watch your daughters when I can. Just ask, okay?"

"Yay! I want Lia to babysit, Daddy."

"Yeah, sure. Okay."

At Ben's Bagels, Olivia opened the door and held it while Gabe steered the stroller through. "Who's ready for breakfast?" Ben's Bagels had the best bagels in New York, as far as Gabe was concerned.

"Morning, Ben," he called to the tall thin man behind the counter that ran the entire length of the shop. He wore a white apron and blue cap.

"Hey, Gabe. What can I get you?"

Gabe pulled out his travel mug. "More coffee. And we'll need half a dozen bagels, all with cream cheese." He suddenly remembered Lia. "Unless you want something else?"

She shook her head. "I like cream cheese. And I like whole wheat."

Cool. Okay, then. "Coffee?"

"Sure."

"That'll be one plain, one everything, one—"

"Rainbow, Daddy!"

"Right. One rainbow. Liv?"

"I want the cinnamon raisin."

"One cinnamon raisin, one whole wheat, and the last one is to-go. That'll be a plain bagel. And a large coffee."

"Coming up. Go have a seat. I'll bring the order out."

"Thanks." Gabe pushed Emmy's stroller over to a corner

table near the window, got the baby fastened into a wooden high chair and headed to a refrigerated case to grab some orange juice containers. When he stepped up to the register to pay, Ben slid his travel mug across the counter, along with a second cup in a to-go container with cardboard sleeve.

"Your fuel, sir."

"Got that right," Gabe replied with a laugh. He brought the juice to their table, poked straws through the holes and handed one to each of the older girls. For Emmy, he poured some into her sippy cup, diluting it with a little water.

"Lia. How do you like your coffee?"

"Milk and sugar."

"Be right back." Gabe went back for the cups, fixed Lia's the way she'd directed, and brought them back to the table. "Girls, be careful of the hot cups."

"Bay-gul, Dad-dee."

"Coming up, Emmy."

Maddie eyed Olivia's bagel. "I like raisins, too. Do you like raisins, Daddy?"

Gabe despised raisins and shook his head. "Uh-uh, no way, no raisins for me."

Giggling, Maddie asked, "Did you ever try raisins? You can't know you don't like them unless you try them first. Right, right?"

He grinned at her attempt to make him eat the words he'd said to her so many times. "I have tried them and don't like them. But if you like raisins, you should eat them."

"Next time, I can get two bagels. A rainbow one and a raisin one. Or three! Do you like raisins, Lia?"

"Love them."

He glanced at Olivia. She was still quieter than normal and he wished he could figure out how to make things right for her. "How about you, Liv? Are you pro-raisin?"

She shrugged. "I think they look disgusting but I like how they taste."

"Okay, that's two pro-raisin, one anti-raisin, and one moderate."

"What's that mean, Daddy?"

"Moderate means Olivia is so-so about raisins. Pro means you and Lia like them. And anti means I'm against them."

"Oh. I'm anti-vegetables 'cause they're 'sgusting."

Lia hid a smile behind her cup but he laughed. "Vegetables may be disgusting, Maddie, but they're super-fuel for your body."

"Here we go, Ivers family." Ben slid a tray covered in bagels to their table. "One rainbow, one plain, one everything, one whole wheat, and one cinnamon raisin."

Lia's smile froze on her face and Gabe wondered why—Oh. Right. *Ivers family.* He shrugged it off. If Ben wanted to think they were a thing, more power to him.

"Yay!" Emmy applauded. Ben bowed and made Maddie giggle.

Ben handed Gabe a paper bag. "That's your to-go order plus a few treats for the girls."

Gabe smiled. "Thanks, man."

"Enjoy."

"Okay, everybody. Dig in."

Olivia ate in silence. Maddie chattered about how good raisins and rainbows tasted. Emmy danced in a wooden high chair. Gabe just kept watching Lia while simultaneously worrying about Kim wanting to sleep and Olivia wanting to skip soccer.

When Olivia finished her juice, she jumped up. "I have to go to the bathroom."

"Me, too! Me, too!" Maddie sprang to attention, but Gabe's hand on her shoulder kept her seated.

"Do you really need to go to the bathroom or do just want to be with Liv?"

Maddie hesitated, just for a moment, and Gabe knew the truth. "Ducky, I know you love your sisters, but you have to give them privacy sometimes. Do you know what that means?"

Brown eyes wide, she shook her head. "Uh-uh. What?"

"Privacy is being private about some things so that only you know about them. Going to the bathroom is private. What's under your clothes is private."

"Oh, like your—"

"And sometimes—" Gabe quickly cut her off before she brought up the whole 'big thing' story in front of Lia "—sometimes, you need to stop asking people a hundred questions and just let them be. Understand?"

Maddie thought about that for a minute and then shook her head. "I like questions. Questions are how I know if someone's my friend or not. Are you my friend, Emmy?" she asked the baby.

Emmy, who was just two, answered as two-year-olds are compelled to do. "No!"

"That's not nice," Maddie protested.

"Eat your breakfast, Maddie." Gabe angled his seat so he could keep an eye on the restroom from here. He hated public bathrooms, hated having to bring the girls into the men's room but hated even more when they insisted on going alone. But he knew Ben's. The restroom here was a single toilet. As long as the door was locked, Liv was safe.

"So, Gabriel. Are you working on any new projects?" Lia asked and he stared at her dumbly. "You mentioned you're an engineer?"

Oh, right. "Funny you should ask that. I just returned to that work. One day a week, but it's cool. We're removing the fire escapes from a downtown residential building and updating all the stairwells to the current fire codes."

She sipped coffee, licked her lips and he shifted on his chair. "Removing the fire escapes?"

"Yeah. Most new structures don't have them. Instead, the stairwells are fireproof."

She nodded. "I never knew that."

He glanced toward the restroom again. Liv was finally on her way back and he relaxed. He told Lia all about his work and it wasn't until Emmy let out a squeal of protest that he realized he was boring all of them. "And that's probably way more than anybody ever needed to hear about structural design."

Lia waved a hand. "Actually, it was interesting. You must be very good at it."

Gabe's face warmed. "I am. But how can you tell?"

"Because you love it. You love talking about it."

He shrugged. "I do love it. Not sure how good I am at it these days." He took a bite of his bagel.

"Why not?" Lia handed Maddie a napkin.

Gabe gave Emmy her cup of juice. "Well, you've seen my

place. I'm keep trying to eke out more space, but it's like squeezing blood from a stone. Five of us in four rooms is tough, but that's the apartment that comes with the superintendent job. I can afford the difference in rent on a bigger unit once I earn some extra money, but for now, I have to make this unit work."

Lia's eyes lit up. "I can help you with that. I helped research a book called *Small Spaces*."

Nodding, he sipped some coffee. "Like your newsletter? Nice job, by the way."

"Thanks. And yes, the newsletter idea sprung from that project."

"I like the life hacks section," he admitted. "Okay." He circled his hand. "Let's hear your ideas for making this apartment work."

"Well, you could give the girls your larger bedroom."

"Dad-dee has a big bed."

Lia exchanged a grin with him and he shrugged. "The girls always want to sleep in my bed."

"It's really comfy, Daddy," Maddie announced.

"There's a lot you can do, Gabriel," Lia continued. "Built-ins, furniture that does double duty."

He nodded. "I've been looking at pull-out sofa beds."

"That's one option. Have you thought about a Murphy bed? They're a great way to gain extra space." Lia took out her phone, tapped the screen, then showed him a website.

He took her phone, scrolled through the pictures. He'd never even thought about hideaway beds. The pictures were impressive. Some were desks, others were bookcases and still others were sofas when the bed was folded.

"They're not that expensive and they install fairly easily—or so I'm told... What?" Lia caught the way he was staring at her.

"I am thoroughly embarrassed that I never thought of this."

"Can I see, Daddy?" Maddie stood up. She studied the pictures and frowned. "I don't want to sleep folded up."

Laughing, he shook his head. "It's okay, Ducky. It's only folded up when you're *not* sleeping." He took Lia's phone back, synapses firing at light speed, and wished he had a sketch pad. If he put a Murphy system on the wall where the living room bookcase stood, that would free up his room—Oh! He could put similar beds in that room so the girls would have not only a place to sleep, but also a place to hang out. Kimberly would be thirteen in a few months. He'd much rather have her home than hanging out in places he couldn't keep an ear—or an eye—on things.

"Dad-dee, pee-pee."

Startled, he froze for a second and then remembered Emmy had no diaper on. "Right! Potty. Hold on, Emmy. Hold on." He grabbed the bag off the stroller, quickly scooped Emmy from the high chair and hurried to the restroom where Emmy hit the bull's-eye. "Good girl. High five!"

"Yay! I tell Ee-uh."

Lia. *Shit*. The girls. He'd... Jeez, he'd just left Liv and Maddie out there. He hadn't thought twice about it. He'd, well, he'd just *assumed* that Lia—

He chased after the baby, found her already on Lia's lap, telling her all about the potty. Maddie was doing her chair-dance thing and then held up a raisin to Lia's mouth that she gobbled up with a little growl. Liv slumped over the table, picking her bagel apart. She brightened considerably when something Lia said impressed her.

"Dad, Lia recorded that interview with LeeAnne Walters. Remember the one I said I wanted to see but you said no? Anyway, she said I could watch it. Can I do that with her later?"

Gabe winced. He was supposed to do that and completely forgot. "Sure thing, Liv." He sat down, grabbed his coffee. Lia looked at him sideways.

"Something wrong?"

He shook his head. "No. Everything's...great."

"I'm sorry. I should have checked with you first. I didn't think." Lia put a hand on his arm, which sent his hormone levels happily into orbit. "If you want, I'll lend you that book so you can figure out what plans would work in your apartment. We could look through it while Liv's watching the documentary."

"Yeah. It's fine. That would be great."

There was that word again. But the really weird part was...he wasn't lying. Not one bit.

❦

ON THE WALK home, Lia held Maddie's hand—but remembered to ask Gabriel first if that was okay.

It was.

Lia tried not to read anything into that, tried not to make a big deal out of it, but this was his *daughter*. He was trusting her with one of his children. What *deal* got any bigger?

Maddie chattered all the way back to the building and Lia admired Gabriel's patience answering questions like why bagels had holes, why raisins were wrinkly, and why she couldn't eat bagels for lunch and dinner, too. Emmy pointed out things of interest along the way, shouting out *Bird! Car! Puppy!* whenever the need arose.

Lia had never had more fun.

"Okay, girls, you stay with Lia. I'll give Kim her bagel and be right back."

"'Kay, Daddy."

In her living room, Lia queued up the recorded documentary she'd made. "Here you go, Liv."

When Olivia said nothing, Lia turned to Maddie.

"Maddie, would you like to read a book or color?"

"Ooo, I love to color."

"Got you covered." Lia took out some paper and markers and set Maddie up in the kitchen. Emmy wanted to color, too, so Lia had a little brainstorm. She shoved her coffee table into the kitchen, grabbed some throw pillows from the sofa, and organized the two younger girls there so Olivia could watch her documentary in peace.

"Olivia, can I get you anything?"

"No."

Lia pressed her lips together.

"Thanks," she added, suddenly remembering manners.

Smiling, Lia opened the rear door when Gabriel knocked. He walked in, grinned at his girls at their little art station.

"Where's Kimberly?"

His smile faded. "She says she's tired but I managed to coax her up for the bagel. I hope she's not coming down with something." He put a large sketch pad on her kitchen table. "I brought this so we could sketch ideas out."

She winced. "Um, yeah. I'm not so good at sketching."

"That's okay. I am. Just give me a second." He stepped into her living room, checked on Olivia. "How's the show?"

"Good."

Lia bit back a grin when Olivia didn't even look at her father. Gabe shook his head and rejoined her in the kitchen.

"That's some desk you got," he said, jerking his finger over his shoulder. "Mission control."

"Yep," she said proudly. "I was going to make an office out of one of the bedrooms, but like working down here more. I really love it, but have to call the store and set up service."

"How come?"

"It's damaged. One of the drawers is warped."

"I'll take a look."

Lia shook her head. "Not necessary."

"It's not a problem. This is what I do."

He crossed in front of Olivia's line of sight, earning a hiss, and examined the three drawers in the desk's base. He opened and closed them, saw the problem immediately. He returned to the kitchen. "You got a flathead screwdriver?"

"Sure." She went to the drawer where she kept her tools, handed him the screwdriver and followed him back to the corner of the living room where the desk was. He opened the drawer as far as it would move, slid his hands along the metal side rails, pressed on something and just like that, the whole drawer came out of the desk.

She watched him crouch down, carefully eye the tracks on both the desk and on the drawer. With the screwdriver, he pressed a spot on the track, then eyeballed it again. Satisfied it was straight, he replaced the drawer and closed it. Lia's mouth dropped open.

"That's it? It's fixed?"

"That's it."

"You really are Super Man. Thank you so much."

"Daddy, I can't hear."

"Oops. Sorry, Liv." He handed Lia back her screwdriver and went back to the kitchen.

"Seriously," Lia began after she put the screwdriver away. "You did that in like three minutes."

He shrugged. "No big deal."

She sat beside him at the kitchen table and began paging through his book, studying the pencil sketches of buildings, houses, a set of bunk beds, and...and a dog house? "These are amazing, Gabriel. Like really good. Have you ever done people?"

His gaze met hers, held. "I have some of the girls," he admitted with a shrug.

"Could I see them?"

He laughed, low and soft. "Are you asking to see my...etchings?"

Lia's face burst into flame. "I'll just go find that book." She hurried into the living room, searched the tall bookcase beside her desk for the *Small Spaces* book she'd help research and took it back to Gabriel, who was on his knees showing

Maddie how to draw a puppy for Emmy.

She froze near the kitchen door, saw the connection that linked them, unmistakably, as a family. Emmy's blue eyes, the shape of Maddie's face—they were Gabriel's. But it wasn't just their DNA. It was the trust that filled the girls' eyes when they looked at him. And it was the naked pride that filled his when he looked back.

She'd never have this. Even if she did take Roseann up on her amazing offer to carry a child for her, half that hypothetical baby's DNA would be a mystery. Whose features would she see on a small face?

Tears gathered behind her eyes as the cold hard fist of that reality squeezed her heart.

"Lia. What's wrong?"

Suddenly, Gabriel was there, his hands on her arms, his face full of concern. Deliberately, she took a step back, shivered when his hands fell to his sides. "It's…silly. I'm being silly. Don't mind me." She waved her hand, swatting at that cold hard reality like it was an insect. "Come on. Let's get to work."

"Yeah. Okay." He took the book she forgot she held, put it on the table. "We don't have much time before Emmy's nap time."

She swallowed hard and managed a smile. She'd forgotten about nap time—just further proof, as if she needed any, that she wasn't mom material. "Oh. Right. Forgot."

"Oh, trust me. She won't." Gabriel slid the book closer, opened the cover. "I read your newsletter," he said, turning pages. "Good stuff in there. Did that come from this book?"

Lia coughed once, cleared her throat, tried to talk over

the lump still inside. "Some did. I have an agreement with the author to use her work. You're already well organized but sometimes, you find a new technique, a new tool in your toolbox that can make a big difference."

He glanced over at her, eyebrows raised. "Um. Thanks. That trick about the dishes? It really helps."

She smiled. "Glad to hear it." She angled the book, flipped pages and slid it back. "This is what I wanted to show you. Transformative furniture. Your table takes up a lot of real estate. Look at this one."

He glanced at the bookcase pictured across the two-page spread she'd indicated and his jaw dropped. It rotated from bookshelf into a table. "How have I never heard of this before? I'm an engineer."

She shrugged. "Probably because it solves problems you didn't have."

"Until now."

"Until now," she agreed. "This shelf unit could go right where your dining table is now. You can keep dishes on the shelves, assuming they're safe around Emmy, and then just swing the shelves into the table formation."

"Very cool. And it locks into position, so E-Rex here won't swing on it."

"Exactly."

"Only downside is that it needs a few feet of clearance to swing from shelf unit to flat table."

Lia nodded. "Okay. Good point. How about this one." She flipped a few pages, showed him another table.

He shot her the side-eye. "There's no way that tiny console table can seat eight for dinner."

"It does, but the extenders aren't self-storing, so what you're saving in real estate, you may be losing in trying to hide those extra pieces."

"Still cool, though. If I had free wall space, I'd hang the panels up as artwork, and just pull them off the wall whenever I needed them."

She stared at him. "That's...pretty brilliant."

"Thanks."

"Okay, let's look at beds," Lia said and then bit her lip. That sounded so...so suggestive. She took a glance at Gabriel from beneath her lashes, found a distinct pink flush crawling up his neck. She turned the pages and showed him the Murphy bed systems. "So, we're looking at what's currently your family's main living space. You need shelves and storage. You also need a sofa for at least the five of you to sit on, but hopefully more so you can have friends over. Something like this incorporates the sofa into the bed."

"Let me see that." Gabriel tugged on his lips as he studied the image and Lia's own lips tingled in response. "All you do is move the cushions and the bed lowers right over the sofa?"

"Exactly. Some of the beds don't lower at all. They rotate."

"Dad-dee, see?" Emmy shoved her drawing into Gabriel's hands.

"Ooo, pretty, Emmy. Lots of blue. I like blue."

"Look at mine, Daddy! Mine's blue, too. I made my bagel. See? There are the raisins."

"Yes, that's a lot of raisins."

"Fridge, Dad-dee." Emmy snagged her drawing and tried

to stick it to Lia's refrigerator door. When it floated to the floor, she began to cry.

"Ooo, Emmy. Look what I have." Lia hurried to a drawer near the sink, took out magnets. "Here we go. Let's put it on the fridge." She retrieved the toddler's scribbles, held it out to her, but Emmy slapped it out of her hands. Lia took the sheet of paper again and stuck it on the door herself.

"Emerson. Not nice." Gabriel stood, scooped her up in his arms and rocked her. He glanced at Lia's oven clock. "Eleven-thirty. Right on cue. Sorry. I need to—"

"No!" Emmy cried, holding her arms out to Lia.

"Oh, I, um. Sure. Okay." Lia caught Emmy as the baby all but pitched herself out of Gabriel's arms. "It's okay, sweetie. Are you sleepy? Put your little head down. That's a girl," Lia murmured softly as the baby burrowed against her shoulder, wiggling her little butt. Emmy snagged a lock of Lia's hair that had come loose from its bun, held on.

Gabriel looked gut-punched. He hovered for a minute. Then he went back to the table and pored over the book, glancing up a few times with a frown. Lia shifted the baby, then swayed gently to the song that Maddie was humming from her pillow on the floor, rubbing soft circles on her tiny back. She couldn't deny that she was honored the baby had wanted her instead of her daddy.

But Gabriel, on the other hand, looked crushed. When Emmy had at last fallen asleep, he stood and held out his arms.

"Here. Let me take her. I'll put her on your couch with Olivia."

"Sure. Thanks."

Carefully, she shifted so Gabriel could take the now-sleeping baby from her arms, brushing against her in the process. They both froze. She lifted her eyes to his, found them wide. God, he smelled nice. Not drenched in whatever expensive cologne or body wash Jared used to buy online, but clean. Sweet. Fabric softener. Who knew that could turn her on this much?

He cuddled Emmy against his chest and took her to the living room, asked Olivia to keep an eye on her as he put her on the other end of the sofa. Lia joined him, scooping another pillow off the back and putting it on the floor, in case she rolled off. She covered Emmy with a light throw she kept folded on the back of the couch.

"Thanks, Lia. She'll be out for a while."

"No problem. She can stay here while you take Olivia to soccer."

"Right. Soccer. Almost forgot. Liv, is your show over yet?"

"Twenty more minutes."

Gabriel smiled tightly so Lia turned and headed back to the kitchen table. Those twenty minutes went by way too fast in her estimation. They went through the book twice and Gabe took notes and even sketched out an idea in his pad.

"It's over, Daddy. It was so good."

"What do you say to Lia?"

"Thanks, Lia."

"Okay. Go home, get your uniform on. We have to go in five minutes."

"Where, Daddy?"

"Olivia has soccer, Maddie."

"Can I stay here with Emmy, too? Please? Please, Lia, can I?"

"Sure. You can help me look things up on my computer."

❧

IT WAS WELL past three o'clock when Emmy stirred, blinking owlishly at Lia. "Hi, Emmy. Did you sleep well?"

Emmy kept blinking.

"Come on. Let's try the potty, okay?"

Lia grabbed the little plastic ring Gabriel kept in his backpack and took the toddler upstairs but wasn't fast enough. She wet her pants and Lia's.

"Uh-oh," she said and Lia laughed.

"Uh-oh is right. Okay, let's find new clothes."

In Gabriel's backpack, she found another pair of pants for Emmy. In her room, she found a pair of dark blue jeans and a white shirt. She changed Emmy on her bed, making funny faces, and tickling her. While Emmy crawled around on the bed, she'd stepped out of her wet jeans, kicked them to the side, and let out a little scream when the baby shrieked, "Dad-dee!"

"Hi, my Emmy. Hi."

Lia whipped around. "Gabriel! How did—"

"Maddie let me in. Everything okay here?"

"Dad-dee! I wet."

"Uh-oh. On the couch?"

"No. On me. But it's okay. She's changed. And I'm—"

His eyes skimmed her from head to toe and back up again. "You're—Oh! Sorry. Right. Thanks for watching them. Bye." He spun around so fast, Emmy shouted "Weee!"

Lia tugged on her clean pants and a new white T-shirt, and hurried after them. He'd already gotten Maddie up and to the door.

"Gabriel, it was no problem. We had fun, right, Maddie?"

"We did! I played the princess game, Daddy. And I told Lia we're gonna be princesses for Halloween. And look, Daddy!" She flipped her hair. "Lia got all the knots out of my hair and it didn't even hurt."

Gabriel blinked and ran his hand down Maddie's head. "Oh, wow. That's great, but it's time to go home now."

Maddie stepped outside. Gabriel was right behind her, holding Emmy and the backpack.

"Gabriel?"

"What?"

Lia jerked at the sharpness in his tone. "Nothing. Sorry."

Lia shut the door after them, wondering what the hell just happened.

Chapter Ten

TODAY WAS TRASH day.

Lia had spent forty minutes with her face pressed to her window, watching Gabriel haul cans, bags, and bins to the curb. He wore well-worn jeans, work boots, and another one of his T-shirts. This one said Daddy Rex.

She knew Emmy's shirt would say E-Rex. It made her smile.

The man was such fun to watch. She wished she could go out there, flirt with him, maybe even take a nice big bite out of him.

But watching was all she'd permit herself to do.

The way he'd practically run from her had convinced her that keeping some distance was the best decision she could make. So she hadn't seen him since Saturday, except for Halloween, when all of the Ivers had knocked on her door wearing various princess costumes. Kimberly was dressed as Belle, Olivia wore a Merida costume, Maddie was Cinderella, and baby Emmy was Ariel complete with little coconut bra tied over her jacket. But winner of the best costume went to Gabriel, who wore a Jasmine costume complete with long black wig and exposed belly button. When she opened the door to their knock, he tossed a scrap of carpet at her feet and smiled. "Flying carpet. Get it?"

She did not smile back.

She gave it a lot of thought. Gabriel was a great guy, but she needed to stay away.

Fifteen minutes went by without a Gabriel sighting, and when Lia saw Mrs. Morgan walk back to her own door, Lia figured it was safe to go out to the curb with her own trash.

"Hey, Lia."

Lia turned, found her next-door neighbor outside. "Hi, Jessica. How's the little guy?"

"Oh, just about fine now. And he really liked the car. Thanks again for picking up his medicine."

"No problem."

"Hey, love the newsletter. Those tips for preparing for flu season are just what I needed after Mason's ear infection."

"I'm so glad you liked it! I'll see you later." Lia turned, headed for her front door, and froze mid-step.

Gabriel stood on the courtyard steps, staring down at her.

She nodded but he said nothing. Taking that as her cue, Lia turned up the path to her front door.

He hurried down the courtyard steps. "Lia, wait. Please."

She waited. He shoved his hands in his pockets and looked at the ground. "Um. I...I need to talk to you."

"I'm busy," she lied.

He glanced at his door and sighed. "Please? I owe you an apology. An explanation. Could you...could we go inside? I left Emmy alone so I could talk to you and—"

Her heart gave a leap of panic at that. "Fine. Give me a second."

He flashed her a lightning-fast smile, there and gone before she could react. She locked her front door and followed him up the stairs to the courtyard and to his front door, waited while he unlocked it.

"Okay, Emmy. I'm back."

"Dad-dee, down. Ee-uh! Hi!"

"Hi, Emmy." Lia moved for the high chair while Gabriel washed his hands in the sink—which, she happily noted, was full of sudsy water and soaking breakfast dishes. "Can I free her?"

"Um, sure. How about some coffee?"

Why not? "Please." She put Emmy down while he got her a cup, inserted a pod, pressed the button, handed her the steaming cup when it finished filling. He moved around the small space, got out milk, sugar, a spoon, and watched in silence while she doctored the coffee to her taste.

He made himself a cup, still not saying a word, so she made herself comfortable at the long oak table that split the two rooms, sat back, crossed her legs, sipped her coffee and waited.

He grabbed a plastic party favor bag. "I can offer you candy with your coffee, but that's about it. Some of it's left over from Halloween and some of it's from a birthday party Maddie went to."

She managed a smile, but shook her head. With a sigh, he tossed the favor bag aside and slumped into the chair next to hers.

"So, hey, there's something I've been meaning to ask you. Maddie's been talking about a princess game? What is that?"

"It's a website I found. Games for kids."

"Oh."

Lia watched the flush crawl slowly up his neck and bit back a smile.

He was nervous.

The thought charmed her down to her toes.

He cleared his throat. "Lia, I really enjoyed hanging out with you the other day. Breakfast, then looking at the furniture book. You're smart. You're awesome. You're...you're beautiful." He said it quickly, like he was afraid he'd chicken out if he waited.

Speechless, Lia could only stare at him.

"I'm sorry," he said with a helpless shrug. "I'm seriously out of practice at this. The truth is, I like you, Lia. I really like you but when Emmy wanted you instead of me, I—well—I—"

"Oh," Lia said, understanding completely. "Gabriel. You have to know that didn't mean anything. I'm novel to her, that's all."

He shook his head. "No, she really likes you, Lia. That should make me relieved. Happy, even. And it does. It's dumb but it...well, it hurt. I've been doing this single parent stuff for a while now—since she was four months old," he admitted, turning to watch Emmy play with her little kitchen set in the corner of the living room. "Most of the time, I think I have it all under control, I got it all handled, and then, there are days when I swear I don't know a damn thing."

"I completely understand." Lia saw the tension in Gabriel's body, the flush on his skin and figured he'd rather be

135

outside hauling more trash than reveal this part of himself. She reached her hand across the table, gave his a squeeze.

He went completely still.

"Gabriel, you've been daddy and mommy to these girls for a long time," she murmured. "It makes me wonder who takes care of you?"

He stared at the hand gripping his with a frown, so Lia drew back. She'd moved no more than an inch when he shook his head, snagged that hand again. When he lifted his eyes to hers, Lia leaned in, touched her lips to his.

GABE WASN'T ENTIRELY sure how it happened. One minute, they were talking and the next, they were kissing and he really hoped he wasn't dreaming this.

Her lips were exactly as he'd imagined.

Soft.

Hot.

Just like the rest of her. He took the kiss deeper and tasted chocolate—had she snuck a piece from that party bag? He smiled against her lips and melted into her like metal under a welder's torch. *Lia*, he thought. This was Lia, who was everything that was soft and warm and smelled like lilacs. Lia, who took such pleasure in helping everyone she met. He wanted her, breathed her, dreamed of her and he knew this was wrong, wrong to do this with anybody but Janey, but God help him, how could it be wrong to feel what he was feeling?

He'd wanted solace, comfort, and maybe, to feel reassured that his last child still loved him. But now, kissing Lia, he thought maybe, just maybe, he'd needed reassurance that he was still alive. As soon as that thought crossed his mind, all he could think about was *more*. More of her heat, more of her hands in his hair, more of her mouth over every inch of his body, more of his heart galloping and his stomach flipping. More lips, more tongue, God, more tongue. More gasps, more moans, more sighs.

All.

She tugged on his hair, pulling him closer and he went, helpless to resist her, kissing her like she was the only thing that could possibly keep him steady in a world that pitched and spun. When they finally broke apart, ending right where they'd started…staring into each other's eyes, clutching each other's hands, pulses pounding like drum beats, he couldn't remember a single reason why he'd ever believed kissing Amelia Blake was wrong.

"Kiss me, Ee-ah." Emmy pounced on Lia, who scooped her up and planted a loud "Mwah" on her cheek.

He couldn't find the words. He'd kissed Lia. He'd kissed her. He hadn't kissed anybody but Janey since college. He waited for the one-two punch from guilt and grief, braced for the knock-out from the bitter fury that always, *always*, followed.

It didn't come.

He studied Lia. Her face was flushed and her hands shook a little and her lips were just a little bit swollen. The emotion that flooded him then wasn't guilt, grief, or anger.

It was…pride. Pure testosterone-driven pride.

Her eyes met his and he grinned.

He'd just opened his mouth when his cell phone rang. He glanced at the screen and spelled out a curse.

"Hello?"

Lia detected a note of worry in his voice but when his entire body went tense, she knew something was wrong.

"Kimberly? What's wrong? Is she okay? Yeah. Um. Sure. I'll pick her up. She was fine this morning. What? She has *what?*" he repeated, his voice a whole octave higher. "She has cramps. Oh, God." Gabe's face went gray as he ended the call.

"I have to go. I have to get Kimberly. She has…"

"I'll stay with Emmy. Go."

Startled, he looked at his youngest daughter and then back at her as if he forgot where he was and what he was doing. Finally, he nodded, suddenly unable to talk. "You— um—God."

And he took off at a dead run, not even bothering to shut the door behind him.

❧

HE REACHED THE school in less than fifteen minutes, his heart beating like a trapped animal behind his ribcage, and found Kimberly curled into a ball in the nurse's office. Her face was pale and she kept clutching her stomach.

"Hey, Cocoa-Pop. How you feeling?"

"Daddy." Her voice was tight.

"What's wrong?"

She shook her head. She couldn't even look at him. "I need to go home, Daddy." And then gasped. "Emmy?"

"She's with Lia. Come on now. I got you." He wrapped an arm around her, collected her stuff, signed her out, and finally got her to the SUV. She curled into the passenger seat while he fastened her seat belt. As he drove, he reached a hand out for hers and she gripped it hard for the rest of the ride. When they got home, he scooped her up into his arms like she was still Emmy's age, but she squeaked.

"Daddy. I can walk."

He hesitated only a moment and put her on her feet.

Lia pulled open the front door before they reached it…and just took over. "Come on, sweetie. Lie here."

Gabe watched Lia lead Kimberly to the couch, cover her with a blanket and run to his kitchen where she took a towel out of a pan of steaming hot water, wrung it out using his barbecue tongs and wrapped it in plastic. She wrapped that inside in a second thick towel and pressed it to Kimberly's middle.

"Better?" she asked.

Kimberly closed her eyes and moaned. "Yeah. The heat feels good."

His stomach twisted. "Aw, honey. I'm sorry." He dropped to his knees, brushed the hair from her face. Did cramps really hurt this bad? Was that normal? Did women endure this every month? He tried to remember Janey's periods but he honestly couldn't remember her complaining about this level of pain. He looked at Lia for help but she was reading her phone's screen. When she saw his face, she quickly put the phone away and spoke to Kim.

"Are you wearing something right now, sweetie?"

Kim's eyes darted to his and back to Lia's. "Um, the

nurse gave me this really big pad but it feels like Emmy's diaper."

She made a disgusted face and Gabe's heart hurt. *Janey should be here for this.* Wait. Emmy!

"Emmy's asleep." Lia answered his unspoken question.

Kimberly made a choking sound. "Lia. It's really a lot," she whispered.

"Okay. We'll fix you up. Are you okay here by yourself for a few minutes?"

"Why? Where are you going?" Panic tainted her voice.

Lia ran a hand down Kimberly's hair. "I'm going to borrow your daddy for just a few minutes and then we'll be back, okay?"

Kimberly nodded but looked scared.

Helpless, Gabe watched her pale face twist into a grimace. She rubbed and pressed on her lower abdomen. Suddenly, Lia's hand was on his arm, tugging him out of the apartment, jerking him out of his thoughts. "Gabriel. Come with me. She'll be okay for a few minutes. Emmy will be up soon so we don't have a lot of time. Come with me now."

He didn't want to leave Kimberly, but he needed to trust Lia, needed to know she'd know what to do because he absolutely didn't. He followed Lia back to her apartment and up the stairs to the bathroom with the big claw-foot tub.

From the wastebasket beside her sink, she removed boxes of feminine products. "It's a good thing I forgot to take these to the curb. How do you feel about tampons?"

His jaw fell open. *Feel about them?* He did his best never to think about them, let alone develop feelings for them.

"Do you know how to work these?" She unwrapped one,

held it out.

He stared it like it might bite. Hell, no, he didn't know how to work them. This was supposed to be Janey, not him, God, not him. Lia huffed in frustration and guided him to toilet, pushing him down, shoving the unwrapped tampon into his hand.

"Honestly, Gabriel. This is all perfectly natural. I know this is hard for you, but it really is okay."

No. No, it *wasn't* okay. Kimberly was writhing in pain on the sofa just when she needed her mommy the most and he was having a damn nervous breakdown. He swallowed hard and stared at the small plastic cylinder in his hand.

And swallowed again. Hard.

"Gabriel, look at me." Lia grabbed his hand. "If your wife were still alive, if she were here right now, do you really think you wouldn't be right there with them the second she told you your daughter was hurting and frightened?"

He flinched and jerked his hand away, but Lia's words arrowed straight to his heart. He could imagine it, could see it all perfectly in his head. He shut his eyes, let it play out. The school would have called Janey first because she was closer. Janey would have called him immediately. They'd have cursed at how fast their baby girl was growing up. They would have laughed at their own embarrassment.

And he would have been on his way home with ice cream and maybe a new movie to watch.

"You're right," he admitted after a minute. He lifted his eyes, not surprised to find Lia smiling down at him. "Okay. You're right. If Janey were here right now, I'd pretty much be doing—"

"Exactly what you *are* doing."

"Yeah." He managed half a laugh. "Okay." He ran a hand over his face. "I can do this."

"Of course you can." Lia put her hands on his shoulders. "This is biology. That's all. Simple biology. Your daughter needs you. She's scared and she's miserably uncomfortable and you're going to help her through this."

He was miserably uncomfortable too. But he ruthlessly shoved it all away. Kimberly needed him. He examined the tampon Lia had pressed into his hand.

"Okay. Right. Um. So, I know this is supposed to go…inside. But it's plastic so I don't—" He shook his head.

"This is an applicator. The tampon is inside it. Press the plunger."

He did and a small wad of cotton on a string emerged from the plastic cylinder and spots appeared in front of his eyes. Somebody groaned and it took him like ten full seconds to realize it was him.

"Do you have any objections to these?"

God, yes! He objected to all of this. Every minute of it. *Objection, objection, objection!*

"Gabriel, are tampons are okay with you?"

He blinked. He heard the words she said, but they just weren't making sense. "Some parents have…objections to tampons because they're worn *internally.*"

He started to nod but stopped when her meaning finally clicked. "Oh." He rolled his shoulders. "No. No objections. It's up to her. Her body. Whatever she decides."

Lia smiled at him and nodded. "Okay. Come on." She grabbed the packages and then led him to her bedroom.

He halted near her bed while Lia rummaged through a drawer in her dresser.

"These will be a bit large for Kimberly, but it shouldn't be a big deal. I used to buy cheap pairs because the leaks almost never wash out." She handed him two pairs of plain white underwear.

Leaks. He collapsed onto her bed, took some deep breaths, and found himself extraordinarily angry. "Christ, Lia. I've never, not once, ever regretted not having sons but I gotta tell you, I don't know how to help with girl problems. If this were voice cracking or—or erections, I could help. You just, you know, carry notebooks and wear long shirts and think about grandmothers—" Gabe broke off when it suddenly dawned on him that he was talking about erections with a tenant while holding a tampon in his hand. He made a sound much like that of a cat choking on its own fur.

"Gabriel, you wear barrettes in your hair and nail polish on your fingers. I've never known a guy *better* able to help with girl problems than you. But can I give you some advice?"

"God, yes." He all but fell to his knees at her feet.

"Don't think of this is a girl problem. In fact, don't treat this as a *problem* at all. It's a normal, healthy, biological process. If you wig out on her, she's going distrust you. And if she distrusts you, she'll pull away from you."

Yeah. He was wigging out.

Her arms came around him, soft and gentle, like everything else about her. Before he could think about what he was doing, his arms banded around her like she was the primary support on one of those structures he used to scale.

He shut his eyes and buried his face against her middle. She ran her hands up and down his back and he sighed, wishing he could stay there forever, wishing he wasn't alone in this.

After a minute, he lifted his face and whispered, "Okay. I should go...um, not fuck this up."

"Come on," she said, stepping out of his arms. "I'll be right there if you need me."

Need her?

He was suddenly afraid he'd never be able to stop.

❧

LIA LEFT GABRIEL'S apartment after reassuring both father and daughter they'd be just fine. Kimberly was comfortably resting with a heating pad, a dose of ibuprofen for her cramps, and well stocked with supplies. Gabriel, while not exactly *comfortable*, was...dealing, she supposed. She'd promised she'd find him a list of gynecologists because yes, it was time for an examination, especially if Kimberly was in this much pain.

She unlocked her front door, tossed her keys to the coffee table and collapsed on the sofa, nibbled on her thumbnail.

She'd *kissed* Gabriel Ivers.

She'd replayed it all day. Even now, her lips tingled when she thought about it, about him. Oh, boy. This was bad. Very, very bad. He loved his wife and missed her so much. How could she even think about trying to fill that void?

And she *was* thinking. What she was thinking had her belly flipping, her pulse racing, and her anxiety levels red-lining.

She needed Roseann. She pulled out her cell, hit the contact.

"Hey, you."

"Ro. I screwed up."

"What? What's wrong?" Roseann's tone instantly changed.

"I kissed him. Gabriel."

"The Super Man? You hussy."

"Jesus, Ro. He's in love with his wife. I'm...oh, God. I'm worse than Candi-with-an-I."

"You are not. First of all, Gabriel's wife is gone, Lia. Second, has it occurred to you that maybe it's time? Maybe he needs to move on and you're *exactly* what he needs?"

"I want to be. I...I really like this guy, Roseann. He is pretty amazing."

"Then stop freaking out. Just go with it. See where it takes you."

"But Janey—"

"Stop," Roseann cut her off. "Don't compare. You're *you*, Lia. You don't need to become her, be better than her, or even resemble her. *You* are what caught his eye. Just keep being you, okay?"

Lia took a deep breath and felt the tension ease. "You know, there are some days I kind of wish I could bottle you and sell you to the mental health industry. Best Friend Therapy."

"Gee. Thanks."

She laughed. "I meant that as a compliment, Ro."

"I repeat. Gee. Thanks. Are you good now?"

"I'm getting there." Guilt kicked Lia in the gut. "Hey.

How are you doing? Ever since I moved, it's been the Solve Lia's Problem Show. I haven't bothered to check in with you. See how you're doing."

Silence answered her.

"That good, Ro?"

"It's...complicated, Lia."

"Guy, parents, or work?"

"Two out of three."

Oh boy. "Want to talk about it?"

Roseann sighed. "My parents have joined forces. As they presented the case to me, I'm not getting any younger and they would like grandchildren. Therefore, they want me to meet this guy that they think is perfect for the job."

Stunned, Lia sat on her sofa with her mouth open. "Um. Wow."

"Yeah."

"And you said what?"

"I said okay," Roseann admitted and then cursed. "I'm thirty years old and they still have this way of making me feel like I deserve to go to bed without dessert. What is so wrong with being choosy?"

"Nothing. And you're not choosy. You're cautious and I happen to think that's smart."

"Exactly!" Roseann said. "Would you call my mom and tell her that?"

Laughing, Lia agreed. "So when do you meet Mr. Wonderful?"

"Friday. We're meeting for coffee."

"Friday," Lia repeated, mentally running through her schedule. "Okay, we'll do the standard drill. Text me his picture. Call me, keep the line open. Remember the codes?"

"Of course I do. I came up with them. Now I have to figure out what to wear. Friday is dress-down day. Do I, in fact, dress down, which could be perceived as not giving a crap? Or do I dress up, which could be perceived as—"

"Desperate?"

"You're right. Dress down it is."

Once they had a plan in place, Lia ended the call, gathered her hair into a ponytail and settled in with her laptop. She'd been so caught up in Gabriel and his family today, she'd let her work slide. She needed food, so she took the laptop to her kitchen table, fixed herself some soup and a sandwich, and opened her email. The chicken noodle soup smelled amazing and set her stomach growling when she ladled it into a bowl. While reading the reviews on Goodreads for a client's latest novel, she ate her dinner, and then spent the next several hours checking in with her clients, sending status reports, handling billing, and examining social media accounts.

Tomorrow, she had appointments with both the local fire department and police precinct for research on a rescue procedural novel one client was developing. Another client, also an author, needed her help identifying things she called *sexy math*. Lia did a quick Google search and jotted down some notes. She'd have to hit the library for this.

By eleven o'clock, her eyes were blurring and she figured it was time to call it a night. She stood up, stretched her neck to each side and almost screeched when a light knock sounded on her kitchen door.

She peered through the glass pane and opened the door,

worry spiking. "Gabriel, is Kim—"

"Fine. They're all fine and asleep," he said quietly. "Can I come in?"

Lia nodded and stepped aside. He took in the laptop and notes spread all over her table while she shut and locked the door.

"I'm interrupting your work." He held a baby monitor in his hand. He put it carefully on the counter, adjusted the volume.

"No, I'm done for the night."

He nodded and studied her. God, she must look like an unmade bed. She smoothed her hair, discovered half of it had escaped its ponytail. She took out the band, started to scoop it into a new tail, but Gabriel stepped closer, covered her hands with his own and shook his head. "Don't. Please."

She swallowed hard. There was a glint in his eye she hadn't seen before. She held her breath and lowered her hands, wondering what he'd do next.

He moved his hands up, tucking hair behind her ears, rubbing soft little circles against her scalp, lifting her hair and letting it fall all around her shoulders. "This was the first thing I noticed about you," he whispered. "Fire I can hold in my hands."

She squeaked and his lips twitched, a breath away from hers.

"Kiss me again." He smiled.

God, she loved when he smiled. His grip on her hair tightened and he touched his mouth to hers.

Lia practically combusted. Gabriel's mouth should be named a wonder of the world. Firm and skilled, that mouth took her from zero to about sixty in a matter of seconds. He cupped her cheeks, angling her face so he could kiss her deeper, and slid one hand down her back, settling on her butt, but the other...oh, he kept that one where it was, stroking and petting her hair. She let out a sound that sounded ridiculously like a purr.

"Gabriel," she whispered. "This is insane."

"I love how you say my name," he said in her ear just before he bit the lobe and sent a jolt of need racing down to her core. "Lia." He kissed her deep, fast. "I never thought I'd say this—feel this again—but please tell me you want me like I want you."

"God, yes."

His arms slid around her. She skimmed her hands under his shirt, felt the long muscles in his back quiver under her fingertips, heard the hitch in his breath. His mouth came back to hers while her hands cruised up and down his body. When she gripped his butt, he moaned into her mouth, lifted her clear off her feet, pressed her hard against his body.

Things got fuzzy and blurry after that.

Lia was one exposed nerve ending. She didn't notice when he set her on top of a countertop until she felt the icy coolness against her bare skin. Then, there was the rasp of his tongue against a nipple followed by the sweet pinch of teeth, the scent of clean male sweat, the gentle strength in those large hands as he stroked, explored, and aroused, the heat of his mouth on her—she couldn't think, couldn't speak, couldn't remember her name. Circuits blew, scattering her into millions of tiny pieces that he caught and put back together.

When she finally managed to wrench her eyes open and focus, she found Gabriel staring down at her with a goofy grin on his face. His shirt dangled from the back of a chair. Her jeans were on the floor, her top shoved up and her bra askew. His unfastened jeans rode low on his hips, his chest heaved as he gulped in huge breaths, but his eyes gleamed with pure joy. "Lia. You...that was... I..." He shook his head, unable to find the words, and kissed her again. Slowly, he pulled away and she squeaked in protest.

"But Gabriel, you didn't—" She reached out for him, but he caught her hand, and shook his head.

"I want to. God, you have no idea. But I can't, Lia. I've left the girls alone too long as it is."

The girls! Her eyes flew to the clock on her microwave.

He'd been here hardly ten minutes.

Ten. Minutes.

She looked back at him in wonder. How was it even possible for her to have—for him to—Lia blew out a shaky breath and began to laugh. "You're not human."

He retrieved his shirt and laughed—actually laughed—and emotion rippled over her in great tidal waves. "Oh, I'm human. Wish I wasn't sometimes." He bent his head down, kissed her stupid again, refastened his pants. "This is not one of those times." He kissed her again. "Mm. I have to go. Lia. God, baby, I have to get back. I'm sorry."

She shook her head. "I'm not."

"I'll do this better next time. I promise. I'll make this right."

He flashed a grin, that grin that tugged on her heart, and he was gone, leaving her still quivering from his touch.

Chapter Eleven

LIA WAS LOSING her mind.

It had been over a week since the first time she and Gabriel…fooled around.

Since then, she'd been unable to think about anything else. She had dreams—daydreams all the time. She couldn't work. She couldn't concentrate. Worse, whenever she saw Gabriel, all she wanted to do was grab him and take a bite out of him.

She'd done just that.

She'd taken her trash down to the building's cellar, saw him pulling on thick work gloves. She dropped her bag, lunged for him, and they were kissing right there. In a trash room.

She should be ashamed of herself.

Ashamed of how much she liked the taste of his lips, the feel of his tongue sliding against hers, the strength in his arms when he'd banded them around her, the scent of his shampoo when he'd lowered his head to hers, and ashamed that their first kiss had happened the day when he was emotionally vulnerable.

But she wasn't. Not one bit.

She gave herself a mental slap. What on earth was *wrong*

with her? It was like she was back in school, unable to concentrate on her classes because her mind was full of daydreams. If she wasn't careful, she might start doodling his name all over her notebook.

When Lia found herself searching for babysitters just so they could... Well. It was clear they needed to do something about this. They needed to feed this need that obviously burned through them both before it killed them.

They talked. They texted.

But they couldn't figure out how to pull this off.

Instead, she watched him. Her apartment overlooked the courtyard. She could see his front door. She knew when he made his apartment rounds, when there was an oil delivery, a meter read, a city inspection. She knew when he took the girls to school and when he picked them up. She knew that Friday nights were typically pizza take-out followed by manicure parties. She watched him rake leaves, loving the way his muscles moved. She was upstairs in her bedroom when he stopped his own work to repair a flat bicycle tire for one of the tenants and then refused any money for the work. Gabriel Ivers was just like her—a man compelled to help. Every morning, after he dropped off his girls, Gabriel and Emmy left little things on Mrs. Morgan's doorstep—a magazine, a treat, or a plant. She saw Mrs. Morgan's delight with each one of them and felt something deep inside her purr.

On Sunday morning, she knocked on the Ivers' door with a bag of warm bagels from Ben's. Maddie lost her mind when she discovered *two* were for her—one cinnamon raisin and one rainbow. Maddie and Emmy were happy to see her.

If they'd been puppies, Lia would have found herself surrounded by wagging tails and exuberant licks. Kim and Liv—not so much. Kimberly was okay with her presence but Olivia ate her bagel with a rigid tension, spearing Lia with searching looks that seemed to see right through that thin excuse she'd given about paying Gabriel back for some favor he'd done for her.

And Gabriel? He couldn't stop smiling. It was a good look on him, Lia decided.

With Gabriel helping Emmy in the bathroom and the other girls scattered around the apartment, Lia made herself useful wiping crumbs from the kitchen table and sweeping the floor.

"I know, you know."

Olivia's quiet voice, not to mention her stealthy approach, had Lia jolting in panic. "What's that, sweetheart?"

"You. My dad. I know you guys like each other," she said with a sneer of disgust.

Lia began to shake her head. "Olivia, I think you're—"

"No," the child said. "I'm not stupid. I saw you. Kissing. It won't work. He'll never forget my mom."

Lia's heart shriveled. A child Olivia's age wasn't supposed to know about sex, let alone that her father was doing it with the neighbor—well, *trying to*, anyway. Lia despised herself for putting both thoughts into her head. But as Lia stared into Olivia's dark eyes, she saw something beneath the accusation, beneath that layer of disgust. Something that looked way too familiar to Lia—grief.

"Oh, Olivia," she said, bending down so they were eye level. "I don't want him to ever forget your mom. I'm not trying to replace her—or make anybody forget her. What I am doing is trying my best to make your dad happy."

"He *is* happy. He has us." And she took off down the hall before Lia could even think of something to say in response.

It was her own fault, really. She'd been entirely too selfish.

Maybe it was time to step back, slow things down, instead of trying to carve out a few minutes here and there for juvenile make-out sessions. Gabriel had responsibilities. He had a life and that life had no room for her.

That's why she elected to work from the library on Monday. She didn't say anything to Gabriel about Olivia, and when he texted her, she simply said she had appointments today.

There'd be no temptation to stare out her window, to knock on his door, to be where she knew he'd be.

Besides, she loved libraries. The internet was a great tool for some research but not even the mighty information superhighway could compete with the skills of a good librarian. She approached the reference desk, asked Dana, the librarian, for help on today's to-do list.

"Hi, Dana. I've got a detailed request that may take a while. Do you have time or would you prefer if I make an appointment to come back later?"

The pretty brunette behind the counter looked up and tucked a pencil behind her ear. "Hey, Lia. How detailed?"

"One of my clients is a mathematics professor on a mission to make math sexy. She wants me to find info on sexy math problems and gave me a list." Lia handed it over.

The woman read her list and looked up with a smirk. "This'll be fun." She put the list aside. "Okay, what's next?"

"Number two is a cookbook author looking for whatever we can find on the history of chocolate—specifically, how it became a decadent treat."

She rubbed her hands together. "I'm always up for chocolate research. Next?"

"Oh, I saved the best for last. I've got a theoretical physics professor over at Queens College who wants me to find out everything I can about the potentiality of flying cars."

The librarian clapped her hands. "Congratulations! You just became my favorite patron ever. Give me about half an hour? I'll find you when I'm ready."

"Deal," Lia said and left Dana for an empty table. From her tote bag, she removed her laptop and journal, checked the rest of the day's to-do list, and settled in to work. She logged onto the library's Wi-Fi and checked her email. Next, she began a basic search on *sexy math*.

Her client, Dr. Susan Abbott, had started off writing a serious paper, but the project had evolved, becoming less serious and much larger than a paper. Much, much larger, Lia thought with a smirk of her own. Dr. Abbott was now writing a book she planned to call *Orgarithmetic*. Inspired by a John Green book, Dr. Abbott decided to apply math equations, theories, and probabilities to finding her perfect sexual partner, represented by X.

Because, math.

Lia fanned her face. It was such a good thing she was a virtual assistant. There was no way she could possibly maintain professional decorum if she'd had to discuss this project face to face. She took a deep breath, found her center, and got to work. Dana proved to be a most excellent librarian, having located half a dozen sources of new content Lia probably never would have discovered through Google searches alone. She took notes, gave her cheeks a few light slaps when her inner child giggled, and sent Dr. Abbott a lengthy email complete with citations and conclusions which, she was forced to admit, were appropriate for nothing more than levity, at best.

She worked for hours, worked past noon, stopping only when her stomach began a noisy growl. She decided a lunch break was in order and collected her belongings. On her way to the exit, she spotted a familiar figure in the children's section.

Olivia.

The girl was hunched over a table, alone, poring over a thick book. She seemed to sense Lia's eyes on her and lifted her head, closing her book with a snap. Lia frowned. She'd expected to see that same accusatory expression on the little girl's face now seared into Lia's brain, but instead, Lia had seen guilt.

She took out her cell phone and called Gabriel.

"Ivers." His tone was brusque.

"Gabriel, it's Lia. I—"

"Not now, Lia."

"But I just saw—"

"Please! I have a crisis here. I'll call you later."

And the line went dead.

Okay, she told herself as her temper spiked. Okay, he's obviously in full panic mode. She could understand that. So she tapped out a quick text.

Olivia is in the library by herself.

She tapped Send. Saw the message was delivered. Waited. Waited some more. She wasn't sure if she should insist Olivia come home with her or go get Gabriel.

Her mind flashed back to the day Maddie had nearly been hit by a car because of her. Okay. She'd leave Olivia here, go get Gabriel.

Her temper faded under the pressing weight of his silence. She walked back to Reference. "Dana, could you email me anything else you find? I have an issue I need to address."

"You got it, Lia."

"One more thing. There's a little girl in Children's by herself. She's skipping school. I need you to keep an eye on her while I go get her father. He's not answering his phone and I know him well enough to know he's probably called in the National Guard. Could you maybe watch her, try to keep her here until we get back?"

"Oh. Oh, wow. I'll do what I can." Dana nodded.

"She's really into women in science," Lia offered.

On the walk home, she told herself it didn't mean anything. He had to be out of his mind with worry. She knew how devoted he was to his daughters—it was the first thing that had attracted her to him.

But this? Lia shoved her hands into her pockets and walked a little faster. This felt different...this felt...ominous. She knew that was ridiculous but the feeling wouldn't leave her.

WHEN GABE WOKE up on Monday morning, the weather outside was chilly and so, apparently was Lia. He was doing his best to figure this all out. He wanted to be with her and miraculously, she wanted him the same way.

So he'd thought.

But she'd put him off today, fed him some line about work. But okay, he could take a hint. He backed off.

The weather *inside* was marked by the thunderous clouds on his daughters' faces. Kimberly was cranky. Madison didn't want pancakes, she wanted French toast only to declare a hunger strike. Olivia stared daggers through Gabe. Only Emmy seemed happy, but she almost always was.

He sang. He'd been singing a lot lately. He felt so damn good, he was bursting with it, so—yeah. He sang. Not well, but who cared? He began singing 'Let It Snow' until he felt the weight of three out of four girls glaring at him.

Jeez, everybody's a critic.

"Kim, you'll need to start going to bed earlier."

Olivia rolled her eyes and shot him a look of such disgust, he froze while stacking pancakes on her plate.

"What?" he demanded, exasperated.

"Nothing. Just wondering if *Lia* likes pancakes."

His eyes narrowed. "I don't actually know but I'll ask since it's clearly important to you."

"It's not. I don't care what she likes."

He cut up Emmy's pancake into bites and sighed in exasperation. "Then why did you bring it up?"

"It doesn't matter!" she screamed. "I hate Lia and I don't

want her here anymore."

Gabe sat down, sipped his coffee, tried damn hard not to show how distressed he was to hear this. "Any particular reason why you hate Lia, who just a few days ago, was the goddess who'd recorded that show you wanted to see?"

She skewered him with another sideways look and Gabe had a feeling Olivia may *not* have been as sound asleep as he'd thought. His face burned and he looked away. He wasn't ready to get into this and most especially, not with his nine-year-old.

"I like Lia, Daddy. She's pretty and nice and she smells really good and she says she's my friend."

He smiled at Maddie. When you're six years old, friendship is a really big deal. "I like her, too."

At that, Olivia flung down her fork, shoved away her plate, knocking over Kimberly's juice glass, which spilled all over her.

"Olivia! What did you do that for? Now I have to change my outfit."

Kim stomped down the hall to their bedroom, grumbling the whole time.

"Dad-dee. Mess."

"Yes, Emmy. Liv made a mess and is going to clean it up." He paused, waited for Olivia to move. "Now, Liv," he snapped.

Her face thunderous, she got up, grabbed some paper towels and started wiping the spilled juice from the table, the chair, and the floor.

"Maddie. Hair?"

She shrugged. "The yellow clips?"

Fine by him. He grabbed the basket, tugged a brush through Maddie's snarls until her dark hair gleamed smooth down her back. He twisted the front of her hair into two ropes and fastened each with one of the yellow clips. God bless YouTube's endless cache of hairstyle videos. He'd watched a bunch after Maddie had informed him that Lia got the knots out of her hair.

If she could do it, so could he.

"Me, Dad-dee!" Emmy patted her head so Gabe took out another clip—a soft one this time—and lifted Emmy's gold curls out of her eyes.

Olivia was still wiping up juice. He got out some spray cleaner, spritzed the floor and the chair, waited while she wiped that, too.

"Braid, Liv?"

She did not answer him. Impatient, he repeated his question.

"I don't care about hair, Dad."

Fine. He was just about out of patience. "Maddie, get your jacket and your backpack."

He strode down the hall for his own jacket and Emmy's. It took ten more minutes to get everybody out of the house and into the car. He wondered what Lia was up to today and glanced at her apartment as he buckled Emmy into her car seat.

"Dad," Liv snapped. "We're gonna be a late."

Clamping down on his temper, he said nothing, just shut the door, climbed into the driver's seat, and started the car. He dropped Kimberly off first, then headed for the elementary school. Olivia took off but at his shout, she came back, waited—not patiently—for Maddie. As they headed inside the school, he took a long slow breath.

"Wow, Emmy. Gonna be a long day."

"Why, Dad-dee?"

"Bad moods. You're not in a bad mood, too, are you?" He glanced in the rearview mirror, laughed when she shook her head.

"Good."

They drove back to the building and Gabe checked his list. A washing machine that wasn't draining, a stuck doorknob on an interior door, and some lightbulbs to change around the building—nothing urgent or too difficult and after the morning he'd had—a hell of a nice gift. He grabbed his tools, Emmy grabbed her pink plastic toolbox, and off they went.

As he worked, he found his thoughts skating in Lia's direction more than once. Damn, she was amazing. But it wasn't just the sheet-clutching, world-rocking sex he kept imagining, dreaming, dying to have with her. It was *her*. He genuinely enjoyed being with her, around her. She was smart, she was gorgeous, and she had endless wells of patience for his girls—and him. Maybe the only reason she blew him off today was because she needed to recharge. He could respect that.

"Gabe, how's it going? Wow, you always grin like that at doorknobs?" Jessica Vella asked as she joined them in the hallway on her second floor.

Gabe shrugged and tried to wipe the grin off his face. "Just Emmy being cute," he lied and forced himself to stop thinking about Lia. When his thoughts turned to Olivia's behavior that morning, he began to worry. She had a serious objection to Lia that had started almost since Lia moved in.

"Here, Emmy. Can you hold this for me?" He handed Emmy the new doorknob he was about to install in Jessica's linen closet door.

"No. I pway."

"It's okay, Gabe," Jessica said. "She can play with Mason. I'll watch them downstairs."

"Great, thanks." He grinned as Emmy took off to play Matchbox cars with Jessica's three-year-old. He had the new doorknob in place in no time at all, jogged down the stairs and found Emmy and Mason making car sounds together.

"Okay, all done. Time to go, Emmy."

"Thanks, Gabe," Jessica said.

"No problem." He scooped up tools and baby and they went off to tackle the next item on the list.

It was about eleven when the school called him. "Uh-oh." The last time a school called, Kimberly was dealing with cramps. He braced himself and said, "Ivers."

"Mr. Ivers? This is the attendance office checking in on Olivia Ivers. How is she feeling?"

A tiny ball of ice formed in his gut. "She was fine when I brought her to school this morning."

"Mr. Ivers, Olivia is *not* in school today. That's why I'm calling."

The words were a kick to the nuts with steel-toed boots. "What do you mean, she's not there?" Jesus, was that his voice? He heard the terror in it and that ball of ice froze everything inside him down to his marrow.

"Mr. Ivers, are you sure she went in?"

"Yes! I dropped off both of my daughters this morn—"

Both of them. Prayers began to play in his head, while the terror turned to throat-choking panic. "What about Maddie? What about Madison Ivers? Is she there? Is she there!"

Paper rustled, voices murmured. "Yes. Yes, Madison is in her class."

Thank you, God. "Pull her out. Ask her where her sister is. Call the police. I'm on my way." He grabbed Emmy and his tools, put them in the car and took off.

At the school, the principal and a security guard were waiting for him at the main entrance, the same entrance he'd watched Liv and Maddie walk through that morning.

"Did you ask Madison?"

"Yes, Mr. Ivers. Madison's safe in her class. I spoke to her myself. She said her sister forgot something in your car and went to get it before you drove away."

A lie. There wasn't anything in the car besides his tools. "What about the cameras?"

"We checked. Seventy-six seconds after Olivia and Madison walk in, Olivia walks back out, alone."

That blind helpless panic took a solid grip on him with sharp claws. He dragged both hands through his hair while Emmy whimpered in her stroller. "Dad-dee. Dad-dee."

"Mr. Ivers, the police are here."

Gabe looked up, found two uniformed officers approaching. The first question they asked was about his marital status.

"Widowed. Their mother died two years ago."

They asked him a dozen questions, a dozen more, and then they sent him home. "It's the best place for you to be right now, in case she calls or comes home."

"Yeah. Yeah, okay."

Somehow, he managed to get Emmy and himself back to the apartment before his hands began to shake. He needed… God! He needed his baby. But he called Mike. Then, he knocked on all the doors in the building, asking if anybody had seen Liv. Nobody had.

His cell rang. Lia. He didn't have time for this.

"Gabriel, it's Lia. I—"

"Not now, Lia."

"But I just saw—"

"Please! I have a crisis here. I'll call you later." He ended the call and searched Jessica Vella's face as she and her little guy returned from their search of the cellar. When she shook her head, he cursed. Where the hell was Olivia? Mrs. Morgan stepped forward while he went out of what was left of his mind.

"Mr. Ivers. Gabriel. Isn't it time for Emmy's lunch? I'll mind her. Give me your key."

Emmy. Lunch. Oh. Christ. He looked at his wrist, but there was no watch there. It had to be well past noon. Yes. Yes, of course, Emmy needed her lunch and her nap. He pulled his keys from his pocket, handed them over and managed a nod.

The old woman patted his arm. "I'll mind her. You take care of this." She unfastened Emmy from her stroller, lifted her up and slowly made her way up the steps that led to the courtyard and Gabe's apartment.

Take care of this? His legs were about to buckle. He glanced toward the street where another squad car pulled up.

His spit dried up, just clean dried up.

"Mr. Ivers?"

He could only nod. *Oh God, Livvie.*

The officer who stepped out of the passenger seat put up both hands. "We have no word, Mr. Ivers. We're still looking. Security footage shows her walking north on Bell Boulevard."

At that, his legs *did* buckle. Why? Why, damn it, would she do this to him? He fell heavily to the courtyard steps, gripping his head in both hands while that monstrous panic pounded him. The second officer stepped forward. "Mr. Ivers, has she been having any problems in school? Anybody picking on her?"

Had she? He shook his head, but that didn't mean…

"What about social networks? Do you have the passwords to her accounts?"

"She doesn't have any. No cell phone either."

The two cops exchanged a glance. "Has she been acting out lately? Out of sorts?"

He started to shake his head, then stopped. "Yeah. She was in a foul mood this morning. No idea why. And she wanted to quit soccer, which is weird. She loves it. Or she used to."

"Who coaches the team?" The officer whose name tag read *Russo* asked.

"Um. A teacher. From her school. His name's Kress. Mr. Kress."

The officer wrote it down on a pad. "We'll need a list of her closest friends, somewhere she'd run to if she were mad at you."

"At me?"

The second cop, Officer Munoz, spoke up. "Has she been mad at you?"

Gabe lowered his head, his hands beginning to shake. Slowly, he nodded.

"Why?"

"The neighbor." He stabbed a finger toward Lia's front door. "She doesn't like the neighbor."

"And?"

"I do," he admitted.

"Are you involved with this neighbor?"

Involved. He swallowed hard. "Um. I like her, and well, we—um. Yeah. It's brand new." Holy God, he was stammering. His daughter was missing and he was stammering with embarrassment.

"Do you have a recent photo of your daughter?"

He nodded, swiped at his phone, opened his photos app and handed the phone to the officer.

"You drove her to school this morning. Did you see her go into the building?"

Had he? He shut his eyes, tried to remember. "No."

"And what was she wearing?"

"Blue jeans. An E=MC2 T-shirt and a black hoodie. Her sneakers have purple laces and her hair was down and kind of snarly. She refused to brush it this morning. Oh, and she's got a tiny scar, right here," he said, pointing just under his chin. "Her sister hit her with a toy when she was four." His voice cracked.

The phone still clutched in his hand buzzed. He glanced at the text message from Mike.

"Any word?"

He texted back a terse, *"No. Cops here now."*

"On my way."

"You said your daughter's mother is dead. How long?"

"She passed away two years ago."

"Would she visit her mother's grave?"

His eyes bulged. "No. Janey's buried upstate in Putnam Valley."

The officer's pencil scraped on his notepad and Gabe wanted to climb out of his skin. How was this happening? How had he lost one of his kids? Ever since Lia had moved in, he'd been distracted, unable to remember his promises, unable to focus on anything except the way she'd felt in his arms, the way she'd tasted.

"Gabriel."

His head snapped up. Lia stood in front of him and the knife-edge sharpness in her tone almost undid him, told him she'd been ready to brawl, but as soon as he lifted his face, the fury in hers changed at once to concern.

To fear.

"Olivia is in the library. She's just fine."

Both cops turned to her in unison. Gabe was on his feet, had her by the shoulders. "What? What do you mean, she's in the library? Why the *hell* didn't you tell me?" He'd given her a good shake until she shoved him back a step.

"I tried! I called you not ten minutes ago," she snapped back. "And, I texted."

He stared at the phone in his hand. Oh God. She had. And he'd hung up on her. He was a dick. He knew it, had to apologize, but right now?

Olivia.

Gabe took off at a dead run. He ran without a thought for anything or anyone but Olivia. The library was easily half a mile away from the apartment and by the time he reached its front doors, so had the police car. The officer who'd asked him for Olivia's photo joined him at the door, put up a hand to stop him.

"Concern, not anger. Understand?"

Gabe blinked, sucking wind, and then nodded. He got it. He strode through the front doors, turned for the children's section. Olivia loved reading the Remarkable Women series. How had he not thought to check here? Gabe headed straight for the 509 stacks and skidded to a halt, gripping a shelf when his knees buckled for the second time that day. There she was, curled on the floor, one of the books opened in her lap, messy hair hanging in front of her face.

Silent prayers tumbled from his lips and his heart seemed to sob even as it floated out of his body. She was safe. She was here. *She was safe.*

Until he got his hands on her.

Maddie running off after Lia that day had scared a year off his life. Olivia may have shaved off a decade, at least.

While he stood there feeling like a total failure as a father, the officer beside him cleared his throat and stepped forward. Olivia's head snapped up, big brown eyes locked on his, an expression of such horror on her face, Gabe almost…key word being *almost*…decided against grounding her until she was thirty. But when that same thunderous expression from breakfast returned, his own temper spiked again.

"She *told*. I knew it. I knew she would."

Gabriel snapped up a hand. He didn't want to hear her say anything except how sorry she was. "Officer? This is my daughter, Olivia." Smiling tightly, he turned back to his daughter and sweetly said, "Olivia. Honey. This nice police officer responded after I called 911 when your school called to ask me why you were absent. He's spent most of that time radioing other officers your description and they've started searching the neighborhood for you."

As he spoke, Olivia's shoulders rose higher and higher and her furious expression turned to shame. She looked down at her hands, said nothing for a long moment. Gabe waited, not patiently, for that apology. Finally, she shut the book in her lap, replaced it carefully back on its shelf and climbed to her feet. She couldn't quite meet the officer's eyes.

"Amber Alert?" she asked.

"Yes. An Amber Alert was issued."

She shrank a little. "I'm sorry, sir."

"What was that?" Gabe barked, making her jump.

"I'm sorry," she repeated, louder.

The cop cleared his throat. "Young lady, if it were up to me, I'd put you in handcuffs and haul you off to reform school, but luckily for you, it's not up to me."

Gabe appreciated the officer's attempt to scare Olivia straight and said nothing as her eyes went saucer wide, snapping to the cuffs hanging from the officer's belt, because he was still shaking.

"I'm sorry," she said a third time.

"Liv, I'd like to know why."

She couldn't meet his eyes either. "Why?"

"Yes. Why."

One shoulder came up in a half-hearted shrug. "I just didn't…"

He leaned over, putting his face eye level with hers. "You just didn't what?" he prodded, far too softly.

Olivia recoiled and Officer Russo cleared his throat again. "I'd like to know why, too. Did somebody at school hurt you?"

Olivia shook her head and if Gabe thought he'd been scared before, he just about needed a crash cart while he waited for her to answer that question.

"Then why?"

His daughter sighed. "I just don't like it, okay?"

Officer Russo turned to Gabe. "Mr. Ivers, I think this is a situation you'll have to address with the school. If you discover something…something more, you call us back."

Gabe nodded. "Thank you. Thank you both for all you did today."

"Our job, sir."

"A hell of a good one."

Gabe shook Officer Russo's hand and watched him walk to the exit. Olivia was running a hand over the books, trying her best to seem interested in them when he knew she was shivering inside.

"Let's go home, Newton."

Her head snapped up, surprise all over her face. Gabe straightened up and held out his hand. When Olivia took it, he tightened his and a little voice inside him screamed, *Never let her go.*

He never would.

BY THE TIME Gabe got Olivia home, he felt like he'd run a marathon. Exhaustion seeped into every muscle, every bone. He knocked softly on his front door, hoping Emmy had gone down for her nap without issues.

Mrs. Morgan opened the door, hand patting her chest and tears filling her eyes. "Oh, thank goodness! My prayers are answered." She wrapped Olivia in a hug, the glasses she wore on a little chain around her neck poking his poor daughter in the cheek.

She held Liv at arm's length and scolded her. "Do you have any idea what you put your poor daddy through, young lady?"

Olivia nodded and said, "I'm really sorry."

Mrs. Morgan patted her shoulder and nodded. "Well, good." She looked at Gabe. "Oh, sit down, young man, before you fall down. Emmy's asleep, God bless her. Ate all her lunch, too. But she refused a diaper."

Gabe groaned. "Okay. Thanks for minding her, Mrs. Morgan."

The old woman waved a hand and moved into Gabe's kitchen, took out a plastic-wrapped plate from his refrigerator and set it on the table. "I fixed this for you. Livvie girl, you look like you could use some fueling up, too. Come sit."

They sat at the table, father and daughter, the weight of things still to be said hanging between them. Mrs. Morgan bustled around the small room, cutting a thick sandwich into halves—one for him and one for Olivia. She poured a tall glass of milk for each of them and he grinned. Gabe suddenly remembered Mike had dropped everything and was on his way.

He drew his phone out, pressed Mike's contact button.

"Got her."

"Jesus God. What the hell, man?"

"Yeah. I know."

"Lemme talk to her."

Gabe handed Liv his phone. "Uncle Mike wants to talk to you."

Cautiously, she took the phone, held it to her ear. "Hello?"

Gabe couldn't hear what Mike was saying but knew it must have been blistering judging by the way Liv's shoulders were inching up to her ears.

"I'm sorry...I will...I do...I promise...okay." She handed the phone back to Gabe.

"I'm crossing the bridge now, sitting in traffic. Should be there in thirty," Mike said. "We'll take the girls to dinner?"

"No. We'll eat here. I don't think going out to dinner—"

"Is appropriate, given what happened. Got it. I didn't think of that. You're right."

Right, huh? So how come he felt like shit? "Uh-huh."

"You are. Don't let this throw you. See you later."

"Later."

He put the phone down and stood up. "Mrs. M., you saved us today. Thank you."

Mrs. Morgan's lips twitched and she swatted him. "Oh, you." She took his keys from the pocket of her warm-up suit, which was blue today, and put them on the counter. "I'll leave you two to talk things over. Now, Miss Olivia, I expect you to mind your daddy." She wagged a finger at his daughter.

Olivia nodded and said, "I will."

Gabe walked her to the door, thanked her again, and as soon as she was gone and the door closed, he sagged against it. "I figure we've got about half an hour before your sister wakes up."

Olivia said nothing, just swallowed hard.

"Now," he began, scratching the back of his neck. "I could ground you. I could assign you enough chores to challenge the child labor laws in this state. I could take you to a good therapist. But let's try something else first."

Curious, she watched him move to the living room, kick back on the sofa.

"What?"

"We could talk. To each other."

Liv rolled her eyes.

"Come on, Newton. You and me. Nobody else to hear." He patted the sofa cushion next to him.

With a groan, she joined him on the sofa.

"Okay, look. I get it. When I was your age, I hated talking to my mom and dad. I could never seem to find the right words and always made things worse. But when I met your mom, she taught me that words matter and even when you can't find the right ones, it's important to try." He took both her hands in his. "Will you do that for me, Liv? Will you promise to try?"

She nodded just the way Emmy did, a single solemn inclination of her head.

"Okay. I'll start. I'll ask you questions and you answer."

Still holding her hands in his, Gabe braced for the question no parent ever wants to ask.

"Is anyone hurting you? Touching your private areas, or bullying you, or even threatening you?"

Liv shook her head. "No, Daddy. Nobody's molesting me."

That his nine-year-old daughter even *knew* that word sent that ice ball inside him sliding downhill, gathering momentum. Focus. *She said no, idiot.* But she hadn't said no to the rest of his question. "But your feelings are hurt?"

She looked down, shrugged. "I know it's stupid."

"No. Your feelings are not stupid. Who hurt your feelings?"

"Well," she began and then bit her lip. "Mr. Kress did, first. And then, this kid named Xander."

Gabe's eyes narrowed but he let her tell the story at her own pace.

"I asked Mr. Kress if we could do projects about women in science. You know, like the books?" When he nodded, she rushed on. "Only he thought that was stupid and some of the kids laughed. Instead, he told us we have to write term papers and Kim helped me pick my topic that was about a woman in science but he said no to that, too. In front of the whole class, Daddy. He said it was stupid, that everything I like is stupid. So now Xander calls me Stupid every day and I'm not stupid! I'm the smartest kid in the whole class, Daddy. I know all the answers, even when Mr. Kress doesn't call on me."

Gabe listened carefully. Olivia was right; she was extremely bright. Beyond her grades and test scores, she had a curiosity inside her that Kimberly lacked. Kim got good grades, too, but she did what she needed to do and no more. Only Liv had ever really immersed herself in the subject matter—whatever it happened to be.

"Why doesn't Mr. Kress call on you?"

She lifted one shoulder in her signature shrug. "Because he hates me!"

Gabe lifted a hand. "Let me understand what's happening. Are you raising your hand?"

"Not anymore. When school first started, I raised my hand all the time. Every day. Then, he started getting mad at me, so I stopped."

"Getting mad? How, exactly?"

"He said I was showing off, trying to make the boys mad that a girl was better than them."

"He said that?"

She nodded and then her words came out in a rush. "Daddy, no matter what I say or ask in class, Mr. Kress makes fun of me and then the class does, too. Like this one time when he was telling us all about the Apollo and Mercury missions and the re-entry blackouts, he said astronauts couldn't talk to NASA on earth because of the heat, but that's not true. It's because of ionization, so I raised my hand and told him but he just made a face and said it was disrespectful to tell a grown-up he's wrong. Then he asked me how I knew about things like ionization.

"I told him I read all about it at the library so he asked all the other girls in my class if any of them heard about ionization and none of them did. He said that's because normal girls like shopping instead of science."

Yep. The picture was crystal clear now.

"Cassidy calls me Olivia Ions instead of Ivers."

"And that hurts you?"

Olivia's little face puckered up.

That did it. He and Mr. Kress needed to have a chat.

Right frigging now.

"Okay, Liv. Here's what I think we should do. I think Mr. Kress is the wrong teacher for you. I'll talk to your principal and ask that you be moved into another teacher's class."

She nodded and scrambled onto his lap. Gabe went still while his daughter wrapped her arms around his neck. "I'm really sorry, Daddy. I just...you know...wanted to learn actual stuff instead of being called names, but Lia ruined everything."

Lia. Understanding dawned. "If Lia hadn't told me you were in the library, that Amber Alert would have frightened a lot of people, Liv. Grandma and Grandpa. Uncle Mike. Your sisters. You made the wrong decision here and shouldn't blame Lia for that."

She clammed up and shifted off his lap.

"Olivia."

She crossed her arms and shook her head.

"Olivia." His tone held a warning.

She blew out a loud sigh. "You said you'd never send me away. Ever. No matter what?"

He drew his finger over his heart. "Promise. I love you. You're part of me, Olivia. I will never send you away. Ever."

She only stared at him, arms still crossed.

"You don't believe me?" The words sent that ball of ice

avalanching down his whole body.

"Daddy, Zoe has *two* parents and both of them don't want her! Her mom got married again and her husband doesn't like Zoe and he wants her to go live with her dad, but her dad has a new girlfriend and said no. Nobody wants Zoe, Daddy. Not her mom or her dad!"

"Liv." His voice broke so he drew her against his heart and held her tight enough to make her squeal. "I love you and I want you. I will *always* want you and nothing and nobody will *ever* change that. I swear. I swear this to you."

The dam finally burst and she cried in his arms while he repeated the words until his voice faded.

Chapter Twelve

LIA SAT AT her kitchen table, an untouched cup of coffee in front of her. The look in Gabriel's eyes today would haunt her until she died. She'd thought he'd looked sad the day they'd met. But this? This wasn't sadness.

This was so much worse. For a moment, she'd been genuinely afraid he was gone and couldn't ever be brought back.

And it was her fault. Olivia knew. She knew Gabriel and she were...circling each other like animals in heat. God in heaven, Olivia was nine years old and knew her father wanted sex with a woman he hardly knew, a woman who was not her mother. What if that child hadn't gone to the library? What if she'd hopped on the train that stopped hardly four blocks away? She could have ended up—

A knock on the kitchen door sounded. She fumbled the coffee, spilling it down her front. At least it wasn't hot anymore.

She flung the door open to Gabriel, his face tight. "Liv's okay?" she asked.

"Yeah. She's eating lunch." He jerked a thumb toward his place.

Lia swallowed back tears. "I'm sorry. I'm so sorry, Gabriel. She knows. This is my fault. She knows."

Frowning, he put his hands on her shoulders. "Knows what, Lia?"

"Us. You and me. She...she saw us kiss, Gabriel. She knows."

His curse was vicious and self-directed. He dropped his hands only to raise them, tearing at his hair. "That explains a lot. Lia, I'm sorry."

She braced herself. She knew what was coming. And the kicker was she couldn't fault him for wanting to dump her. He had children to protect. "You don't have to say anything. I understand. But if you could please give me a couple of weeks to find a new place—"

He moved so fast, she gasped out loud when his hands clutched her shoulders. "A new place? No. No, Lia. I don't want you to leave. I'm sorry I didn't pick up on the clues. And I'm sorry I bit your head off before. But I am not sorry about wanting to be with you. Not one bit."

"You're not?"

He shook his head, stepping closer. "Lia, this last week with you...you have to know it's been amazing. Incredible." His lips lifted a bit. "I...like you, Amelia. I know I shouldn't. But I do. You...unsettle me."

Wow. She wasn't sure that was flattering and she really didn't like the way he grimaced when he said it. "Well, get over it. Your daughter doesn't like me."

His eyes lifted at that and she could see the determination in them. "But I do. Lia, do you have any idea what you've done for me? You've brought me back to life."

The tears that had been choking her found a way out. "I...what?"

He tugged her into his arms, kissed the tears falling down one cheek. "I thought this was gone for me, Lia. Attraction. Chemistry. Sex. I thought that part of me died with my wife. But you showed me I've still got love to give."

Oh God. *Love?*

"We'll talk more about this later." He put her firmly away from him when her arms snaked around his waist. "Can you stay with Emmy and Liv? I have to go back to the school and kick some ass."

"But Olivia… She…"

"We'll all talk when I get back."

Lia nodded. "Okay. Go kick some ass."

She followed him out through her front door, walking up the courtyard steps while he ran for his SUV. Outside the Ivers' apartment, Lia took a deep breath and knocked.

"Who's there?"

"It's Lia from next door. Your dad asked me to come sit with you." When the door opened, Lia put up a hand. "Okay. Let's get this over and done with. I know you don't like me and that's okay. You don't have to. But you do have to mind what I say while I'm in charge. Deal?"

Olivia nodded once. "Deal."

Lia stepped inside. "Emmy's still sleeping?"

"Yeah."

"Is there anything you're supposed to be doing right now? Chores or homework?"

She shook her head and grabbed the TV remote, slanting Lia a look. Lia bit back a smile. She was pretty sure Gabe wouldn't permit television after what happened today, but since he hadn't left her any instructions, she said nothing.

So, she sat down on the sofa and watched the little girl surf through channels before finally settling on a sitcom rerun.

They watched in silence until the commercial break. Lia turned to Olivia and cleared her throat. "So…I'm not sure if this will help or not, but I'm a good listener and I like to help people. If you want…"

Olivia ignored her.

Okay, then. She'd tried. She took out her phone and checked her messages, then her email. Dr. Abbott was thrilled with the research notes Lia had sent and left her a voice mail. Lia decided to call her back.

"Dr. Abbott? It's Lia Blake. I just got your message. I'm so happy to hear you like the work I did."

"Like it? It's inspired a whole new direction for this book. If you're willing, I'm going to keep you extremely busy."

"Absolutely. Tell me what you need." Lia glanced around, wondering where Gabe kept paper and pens. "Hold on one moment. Olivia, is there a pen and paper handy?" To Lia's astonishment, Olivia got up and fetched her both. Lia smiled. "Thanks. Okay. I'm ready." She jotted down some notes as Dr. Abbott spoke. "More on the Cox-Zucker machine, Gabriel's Horn, and the Ada computer language."

Lia took careful notes. When she hung up, she found Olivia staring at her.

"I know all about Ada Lovelace," she said and took back her notebook. "See?"

Lia read the notes Gabe's daughter pointed out. "I've heard of Ada Lovelace, but I had no idea there was an entire computer language named for her. Thank you, Olivia.

You've just given me a head start on my research."

"You do research?"

"Yes, that's my job. People hire me to do research for projects they're working on. The doctor I was just talking to? She's writing a new math textbook and wants my help on several sections."

"I know about Gabriel's Horn, too. It's a paradox," she explained.

"No kidding?"

"Uh-huh. Look."

Lia watched in awe as Olivia drew a simple XY graph and carefully plotted a shape.

"It's one over x to infinity, rotated around the X axis. And it looks just like a trumpet."

Lia was speechless and not sure she'd understood a word of what the little girl just said. "That's impressive."

Olivia shrugged. "I learned that last year because it has my dad's name." She shut her book and her dark eyes met Lia's. "You like him."

Lia shut her eyes. "I do. Very much. I know that upsets you so your dad and I will talk when he gets back."

"He likes you back. A lot. He…sings now." Those intense brown eyes rolled skyward. "He's pretty bad at it, but he sings." She shrugged. "I guess that means he's happy."

They both jumped when a loud knock sounded at the door. Heart pounding, Lia called out, "Who is it?"

"It's Uncle Mike, Olivia."

Olivia ran to the door.

"Wait, I—"

"It's okay, Lia. He's my dad's best friend."

But Olivia had already opened the door.

"Livvie, munchkin, what the hell were you thinking? You nearly killed us today." The man in the doorway bent down and hauled Olivia into his arms.

"I'm sorry, Uncle Mike." She wriggled free. "This is Lia. She lives next door."

"Oh, right. You're Amelia? I'm Mike Kinsella, Vince's nephew."

"Yes, of course. It's nice to finally meet you."

Lia shook his hand and stood aside. He stepped into Gabe's living room and shut the door. He was a tall man, as tall as Gabe. Dark hair and dark eyes gave him a mysterious air but it was his smile that made Lia sit up a little straighter. He wore work boots and jeans with a tape measure clipped to his belt. Across the left side of his windbreaker, a logo for Kinsella Properties was embroidered in white thread.

"Where's your dad?" he asked Olivia.

"He went to my school."

"Ah. Gonna tell me why?"

Olivia shrugged. "He said Mr. Kress shouldn't be my teacher anymore."

Mike's eyes narrowed to slits. "Why not?"

"He's not a very good teacher. He lets the other kids call me stupid and I'm not."

Oh, she definitely was not—Lia could attest to that. Relief was obvious in the way Mike nodded, all the tension leaving his body. Lia had no doubt he'd have turned around and fought at Gabe's side had Olivia's answer verified the horrible thought that had clearly struck them both.

"And Emmy?"

"Still napping," Lia replied.

"I'll be right back. I've been in the car for hours and need to use the potty."

"It's okay, Uncle Mike. You can say you have to piss. I'm not a baby."

"Oh, I see." His eyebrows rose. "Well, if it's all the same time you, I like saying potty."

Olivia laughed. Mike winked at Lia as he strode down the hall to Gabe's bathroom. Lia wondered if she should leave now, since Gabe's friend was here. But Gabe hadn't mentioned Mike coming over when he asked her to babysit, so perhaps she'd better stay.

Mike rejoined them just as Emmy called out, "Dad-dee!"

"Oh, good! The littlest munchkin is up."

Lia glanced at her watch. "I'll get her. Why don't you get yourself something to drink, since you've been driving so long?"

"Great. Thanks, Lia."

Lia opened the bedroom door, found Emmy standing up in her crib, hair standing on end. "Hi, Emmy."

"Eeee-ah!"

"Yes, baby. I came to see you. Did you have a nice nap?"

"Where Dad-dee?"

"He went to Olivia's school. But Olivia is here and so is your Uncle Mike."

"Un-co Mike? Yay!" Emmy clapped. Lia lifted her out of the crib, surprised to find no extra padding on her little bottom. "No diaper, Emmy? Do you need to potty?"

"Potty."

Lia hurried across the hall, carefully balanced the baby on

the bowl and lavished praise on her when she finished. "Oh, great job, Emmy. Let's wash our hands and go see Uncle Mike." She carefully straightened the child's clothes, helped her wash her hands so she could take off like a bullet to see her father's friend.

"Un-co Mike!"

"Hey, there's my sweet girl." He lifted her high into his arms and pressed a noisy kiss to her cheek, making the baby giggle.

Lia went to the kitchen, found Emmy's favorite cup and poured milk into it. She wasn't sure what the routine was but figured a little snack after a nap couldn't hurt. She found cookies, plated two, put the cup and plate on the coffee table for the toddler and then offered the package to Mike.

"So how do you like the apartment?" Mike asked as he put Emmy down and took a cookie.

"Oh, it's lovely. Really lovely. I work from home so the extra rooms are a help."

"Yeah? What do you do?"

"I'm a virtual assistant. I do research, social media, and other time-consuming things people don't have time for themselves."

Mike's dark eyes widened. "Wow. I didn't know that was even a thing. I should hire you myself."

"For?"

"I'm in the family business," he said, waving a hand around Gabe's apartment. "Property investment. Flipping houses. That kind of thing. Finding out all the codes, laws, and rules about a particular property takes forever. I bought a place right across the street from another place I'd just sold.

Figured I knew everything about the neighborhood, about the town and county."

Olivia, sitting on the floor with Emmy, cut in. "Oh, I remember! Daddy said you almost lost your shirt."

"Got that right. Turns out the street was the border from one town to another. Different tax structure, different codes. Everything I'd learned on the first house was moot on the second."

"Uncle Mike? How could you lose your shirt if it's buttoned?"

Laughing, Mike leaned over and touched her nose. "It's an expression, Newton. Goes back to gambling. You should look it up."

Olivia's dark eyes sparkled and she hopped up, disappeared down the hall into Gabriel's bedroom and returned a minute later holding a tablet.

"Me! Me!" Emmy scrambled up when she saw what was in her sister's hands.

"Emmy, where's your cup and your cookie?" Lia tried to distract her.

"Cook-ee." She looked around, found her snack on the coffee table and grabbed it.

"Liv, maybe you should use that in your dad's room so she doesn't break it."

"Okay."

When Olivia left the room, Lia turned to Mike. "If you're serious, that's exactly the sort of work I can help you with. I'll give you my contact info and rates and you can decide."

"Sounds great."

He smiled and Lia melted a little. He really did have the most amazing grin. It transformed his entire face.

A long silence filled the space while both adults watched Emmy dance with a cookie in her hand.

"Uh, so how do you know Gabriel?" Lia finally asked.

"We go way back. All the way to grade school. Met in first grade and been buds ever since."

Lia nodded. She and Roseann went that far back, too. She met Vivian in college but even though they didn't have the benefit of time, they were just as close. When you find someone who gets you, understands your particular level of *weird*, it just works. She'd thought she'd found that with Jared.

"What?"

She looked up, found Mike looking at her with concern. "Oh. Sorry. Just thought about something."

"Well, whatever it was that made you that sad? Never think about it again."

She had to laugh at that. "I was thinking of my ex-husband."

"There you go. Exes don't deserve neuron activity."

She laughed again. "You sound like you've had some experience in the area yourself."

"Oh, don't get me started. I was about to walk down the aisle with a woman who thought I was some kind of down-to-earth billionaire. Gabe tried to warn me but I was too far gone over her to listen. Three weeks before the wedding, we sit down to go over finances and stuff and she gives me this look. I ask her what's wrong and she asks me where the rest is."

"The rest?"

"The rest of the money." He rolled his dark eyes and shook his head. "When I explained to her that there was no 'more', she actually suggested I liquidate all the properties, so we'd have a, quote, *nice foundation* to build on."

"But...what would you do?"

Mike clapped his hands, which made Emmy clap hers, too. "Exactly! She expected me to get a *real* job after I liquidated everything."

Entertained, Lia leaned over. "What did you do?"

"I demanded back my ring and told her to cancel all the plans, took Gabe and few other guys on the honeymoon that we turned into a fishing expedition, and never gave her a thought."

"Until now."

"Until now," he conceded.

Lia studied him. "You've stayed single all this time?"

He shrugged. "I like my life. I don't need to change it and I sure as hell don't *want* to change it for someone who thinks money is more important than purpose. I enjoy taking old buildings and restoring them, filling them with families and people who'll make homes out of them. I guess I'm like you that way."

Shock sent Lia's eyebrows climbing. "Me? You just met me."

"True, but I can tell you love what you do. Assisting people. You like to help. You wouldn't be sitting here in Gabe's apartment if you didn't."

"That's...that's—" Presumptuous. True, but presumptuous.

"I'm sorry. To me, it's clear so I'm just stating a fact." Mike stood up, grabbed a beer from the refrigerator, tossed the cap into the trash. "You like helping people. I like rehabbing buildings. Everybody should do what they like."

She couldn't find fault in that logic.

Her phone buzzed and she found a message from another client, a teacher in a private school who taught gifted students.

Gifted students. Hmm.

She read the message: *Good news, Lia! The proposal you helped me develop was approved. I got funding to build a Maker Space. Need help finding grants, etc. to help me stock the space. Legos, Snap Circuits, any other games you can find that support education.*

Lia grinned. *Yes.* She texted back a congratulatory message. Then, she sent a text to Gabriel.

Ask Olivia's school about enrichment programs or gifted classes.

"Good news?" Mike asked.

"Very. A teacher client of mine just got funding to build a Maker Space."

"Right. I've heard of them. Robotics and stuff?"

"It could be anything, really." Lia elaborated. "It's space for students to work with their hands instead of just listening to teachers talk."

"And what does she need you to do for her?"

Emmy brought her book so Lia hauled the baby up to her lap and opened the book. "Find her some programs like grants and awards to help her stock the new space."

"Try tomorrow's builders clubs. There are a bunch across

the country. They may offer you supplies like Legos and Tinker Toys to start with."

Lia made a note. "Thanks. I will." She turned to Emmy. "What book is this? Oh, this is a good one." Lia smelled her little head and did her best to ignore the clutch in her center when the baby gripped her hair and laid her head on her breast.

Emmy enjoyed the book, clapping her hands and saying "Again!" when Lia finished.

She and Mike chatted about Gabe, about their work, about their exes for the rest of the afternoon. Lia angled her head and studied Mike. He was an interesting man. Attractive.

And totally Roseann's type.

A slow smile spread across her face.

GABE TURNED THE key in his front door.

"Uncle Mike!" Kimberly shouted.

"Lia!" Madison shouted.

Gabe had picked up both girls while he was out fighting for Olivia. He needed to make sure everyone was safe.

"Hey, girls." Mike stood up, hugged Maddie and Kimberly and to Gabe's mortification, Gabe.

"Mike."

"So you had a hell of a day."

"Yeah."

"Come on. Got beer. Sit down before you collapse."

God, it was good to see him. "Glad you're here, man."

"Yeah, you are." Mike smirked.

Kim dropped her backpack on one of the kitchen chairs. Maddie opened the refrigerator, humming a song. Olivia, still clutching the tablet, wandered back into the living room and sat on the floor. Gabe sat on the sofa where Lia and Emmy were cuddled together.

"Hi, Dad-dee."

"Hi, E-Rex. Are you reading a book?"

"Ee-ah."

"Oh, Lia's reading to you. Thanks for watching them, Lia. Sincerely."

She smiled and kept reading.

"Who has homework?" Mike asked.

"Me!"

"Well, step on up, Miss Maddie. I'll help you with it while your daddy enjoys his beer. Kim?"

"I don't need help."

"Then you can do yours on your own while I help Maddie. Come on."

Maddie eagerly dumped books on the kitchen table but Kimberly looked from Mike to Gabe to Lia. "What's...what's going on?"

Shit. His eyes cut to Olivia but she wouldn't look at him. "Olivia cut school today," Gabe began.

Kim spun on Olivia. "Are you crazy?"

"Your dad flipped out when the school called him," Mike explained. "Called the police, called me."

"And you came," Gabe added, voice gruff with emotion.

"No question. I nearly drove into a ditch when I saw the Amber Alert on one of the road signs."

"Olivia. Jeez." Kimberly gave her sister a look.

Olivia squirmed under everybody's scrutiny. "Okay, I messed up. I'm sorry. I promised Daddy I won't do it again."

Kimberly wasn't convinced. "Did you have to talk to the principal, Dad?"

"Yeah. I got Olivia moved to Mrs. Salony's class."

Olivia's gaze snapped to Gabe's. "You did?"

Nodding, Gabe elaborated. "Yes, Newton, I did. Mr. Kress doesn't understand you. I talked to Mrs. Salony and I think she will. I also asked about enrichment programs. Thanks for that suggestion, Lia," he added. "But you need to understand something, too. School isn't playtime. There are certain lessons you *have* to do, no matter what."

Olivia sighed. "I know but—"

"Uh-uh. No buts."

"Dad-dee, shush."

Everybody laughed when Emmy put a chubby hand over Gabe's mouth. He pretended to bite it, making her shriek with giggles. When she slid off Lia's lap to pounce on top of him, he figured things were as normal as they got around here.

"Okay, okay. Easy on Dad, E-Rex. I've had a tough day." He stood, hitched the baby on to his hip and remembered her diaper...or lack of one. "Hey, are your pants dry?"

"Dwy, Dad-dee."

"High five." He held up a hand that she smacked and took her into the kitchen.

"Oh, I already gave her a snack. She had a cup of milk and a cookie."

Gabe nodded and handed the baby to Mike, who was

sitting at the table with Maddie doing math homework. "Thanks. I've got a chicken to roast. You'll stay?" he asked her.

Lia blinked at him, looking lost on the sofa, still clutching Emmy's Dr. Seuss book.

"Oh, I've got a ton of things—"

"Stay, please, please, pleeeeeeeease?" Maddie pressed both hands together.

Lia's eyes stayed glue to his and Gabe began to sweat. They obviously needed to talk—about Olivia, about them. He really hoped they were still a *them*.

Mike cleared his throat. Gabe tore his gaze from Lia and shook his head at the question in his friend's eyes. He wished he could get Lia alone for five damn minutes. He needed to talk to her, needed to touch her, to reassure both of them that they could handle this...that they were worth this. But he needed to talk to the girls first. He couldn't blindside any of them.

So maybe it would be best if Lia...didn't stay.

Chapter Thirteen

E MOTIONS PLAYED ACROSS Gabriel's face. It both stunned and delighted Lia how quickly she'd learned to read that face. It was already so dear to her.

She hoped to never again see that stark blank stare he'd worn when he'd believed Olivia was missing. She wanted to see the tenderness when he kissed his daughter's head, the easy grins he gave to the building's tenants, and that blaze of desire when he turned those blue eyes on her. She wanted to see those. Oh, she *ached* to see those for a very long time.

But…

She studied his face, saw his indecision, and understood he didn't feel the same way. She'd acted too fast once before and that had ended with some other woman living the life she'd dreamed of.

"I have work of my own to finish today. Another time." Yeah, they definitely had a lot to talk about. If Olivia didn't want Lia in her dad's life, Gabriel would honor that and Lia could never fault him for that. When the pain of that knowledge spiked, she turned to go.

To her surprise, all of the girls moaned objections, even Olivia.

"Lia, I'm really sorry I wasn't nice to you. I promise to be nice from now on."

Well, that was something. Lia glanced at Gabe but he seemed as surprised as she was.

Taking in the awkward moment, Mike groaned. "Jeez, Ivers, you really have lost your touch. Here's how it works." He got up, took Lia's hands in his and smiled wide. "Please stay, Amelia. Allow me to repay your kindness for babysitting my children today."

The girls laughed and Maddie got in on the act. She dropped to her knees and batted her eyes. "Pleeeeeeease stay?" And then she let out one of her excited little gasps. "Oh! I know! We could do manicure night tonight with Uncle Mike and Lia!"

Mike snatched his hands back. "Oh, um—"

Gabe's grin was quick and lethal. "That's a great idea, Maddie. Show Uncle Mike the new color we got. He'll love it."

Maddie took off down the hall with a squeal. Mike skewered Gabe with a look.

"Oh, you so owe me for this."

Gabe only laughed. When he looked at Lia, his mirth faded a bit. "What do you say, Lia? Will you stay?"

She looked from Gabe to Mike to the girls and nodded. "Um. Yeah. I guess I can't miss manicure night." His smile flashed in response, quick as lightning and ten times as bright, staggering her with its meaning.

He was happy. *She'd* made him happy. The thought was humbling.

"Okay, girls. Better finish homework fast so we can get this party started."

By six o'clock, everyone's homework had been completed and Gabe had the meal served. Maddie kept up a running commentary on everything from her classmates to the neighbors.

"Daddy, can I play with Mason tomorrow?"

"No, you have school tomorrow."

"After school, I can play, right? Right, Daddy?"

"Yes, Ducky."

Lia smiled at the nickname. "I've been meaning to ask about your girls' nicknames. Kimberly is Cocoa-Pop. Olivia is Newton and I think I know why. Maddie is Ducky and Emmy is E-Rex."

"Oh! Oh! Tell her mine, Daddy! Tell her mine first."

Gabe sipped his beer. "No, no. Kimberly is the oldest so she's first."

"Janey and I were completely overwhelmed when Kimberly came home. She had colic and cried a lot. Nobody got any sleep. Until the day when that song came on…shimmy, shimmy."

"I remember that song," Lia said, laughing.

"I danced around the house with her, singing Kimmy, Kimmy, Cocoa-Pop and it—"

"You *sang* it to her? Oh my God, that's so cute." Entranced, Lia leaned forward, but Gabriel's face went pink.

"Everybody calls me Cocoa-Pop now," Kimberly complained.

"Nothing wrong with that. It's cute," Mike said emphatically.

"I'm almost thirteen. That's too old for cute," she announced, wrinkling her nose. Lia couldn't help but notice the pain flash in Gabriel's eyes.

"Right." Mike nodded. "The big thirteen is coming up."

"That's exciting. When is your birthday?" Lia asked.

"January."

"You'll always be my Cocoa-Pop, even when you're thirty," Gabriel said. "Now, you think you know why Olivia's Newton?"

"Sure. Olivia Newton John."

"Nope."

Lia noticed Olivia leaning closer. It was clear all the girls had heard these stories many times before and never got bored. Playing along, Lia frowned and said, "I give up. Why?"

"Well, Olivia's smart."

"Really smart," Olivia added. "Daddy likes to call me Professor sometimes."

"But Newton is in reference to Isaac Newton," Gabriel said.

"The guy with the apple and gravity?"

"Exactly."

"Why?"

"Go get the picture, Liv."

Olivia was already up. She plucked a photo album from the bookcase in the living room and showed Lia a picture.

"Oh wow. Cuteness overload!" The picture showed Olivia as an infant of about six month, wearing a pair of horn-rimmed glasses and holding an apple.

"You always leave out the best part," Mike complained. "Olivia would watch everything going on around her. Just watch with those big dark eyes."

"Used to freak out Janey," Gabriel added.

"How come?"

"Janey always believed that Liv was a full-grown adult born into a kid's body."

Oh, yeah. Lia had no trouble believing that.

"Does that mean I can stay up—"

"It does not." Gabriel cut her off before she finished asking the question. "Janey found Olivia conducting her first experiment before she could walk. She was throwing a ball into the air and watching it fall. Janey said it was like Olivia had discovered gravity all on her own."

"So...Newton. I love it." Lia smiled at Olivia. "That's a great nickname."

"My turn! My turn!" Maddie thrust her hand in the air. "I'm a dinosaur."

At Lia's look of confusion, Gabe asked, "You've never seen *The Land Before Time*, have you?"

Lia shook her head. "I don't remember."

"Oh, trust me. You'd know." Mike leaned against the sink, crossed one leg over the other, and tapped the screen on his phone. "Here." He handed his phone to Lia and pressed play on a video of one of the movie's scenes that introduces Ducky the dinosaur.

"Can we watch it, Daddy? Lia needs to see my movie so can we watch it together? Can we? Please? Please?"

"Not tonight. We have nails to paint."

Maddie gasped. "I'll get the stuff!" She streaked down the hall.

"Yep. Totally see it now." Charmed down to her toes, Lia asked, "I'm guessing Emerson's unique name has a similar story?"

"I nicknamed her E-Rex to go along with Maddie's *Ducky* dinosaur. E-Rex isn't a character in the movie but, well, you've met Emmy. She's kind of a terror."

Everybody turned to look at Emmy, who was busy putting chicken pieces on top of her head.

"I think they're adorable names."

"Found it!" Maddie ran back in carrying a clear plastic storage box containing nail polish bottles, cotton balls, files and clippers.

"Wow, look at the time." Mike looked at his wrist. It was bare.

Gabriel pointed a finger at him. "You're not going anywhere."

"You promised," Maddie reminded Mike.

"Okay, okay."

The older girls hopped up, began collecting plates and scraping food into the trash bin. Lia got up and did the same, delighted when she noticed the sink was already full of soapy water. God, she was ridiculous. When a sink full of soapy water made you happy, you had issues.

"Lia, what's your nickname?"

She glanced over her shoulder at Mike but met Gabriel's eyes instead.

"Besides *Lia*, I haven't got one."

"Really? Your dad didn't give you some cutesy name like Kitten or Princess?" Mike teased.

She shrugged. Her father had been far too busy cheating on her mother to develop the close relationship Gabriel had with his daughters. "My mom calls me *Amie*."

PATTY BLOUNT

"Oh, that sounds just like Emmy," Kimberly noted.

"*Amie* is French for *friend*," Olivia said.

Lia nodded. "That's what she always said, too. I despised it."

"How come?" Gabriel asked.

She shrugged and smiled at Mike, who'd grabbed a towel to start drying dishes. "She didn't mean it fondly. It was…criticism. Does anybody want coffee?"

Definitely not the deftest of subject changes, but it worked.

She snuck a glance at Gabriel. Lia knew he had to be absolutely exhausted after the brutal day he'd had. But he sat patiently while Olivia removed the pink polish from his nails and Kimberly worked on Maddie's. Baby Emmy waved her hands from her high chair and said, "Mine!"

"No, it's bedtime for you, E-Rex. Say good night."

"Night, night!" The baby waved and after good-night kisses had been exchanged with everybody, Gabriel walked her down the hall.

Lia happened to glance at Olivia and squirmed under the little girl's steady scrutiny. She wished she could find an excuse to leave. She didn't belong here, in this room so full of love, it practically burst through the windows. Her father had never loved her like Gabriel loved his daughters. Jared had never loved her like Gabriel loved his wife. It didn't matter how hard she tried. It didn't matter how helpful she was, or how funny she was, or even how generous she was. People just couldn't seem to love her. Except for Roseann. Roseann loved her. Lia tried to remember that, tried to take comfort in that.

"What color do you like, Lia? I like this one. And this one. And this one." Maddie took out several small bottles.

"I like them all, but I think I should go now."

They didn't seem to hear her.

"Uncle Mike, which one do you want?"

"Too much to hope for that you'd actually buy clear nail polish once in a while?" Mike complained.

"Uncle Mike wants the blue one, Maddie," Gabriel called as he left the girls' bedroom.

Kimberly held up the bottle of blue so bright, it practically glowed in the dark.

"Oh no, Mike doesn't," Mike shot back.

"What's the matter, Mike? Afraid a little nail polish will make you less of a man?" Gabriel asked when he retook his seat.

Mike ignored the jab. "She go down already?"

"Out like a light as soon as I started rubbing her little back."

Oh, God. He rubbed her back? Even after a nightmare, her parents hadn't done that for her. When she was about seven, she'd crawled in bed with them one night after a particularly scary dream and her father had threatened to punish her.

"Lia, you okay?" Gabriel asked.

She jumped up, headed for the coffee machine. "Sure. Fine."

"Wow, feels like she just woke up," Mike said, reclaiming Gabriel's attention.

"She can't seem to give up the afternoon nap yet, which is fine by me."

"This color, Uncle Mike!" Maddie held up fuchsia.

Mike let out a low moan.

Lia sipped from her cup, standing against the counter, face burning. She was miserably out of place and keenly aware just how much she did not belong here.

"Daddy, I've been thinking about my birthday," Kimberly began. "I want to do something really special because I'm becoming a teenager. I'm growing up."

She saw the flinch Gabriel did his best to quell while smearing petroleum jelly around his fingertips. The cup in her hand trembled and she spilled a drop or two of coffee on her hand, the sting of it hardly a blip compared to the pain she was doing her best to keep hidden.

"What'd you have in mind?"

"Can we do something? Just you and me, I mean."

His forehead puckered. "But what about your sisters?"

"They can stay home with Uncle Mike. Or Mrs. Morgan. Or Lia."

"What would we do?"

"We could get dressed up and go out to dinner that's not at the pizza place? Or we could go get real manicures. Like at a salon with the fancy chairs you dip your feet in."

Kimberly leaned so low over Mike's fingernails, it was hard to hear her, especially with Maddie chattering about how pretty Gabriel's hands looked. But somehow, Gabriel heard every thing his daughter had said.

And everything she hadn't.

Don't say no, don't say no, Lia silently begged. Little girls adore their daddies. They look up to them, admire them, and respect them. And when little girls become young women, they need the man—the first man they've *ever* loved—to model the kind of man those young women could trust with their hearts. She squeezed her eyes shut, wishing she could offer her suggestions, her ideas, because yes! Yes, Lia completely understood what Kimberly wanted.

She'd wanted it, too.

Gabriel cleared his throat. "I think that's a fine idea. In fact, we should make it a new tradition."

Lia's eyes snapped to his when she heard the husky note in his voice, but he was smiling softly at his oldest daughter.

It just about *undid* her. She practically dropped her mug into the sink. "I'm sorry, everybody, but I need to leave. Thanks for dinner. Mike, it was lovely to meet you. Good night." With emotion choking her, she bolted across the courtyard to her own unit and made it all the way to the living room before the tears overflowed their locks.

❧

MIKE JERKED HIS thumb at the door as it shut behind Lia. "Go after her."

Gabe made a sound of frustration. "I will. In a minute." Guilt swam inside him. He shifted, sighed, blew on the fingernails Maddie painted. Then his eyes lifted, settling on the photograph stuck to the refrigerator door.

"Girls," he began. "Do you remember what I said about Lia, about not knowing her? If that changed, we'd talk?"

Olivia's head came up from the swirl she was painting across one blue nail. Gabe watched her carefully but his smart, serious little girl gave nothing away.

Maddie was the first one to ask the big question. She gasped loudly. "Daddy! Do you want to kiss Lia?"

Gabe's face burned but he nodded. "Um. Yeah. I really do." God, he loved kissing Lia.

"Yay! Lia's gonna be your girlfriend?"

"Well, that depends. Here's the thing. I like Lia. A lot." Gabe tried not to roll his eyes because *like* was such a half-assed word. He was crazy about Lia. "And I need to know what you think about that."

"Are you gonna get married?" Maddie clapped. "Oh! Can I be flower girl? I want to wear a tiara!"

"Slow down there, Maddie. Your dad's not sure he's ready to date yet until he knows it's okay with you." Mike put a hand on Maddie's head.

"Daddy," Kimberly cut in. "I think Lia's pretty awesome. I'm totally okay with you guys dating."

Gabe smiled at his oldest daughter. Her blue eyes were earnest and her smile wasn't forced. Nodding, he said, "I think she's pretty awesome, too." Then he turned to Olivia.

"Liv. What do you think?"

Olivia had returned to her nails, drawing the brush slowly over the same nail. He waited, dread pooling in his gut. If Kimberly was his mini-me, Olivia was surely Janey's.

"What about Mommy?"

She may as well have shot him.

Speechless, he gaped at her, his heart deflating like a punctured old bicycle tire. He squeezed his eyes shut. Guess he had his answer.

"You know, I was there the first time your dad saw your mom," Mike began.

Olivia's eyes shifted to Mike's. "You were?"

"Yep. We were just a few years older than Kimberly. It was in our second year of high school. Dad and I were shooting some hoops and your mom ran by in her gym clothes. She ran track. The ball hit your dad right in the head. Remember that, Gabe?"

How could he forget? He never felt the ball hit him. All he felt was a jolt of awareness, followed by profound dizziness when he forgot to breathe.

"Your mom had long dark hair, just like yours," Mike continued.

"And mine!" Maddie reminded him.

Laughing, he acknowledged, "And yours. She ran right by us, never even noticed. It took me close to five solid minutes of calling his name to bring your dad back down to earth."

"Was it love at first sight, Daddy?" Maddie wanted to know.

The question shocked Gabe out of his stupor. "Where did you learn that phrase?"

"TV. Was it, Daddy?"

"Not exactly. I didn't have the guts to talk to your mom for a while."

"A while?" Mike snorted. "Try three years."

Olivia's lips twitched.

"Your old man didn't make his move in high school and somebody else got to your mom first. She dated that loser for a couple of years."

"What did you do, Daddy?" Olivia asked.

Mike answered for him. "He moped around, regretting

his life choices."

Gabe wadded up a napkin and threw it Mike. "Hey, I dated."

"Yeah, yeah. You took Abbie Grimes to one dance, and went with Melanie Abrams to the prom. That is not dating." Mike tossed the napkin back and continued his story. "He tried to forget your mom. He tried to go on without her. And you know what happened?"

"What?" Maddie leaned forward, eyes round.

"He was miserable. He got into some trouble—"

Maddie gasped.

Gabe put up both hands. "Uncle Mike is exaggerating. Right, Uncle Mike?" Gabe asked, pointedly. There was no way in hell he wanted the girls to know about the time he nearly got arrested for brawling, or the time he got so drunk after he saw Janey kiss that loser she was dating instead of him, he couldn't stand up. Mike had to haul his ass home.

Mike said, "Right." Then he shook his head. "Anyway, in our first year of college, we happened to see your mom walking into a dorm. We didn't even know she was at our school until that exact moment. Your dad froze right where he stood. It wasn't until I gave him a shove and told him not to waste three more years that he made his move."

"And then what?" Olivia leaned forward.

"Your mom said yes." Mike paused, let that sink in. "He had this look on his face." Mike arranged his own features into happy amazement, making the girls laugh. "Did you see it, Olivia?"

"How could I? I wasn't born yet."

"That's true. But I was talking about tonight. Whenever

he looked at Lia."

"What look? There was no look." Mortified, Gabe stood, threw that balled-up napkin in the trash so he wouldn't have to see Liv's face crumble.

"There was definitely a look. When Lia finally agreed to stay for dinner, you smiled at her the same way you smiled at Janey when she said she'd go out with you. It's this look like...I don't know. Like you just got a suitcase full of cash or something."

"You're stretching things here, Mike," Gabe said, shaking his head. "I hardly know Lia."

"But you want to."

"Okay. Yes. I do. I admit, I like her a lot. I think she's beautiful and smart and...and *good*, you know? A truly good person."

"But?"

Gabe sighed. "But my girls have to come first."

"You deserve to be happy again, Gabe. Kimberly and Maddie get that and I think Liv gets it, too. Right, Liv?"

Olivia didn't respond.

Gabe sighed. Mike made it all sound so damn easy. Just knock on the door, draw Lia into his arms, and magically, life would be puppies and unicorns. There were children in the picture. Four beautiful daughters who deserved to keep whatever memories they had of their mom. And then, there were logistics like jobs and money and where they'd live and chores and stress and—

With a start, Gabe shook himself out of that train of thought. Jeez, he was picturing life married to Lia. Where the hell had that come from? He glowered at his best friend,

207

who merely grinned back, like he'd been able to read his thoughts.

"Maddie, bedtime for you," Gabe finally said.

"Aw." She moaned the word out into three long syllables.

"Say good night."

Gabe was grateful that Maddie cooperated through her bath and bedtime. He was wiped out—physically and emotionally wrecked. By the time he returned to the living room, he swore he could hear his muscles crying for bed. To his immense shock, Olivia decided to go to bed, and Kimberly went into Gabe's room to read for an hour before bed.

When it was only Mike and Gabe in the room, Mike folded his arms and cocked his head. "Go ahead. You know you want to say it."

Gabe made a sound of exasperation. "Fine. You were out of line tonight. I get what you were trying to do. But don't press Olivia like that."

"Why not? You want to be with Lia. I don't think it's fair that you're letting a nine-year-old decide who you get to date."

"Yeah, well, nobody ever said life was fair."

"Ivers, you are completely *gone* over that girl and she's just as crazy about you. I watched you both tonight. You two have this…I don't know…this gravitational pull. I get why you're scared, but—"

"I'm not scared, exactly." Gabe cut him off. "Mike, losing Janey *shredded* me." He stopped, pressed his lips together when his voice cracked. "I thought that part of me was gone for good, you know? The part who could trust someone enough to let all the walls down and know that even at your worst, you were loved absolutely? I thought it died with her. But from the day Lia moved in, I've been…aware, I guess. I feel like she brought me back to life."

"You slept with her."

It wasn't a question. Gabe lifted a brow, and when he saw that Mike wasn't accusing him of anything, just trying to collect the facts, he shrugged.

"I want to. We've had some…logistics issues. Being with Lia is…it's amazing. *She's* amazing. Mike, I know you think this is lame but I never wanted anybody but Janey. I didn't think I could do it with anybody else."

Gabe squirmed. It was hard to admit to somebody who'd slept with a dozen women that he'd been with only one. He wasn't passing judgment—or trying not to, at least.

"Okay," Mike finally said. "I get that losing Janey turned you inside out. But, Gabe. You can't keep yourself and those girls in…in some kind of emotional bubble wrap. The risk is the reward. You were the one who told me that, remember? The more you risk, the greater the value of the return. You risked it all with Janey and yeah, you lost a lot and it fucking hurts, but look at everything you gained, Gabe. Look at it and tell me it wasn't worth it, that you wouldn't do it all over again even if you knew the outcome."

Gabe couldn't answer him because Mike was right. He *would* do it all over again. "Mike, it's hard. It's so damn hard."

"Yeah, well, nobody said it'd be easy, either. What if Lia is worth it? Gabe, I wasn't bullshitting you—the way you looked at her? I think you're already in love with her. I don't know how you can walk away from that, even for Liv. I think you owe it to her, to all of them, and to yourself to see this through. You deserve to get a life."

Gabe's mouth fell open.

Mike stood up, headed for the hall. "I'm sleeping on your couch tonight so get off it."

Gabe sat on the sofa, staring at the front door, hoping Lia would walk through it. Then a movement in the hall caught his attention.

"Daddy?"

"Yeah, Liv. What's wrong?"

She was in her pajamas already and had obviously put herself to bed. He tried not to let that bother him. When she didn't answer him, he just held out his arms. She ran into his hug, buried her face in his shoulder and his heart twisted. "If you're nervous about school tomorrow, don't be. I'll come in with you when you meet Mrs. Salony. It'll be fine, I promise."

"No, it's not school." She shook her head, pulling away so she could look up at him. "Daddy, did I break your heart?"

He froze for a second, not entirely understanding the question. Then he cursed silently. She'd *heard* them. Damn it.

"Liv, you don't need to worry about my heart. You just focus on Liv things, like school and science—"

"Daddy, Uncle Mike said you have a look. Is this it?"

She held up a hand. Clutched inside it was a photo. He took it from her, not surprised to find it was one of him with Janey. It was taken back in college—probably by Mike. He laughed once because yeah, he looked like a goofball with a big dopey grin and adoration in his eyes. "Yeah, I guess it is."

She bit her lip, nodded, and took the picture back. "That's what I thought." She scrambled out of his arms and took his jacket from the hook near the front door. "Here."

"What's this for?"

"Go tell Lia it's okay, Daddy. Uncle Mike's here in case Emmy wakes up."

A whole storm of emotions swamped him but mortification won out. "Um, Liv, it's okay. I'll talk to Lia tomorrow, as long as you're sure."

She shrugged. "I'm almost sure."

Uh-oh. "Almost?"

"Lia's nice."

Right. "But?"

"She's not Mommy."

"No. She's not," he was forced to agree.

"Mom's dead. She's always gonna be dead."

The breath left Gabe's body with the force of a groin-kick, but he nodded.

"I don't want you to be sad 'cause of me. If you want to kiss Lia or, you know, marry her or whatever, I guess it's okay."

Pride tangled with love to form a lump in his throat. He couldn't speak for a minute or two, so he scooped Olivia up into his arms and held her to his heart.

A KNOCK SOUNDED on the rear door. Lia sighed and unbolted it, knowing who was there without bothering to look.

"Lia. Can I come in?"

The punch to her core almost doubled her in half. Gabriel looked like he'd been dragged through hell. There were purple circles under his eyes, his hair was a mess, and his face was way too pale.

So why the hell did her pulse race at the sight of him?

"Um. Well, I was just on my way out." That wasn't a lie. She needed Roseann.

Gabriel's eyes went wide and then narrowed as he took in her overnight bag. He opened his mouth, shut it, shook his head. "Lia, can I just tell you I'm sorry before you leave? I'm sorry for Olivia, what she said. I know it hurt you. And I'm sorry I'm too tired to do much more than ramble right now so just let me get it all out and I'll say good night, okay?"

She stood aside, let him in.

Waited.

He looked ready to fall over. She pulled out a chair, guided him into it, but remained standing herself. If he was going to tell her good-bye, she wanted to be ready with her exit strategy.

"The day Maddie took off after you, I grounded Liv, too. She mouthed off to me and it pissed me off. She said something about you."

"Me?" That snagged her attention.

"Yeah. She uh…she doesn't want a stepmom."

His hands shot up when Lia's eyes bulged. "I told her she was way out of line. If and when I ever fell in love with somebody, we'd talk about it then, so we had that conversation tonight, after you left, because…well, because that time is now."

Oh, God. A strange buzzing began to fill her ears. But he…they…that meant… Lia shook her head, unable to grasp what he was trying to say. "So you're not breaking up with me?"

Gabriel stood then, took her in his arms. "No!" And then he held her away from him. "Wait. Is that what you want?"

She shook her head. "No. God, no."

"Good. Okay. This is good." He managed a sweet and awkward grin.

She couldn't find her voice. Couldn't think. She pulled him in, laid her head over his heart. Silently, she told Janey she'd take care of him, take care of all of them. When she felt him kiss the top of her head, she felt peace fill her.

Lia lifted her head, pulled his down and kissed him. She'd lost track of how many kisses they'd shared, stolen, or snuck. At some point, she'd stopped counting and wasn't that too bad? She'd always believed a first kiss was the most magical, most hopeful thing there was in this world. Maybe she was wrong. Maybe it wasn't the first kiss, but the *next* kiss.

"Lia," he whispered, sliding his fingertips through her hair. "Lia. Mike is staying tonight. That means…"

Oh. God.

Anticipation built in her so fast, it made her knees buckle.

"Can I stay?"

She didn't hesitate, didn't think, didn't worry, didn't obsess. She nodded and led him upstairs.

Chapter Fourteen

THEY HURRIED, LAUGHING and whispering, to her bedroom.

He couldn't wait to get his hands on Lia again. But as soon as they entered her bedroom, he lost his nerve. He dropped his hands, stuffed them into the pockets of his jeans, uncomfortable with even bringing up the subject but it had to be done. "Uh, I need to apologize to you, Lia. I didn't knock on your door for this."

Her smile froze and then faded. She nodded once and stepped back and Gabriel understood he'd hurt her.

"No! That doesn't mean I don't want you." He snapped up both hands. "I wanted to talk, to thank you for everything you did today."

Lia nodded once, smiled tight-lipped. "So...this is just a...a gratuity."

"No. No, Lia." God, he was making a mess of this, a total mess. "I'm out of practice with this sort of thing."

"What sort of thing is that?"

He looked at her sideways because her tone was way too sweet and he wasn't buying it for a second. "Can we sit? Please?" He waved a hand toward her bed.

She pursed her lips, but nodded.

"Lia, today…well, it sucked," he said with a laugh. "I feel like I went through some sort of high-octane parenting boot camp. I'm exhausted and raw and, and so damn scared I can hardly stand it, but I needed to see you."

He hadn't stopped reeling since the school called that morning, but he swallowed hard and studied her carefully. She still wore the jacket she'd put on before the fast run across the courtyard from his door to hers. Her cheeks were red from twin blotches of embarrassment. He smiled again. Look at the pair of them. Like two adolescents at a middle school dance, trying to adult.

"Lia, you knocked me sideways the second I saw you and I still haven't regained my balance. You have to know that pissed me off."

Her eyes glittered with something he sure as hell hoped weren't tears. When he saw her lips twitch, he relaxed.

"Pissed you off," she echoed.

He joined her at the bed and sat down before his knees buckled. "Losing Janey…it pretty much killed me. You know how everybody talks about crap like anger and denial and acceptance?"

"Yes. The stages of grief. They're a well-established part of the process."

He held up a hand. "Oh, trust me. They're true. I got hit with all of them at once. Denial, anger, sadness, bargaining—I couldn't deal, so I…didn't. I went through the motions for my girls but I checked out until you moved in." He lifted his eyes to hers, found her listening intently, head angled.

"Tell me about her. Your Janey."

215

She might as well have clobbered him with a two-by-four. God, this woman confused the hell out of him.

"Um. What do you want to know?"

"Anything. Everything."

Okay. He could do this. "We met in school. Upstate. We had no classes together. I noticed her in freshman year but we didn't start dating until college because some asshole got to her first."

Lia's lips curved. "What did you do?"

"I got over her. Or tried to, at least. I did a halfway decent job until we met again in college. This time, I didn't wait. We got married right after graduation, had Kimberly by our first anniversary."

"Wow. You work fast."

He shrugged. "Not very. Four kids in ten years and then…four months after Emmy was born, she died. Aneurism. They say she was born with it."

Lia suddenly gasped, pressing both hands to her heart. "Your girls?" And another gasp. "I'm sorry. It's none of my business."

"They're fine." He smiled, touched. "I had them all immediately tested. I lied to them. Emerson and Madison were easy. But Olivia and Kimberly knew something was up. I swear to God, I didn't sleep for two full days while I waited for the results. Couldn't take my eyes off them. Whatever Janey had, it doesn't seem to be hereditary."

There was a long silence. Comfortable. Easy. She looked up. "Gabriel?"

God, he loved when she called him by his full name. "Hmm?"

"You said I knocked you sideways. Is that a good thing?"

Eyes pinned on hers, he spread his hands apart. "It is now. It wasn't when we first met."

"Oh."

He laughed when her cheeks went pink again. "Okay, Lia, the truth is, I loved my wife. I haven't looked at anybody else since I was a kid. Until now." He paused, let that sink in for a minute. "I don't know how it happened. I didn't want it to happen but now…"

"Now?" she repeated.

"I never saw you coming but now that you're here…that we're here…I want us to be together."

She bit her lip, opened her mouth and closed it. He'd dropped a bomb on her. He understood that.

"Am I very much like her? Janey?"

Christ, talk about bombs. He drew in a deep breath, tried to answer and laughed. "You're you. You're not a Janey replacement. Janey was a mess. Disorganized, scatter-brained, always losing stuff. She was smart and kind of shy but had tons of friends. She was beautiful to me but we fought a lot about things she'd swear on a stack of Bibles she'd told me, but never had, and she bought way too many shoes and I loved her," he finished simply. "You're so friendly and helpful and organized and—and brilliant. It's actually scary because I was afraid you were perfect."

She made a face that made him smile.

"You're full of love you don't know what to do with. It pours out of you, Lia. I know we haven't known each other that long but I've never met anybody who spreads smiles the way you do. Every place I go, a smile appears at the sound of your name. Ben the bagel guy lights up like a neon sign when you walk in. So does Sal at the pizza store. My tenants adore you. My daughters love you. And I want to be with you if you'll have me."

A slow flush spread across her face and Gabe needed to believe that was a good thing.

"Your turn, Lia. Tell me about him. The ex."

Her lips pulled into a thin, tight line.

"Jared." She sighed in disgust. "We met in college. We were married for four years. We lived in the city in this great co-op. Then, this girl moved in, one floor above us. Candi. With an I." She said it with a sneer.

Uh-oh. Gabe was pretty sure he knew how this story ended.

"We were trying to have a baby. While I was busy with temperature charts and ovulation predictor kits, Jared hooked up with Candi-with-an-I."

"When did you find out?" Gabe asked but Lia squirmed.

"I didn't. He told me when I was almost ten weeks pregnant."

Gabe's jaw dropped. Pregnant? But…

Oh no. Oh God.

He opened his arms to her, held her against his heart. "Lia."

Her arms came around him. Held him tight. "We didn't know it was ectopic. He was working. I had a cramp that wouldn't let up. And then I started bleeding. Roseann—you met her—she took me to the hospital. I had to have emergency surgery. They couldn't save my baby. They almost didn't save me. I couldn't reach Jared. He wasn't answering his cell."

Her flat tone couldn't hide her pain. Gabriel stroked a hand down her hair.

"I called him at work. They told me he wasn't there. He'd taken a personal day. I thought I just forgot, that maybe he'd told me and it just slipped my mind. He showed up at the hospital the next day, looking like hell. At first, I convinced myself it was because we'd lost our baby, but that wasn't why and I think on some level, I knew it. He wouldn't touch me, wouldn't sit near me. He just stood there while I kept babbling apologies and stupid promises about how we'd try again, we'd keep trying. Finally, he put up his hand, shook his head, and said something happened, something he never expected, never planned on.

"He'd fallen in love with Candi and wanted a divorce. He said he wanted to tell me weeks earlier, but couldn't do it after we learned I was pregnant. He wanted me to know he tried to break things off with her, tried to do the right thing, but after I lost the baby, he realized life is too short to not be happy in it. He said I could keep our apartment."

Big of him, Gabriel thought, biting his tongue to keep from cursing.

"I was devastated. I left the hospital against medical advice and went home. I ended up—" Lia pulled away and shrugged. "Well. That doesn't matter now. I called Roseann in a panic when I noticed Candi's baby bump and moved out within the week."

"Oh, baby, I'm so sorry," Gabriel whispered. He wished he could hit something. What a tool this Jared was. He had a great woman like Lia and he pulled shit like that? Swallowing hard, he cradled her face in his hands. "I am so sorry," he repeated. "We don't have to do this now, or at all, if you're not ready or if you don't want me."

"I do but…"

But.

So not the word a man barely holding on to his self-control wants to hear. "How long has it been?"

"The divorce was final almost a year and a half ago."

So he'd be her rebound guy. Suddenly, Janey popped into his head. Lia would be *his* rebound. That realization sawed through him with a rusty knife.

"Do you still think about him?"

"Not with fondness. When I do think about him, there's a bad word or two. Maybe a revenge fantasy."

He couldn't help it. He laughed. And when he saw the same question in her eyes, he knew he had to give her the truth. "I think about Janey every day, Lia. I always will. The girls…they're so much like her, in a dozen different ways. But I think about you, too. This is new for me. There hasn't been anybody since Janey until now. Until you. So now, I'm thinking…maybe my heart's big enough, healed enough, to hold you both and I really need to know if this is okay with you."

That was all of it. Cards out on the table. He'd told her everything. He also knew it wasn't exactly the love song every girl dreamed of hearing. But she had a past, too. If he could take the chance, couldn't she? Did she know she was killing him slowly with all this waiting?

Finally, she moved and he had just enough time to suck in a breath before her mouth covered his and his brain downshifted into first gear. All he could think was *yes*. He'd wanted to feel all that softness for weeks. Sink into it like a pile of fresh-fallen snow. Soft. *Yes*. God, yes.

Her mouth was hot on his and when she made a sound, his brain re-engaged enough to tell him it was a happy sound and urged him to make her do it again. He ran his hands through her hair, lifting it, smoothing it, rubbing handfuls of it against his face. A jolt hit him square in the solar plexus. This was *Lia*.

She ran her hands from his hair to his arms, to his chest, down his stomach and this time, he was the one who made a happy sound.

"Lia," he murmured. "Lia." He trapped her hands, held her away from him while he could still form words. "Let me. Please let me."

Her eyes met his and he held his breath, waiting.

TIME STOPPED UNTIL she nodded. Her consent was all he needed to lose his mind.

The way those lips felt, the way that hair smelled, the way her hands moved on him…he didn't just kiss her—he feasted on her like she was his first meal in…well, years. He tumbled into this kiss, let it consume him, let it take over until all the world faded away and all that was left was this. *Her*.

He tugged her down to the pillow, rolled over her body and settled his erection there—*right there*—where she was made for him, just for him and kissed her until he couldn't stand it another second. He stripped off her clothes, the jacket she still wore—he tossed that to the floor and before it even landed, he had his hands under her the hem of her top, and the tingle that rippled under his fingertips stirred something in him.

This woman was magic. Being with her like this was a gift he wasn't sure he deserved but damn it, he *wanted* it. He couldn't get enough of her taste and kissed her again with his fingers fumbling the button on her jeans.

"Gabriel," she whispered, pushing on his shoulder. "Clothes. Off."

He was working on it. Cursing, he left that perfect cradle of her hips so he could peel the jeans from her body. Then he stood up, ripped his own clothes off, scattering them all over the floor. Condoms. He'd blushed like a twelve-year-old when he bought them last week.

Been carrying some around ever since.

Thank God.

He knelt on the bed as he covered himself, shaking from anticipation. Did she feel it, he wondered? Did she feel the same toe-curling want that was currently gushing through him like the tidal surge during a hurricane? He shifted his gaze to meet hers and even though her eyes were blurred by lust, she bit her lip.

No. Oh, no, no, no.

He cocked his head to one side, did the play-by-play in his mind, hunting for the moment when he'd messed up so he could obliterate it from her memory. When he noticed her hands had slipped from his body to her own, to spread over her abdomen, to *hide*—he understood *he* wasn't what was wrong and a spike of anger aimed at her dumbass ex arrowed through him.

"Let me see, Lia. Please?"

She shut her eyes, but slid her hand away.

Okay, then. Time to make her forget. He took her hand in his, slowed his breathing, even though he was sure it would kill him to slow down. But he would. He'd give her that; he'd do that for her. He kissed the hand he held and looked.

The scars were hardly visible, three of them riding low under her navel. He bent his head, licked, nibbled, and kissed each one. "You're beautiful," he said between kisses. When she tried to squirm away, he said it again and again and again, until she shivered and moaned and begged. "I think you're beautiful exactly as you are." He let go of her hand. "Touch me, Lia. *Please*." He practically hissed out that last word.

She did, taking her hands on a slow tour of his lines and curves, stopping here and there to clutch, to squeeze, to torture. Every time she neared the prize, his pulse would leap, but she'd back off, leaving him dying by degrees.

"More, Lia. More." He dragged her up to her knees, wrapped himself around her, kissed her again. Always, again. He was hard and hungry. Lia met him kiss for kiss but it wasn't enough, not nearly enough to soothe what he had inside him for her—what he thought had died. "Touch *me*, Lia. Please."

When her hand closed on him, his eyes crossed and he let out a sound that made her gasp. "Now?" he mumbled into her hand, the sound a ragged, breathless plea.

"Yes," she whispered. She sank back down to the mattress, hands taking him with her, guiding him into her, welcoming him. She clenched, surrounded him with heat and softness and he suddenly couldn't shut up. "So soft, Lia. God, I love how you feel…soft and hot and I never want to leave." He buried his face in her hair. "Mm. Lilacs." His thoughts scattered and with his lips, hands, and body, he did his best to scatter hers, too. He left no part of her unexplored, running his hands up to her breasts and then down, down to her center, moaning whenever something she did pleased him or when something he did pleased her because it was the same now. His pleasure, her pleasure. His body, her body. Them. One.

His body sang to hers. She kissed him, let her hands roam, caress, and squeeze. His words became incoherent and he laughed—actually laughed. He fused their lips together when he felt that long-lost heat deep inside him ignite and then detonate. She grew impossibly tighter around him. She held him, held him tight as he chased the explosion, rode the after-shocks, and held him together until he returned to solid ground.

LIA LAY SPRAWLED on Gabe's chest, listening to the solid thud of his heartbeat under her ear.

It galloped. She smiled.

So did her own, she noted, and her smile grew.

He ran one big hand up and down her spine and she wanted to arch and purr like a kitten. She lifted her face to his, kissed him again.

"Mmmm. You taste so good," she whispered.

"So do you." He grinned and then he yawned. "Sorry, sorry. It's not the company."

She smiled. "Had a long day?"

Laughing, he pressed a kiss to the top of her head, and pulled the covers over them. "God, yeah. They're all long but never a day like this."

Lia put her hand over Gabe's heart. "You are amazingly good at this."

"What," he asked with an eye-roll. "Sexy pillow talk?"

"No, balancing everything. I'm going to say something that will sound weird, given what we just did, but I wish I had a dad like you."

"Yep. Weird." Gabe tightened his hold on her. "But thanks. So, does that mean you and your dad aren't close?"

Lia shook her head and snuggled closer. "No. He was too busy serial cheating to become as involved in my life as you are in your daughters'."

Gabe played with her hair. "How old were you when you found out?"

She thought about it. "I'm not really sure. It was just sort of always there, you know? That tension. The constant passive-aggressive sniping they'd do to each other, the long unexplained absences, the whispered telephone calls."

"What about your mom?"

Lia shifted under the sheet. "That's more…complicated," she finally said. "She blames me."

Gabe's hand went to her chin, tilted her face up to his. "No way. How?"

"Well, my arrival wasn't exactly planned. I think my father felt trapped and rebelled. And my mother used all of my various flaws and shortcomings as justification for his rebellions. She is hyper-critical of everything about me."

"I see no flaws." He laughed and took his thumb over the curve of her breast.

But Lia didn't laugh. She sat up, swung her legs over the side of the bed, looked at him over her shoulder. "There are many."

"Give me one." He sat up, too, adjusting a pillow behind his back.

She shook her head. "If I give you the list, you'll run."

His smile broadened. "I live here. Not going anywhere."

"Good." She said it simply. And then, she panicked. "I know I shouldn't press you because you have your hands full, and I totally understand if you don't want to take this further," she babbled. "But I—"

"I do." He cut her off, tugged her back down, kissed her again. He rolled her underneath him, pressed his lips to her neck, her shoulder. "Lia, I don't know about you, but I thought we were pretty damn amazing."

She clapped both hands to his face. "Yes! Yes, it…you…this was amazing."

His smile lit the dim room. "Damn right." His arms snaked around her waist, fingers caressing skin. "So let's just…enjoy it, see where it takes us."

He bent his head and kissed her breast and Lia stirred, the need already building again. They made love a second time…and a third before sleep finally took them but even in sleep, he never let her go.

Chapter Fifteen

GABE SMILED AT the conductor on the train and almost blushed.

He did that a lot lately. Smiled. He smiled at total strangers. Smiled at his girls, at the people in the bank, in the grocery store and at the bus stop. Smiling was cool. He liked smiling.

He'd missed smiling and didn't even know he'd missed it until he had a reason to start again.

Lia.

He pulled out his phone, shot her a quick text message.

Gabe: *I miss you.*

Lia: *You saw me twelve hours ago!*

His grin stretched wider. Oh, he'd seen her all right. God, did she have any idea how hot, how gorgeous she looked when he made love to her?

Gabe: *I'll bring you back a present from the city tonight.*

Lia: *Something delicious?*

He stopped breathing for a second.

Lia: *OMG! That didn't come out right. Sorry.*

He snorted out a laugh, got his seat mates giving him the side-eye.

Gabe: *See you later?*
Lia: *Definitely.*

He put the phone back in his pocket and stared out the window, but his thoughts were still on Lia. Thanksgiving was coming up. He wanted to spend it at home, with Lia, but Janey's parents had called and he didn't know how to explain Lia to them just yet. Instead, he blamed his work schedule and asked if they'd mind taking the girls during the Christmas break so he could start building the transforming furniture he'd ordered.

With Lia's help, he'd ordered a pair of twin beds for Kim and Liv that would go in what was currently his bedroom and a larger bed for himself that would go in the living room. He'd do the kitchen another time. If he got them built and installed easily enough, maybe there'd be time to…to test out his bed before he had to pick up the girls.

Time. Frowning, he pursed his lips and thought about last night. Mike had gone home and since that first night, it had been difficult to find time to be together again. Gabriel could not risk staying at Lia's place with the girls home alone. And she wasn't comfortable staying at his. What if one of the girls woke up and discovered her there? Even though he'd talked to them and they'd said they were on board, he figured some things needed to be private. Daddy and Lia having sleepover parties was definitely one of them.

Still, though. He wanted more time with her. Needed it. He woke up in the morning with energy, with…with anticipation instead of dread. It was Lia. All Lia.

Jeez, he almost groaned out load. This woman had turned his world upside down in a dozen different really good ways and he hadn't so much as taken her to a movie. Well, he'd damn well fix that starting tonight. She'd be there when he got home because Mrs. Morgan couldn't watch the girls after school.

Home. Warmth spread inside him at the thought. Lia and home. Yeah. Yeah, that really worked. Oh, boy. *Slow down, Ivers.* The pragmatic part of him urged him to be careful. But the other part, the part that knew just how fast life could lob those curveballs at you, circled its hands and said, *better hurry.* You never know how much time you'll have together.

Make it count.

Did he see Lia in his life? Yeah. He did. So he tried to imagine living what was left of his life *without* her.

And there it was. That white-hot pain straight through his soul. The same pain he'd said, he'd *vowed,* never to feel again, was back as strong as ever. He didn't know how it happened. He never wanted it to happen.

But it did.

He was in love with her, completely and totally in love with Amelia Blake. *Whoa.* The power of those words, that realization, shot through him like an electric shock. And then he squirmed. She wasn't anything like Janey. Okay, yes, it wasn't fair of him to compare them but he couldn't help it. He'd only been with Janey, had never wanted anyone else— until now. Lia wasn't a handy replacement. She wasn't the sequel, and she wasn't the runner-up. She was Lia. She was herself and she was amazing.

He caught his lip between his teeth, forced himself to answer the unthinkable question: How the hell would he survive losing her, too? Thinking of her as…gone…sent chills rolling all the way down to his bone marrow. He wasn't a morbid person—or at least he wasn't until he'd lost Janey.

He didn't have to lose Lia. He didn't have to.

The train pulled into Penn Station. Gabe grabbed his backpack and stepped onto the platform and walked fast. He didn't know how they'd make it work and he didn't know if she felt the same way. There was only one thing he *did* know.

He had some time before he was due at the job site. He headed for 47th Street. Now that he knew what he knew, he damn well would make it count.

ↄ

BY THE TIME Gabe made it home, he was dragging. He unlocked his door, found not the usual afternoon chaos, but four beautiful girls smiling at him…and one beautiful woman smiling at him, too.

He blinked, not sure he was in the right apartment.

Emmy was in her high chair, scribbling madly with a bright orange crayon. Olivia tapped at the iPad. Kimberly lounged on the couch, reading a book. Maddie was already in pajamas, hair wet and streaming down her back, while Lia sat behind her on the couch, armed with a strange-looking brush and a spray bottle.

"Daddy's home!" Maddie said with a gasp. "Hi, Daddy. Did you miss me? I missed you this much." She spread her arms out wide and he couldn't help but grin.

"I did. I missed all of you. Hi, Emmy." He went to her first before she knocked over the high chair. "Want to get down?"

"Dad-dee, ook!"

"I see. What did you make?"

"A punk-in."

"It's a great pumpkin." He smiled and liberated her from the high chair.

Liv held out a fist for a bump, which he gave, but added a loud smacking kiss to her cheek. He glanced at the screen and saw she was looking at the NASA site.

Kimberly didn't look up from her book, so he kissed her head.

"Daddy, I got a hundred on my spelling and there's a note from my teacher about lice—"

The color drained from Gabe's face. "Lice?" No. Not lice. Please God, no.

"It's okay, Gabriel. It's okay. No lice. I checked."

Of course she did. He put a hand on hers, tugged her closer and kissed her, too. Right in front of everybody.

"Ewwww. You kissed on the lips." Maddie made a face.

The other girls hardly noticed.

"No lice. Thank God. So why are you wet?"

"Lia said she'll put my hair in braids but it was so tangled up, she couldn't."

"I washed her hair and now we're detangling it," Lia explained.

"Detangling it. And nobody's crying? You're magic." He kissed her again, making Lia and Maddie giggle.

"Nope. Just well armed." Lia handed him the plastic brush. "This is wonderful on my hair so I bought one for you."

He took the brush, examined it. It looked like a rock—a purple rock with lots of legs.

"Here. I'll show you." Lia took the brush back and lifted a section of Maddie's hair. The rest, she clipped up and out of the way. She sprayed whatever was in the bottle on the lock of hair in her hand, then began brushing from the middle down instead of the top. When she hit a knot, she slowly worked the brush through it. When the hair was tangle free, she brushed it from the top down.

"How long you been at this?"

Lia lifted a shoulder. "Ten minutes maybe? That's why Emmy's in her high chair. I wanted to make sure she stayed where I could see her."

"What's in the bottle?"

"Diluted conditioner. Leave it in."

Gabe sat next to Lia, draped an arm around her while she worked on the rest of Maddie's hair, and sank into a feeling of...comfort. Jeez, that sounded lame. But it was true. This was normal. This felt like the way things were supposed to be. He wondered about homework and still had to deal with dinner, but for five more minutes, he sat. Enjoyed. Okay, he basked.

A knock on the door triggered the chaos that typically marked this time of day. Maddie, Olivia and Kimberly all charged to the door and before Gabe could react, an earsplitting whistle cut through the air and everybody froze.

His gaze whipped to Lia.

"Check who it is first," she reminded them.

"Where did you learn to do that?" he asked, voice awed. That was the single most impressive thing he'd ever seen— er, well—heard.

She shrugged. "I did some research for a client once on whistling techniques. That one stuck."

"Um. Wow."

"Delivery guy's here, Lia," Kimberly announced.

Delivery of what? Kimberly opened the front door, accepted two large bags and a cardboard box that she took into the kitchen while Lia stood up. From the back pocket of her jeans, Lia removed a few bills, told the guy at the door, "Here you go, Bao. Keep the change."

In the kitchen, she and Kimberly unpacked cartons of steaming fragrant rice, dumplings, and vegetables, a plastic container of soup, a foil bag of ribs, and a plastic box of chicken. From one of the upper cabinets, she took down bowls, put those on the table that Gabe only just now noticed was spotless. Olivia had already put the tablet and Emmy's crayons away.

Without being nagged.

This was Hogwarts. Obviously.

"Emmy, come here, sweetheart. Tell Lia what you want to eat."

Emmy ran to Lia, lifted her arms and once lifted to Lia's hip, examined everything on the counter. "Dis!"

"Chicken. Yum."

Lia fastened Emmy back in her high chair. Gabe watched

her efficiently plate six meals and put them on the table. "Gabriel, beer?"

When he didn't answer, she halted, angled her head and studied him. "You're pale. You're feeling okay?"

"I'm fine." *So* fine. The scene was ordinary and normal but felt right. It took him a second or two to understand why.

This place had never felt like a home—until now.

He shed his jacket, slid off his boots, walked to her, and pulled her into his arms. She smelled like hair conditioner and fried rice and his heart clenched behind his ribs. "How was everybody's day?" Olivia left the table to pull a folder from her backpack to show him.

"Mrs. Salony is amazing, Daddy. She gave me this today 'cause she knew I'd like it. Can I do this? Please?"

Gabe laughed. "Wow, Liv. You sound like Maddie."

"Go where?" Maddie demanded. "I can come, too. Right, Daddy? Right?"

He read the flyer Olivia handed him. "No, Ducky. This isn't a place. It's homework for extra credit. It's also a lot of work," he said to Olivia. "You sure you can handle it?" The flyer was for an essay and poster contest to promote the International Day of Women to be held in February.

"I can handle it. I already know what I'm doing." She flashed him a fierce grin. "A collage made up of the scientific contributions of women."

"Like chocolate chips for Ruth Graves Wakefield?" Lia asked, spooning wonton soup into a bowl.

Olivia's eyes went saucer-round. "That's a good one, Lia."

"Okay." Gabe held up a hand. "As long as your actual school work doesn't suffer. Deal?"

"Deal. Thanks, Daddy."

He had to laugh. Liv was the only kid he knew who thanked you for giving her more work.

They ate dinner, everybody laughing when Gabe told them about running for the train and almost skating on someone's spilled soda. He told them about his project and the girls told him about school. Throughout the evening, his eyes kept bouncing to Maddie, whose hair fell down her back in soft shining waves instead of its usual wild nest. Diluted conditioner? How had he not heard of that before?

After dinner, everybody headed to their separate interests while Gabe gave Emmy her bath. By the time Emmy was tucked in her crib, Lia had Maddie's hair woven in several braids—one in the front like a headband, and two thin ones down each side. She'd gathered the rest of Maddie's hair into a ponytail fastened with a—a sock? He peered closer and yep. It was a sock. She'd cut the toe off, rolled Maddie's hair all up inside the tube that remained.

"Gabriel, in the morning, take her hair out of the sock, brush it again with more of this spray if you need to, then just twist the two braids and the loose hair together into one coil like this," she said, twisting her own hair. "Then pin it in place. Maddie, you remember what I told you?"

"Yep. Not to use anybody's brush or hat." And then, Maddie kissed them each on the cheek and...and took herself to bed. He stared after her, jaw dangling. This wasn't Hogwarts, Gabe decided. It was Wonderland.

No. It was *Lia*.

"You should keep her hair up until the lice threat is over."

Pin it up? He was lucky he could fasten the ponytails. But he nodded because she was right and he really didn't want to cut Maddie's hair. Thought about it a hundred times and always backed off.

He leaned toward her, sitting on the couch beside him, and wrapped both arms around her. "Can I keep you?" he murmured into her ear.

She froze in his arms. He held her away from him so he could see her face and yep—total shock. The gawky teen he used to be showed up, filled him with misgivings. He'd screwed up. He was rushing things. He was—hell with it. Throwing caution to the wind, he plowed straight ahead. "Lia, I know this is moving fast but you have to know how I feel about you."

Brown eyes huge, she kept them glued to his and slowly shook her head.

He leaned in until his lips were a breath from hers. "I'm in love with you." He felt her gasp and kissed her. "So in love with you."

Her arms curled around his back, squeezed so hard, she cut off his air supply. "Really?"

"Yes. Ow. Yes." He kissed her again as soon as he could breathe.

And again.

"Daddy. Oh."

He lifted his head, found Kimberly standing in the hall, biting her lip. "Hey, Cocoa-Pop." He held out his hand, motioned her closer. "You okay?"

"Um, well…" She trailed off, shifting her weight from one leg to the other. "I'm out of…supplies."

It took him a minute. "Oh! Yeah. Okay." He got up, grabbed his jacket, put on his boots.

"Okay if I walk with you?"

He looked up in surprise. Lia's voice was soft and tentative. He turned to Kim. "You okay keeping an eye on your sisters for a bit?"

Kimberly nodded, still biting her lip. "Sorry, Daddy."

"No problem."

Outside in the cool evening air, he and Lia walked in silence, huddled deep inside jackets. They'd reached the corner when inspiration struck.

He held out his hand.

She took it with a sudden smile, kept hold of it all the way to the pharmacy. That was nearly as great as the sex.

"Thank you. For everything today—Maddie's hair, dinner, babysitting."

"You're very welcome. I enjoy spending time with them, Gabriel. Your daughters are incredible."

Yep. Hard to argue with that.

Inside the store, they headed for the aisle where all the feminine products lined the shelves. He'd just reached for the same package Lia had given him the day he'd had to pick Kimberly up from school and froze. "Crap. Lia, I'm so sorry. I never replaced the supplies you gave us."

"No, it's okay. I'm good."

"This stuff is expensive." He pulled two packages of everything he remembered. "Is this it? Oh, wait. You said baby wipes, too. Those are in the next aisle."

"Gabriel." Her hand on his arm stopped him. She wouldn't meet his gaze. She returned the second packages to their spaces on the shelves.

"Lia, I don't expect you to pay for my—"

"It's not the money, Gabriel. I don't need these things anymore."

Confusion clouded his mind. She was too young for—

Oh God.

His mind shot back to the day Kimberly had been sent home from school. He'd been a hot mess but Lia had taken control of the situation. She'd brought him to her apartment. He'd watched her pull those packages out of her bathroom *wastebasket*, heard her say it was a good thing she hadn't thrown them away but the significance of her words never penetrated the haze of his panic.

Until now.

That night, the first night they'd been together, she'd tried to hide the scars on her belly.

He spelled out a bad word, let the packages fall to the ground at their feet so he could grip her, his heart twisting behind his ribs. She hadn't lost *a baby*. She'd lost *all her babies*.

"Amelia," he whispered when she wriggled out of his arms, but not before he saw the tears in her eyes. "Oh, God. I am so sorry." His hands itched to hold her, to comfort her.

"Yeah. Me, too." She swiped a hand over her eyes, smeared some of her makeup. "We shouldn't leave the girls alone too long."

"Yeah. Okay." He picked up the packages from the floor and followed Lia to the register line. He grabbed some chocolate, too.

The walk home was uncomfortable. Once back at the building, she headed for her own front door instead of his.

"Lia. Talk to me."

"It's been a long day, Gabriel. I'm sure you're tired and so am I."

Bullshit. She was hiding again. He followed her up the steps to her door, turned her to face him. "I told you I love you. That doesn't just stop, Lia."

She shook her head. "You don't have to keep saying that."

"I do. I will. Until you believe it."

She sighed loudly, a cloud of vapor visible between them. "Gabriel, you are the best father I've ever seen. When Emmy's a little older, you'll want more babies—a son, to carry on your name. I can't give you that."

She tried to pull away so he tightened his grip. He was shaking his head before she finished talking. "No. I don't want more kids. I have all the children I need. What I need is you. Us."

He saw the wish flash naked and undisguised in her eyes so he moved in, kissing her just under her jaw, the spot that always made her melt. "I told you the first time I touched you, the first time I saw those scars, I want you exactly as you are."

When he felt her body vibrate, then relax, he knew he had her. "Come home with me, Lia. Come home and let me show you."

He took her hand, tugged gently. When she stepped down with him, he silently cheered.

239

THEY SAT ON Gabriel's sofa, pretending to watch TV and Gabriel was in love with her. The girls were in their beds and Lia knew she should return to her own apartment but Gabriel was in love with her. She'd gotten no work of her own done today and now that it was nearly eleven o'clock, was too tired to think about anything—except Gabriel being in love with her.

Holy God.

He loved her. He said the words, all three of them. This…this was unreal.

She peeked at him from the corner of her eye. He had an arm around her shoulders, rubbed a thumb in soft little circles on her upper arm, occasionally moving higher to touch her hair.

He was a toucher. He enjoyed it, reveled in it like a man…

Oh, God. She forced herself to finish the thought. *Like a man starved for affection.* It was so on the nose, she felt her face blaze guiltily for thinking it. Since they'd begun sleeping together, he couldn't keep his hands off her—not that she was complaining. She loved being the focus, the object, and the target of his desire. But it was hard to ignore that little voice inside her that kept asking if this was real. He hardly knew her. She hardly knew him. When was his birthday? What was his favorite meal, his favorite movie, his favorite book? Was he allergic to anything? She didn't even know what faith he practiced, what political party he supported, what music he listened to. But she wanted to. She wanted to know every little thing about him.

"I can hear your brain working all the way over here."

His voice, rough with fatigue, startled her. She looked at him, managed a close-lipped smile and a shrug.

"Problem?"

She shook her head.

"Uh-huh." He gave her the side-eye. "I'm not buying that." He shifted on the sofa so he could face her. "Spill."

Oh, God! She scooted back and shook her head. He moved closer, cradled her face between his hands.

"Lia. Talk to me. Please?"

She wasn't sure if it was the concern she heard in his voice or the *please* he tacked on to his demand, but suddenly, she was blabbering. "You said you love me. You're in love with me. How? Why? I mean, we hardly know each other, except for, you know, *biblically*. I could be an ax murderer. I could be a champion yodeler or a clingy, suspicious witch or—or—I don't know, a compulsive shopper. You can't know!"

The frown between his eyebrows disappeared as his expression turned to one of shock. "Lia, I *do* love you. I *am* in love with you." He kissed her cheeks. "I know everything I need to know. The rest is part of the thrill." He kissed her mouth.

"But—"

"Stop. You know I've done this before. I know how I feel."

Rather than reassuring her, that only made her feel more worried. "So you love me because I'm like her? Janey?"

"No!" Gabriel's blue eyes popped wide. "We've already

had this conversation. Come on. Tell me why you're really freaking out."

Freaking out, was that was she was doing? Insulted she narrowed her eyes. "I'm trying to understand, Gabriel. Jared said he loved me, he was in love with me—"

"I am not Jared. You are not Janey." His voice held the distinct tone of impatience.

"Shhh!" Lia waved a hand and indicated the hallway where the girls' bedroom was.

He blew out a sigh, took her hands in both of his, and lowered his voice. "Lia, I know what I need to know," he repeated. "You love kids. I happen to have four, so that's a plus. You're smart, which is also handy. I like being able to tell you about my work without having to explain all the basics first. I love having you teach me stuff I never knew."

She lifted her eyes to his at that. Jared always hated when she tried to make things easier for him.

Gabriel's eyes narrowed. "I get that your ex-husband hurt you bad. But I'm not him and it's not fair for you to judge *me* by *his* mistakes. He's a scar for you. And maybe I rushed things by telling you how I feel—" At her raised eyebrow, he raised his hands, palms up. "Okay, fine. Let's just admit I did. That's a scar for me. Now that we know this about each other, we can work around it."

"How?" she asked over the lump of dread blocking her throat.

"By committing, Lia. By giving this," he answered, waving a hand between them. "Us. Our relationship. Whatever you want to call us, Lia, we promise to make it a priority until you're sure."

"*I'm* sure?" she echoed.

"I already am."

"But how?" she asked again. "I mean, you had a legitimate freak-out when Emmy ran to me instead of you."

He nodded. "I did. That's true. That was a daddy reaction. But now it factors in to the whole in love with you thing."

Frowning, she shook her head. "How?"

"It means I'm right to trust you. Those girls," he continued, stabbing a finger toward the hall, "are my life. When I leave them with you, I am literally putting my life in your hands."

She shook her head again. "You do that with Mike and with Mrs. Morgan, too. But you're not in love with them."

"Maybe not *in love* with them but I love them, Lia. Don't doubt that for a second."

Mollified, she managed a shaky smile. "You confuse me, Gabriel."

His eyebrows shot up at that.

"You talk about love and commitment like most guys talk about sports and—"

He slapped a hand in the air. "Hold it. I have this really strong suspicions you're about to lay another Jared comparison on me."

"Not just Jared. Every man I've known," she responded on a furious whisper. "Starting with my father. Boys I knew in college. Scars, remember?"

She'd tossed his own words back at him and he had to pull in a slow breath to steady his temper. "Right. You're right," he conceded. "What you're saying is you need time."

Relieved, she nodded. "Yes."

"Okay. I'll do my best to be patient, but you need to understand my scar, Lia."

"I do—"

He shook his head. "No. You can't because you haven't lived it. I was deeply, certainly, completely in love once before. I waited too long to tell her and almost lost her. When I did get her, we got only ten years of that *rest of our lives* we'd so naively thought would be forever. That one stingy decade taught me that nothing is promised, Lia."

Gabriel paused, and slid closer to her, ran his hands up her arms to her face, cradled it gently in his hands. "Lia, I'm thirty-seven years old. If I make it to seventy or eighty, that gives me three, maybe four decades left, if I'm lucky."

She felt that quick punch of fear shudder through her. She got his point. The years go by fast...and there was no guarantee anybody got that many.

"I never planned on doing this again. I didn't believe it was possible for me to love again but now that I know I can, wasting a single second of that time is like asking me to cut off a limb."

She nodded, put her hand to his cheek. "*Your* scar." She could understand his rush, maybe try to meet him somewhere in the middle. "Okay, Gabriel. Okay." She kissed him. "Give me your patience and I'll try to stop looking for your way out."

He grinned, kissed her quick. "Deal."

He pulled back, but she held him longer, took the kiss deep. Slow and steady. She needed to feel more than lust tonight. She needed to feel connected, feel treasured, feel sure. Under her fingertips, Gabriel's blood thrummed and his pulse galloped. When he groaned in her mouth for more, she hushed him, and pressed a series of feather-light kisses to the bare skin of his belly after she slowly slid off his shirt. By the time they finally made it to his bed, he was almost incoherent but still, she moved with deliberation. She planned to stay tonight. She planned to make this last all night.

But after they were done, long after Gabriel had fallen asleep, sprawled naked on his stomach with one arm thrown over her waist, she couldn't relax, couldn't turn off her mind. Shortly after three a.m., she slid out of Gabriel's bed and went back to her own apartment, collapsed on her sofa, and told herself to stop questioning it. He loved her.

So why was she unable to sleep?

Chapter Sixteen

As the holidays and school vacation loomed closer, Gabe's daughters seemed to sleep less. At least, that's how it felt to him. He wanted more time with Lia, but circumstances seemed to conspire against him. Besides his building manager duties, there were presents to wrap and decorations to hang and cookies to bake and various parties and gatherings to attend, like Maddie's class party, at which he was expected to supply a game of some sort.

Games. He shook his head. When he was in school, parents supplied cupcakes and donuts and candy. Today, it was all about alternatives. He had no idea what kind of game a classroom full of first graders could play so he grabbed his tablet while Emmy took her nap and started browsing.

Just as he got settled, a knock sounded on his door. He opened it to find Lia on his doorstep, looking hot in a pair of jeans and red jacket. "Hey."

"Hey," she replied and pushed him against the door as it closed.

"Whoa. Someone's happy to see me." Gabe grinned. "What was that for?"

"Congratulate me. I just landed a new client. A big new client."

Gabe's grin widened. "You did it? The recruiting company? Holy cow, that's awesome." He spun her around. "This calls for a celebration." He put her down, headed for the kitchen. "How about coffee?"

Shaking her head, she unzipped her jacket and tossed it over a kitchen chair. "I'm too buzzed for caffeine. Gabriel, this is huge! Rave Recruiting wants me to manage their LinkedIn presence. I'll be writing articles, setting up a calendar of posts, tracking engagement. And, they're planning some job fairs they want me to help organize, which will really put my name in the right ears..."

He was happy for her. Of course he was. Okay, no. He wasn't. Time was already stretched so thin between them, he practically needed to hire her just so they could get together. He wanted more time, not less and—

And he was an ass.

Look at her. Just look at her. She paced his living room, talking with huge hand gestures, her face flushed and that soft husky voice dripping with pride and enthusiasm.

"...And if that goes as well as I have every reason to believe it will, she says she knows two other good matches, one who's got a real knack for PR and the other who's a former librarian who's a demon with research."

Patience, he reminded himself. *Patience.* He went back to the sofa, grabbed his tablet. "You'll get it done. You're magic, remember?"

She flashed him that smile, the one that screamed *I already know that but thanks for agreeing* and he grinned right back, the one that said *Oh yeah, I'm sure.*

She went still, eyes glued to his. Yep. She was starting to

believe him. The ring tucked in his underwear drawer suddenly called to him.

Not yet.

"What are you up to?" she asked, joining him on the sofa, angling her head to see the screen.

"Research. Maddie's holiday party at school."

"Oh, fun! I've got a really easy Santa Claus snack you can make out of strawberries, grapes, and banana slices."

He grinned. Of course she did. He hadn't missed the way her eyes lit up when he said the R word. Research was fun to her. "Nope. I have to provide a game."

"Ooo, for how many kids?"

"Uh, twenty-eight."

"Okay. I got you covered. Don't go away." She leaped up, grabbed her jacket and disappeared out the door and Gabe kicked himself. Why the hell had he said anything? Lia had knocked on his door in the middle of the afternoon, three out of four kids were in school and the fourth was asleep and he'd let the opportunity go?

Oh, he was definitely off his game.

Lia was back in ten minutes, handing him a plastic bag. "Here."

"What's all this?" he said, peeking inside the bag.

"Everything you need to make a holiday punch board."

His eyebrows shot up. "What—Never mind." He dropped the bag and lunged for her, got his mouth on hers before she could squeal, backed her up toward his bedroom. By his estimate, they had forty minutes before Emmy would wake up and he planned to use every one of them.

"But what about—"

"Later. Naked now," he whispered, locking his bedroom door.

It didn't take forty minutes.

Twenty minutes later, they were both sweaty, panting, and smiling just as Emmy let out a cry. Lia was still wearing one sock.

"Dad-dee!"

∾

WITH A GRUNT, Gabriel crawled over Lia, tugged on his pants and went to free his youngest daughter. Lia lay there for another minute, trying to catch her breath. Good Lord, what *was* that? How did he do all those amazing things to her so fast? She remained there for five more minutes, listening to Gabriel help Emmy use the potty.

"Bye-bye, poo!"

"We really don't need to wave good-bye to it, E-Rex."

"Where go, Dad-dee?"

"It goes in the sewer."

"Aww."

"It's okay. It likes it there."

Lia giggled helplessly in his bed.

Emmy gasped. "Whas dat?"

"Emmy, no—"

"Eee-uh!" A half-naked toddler climbed up on Gabriel's bed and pounced on Lia. "Hi! Hi, Eee-uh. Mwah." Emmy kissed Lia's face with a loud smack. "Dad-dee! Eee-uh's in da big bed."

"Okay, okay, let's let Lia get dressed, Emmy."

The expression on the baby's face turned comical and before he could stop her, she'd lifted the covers and exposed Lia's naked body. Her eyes and her little mouth formed perfect circles of shock. "Eee-uh's nake-y, Dad-dee."

"Come here, you little mood-killer." Gabriel snagged Emmy, lifted her high in the air, making her squeal.

Lia, still giggling, met Gabriel's eyes over the baby's sleep-tousled head.

This is gonna get complicated, they told her.

Bring it, she said with her own.

He strode out of the room with a laugh.

SAFELY REDRESSED, LIA met Gabriel and Emmy in the kitchen where he was unpacking the bag she'd brought over. Emmy was buckled into her high chair with a cup and apple slices. Gabriel was still half-dressed.

"Okay, so what's this poke game you mentioned?"

"Super easy," she assured him, digging into the bag herself. "I've got some inexpensive ornaments and holiday treats. We put one item inside each of these cups, cover the mouth of the cup with tissue paper in assorted colors, and then glue the cups to a large piece of poster or cardboard. The children earn a punch through the tissue-paper by correctly answering a question and win whatever's inside."

Gabriel blinked at her. "This…you…this is awesome. Thank you."

Lia smiled. "I was thinking we could do a snowflake, to make it more universal."

"Snowflake." He decided, pulling out white, silver, and blue tissue paper. "Wait." He put the papers down, turned to her. "What were you planning to use all this stuff for?"

Lia waved a hand. "For the kids in the building. I was going to invite little Mason from next door, plus the Danners' son and your girls over for some cookies and games."

He studied her face and she had to fight the urge to squirm.

"Lia. I'll find something else."

No. She needed to do this. "Gabriel, it's okay. I want to help. Really. Come on. Let's get started. We've got a lot of cups to fill."

He took her hand, drew her into his arms, hugged her. "Are you sure about this?"

"Absolutely."

"Then let's get started."

She laughed, pecked his nose. "First, you need to get dressed. You're entirely too distracting like this."

"Oh. Am I?" His voice went deeper and that look came back into his eyes.

"Dress. Now."

"Yes, ma'am." He gave her a little salute and took off down the hall.

"Me! Kiss." Emmy demanded from her high chair so Lia went to her and kissed her little nose.

Gabriel had a large foam board left over from one of Liv's science projects. He grabbed a pencil and sketched out a snowflake pattern. Watching him sketch was an unexpected thrill. The way he held the pencil, the way figures took shape under his hand, mesmerized her. It didn't take them long to cover the cups with tissue paper and glue them down.

"This is great, Lia. I'll stick this on top of my dresser so it doesn't get Emmy-fied."

Lia laughed. "Good idea." She began cleaning all the scraps, tossing them into the trash. She glanced at the clock on the oven and called back to Gabriel, "Hey, when are you picking up the girls?"

"About half an hour." He walked back into the kitchen as Emmy ran into her bedroom.

"Have you shopped for them yet? For the holidays?"

Gabriel frowned. "Um, well." He scratched his neck, something she noted he did when he was uncomfortable. "Some. I ordered a bunch of stuff online."

"You can use my place to hide it all. I can even wrap it for you."

"Oh, well I just shipped it upstate to their grandparents' house. We're spending Christmas there."

A pang of longing squeezed her heart. "Oh." Of course he'd have traditions and plans. He had a family.

"Hey, why don't you see if you can clear your Friday afternoon to bake with us. That's what we're doing on Friday. The girls are off for two weeks, so I wanted some time with them before I drop them upstate with Janey's parents."

At her blank expression, he elaborated. "You know…so I can build those beds."

Lia opened her mouth only to close it. She'd completely forgotten about the built-ins. The materials were stacked in the building's garage.

"We'll bake some cookies and then trim the tree I got—

potted, which you'll be happy to know." He shot her a grin.

A potted tree? Joy replaced the pain she'd felt a minute before. Decorating potted Christmas trees was a tip she'd included in the last edition of her building newsletter and hearing that he didn't just read the newsletter, but followed her advice put another crack in the wall around her heart.

"Gabriel, you're...you won't be with your daughters for Christmas?"

"Sure I will. But I'll be driving back and forth between here and there. I have a ton of work to do and can't keep one eye on them while I'm doing it." His eyes lit up. "Did I show you my latest plans?" He stretched to the top of the refrigerator and took down some papers. They were more of his amazing sketches. "Mine is going there, on that wall. Kim and Liv get my room. Their beds will fold up into these sofas. Remember? You picked this one."

She flipped through his sketches, saw he'd added desks and shelves and felt his excitement. "You should just take my unit. That one has three bedrooms. Would it help if I spoke to Mr. Kinsella?"

"No," he said firmly. "It wouldn't. Look, I know this isn't an ideal arrangement, but I'm doing the best I can."

She gasped and squeezed his hand. "I'm not judging."

Emmy ran in, clutching books in each hand. "Weed, Eee-uh."

Lia crouched down, examined the books. "You want to read? Okay. Go sit down. I'll be there in a minute." She stood up, looked into Gabe's stony face. "I know better than anybody just how hard you work to make a good life for your daughters. I can see it. Gabriel. I feel it."

He winced and looked away. "I'm sorry for that." He put the plans back on top of the refrigerator. "The whole reason I said yes to helping Paradigm part-time was so I can afford the difference in rent between this unit and the duplex. But, Lia, that's a long way off. Years, especially after I bought—" He bit his lip and shrugged. "For right now, remodeling this unit will give us more privacy."

"Privacy? You'll be sleeping in your living room while I have two unused bedrooms across the courtyard." She folded her arms and shook her head. "That hardly seems fair."

"It's business." He shrugged. "I'm not taking it personally."

Lia took a deep breath, smarting at his implication that *she* was taking it personally. "I hate feeling that you need help, but there's nothing I can do for you."

"Sure there is," he said with a gleam in his eye. "You said you have two extra rooms next door. Can you store some of my stuff? If I can get this room and maybe the bedroom empty, that will really help make the work go smoothly."

She thought about that for a minute. "I have one room set up as a guest room. We could stack all the mattresses in there, maybe boxes for this stuff." She waved a hand at the shelf unit currently in his living room.

"Great. Thanks. See? You helped." He pecked her on the cheek, then joined Emmy on the sofa and began reading her books. She watched him, her heart swelling.

He'd given her the words.

And now, he was backing them up with actions. Little ones, like reading her newsletter. Big ones, like supporting her wins, trusting her judgment...and paying close attention to the things that scared her the most.

Yes, she thought. Yes.

THE DAYS PASSED painfully slowly—if you asked the Ivers girls.

Lia's punch board game was a hit with the first-graders in Maddie's class, and her cookie-baking skills thoroughly impressed Gabe's girls—even Olivia. She'd once told him she didn't cook, but apparently, baking was a whole different set of skills for her.

He wasn't sure how he did it all, but he managed to get cookies, presents, decorations, and daughters all up to their grandparents' house without losing his temper (the curses he spelled didn't count) or forgetting anything critical. He'd told Jim at Paradigm he couldn't make it into the city at all over the next few weeks because of the girls' holiday break, and he'd told the tenants he'd be available only for emergencies. Any general maintenance would have to wait until after construction.

It was Day Two of construction.

Mike arrived on Day One along with two of his buddies that Gabe knew well. With all four of them helping, they got the furniture in Gabe's living room and bedroom moved to Lia's. Today, they'd start assembling the hideaway beds in the bedroom for Kim and Liv. He'd ordered white cabinets for the girls' beds. Each unit had two side bookcases that remained stationary and the doors were concealed by small love seats that folded down when the beds were opened. The two units would be assembled where his bed had stood. There'd be a wardrobe plus a desk and more shelving on the wall surrounding the room's two windows.

Alphonse and Isaac, Mike's pals from his upstate town, hauled up the materials from the locked area in the garage. Tools sat on nearly every flat surface in the apartment. Gabe was standing on a ladder when Mike asked, "So how's Lia?"

"Fine," Gabe snapped, embarrassed to feel his face burn at the question.

"You guys are good?"

"We're fine," he said again.

Alphonse exchanged a grin with Mike. "I got a glimpse of her a little while ago. You're right. She *is* fine."

Embarrassment gave way to annoyance. "Can we just work, please? I gotta leave at three. The in-laws expect me for dinner tonight."

"Slacker." Mike tossed a piece of plastic at him. Gabe just pressed his lips together, fastened another screw into the first bed's cabinet.

On the other side of the room, Isaac drilled a hole through the wall for the cable TV. "How many kids you got, man?"

"Four."

He let out a whistle. "They must miss their mom."

Gabe's patience was thinning out. "Sure do." He stepped off the ladder, called out to Mike. "Okay. Let's bolt these to the wall and then get the mechanism in place."

Mike put his power drill on a windowsill. "Let me check the level first."

With a grunt, Gabe grabbed a stud finder while Mike

picked up the level. He marked the locations of the studs in the wall. Mike marked the positions where they'd need to drill in the cabinet to hold the mechanism. After Gabe drilled the holes, Alphonse and Mike fastened the bolts.

"This kit is great. Pretty easy, actually," Al said. Gabe merely grunted.

Isaac sanded the edges of the mattress platform and then fastened the foldaway legs that would support the bed when it was lowered. They'd just gotten the mattress platform connected to the mechanism when a knock sounded on the door.

Gabe cursed and left the bedroom to answer it.

"Hi!" Lia said brightly. "I brought you some food." She held up a pizza box and a six-pack.

"Oh. Yeah. Thanks," Gabe muttered. He didn't want her here. Not now when he'd practically taken off Al's head.

Still smiling, she stepped inside, kissed his cheek, and dropped the refreshments on his kitchen counter. "Do I get a sneak preview?"

Sighing, he shrugged. "If you want." He led her into what used to be his bedroom. "Guys, this is Amelia Blake. Lia, you know Mike. That's Alphonse and this is Isaac."

"Hi, guys. I brought you some pizza and beer."

"Yes!" Isaac disappeared.

Lia examined the cabinet of the first bed. "Wow. You got a lot done. This looks great. And the girls can operate it alone?"

"Sure." Gabe raised and lowered the bed, showed her how the legs that would hold the mattress rotated inside. "I'm using the mattresses I already have. They'll fit and it saves me some money."

"Good idea. Can I help you with anything?" she asked but he shook his head, willing her to just go and let him do what he needed to do.

"Okay. You drive safely, okay? Before you go, will you knock on my door? I've got something for you."

Something else? Jeez. She'd already brought food. Swallowing back a sound of frustration, Gabe nodded. "Sure."

"Okay. See you." She turned to leave, hesitated and then shot him a wicked grin over her a shoulder. "You know," she whispered. "I never thought I was the kind of girl who got turned on by a guy in a tool belt…"

Gabe felt his spirits rising. "Yeah?"

"Oh, yeah. Maybe we'll play super and tenant one night? I'll call you to hang a shelf for me. You can bring your…hammer."

He snorted and gave her bottom a swat. "Get out of here before I embarrass myself in front of the guys."

She kissed his cheek again but that suddenly wasn't good enough. He caught her before she could disappear and charged. By the time he lifted his head, she was swaying.

He walked her out. "Bye, guys." She waved when she reached the door. "Nice meeting you."

"Thanks for the pizza," Mike called after her. "Ivers, what the hell did you do? She ran out of here like a bat outta hell," he demanded when Gabe shut the door.

"Bite me." He snagged a slice and popped the cap off a longneck. "Eat fast. I want the second bed up before I go."

Alphonse's dark eyebrows shot up. "Jeez, sure Ebenezer Ivers."

As the other guys laughed at that, Gabe lifted his middle finger.

~

LATER THAT AFTERNOON, he knocked on Lia's back door, as promised. She came to the door wearing jingle bells on her socks. It made him smile.

"I gotta run. I'm gonna be sitting in a ton of traffic and they're expecting me for dinner."

"I won't keep you. This is for you and your girls." She grabbed an enormous shopping bag from a chair in her kitchen and handed it to him. "Open it on Christmas Eve." She winked.

"Um. Wow. Yeah. Okay." He felt like a dick. "Thanks, Lia. Really. But I'll see you tomorrow." He pulled her toward him for a kiss that wiped his mind clear.

"I know. I just wanted the girls to see more presents and build their excitement, you know?"

Building excitement? Oh, he knew a lot about that.

He walked down the courtyard steps to his SUV, put the bag inside, and started the engine. He thought about Lia, about her kindness, her softness, her desire to help. And then he got out of the SUV and knocked on her door again—the front one, this time.

"Gabriel? What's—"

"Okay, I get that this is completely spur of the moment and understand if you can't just drop everything, but...um... Do you...uh... I'd really like... Shit. Okay, would you like to come with me upstate? Have dinner with

Janey's parents? I want everybody to meet you. I want them to know I'm *with* you."

Her jaw dropped and a moment later, her eyes filled. Suddenly, her arms were around his neck. "Oh my God! That...this...oh, Gabriel. You couldn't have given me a better gift."

A feeling of warmth floated over him. "Yeah?" He grinned. Shrugged. "If you say so. So how about it? Can you throw some stuff in a bag and come with?"

She let him go and beamed up at him. Didn't hesitate. "I can and I will."

And she disappeared up the stairs, coming down barely five minutes later with a large bag on her shoulder. She moved to the kitchen next, tucked more cookies into a fancy gift bag, and then dove into her refrigerator for a bottle of wine. "Okay. I'm ready."

Ready, he repeated silently.

Yeah...so was he. He'd been ready since Thanksgiving. Was she?

Chapter Seventeen

"DADDY!"

Gabe hardly had time to close his door before Maddie was running down the driveway toward him. "Hey, Ducky. How are you? I missed you." He boosted her to one hip and walked around to the passenger door.

"I missed you, too. This much!" She let go of him long enough to spread her arms apart as far as they would go.

"How's Emmy?" he asked.

"Emmy wet Grandma's couch and Grandma got mad like this." Maddie pulled a face that made Gabe roll his eyes and groan, but Lia laughed as she stepped out of the SUV.

Maddie gasped. "Lia! Hi!" She wriggled free of Gabe so she could fling herself into Lia's arms. "Did you bring cookies?"

"Yes, I sure did."

"Yay! I'll tell Grandma."

Maddie ran off, shrieking happily into the house while Gabe moved to the rear of the SUV and started unloading the bags Lia had given him.

"You, uh, ready for this?" he asked her. "Chatty Maddie's in there right now, spreading good cheer." He wriggled his fingers. "I figure you've got about ten seconds before we're surrounded."

Lia tossed hair that shined like fire over her shoulder, looked at him with a smile. "I'm ready."

Gabe glanced toward the house as the laughter and shrieks got louder. "Five seconds."

"Gabriel." She gave him a stern look. "I'm not going anywhere."

Her words gave him a much-needed shot in the arm. Or maybe, it was a kick in the ass.

Okay then.

He flashed her a grin, took her hand and strode up the front steps and through the door with her at his side. "Hi, everybody."

"Gabe?"

His grip tightened on Lia's hand when his mother-in-law stood up from her spot beside Emmy on the sofa.

"Dad-dee! Hi!" Emmy slid off the sofa, ran to the Christmas tree in front of a window and grabbed a toy.

"Linda. This is Amelia. She's…um, well. I—"

"But we call her Lia 'cause we're friends, right Daddy? Right? Right?"

"Yes, Ducky."

"Dad-dee!" Emmy ran over to him. "See?" She batted him with a stuffed reindeer.

He scooped her up, propped her on a hip and reclaimed Lia's hand.

Linda's gaze landed on their hands. When she gasped, Gabe knew there'd be no hiding it now. "Lia is Daddy's girlfriend, Grandma. Right, Daddy? Is she? Lia, are you? Are you my daddy's girlfriend now?"

Gabe never took his eyes from Linda. "Yes," he said simply.

Linda's lips wobbled...then curved into a smile that slowly spread. "It's about damn time, Gabe." She grabbed him in a tight hug and then turned to Lia. "Hi. Welcome. I'm Linda Haggerty, Gabe's mother-in-law." She hugged Lia, too.

It took Lia a few seconds to catch up but she returned the hug. "I hope it's okay that I'm here." Maddie and Emmy hugged her, too.

"Honey, like I said. It's about damn time. Let me take your coat."

"Oh, um, these are for you." Lia handed Linda the bag of cookies and bottle of wine.

"Thank you. That's so thoughtful."

"Where are Kim and Liv?" Gabe asked.

"Upstairs, honey. They're braiding hair."

"Be right back." Gabe put the baby down and kissed Lia's cheek.

He headed upstairs to the room Linda kept for her granddaughters, found Kim brushing Olivia's dark tresses on one of the room's twin beds.

"Ow, Kimberly! Not so hard."

"Well, if you tried brushing it once in a while, it wouldn't get all snarled up like this."

"I wish it were blonde like yours."

"The color doesn't matter. You have to take care of it. Use that brush Lia bought us."

"Lia's hair isn't like ours." Olivia moved the clip so she could see. "It's like, red."

"It's called auburn."

"Daddy likes it."

The smile on Gabe's face dimmed. Kimberly clipped a huge section of Olivia's hair in front of her face.

"So what?"

Olivia shrugged. Kim took out the clip and started weaving sections into a French braid. "Maybe he likes it better than brown hair."

This time, it was Kim's turn to shrug. "That's dumb."

Gabe might have laughed if that hadn't hurt so damn much. He cleared his throat. "Not dumb. But it's impossible."

"Hey, Dad."

"Hi, Daddy."

He stepped inside, hugged both girls, and sat next to them on the bed. "Girls, just because Lia's hair isn't like yours does not mean I want yours to be different," he began just as Maddie ran into the room, shouting the news.

"Kimby! Livvie! Lia's here and she's got cookies and more presents!"

Maddie skidded to a stop, a sheepish expression on her face when she found Gabe already talking to her sisters.

"Madison. What have we talked about?"

She held out her hand. "Want a bite of my cookie?"

Gabe folded his arms. "Maddie."

"'Christmas is about giving, not getting,'" she recited.

He sighed, too tired to make a big deal out of this.

Olivia pulled away from Kimberly's hands, shook her hair out. "You brought Lia?" she asked, not meeting his eyes.

Gabe put an arm around her shoulders. "I did. Is that a

problem?"

She folded her arms and said nothing.

"Daddy. It's cool. We really like Lia," Kimberly said. "Right, Liv?"

It took her a minute, but finally, Liv nodded. Gabe exhaled slowly. Good. This was good news. Not that he was anxious about it. Okay. Maybe a little. "Thanks, Cocoa-Pop."

"You're not gonna forget Mommy, are you?" Olivia asked.

Maddie laughed. "That's silly. Daddy can't ever forget Mommy 'cause he has us."

Gabe pointed a finger at Maddie. "What she said." That pulled a small smile out of Olivia. "Come on. Let's go say hi to Lia, okay?"

"Daddy, will you braid my hair? Kim can't do it."

"I could if you'd stop moving," she shot back.

"Sure, Newton. Come on."

"Me, too, Daddy? Can I have a braid, too? Please?"

Gabe had a thought. "Maybe Lia knows how to do braids."

Maddie's eyes lit up and she ran downstairs. To his surprise, Olivia grabbed the hairbrush and some elastics and followed.

Okay then. Time to spread some holiday cheer.

THAT EVENING, DURING dinner, conversation was lively and loud as the girls requested updates on the construction. Gabe showed them pictures he'd taken on his phone of the bed frames. The girls wore matching reindeer pajamas—a tradition Linda and Stuart began back when Kimberly was born—and matching braids Lia had done for them. Except Emmy, whose hair wasn't long enough for much yet.

After the girls had been read to, tucked in, and kissed good night, Gabe sank tiredly to the sofa in the family room next to Lia.

"They go down for you okay, Gabe?" Stuart asked.

"Yeah." Gabe yawned. "Except Maddie. She wouldn't let me undo the braid Lia did for her."

"Oh! I'm sorry. I'll do another one for her."

"She was asleep before I left the room so I think she'll be okay."

"Well," Linda said, stretching her arms overhead. "Your girls have worn me out. I'm going up. See you in the morning. Lia, I'm so glad you're here. Gabriel has been on his own for way too long."

After Linda and Stuart went up to bed, Gabe smiled at Lia. "I'm glad you're here, too."

"So you've said." She sat beside him on the sofa, muffled a squeal when he hauled her onto his lap. "Where's *your* family, Gabriel? You don't talk much about them."

He shrugged. "Not much to tell. I'm an only child. My dad died about ten years ago and my mother's been 'finding herself' ever since."

"You're not close."

It wasn't a question, he noticed. But he answered her anyway. "Never were. I don't think she ever wanted kids and she damn well doesn't want to be a grandma, so I stopped putting in the effort. It was easy after that. Turns out I was the only one trying."

She laid a hand against his cheek. "I have some experience in the absent parent arena. Mine was too busy chasing ass to bother with me."

Gabe's eyes bulged. "Chasing ass?" When Lia said nothing, he smiled. "You always speak like a teacher. I don't think I've ever heard you use bad language before."

Lia's own grin was rueful. "Yes, well, all I can say in my own defense is he brings out the worst in me."

He took her hand and pressed a kiss to the palm. Silk, he thought. Everything about Lia was silk, satin, and velvet. Soft, sweet, and warm.

"Do you think your mother's inattention is why you had so many children yourself?"

What the hell? Gabe opened his mouth, about to snap at her. He'd had so many children because Janey had wanted to. End of story.

Then he closed it.

Lia wasn't judging him.

He'd made that mistake before—several times, in fact. So he was honest. "No. I have so many children because Janey wanted them and I did whatever I could do to make her happy."

"I upset you. I'm sorry." She moved to slide off his lap but he held her there, shook his head, decided to give this honesty thing another go.

"For a minute, yeah. I was pissed off. You have a way of asking questions that feels like you're judging me and I don't like it."

"I wasn't—"

He held up a hand. "I know. I know you better now. I know you were just curious, so I answered your question."

Her lips curled. "Oh. So that's why I felt the tension in your body for only a couple of seconds."

"That's why." He drew her head down to his shoulder, kissed her head, happy with himself. He was getting better at this communication thing. "I promised you patience, remember?"

When she nodded, he wrapped both arms around her. "I will tell you this, though, since you asked. My mom's inattention is why I'm so involved in the girls' lives. Even before Janey died, I was there for all of it. Pediatrician appointments, soccer games, school plays, and parent-teacher conferences. I worked all damn day and so did Janey but we both made sure the girls knew they were loved unconditionally."

Her breath tickled him when she laughed once. "Yes, you are involved. I think that's the first thing about you that attracted me."

"Oh, well that kind of sucks. I was hoping you noticed my ass. Or my rippling muscles."

Laughing now, Lia poked him in the ribs. "Or, it could have been your staggering humility."

"First thing I noticed about you was your hair. I was cursing my luck that day when the car died and then you walked toward me with the sun behind you. It was like watching a fire start." He ran a hand down her mane, lifting it, holding it up on top of her head and letting it fall.

A sudden thought struck him and he wondered if she'd

think it was weird. If *he* was weird.

"What?" Lia sat up in alarm, sliding off his lap.

"Nothing. I just thought of something."

Frowning, she angled her head. "What? What's wrong?"

"Nothing's wrong. I just... Okay, this may sound weird, but father of four daughters here so I've got some experience." Shit, this sounded weird even to him. "Never mind." He waved a hand.

"No, tell me. I won't laugh, if that's what you're worried about."

Laughing would be fine by him. As long as she didn't recoil and think he had some kind of fetish. "I want to braid *your* hair."

She stared at him. "You want to...braid my hair. Why?"

"Because it's amazing. Because every time I see you, I have to remind myself not to touch. Because we're together now and this is what couples do."

"Braid each other's hair? Um. No. That's not what couples do."

"Well, maybe they should," he shot back. "You think it's weird, don't you?"

"No!" Her eyes went wide. And then her cheeks went pink. "I kind of love when you touch my hair."

His grin flashed, just for a second. "Then you'll love this." He grabbed the brush Kimberly had left on the coffee table, took one of the elastics from the pile beside it. "Sit here." He spread his legs, patted the space between his thighs.

She looked doubtful but obeyed, fitting her hips in the spot he indicated. A flare ignited inside him. He drew the brush slowly through all that luxurious auburn hair, parting it into sections. He dropped the brush in his lap, lifted the first section, held it between his fingers for a moment before twisting it around the next. He was good at this. He'd had plenty of practice.

But with Lia?

It was new. And almost frighteningly erotic. By the time he'd exposed her ears, he was hard. He lowered his head, bit her lobe. Lia gasped. He flicked out his tongue, pressed hot kisses along her neck as he braided. He lifted another section, found her other ear and bit that one, too.

Another gasp. Then her hands came down on his thighs. He could do this for hours, he thought, as he ran the brush through another section of her hair.

"Your hair isn't just red," he whispered into the ear he'd just bitten. "It's gold and brown and the color of cinnamon and I swear, the part I just braided is black cherry. Never cut it. Never color it. Promise me." He kissed her neck, her jaw, her shoulder as her hands tightened on his thighs.

"It's my hair," she reminded him.

Right. Of course it was. He cleared his throat, grabbed the elastic, fastened it around the end of the braid he'd made, and loosened her grip on his legs. She stood up, turned and stared at him for a long moment, face revealed by the hairstyle he'd created. Her eyes were dark, her lips parted and face flushed.

"You're as turned on as I am," she murmured.

He didn't reply. Thought it superfluous, under the circumstances. "I'm really glad you came with."

"Me, too," she whispered and bent to kiss him with a

slow, deliberate thoroughness that came damn close to making him beg.

"More," he whispered. "Now."

"Gabriel. Shhh. We can't do anything more. We're in your in-laws' home. So let's just enjoy this, okay?"

Just kiss…he hadn't done that since he was fifteen.

"Okay," he agreed but as soon as he tugged her to his lap, she put a hand on his chest.

"Gabriel. Let me," she whispered, kissing him softly. "Let me."

Oh, God. She was killing him. He dropped his head back to the sofa and had to fight his instincts to take over. Her lips skimmed over him and his bones melted. He wanted all of that sweet, sweet mouth and he moved, just an inch, catching her lips with his. She indulged him for a moment and then pushed him back, a clear demand to let her do what she wanted.

She wanted a lot and yet, not enough. She took her hands on a cruise of his arms, his shoulders, his chest, and then up into his hair. Slowly, so slowly it actually ached, she rubbed her thumbs along his jaw, kissing him deeply. She moaned and his entire body clenched. He wasn't doing a thing except sitting back and letting her do what she wanted and she'd *moaned*. What kind of magic was this?

She shifted, just sort of *oozed* over him, around him. She was loose and liquid and so soft. His hands moved to her breasts and she moaned again but gently nudged his hands away and back to the sofa.

Right.

Just kissing. He remembered. And a funny thing happened. For the first time in his life, Gabriel found himself enjoying the scenery instead of racing to the finish line.

〜

"WHERE HAVE YOU been?" her mother demanded the following morning. "I called you at least three times yesterday."

Lia excused herself from the breakfast table and braced for impact. "Oh, well, as it happens, I'm not home. I'm upstate, in Putnam Valley."

She had thoroughly enjoyed her spontaneous trip with Gabriel. He was a good driver, didn't lose his temper when they hit traffic, and didn't speed or tailgate—which kind of shocked her. He was so impatient most times, she figured he'd be the same kind of driver as Jared, whose temper spiked whenever brake lights appeared. Lia had grown to loathe long trips. But Gabe and Lia had spent the time talking about the various holiday traditions they'd both loved and despised as children, which evolved into a spirited debate about the best gifts they'd received. For Gabriel, it was a prized baseball signed by Mike Piazza himself and for Lia, it was a diorama featuring a scene from her favorite novel.

Gabe had guessed that favorite novel was *Pride and Prejudice*. Lia couldn't remember if she'd told him that but even if she had, she still gave him points for remembering.

They talked about the future, too. Lia was touched when Gabriel said he hoped she'd be able to join his family on a summer trip to Montauk. The warm welcome she'd received from Gabe's daughters as well as his in-laws both delighted and bewildered her. And sleeping the entire night with Gabriel's arms around her had been a welcome change of pace from their usual rushed and stolen moments. She'd had the sweetest of dreams.

Her mood evaporated with her mother's next words. "Putnam, as in upstate New York? What on earth are you doing there and why didn't you tell me you were going out of town?"

She smiled tightly at the Ivers family gathered for breakfast in Linda and Stuart's enormous kitchen and stepped into the formal living room, where a gorgeous Douglas fir stood in the center window. "It was a spur-of-the-moment thing. Plus, I didn't realize I was still required to check in with you."

Victoria Blake didn't miss that note of petulance. "Well, you'll just have to forgive me for worrying."

"I'm fine, Mom. I'm with Gabriel and his family."

A long silence spread between them. "You went away, overnight, with the superintendent of your building and his children? Things have gotten serious pretty fast, then."

Lia supposed they had. But she didn't want to ruin anything by speculating about it with her mother.

Gabriel…loved her.

It was too new. Too special. Too…amazing.

"What did you need to speak to me about?"

"The holidays. When are you coming?"

A pit the size of a ball suddenly formed in her belly. Tension always hung in the air at her parents' home…cloying and overpowering—much like the perfume her mother favored. If her father was actually present, there'd be some

273

disagreement, some argument about which she was expected to pick a side. Just thinking about dragging Gabriel and his daughters into that environment seemed to triple the size of that pit.

"I'm not sure I can make it this year, Mom."

"If things are this serious between you and your super, you can bring him along."

"He has four children, Mom. They can't be left home by themselves."

"Well, I suppose you can bring them, too. If you must."

"I'll check my work schedule when I get home and let you know."

"Gee, thank you."

Victoria's sarcasm was thick and for a minute, Lia felt guilty. But then she spotted her reflection in a mirror hanging over a demi-lune table against a wall. Her shoulders were hunched nearly to her ears and her stomach roiled. Temper suddenly replaced guilt.

"Mom, please don't guilt me. I have been through hell over the last couple of years. My husband decided he'd rather have somebody else, I lost a baby I wanted desperately, and I lost the ability to ever have another one. So you'll have to excuse me if I'd rather spend time with the incredible man I met and his wonderful, interesting, and loving family than drive for four hours to visit you, where I'll be forced to listen while you and Dad lob insults at each other and by extension, me. *If* I decide that's how I want to spend the holiday, I'll let you know. Meanwhile, you might consider visiting me for once."

She disconnected before her mother could say a word in

response.

When she looked up, she found Linda standing in the hall.

"Oh!" Lia's face burst into flames. She was an unexpected guest in this house and had been warmly welcomed and would probably never be asked to return after that phone call. Then again, she'd left the kitchen to avoid being overheard.

"I'm sorry." She lifted her chin. "I'd tried not to interrupt breakfast."

Linda didn't say anything. She just walked into the room and put her arms around Lia. "Sweet girl. You don't have to apologize to me. But if you ever want to talk, you know where I live."

Lia blinked, surprised to feel the sting of tears in her eyes. "I do. Thank you for that." And she hugged back.

"Amelia."

Lia looked over, found Gabriel standing in the hall, a frown marring his forehead.

"You okay?"

"I am. I'm completely fine now." She smiled at Linda and gave her another squeeze. "Thank you."

Gabriel gave Linda's shoulder an affectionate squeeze. "Okay, okay, you two. Breakfast is getting cold and I've got to get back to Bayside before Mike goes on strike."

"Gabe." Linda stopped him with a hand on his arm. "Bring this girl back to visit me. I like her."

"Yeah?" He flung his arms around both of them. "I do, too."

Lia swiped a fingertip under her eyes and laughed.

GABRIEL HAD DELAYED leaving until after breakfast, after the morning rush hour. Emmy cried; she wanted her daddy to stay with her. Maddie wanted a new braid, just like the one Gabriel arranged for Lia the night before.

She had to admit, the man knew his way around a hairstyle. That had been the single, sexiest, most intimate moment of her life—and she'd been *married*.

Gabriel's hand reached over the center console to cover hers. "What are you smiling about over there?"

"Oh, um, well—" she stammered, embarrassed that he'd caught her.

"Come on. Spill." He grinned and then checked traffic behind him to merge onto the highway.

"I was thinking about you braiding my hair last night," she finally admitted. Dear God, was that her voice? It had dropped a full octave, sounding husky and well…sexy—even to her.

"You liked it."

It wasn't a question, just a reaffirmation of what he already knew, given the wide, self-satisfied grin on his face.

Liked it? Lia loosened her jacket and scarf. Liked it? She'd been on sensory overload ever since. Who knew hair could be so…so erogenous? Gabriel's thumb made slow circles against the hand he still held and she wondered how on earth she was going to survive the drive home. She cleared her throat. "Um, Gabriel?"

"Yes, Amelia?"

He knew exactly what he was doing to her, the beast.

"Is there any place we might, ah, you know. Pull over? Some place quiet and private, I mean?"

At that, both of his hands gripped the wheel and the car's speed increased. Fifteen minutes later, he pulled into the drive of a large rambling home. Lia looked at him in total shock. "In someone's *driveway?*" she whispered.

❧

GABE LAUGHED AT the scandalized tone in Lia's voice.

He'd been doing a lot of that lately. Laughing.

Weird. He hadn't missed laughing until now. Now he was so damn glad he had a reason to laugh again. Oh, sure. The girls made him laugh. But under those laughs, there was always pain and grief. But Lia? She entertained him. Braiding her hair last night had been the kinkiest bit of foreplay he'd ever engaged in. She'd sighed and squirmed against him, those beautiful dark chocolate eyes of hers almost black with desire.

He wished he'd had a camera.

Okay, he did have a camera. He'd wished he'd thought to use it.

He had to admit, there was a part of him—probably the part that was still sixteen years old—that enjoyed seeing her walk into the kitchen this morning still wearing that braid. It told him he she'd definitely enjoyed his attention.

It told him that he wasn't alone in this.

He shut off the engine, held up the keys and waggled his eyebrows. "This is Mike's place."

Her eyes went even wider. "Oh, we can't. He's on his

way to your apartment right now. It wouldn't be right."

"We'll be fast. He'll never know." He snaked a hand around her neck, drew her closer, kissed her because if he didn't, he was going to explode. There it was again. That punch of heat. That instant ignition. The sighs, the hums she made. When he pulled back and saw her eyes, he knew she was on board. "But if you'd rather wait…"

"Let's go," she said in that deep husky voice that made him immediately hard.

He was out the door before she finished talking. He helped her from the car, led her up the walk to Mike's front door, inserted his key. "Mike's a bit of a neat freak so, wipe your feet, take off your shoes."

Lia did so while Gabe called out. "Hey, it's Gabe. Anybody home?"

When nobody answered, he lunged. He had them peeled out of jackets, scarves and clothes in two seconds flat and kissed Lia thoroughly senseless up against the door. He boosted her up and over his shoulder, gave her bottom a whack that made her squeal, and headed for the stairs.

Not Mike's bed. That really wouldn't be right. Gabe headed for the small room, the one where he usually crashed whenever he visited. He put Lia back on her feet, steadied her when she swayed, and then said, "Okay. I've pulled over somewhere quiet and private. Now what?"

Her grin was slow and yeah, maybe just a little dirty. "On your knees, please."

Both of his eyebrows shot up and he was pretty sure his heart stopped for a few seconds. Then his own grin flashed when he reached for the zipper on her jeans. "You'd better hold on."

∾

THEY'D MADE IT back to Bayside only twenty minutes after Mike had unlocked Gabe's apartment.

"Good morning," Mike greeted them.

It sure was.

"What?" Mike asked, eyes darting from Gabe's to Lia's.

Lia jerked a thumb over her shoulder. "I've got to get to work, too. Give me a call if you need something. I can pick up food for you later or whatever."

"Sure. Whatever," Gabe echoed, smiling at her.

"Bye, guys!"

"Bye."

When the door closed after Lia, Mike snapped his fingers at Gabe. "Okay, break time's over, you slacker. Jesus, you're like almost half an hour late. What did you do, stop for sex somewhere?"

Gabe headed for the bedroom, saying nothing. Mike followed him.

"You did. Shit, Ivers, you *did* stop for sex somewhere. You son of a bitch."

"You got laid, man? Nice," Alphonse said with a nod of approval. He and Isaac were finishing the long desk opposite the beds. The TV was already fastened to the wall. All three guys ragged on him some but Gabe didn't divulge a single detail. In an hour, they managed to get the work all done, raised and lowered the beds a few times to test them, and then shifted focus to finishing details like covering all the exposed screw heads, sanding any rough edges.

"Well, that's that." Mike stepped back, scrutinized the work. The beds in their cabinets lined the wall opposite the door. In front of each bed, when closed, were two small love seats covered in a bright blue fabric, surrounded by shelves. The beds opened right over each love seat, between the shelf units. The shelves could hold knick-knacks or books.

On the short wall, between the windows, they'd built a desk with more shelving. The girls' dresser that Gabe had refinished back when Kimberly was first born stood opposite the beds. Above that, bolted to the wall, was a new TV. The large closet in this room had also been revamped with new organizers to help separate Kimberly and Olivia's clothing, as well as store some of Gabe's large items, like his tools.

"I like the white wash finish on the bed cabinets." Mike ran a hand down one of the doors.

"Figured it was easiest. The girls can do what they want with colors. I can pick them up a rug or two."

"Hey, Gabe. Want me to run power to this desk for their hair curlers and stuff?" Isaac asked.

He was a tall, lanky kid with serious eyes who looked barely old enough to drive. Gabe liked him. He was quiet, did the work, left the wisecracks to Alphonse. Gabe joined him at the desk, studied it. "What'd you have in mind?"

"Drill a hole here and here, run a power strip up through here, screw it in place, add the extension cord. Might want to do the same for the beds. You're blocking four outlets with these built-ins."

"Good idea," Mike put in.

"Do it. It's a great idea. Mike, let's take a look at the bed cabinets."

"I did already. All we have to do is put some power strips up on the shelf, screw them down. The girls can plug in reading lights, alarm clocks, whatever."

"Great. I'll pick up some strips later. Let's start the living room."

Gabe and Mike worked in silence for a while, unpacking materials, organizing tools and hardware. Gabe's conscience began to prickle.

"Mike."

"What?"

"We did stop."

Mike looked over at Gabe. "Figured as much. Can't hold it against you. That girl is pretty awesome and you deserve it."

Gabe nodded. Sighed. "We stopped at your place."

Mike's hand froze on the plastic wrap he was cutting. "My place? Hell, Ivers. Did you at least change my sheets when you were done?"

"Yeah, I did, but we didn't use your bed." Miserably uncomfortable, Gabe admitted, "I...I just wasn't sure I could drive all the way here without—"

"Understood. Also, understandable. Like I said. Lia's awesome."

"Thanks, man."

"Yeah, yeah. Now, lift that end of the carton."

"No. Seriously. Thank you. For all of this."

Mike shifted his weight, scowled. "You're welcome. We done with the chick shit or do we need to friggin' hug first to get some work out of you today?"

Alphonse walked into the room at just that moment. "Um, not that there's anything wrong with that, but not sure Isaac can handle it."

Gabe chucked a rag at Mike's head, laughing. "Okay. Won't say another word."

"Thank God," Mike said with an eye-roll. "Yo! Isaac. You done in there?"

"Be there in two."

"Al, give us a hand unwrapping the last carton."

He did and by late afternoon, the four men had Gabe's bed assembled and bolted to the wall opposite his kitchen. When the cabinet was closed, the unit resembled built-in shelf units. Unlike the girls' beds, this unit did not fold. Instead, the two bookcases in the center slid across the two bookcases on either end, revealing his bed.

"This is awesome. I want one of these things at my place," Alphonse said, running a hand over the dark walnut finish Gabe had chosen.

"Name the time, I'll be there. Owe you guys." Gabe wiped the dust off one of the shelves.

A knock on the door interrupted them.

"Bet I know who that is," Al said with a chuckle. Gabe shot him his middle finger and opened the door to find Lia struggling with several bags.

"Got heroes, soda, and beer for you hardworking men."

"Yes! Thank you, nice lady. The boss wouldn't let us take a break until everything was done." Al grabbed two of Lia's bags, dumped them on the counter in the kitchen while Gabe grabbed the others.

"This looks wonderful! Show me how the bed works."

There was a snicker from the kitchen. Gabe glared at Alphonse, who held up his hands, surrender-style.

"Like this." Gabe slid the center shelves apart until they stood directly in front of the outer shelf units. Then, he pulled down the platform that would hold the bed.

"Impressive."

"Gabe, want to get the mattresses in place?"

"Yeah. Good idea. Lia, can you let us in?"

Lia had agreed to store most of Gabe's stuff. "Sure." She reached a hand into her pocket, pulled out her key ring and handed it over to Mike. "I'll get these served up. You head over to my place and grab your stuff."

Next door, Mike and Gabe wrestled his mattress down the stairs.

"Gabe." Mike stopped halfway down the steps.

"What?"

"You need to know how lucky you are."

"Lucky?"

"Yeah. You loved twice in one lifetime. Nobody's loved me once yet." Mike wouldn't meet Gabe's eyes and Gabe wished he could find him someone great—as great as Lia because Mike was right. He *was* lucky. He lifted his end of the mattress, hoping like hell it would last forever this time. The thought made him fumble his end.

"Easy. Let's not break Lia's place, okay?"

"Yeah. Okay," Gabe agreed and decided to ask Lia as soon as he could if she had any friends for Mike.

Chapter Eighteen

CHRISTMAS MORNING DAWNED at…five a.m. Lia was afraid Gabe might cry when the girls came downstairs. The construction was finished and everything was back in place at his apartment so he stayed overnight at Linda and Stuart's, falling asleep the minute he'd sat down.

She sat beside him on the sofa, the girls buzzing around the room with anticipation, even the logical and practical Olivia, who poked into bags and examined the labels on presents.

"Can I go first, Daddy? Please, can I? Huh?"

"Hold on, Maddie. My ears aren't awake yet." Gabe stuck a finger in one, wriggled it around.

Stuart and Linda came down the stairs wrapped in robes and wearing delighted smiles. "Good morning. Merry Christmas."

The girls exchanged greetings, managed to sit still long enough for a pre-present photo. Then Gabriel sighed and said, "Okay. One at a time."

"Yes, Daddy," Maddie agreed.

Soon, the room was littered with ribbon, bows, and paper scraps as the girls unwrapped gifts. Lia began to fidget and worry as the girls' attention turned to the bag of gifts she'd brought for them.

Maybe she should have asked Gabriel before she'd shopped.

Maybe she should have played it safe with gift cards for everybody.

Gabriel's arm snaked around her shoulders as she nibbled on a fingernail. She cleared her throat. Okay, then. Too late to second-guess now. "Um, Kimberly this one's for you." She lifted a heavy box wrapped in red paper and gave it to her. "Olivia, this one's yours." For Olivia, she slid her a light flat package. "And Maddie, this one's yours." Maddie's present was small and wrapped in green paper. "And last but never least, baby Emmy gets this one." Lia handed the toddler a package of her own.

"What about Daddy, Lia?" Maddie wanted to know.

"I have a present for Daddy, too." Lia stood up, found her handbag, and handed Gabriel the thick envelope she pulled from it.

Emmy loved the pop-up house and spent the rest of the morning inside it. Kimberly adored her books, a collection of teen best-sellers. Maddie showed her father what was inside her box. Gabriel looked at her in astonishment. "You enrolled her in acting classes?"

Lia swallowed hard. Oh, she definitely should have checked with him first. "It was just an idea. It's a six-week offer. If she doesn't like it, she doesn't have to continue. I just thought—"

"I think it's a great idea." Gabriel smiled. "Maddie, you get to be on stage."

Maddie gasped at this news. "I do? Do I get to wear a

285

costume and—and my tiara, Daddy? Can I sing and twirl, too?"

"You can ask when you go."

"Yay! Thank you, Lia!"

"You're welcome, Maddie." Lia turned to Olivia, who hadn't said a word.

"What did you get, Liv?"

She held up two tickets Lia had printed herself.

"Let me see." Gabriel held out his hand. "It says 'This entitles Miss Olivia Ivers and her father to see the Women in Design exhibit at the Cooper Hewitt on the date of her choosing while Lia Blake babysits.' Whoa. Sounds cool." He grinned at Lia. "What do you think, Liv?"

She shrugged. "It's not...like clothes, is it?"

Lia bit back a grin. "Well, I don't think it's fashion design. But design can be lots of things. Graphic design, industrial design, even the design of prosthetics. I know you're really into the scientific contributions women have made so when I heard about this, thought you might enjoy an outing with your dad."

Olivia didn't look convinced but said, "Thank you."

Lia's heart sank. Well, that was a bust. She'd have to find another exhibit, maybe at one of the city's science museums instead.

"Okay, my turn," Gabriel announced and tore into the envelope Lia had given him. Inside was a thin hardcover photo album called *Daddy and His Girls*. Lia noticed the moment Gabriel realized the cover wasn't just some stock photograph.

It was him.

"Oh, wow," he murmured, flipping through the pages. She'd filled it with pictures of Gabriel and his daughters, one at a time, that he'd never noticed her snap. The pages were thick and glossy. Some had small images; some had full-page shots. There was one of him kissing Kimberly's head, taken the day she was sent home from school. Another shot showed just Gabriel's legs out poking out from under Mrs. Morgan's sink, Emmy's legs in the identical position right beside him. A laugh burst out of his mouth and Lia warmed. He liked it.

He turned the page and stopped at a two-page spread of Maddie captured in mid-twirl, hair flying and huge open-mouth grin on her face. Right after that, Lia had placed a serious photo of Olivia, a thick textbook in her lap, with the most fierce expression on her face. Lia had captured it because she thought it was pure Olivia. That child was going to change the world.

She'd managed to get Mike in there, too. There was a snapshot of Mike and Gabe clinking beer bottles and laughing. Mike held Maddie and Gabe held Emmy. The next page had a series of pictures arranged like a filmstrip. They were from one of the Ivers' manicure nights. He laughed again. His hair was pinned up in clips and Maddie held one hand while Liv held the other, each carefully painting his nails. It was one of Lia's favorite pictures of Gabriel because it was how he looked the day they'd met.

Finally, he looked up, looked at her. "Lia, this is…awesome. Seriously amazing. How did you get all these pictures?"

"I got Mrs. Morgan and Jessica Vella to pass the word.

Some of the outdoor shots came from them."

"It's... This is..." He gave up and hauled her in for a kiss, which entertained their audience. Emmy squeezed between them, shouting, "Me, too!" Maddie applauded. Kim and Liv exchanged disgusted looks. Stuart and Linda just grinned.

When all the presents had been unwrapped and all the debris scooped up, they'd had an enormous breakfast with Linda's famous French toast casserole, scrambled eggs and sausage, enough potatoes to end a small famine, and yummy Mimosas for the grown-ups. Lia had never had a sweeter holiday. It was like something out of a Norman Rockwell scene.

No icy words. No pointed glares. No passive-aggressive digs disguised as thoughtful gifts. No broken promises and no tears. Nothing but smiles and hugs.

"What's wrong?" Gabe whispered, rubbing a large hand over her leg.

She shook her head. She didn't want to explain it...didn't even want to keep thinking as she'd been thinking. The day was perfect. She wanted to enjoy it for as long as she could...as long he'd allow her. At some point, she knew he'd get bored. Or want more than she could give him—like a son. And he'd sit her down in that serious way of his, take her hands in his, and apologize before cutting her loose. He was honorable. That's how an honorable man would break things off.

"Whatever you're thinking, stop. Okay? Everything's fine. Everything's great exactly the way it is, so stop bracing for Armageddon."

She looked at him then, managed a wobbly smile. She was being ridiculous and he was right. It was a perfect day. She'd enjoy it to the last second.

❧

THE LAST SECOND, it turned out, was shortly after Emmy's nap, when she woke up after just twenty minutes of sleep with a fever. Gabriel freaked out.

Lia thought it was sweet until she understood *why*.

Janey died. She died after complaining of a headache.

She took Gabriel's hands, gave them a squeeze. "Gabriel, look at me. It's a slight fever. You cannot panic. You need to hold it together so the other girls see this is nothing serious, okay? There's no rash, no cough, no other symptoms, so let's just treat what we know."

"When Janey had fevers, we always rubbed her down with alcohol. That did the trick," Linda said and Lia felt a shiver run through Gabriel.

"Oh, no. Rubbing alcohol can cause comas and poisoning," Lia told her.

"Still, it can't hurt to at least try."

"Linda. It can hurt," Lia insisted. "Please look it up. Here. Take my phone."

Linda did and a minute later said, "Hmmm. Well, you do what you think is best." She looked doubtful, though. "Who wants to play in the snow?" she asked, getting Maddie up and shrieking through the house to find her coat.

"I'll get the medication from your backpack," Lia told Gabriel.

His throat worked but he gave her a single nod, so much like Emmy always did, it sent an arrow of sweetness straight to her heart.

She fetched the Children's Tylenol, brought it to him. He filled the dropper, carefully checked to make sure it was the right amount, and coaxed Emmy into swallowing it. She cried, a pitiful uncomfortable sound, and burrowed into Gabriel's chest.

"Maybe we should put her in a diaper?"

"No!" Emmy shouted.

"Okay, sweetheart. Let's use the potty then. Come on." Gabriel took Emmy into Linda's bathroom, helped her go, then changed her pajamas and wrapped her in her blanket.

"Gabriel, tell me what you need me to do," Lia begged, needing to help, needing to make that horrified look in his eyes go away.

"Just be with my girls, okay?"

She nodded, went back downstairs and played games with Maddie, talked to Liv and Kim about books and TV shows, and talked to Stuart and Linda about their plans for a European vacation that summer. Twenty minutes went by, then forty. Lia excused herself and went upstairs to check on them.

She found Gabriel sitting on the floor, staring at a sleeping Emmy, curled up in a portable crib, hugging her favorite blanket. Lia approached quietly, touched Emmy's forehead, found it cool and let out a breath.

"She's good, Gabriel. Come downstairs, let her rest."

He shook his head, not taking his eyes off Emmy. "I need to watch."

Lia walked to him, put her hands on his shoulders, found the muscles there coiled with tension. She dug her thumbs into those muscles, tried to massage away his worry, but understood this was part of that scar he'd told her about. "This isn't your fault, Gabriel. Kids get sick all the time."

He made a sound of impatience and shrugged away from her. "Lia. I get what you're trying to do but please. Just don't, okay?"

"No. No, it's not okay. It's Christmas and the rest of your family is terrified. Emmy is sleeping peacefully. Her fever is down."

"But what if—"

"No. No what-ifs. You told me you had all four of them tested and there's no danger. This is a fever that you treated appropriately. If she starts coughing, scratching at a rash, complaining something hurts, *then* you ask those questions. But not now."

Gabriel looked up at her with wide scared eyes. "Yeah. Yeah, okay. You're right." He climbed to his feet, checked Emmy's temperature and adjusted her blanket. "Thank you. For what you said downstairs. I can't—Christ." He dragged a hand over his face. "Janey died because I didn't listen to her, Lia. I didn't think a headache was a big deal. Linda and Stuart, they've never said it. Not once have they ever said it was my fault, but it was, Lia. It was. If I'd checked in with her, if I'd—I don't know—kept an eye on her—maybe she'd still be alive today."

"That's a lot of maybes, Gabriel." Lia put her palms on his chest, felt his heart race. "Is this why you can't tell Linda or Stuart no?"

Gabriel laughed but the sound was anything but happy. "They're used to doing things their way, so how do I say it, Lia? How do I tell the people who trusted me with their daughter that I'm too scared to trust them with mine?"

A gasp at the door had them both whipping around.

"Linda. Oh, Jeez, I'm—"

"Gabe, is this why you don't visit us more often? Is this—Oh my God. This is why you moved, isn't it."

"Linda, please." He moved to her and to Lia's surprise, Linda wrapped him in a hug.

"Gabe, what happened to my daughter wasn't your fault. She was born with that blood clot. I have never held you responsible—"

"If I'd been home—"

"No. You heard what the doctors told us. The bleeding was too extensive and too deep inside her head. There was nothing we could have done even if she'd collapsed inside a hospital."

"But—"

"No. Gabe, I read the internet information about alcohol rub-downs. It's been almost forty years since my child was born and yeah, a lot's changed. We used to put kids to sleep on their stomachs, never imagined they should have helmets to ride bikes, and smoked in front of them. But we changed, Gabe. Have you noticed I haven't had a cigarette since Janey was pregnant with Kimberly?"

Gabe's mouth fell open when he pulled away from Linda and Lia knew he hadn't noticed.

"Janey told me it's dangerous to give babies honey, so I never did that. All you have to do is tell me, Gabe. I won't do anything you wouldn't. I love my granddaughters."

His arms went around Linda. "I know. I know. I'm sorry. I—I was too afraid you'd tell me it was my fault. I'm sorry."

As they held each other, Lia watched Gabriel shed months of guilt and Linda laughed.

"Please tell me this means you'll visit every weekend," she said against his chest and he snorted. "Kidding. Come on now. Let Emmy sleep. Lia's right, Gabe. You can't freak out over every little sniffle." She guided him to the door.

Before Lia followed, she put a hand to Emmy's forehead one more time.

It never hurt to be sure.

⁓

"DADDY! LOOK, WE'RE making snowmen! Do you like mine? Do you?" Maddie waved her hands over the lumps of snow the girls were shaping into balls, sending a flurry over his head.

"Um. Yeah. They look great."

"How's Emmy, Dad?"

Gabe smiled at Kimberly. "She's got a fever but she's sleeping again."

"Maybe it's her teeth. She's been drooling a lot again. Don't molars come in at her age?"

He thought about that. "Yeah, you could be right. I'll check when she wakes up." The last of his anxiety faded at that suggestion. He drew on gloves and prepared to show the girls how engineers build a snowman. He was just about to heft the body on top of the base when Lia joined them.

"Can I help?"

"Hmm. I don't know, girls. What do you think?" He was grinning like an idiot because Lia was dressed in boots, puffy coat, and hat that ruined her hair. Janey hated snow and cold weather and couldn't be convinced to play in the snow if he'd promised her hot chocolate in bed for a week.

"Dad's an expert at snowmen, Lia," Olivia informed her. "Just listen to what he says."

"Oh." She shot him a look that clearly said, *Oh, Really?* He just laughed.

They rolled and packed and stacked for the next forty minutes and then a little voice in the doorway broke his focus.

"Dad-dee."

He spun, found Emmy in Linda's arms. "Hey, E-Rex. Are you better?" He ran up the porch steps to see for himself.

"Uh-huh," she said with a single nod.

"High five."

"No fever, Gabe," Linda announced. "She wants a snack. I have cookies, but…" She trailed off with a meaningful look and ruffled his hair like a little boy when he caved.

"It's Christmas. I think cookies are good just for today."

Chapter Nineteen

WHEN THE HOLIDAYS were over and the girls once again back in their apartment, nobody could stop talking about their new beds. Every time Lia visited Gabriel's apartment, one of his daughters showed her one of the beds. She had to admit, they were pretty cool.

Lia was currently sitting beside Kimberly on one of the two sofas in what used to be Gabriel's bedroom, flipping through Pinterest for birthday ideas. Her birthday was just a few weeks away, toward the end of January, and she'd been unable to decide how she wanted to celebrate turning thirteen.

"...I really want to go somewhere super nice, just me and Dad, you know? No sisters, but I'm not into museums like Olivia is and I think thirteen is too old to do kid stuff like bowling, you know?"

"Oh. Um. Sure."

"I love this!" She showed Lia the image on her screen. Lia examined it, found a complicated hairstyle.

"Oh, so you want to get all dressed up fancy?"

Kimberly nodded. "I do. Is that totally dorky? I mean, he's my dad, not my boyfriend, but I really want to do that. Dress up, go someplace where they don't serve you chicken fingers in a basket."

Lia laughed. "I completely understand."

"When's your birthday, Lia?"

"April."

"Really? So is my dad's."

There it was again...that little *ping* in her heart. She was feeling a lot of them lately.

"Lia, what would your perfect night be?"

"Oh, I don't know. I kind of like just hanging here with your dad and you."

"No, seriously. You and Daddy never go out. What if you could have like the most perfect date you could imagine? What would it be?"

Getting into the spirit of things, Lia squished her lips and considered. "Well, I agree with you. It has to be fancy. Dress up in a new dress, new hairstyle, so that you don't just look pretty, you feel it inside. And go some place where there's china dishes and too many forks."

That made Kimberly giggle. "What else?"

"Oh, maybe a limousine to pick us up with champagne in the back. And dancing."

"Boys don't like to dance."

"That's because few know how. But hey, this is my perfect date, right? So in my mind, your dad knows how and likes to dance. And he has to dress up, too."

"Like a suit?"

"Of course." Lia waved a hand. "Otherwise, what would be the point?"

"What about presents?"

"Something thoughtful and special that I'd keep forever.

Oh, wait. This is a date, not my birthday. So no presents—
except for flowers."

"Ooo, a corsage."

"Perfect!"

"Hey."

Kimberly and Lia looked up, found Olivia standing in
the bedroom doorway.

"Daddy says get your butts to the table or no spaghetti
and meatballs for you."

They'd just sat down when Gabriel's phone rang. "Sorry,
ladies. Duty calls. I've got a blocked drain to fix. Eat without
me. Lia, you can stay?"

"Of course."

"See you later."

"Bye, Dad-dee." Emmy waved from her high chair.

❧

GABRIEL DIDN'T GET back until after the girls had gone to
bed.

"Hey, sorry. I had to change out the pipe, took forever."
He headed for the kitchen sink, washed his hands. "Girls are
asleep already?"

"Yes. I gave Emmy and Maddie baths, but Olivia and
Kimberly said they'd shower on their own."

"You're amazing." He took the cover off the pot still on
the stove, fixed himself a plate and sat down to eat.

"Gabriel, I know what you can do for Kimberly's birthday." She joined him at the table, tablet in hand.

He squeezed his eyes shut. "Okay. I'm ready. Tell me

how much this is gonna cost me."

Lia slid over a list.

"Oh, God, there's a list?"

"Try to keep an open mind."

He studied the list. "Open mind, huh? Okay. New dress, made to order? Lia, I can't—"

"Keep reading."

"Limo. Hair-do. Fancy restaurant. Suit. Corsage. Jeez, she's thirteen. What's she gonna want at sixteen, an orchestra?"

"Now, before you say no, take a look at this." Lia handed him the tablet, showed him a website that makes custom dresses, tapped the one she'd saved. They discussed it for an hour or so and agreed on a plan.

❧

THEIR CAREFULLY CONSIDERED plans were almost derailed by a blizzard that dumped a foot of snow on the city on Kimberly's birthday, but Gabriel, fearing that a late outing on a school night would impact the whole household, had promised her a big night on Saturday night. While her father had spent most of that day pushing the snow plow to clear the building's walkways and stairs, Kimberly fretted about earthquakes or blackouts or some other natural calamity that would force him to cancel.

Lia knew nothing could make Gabriel do that. He appeared to be as excited as his daughter. The new dress he'd ordered was wrapped in a fancy box and currently sitting on Lia's bed. There was a matching corsage waiting in her kitchen. He asked Lia if she would mind styling Kimberly's hair, since the salon had unexpectedly closed for the storm. Lia had spent hours that morning watching YouTube video instructions for appropriate up-dos and practiced one soft style on her own hair. Gabriel promised to send Kimberly over at four o'clock. That would give her plenty of time to style his daughter's hair, help her apply her mascara and lip gloss, and let her unwrap the new dress.

Lia rubbed her hands together. This was so exciting. Oh, she'd have melted into a puddle if her father had ever done something so wonderful for her own birthdays. Her mother had tried to make up for it by planning outrageous birthday parties every year. On her thirteenth birthday, her mother had rented a planetarium and invited Lia's entire eighth grade class.

She'd been popular that year.

Her sixteenth birthday had been the most elaborate by far. Mom had rented a hall, hired a band who'd actually written a song just for Amelia. There was supposed to be a candle-lighting ceremony where Lia had been expected to honor all the people in her life who mattered, only she told her mother she didn't have sixteen people to name so she hadn't done it.

The truth was she didn't want to include her father but couldn't speak it out loud.

Lia shook off her depressing thoughts and made sure her phone was charged so she could take lots of pictures for Linda and Stuart.

❧

AT FOUR O'CLOCK on the dot, a knock sounded on her back door and Lia let an excited Kimberly into her kitchen.

"Dad sent me over. He said you can do my hair for me? And he said there was a surprise?"

Or two or three, Lia thought.

"Yes. Come on. Let's do your hair first." Lia took Kimberly into the living room, showed her a few photos on her computer and started arranging Kimberly's long blonde hair into the style she liked best. It took Lia about half an hour.

"Okay. Finished. Ready to see?"

"Yeah!" Kimberly jumped up, ran to the mirror Lia had near her front door. "Oh my gosh. I look…"

"Grown up."

"Yeah." With her eyes shining, Kimberly angled her head this way and that to see her hair from all sides.

"Try this." Lia opened the door to the closet just beside the front door. On the inside of the door hung a full-length mirror. She held the door so that Kimberly could see her reflection in both mirrors. Lia had woven several tiny braids down the length of Kimberly's hair, pulled up the rest of her hair into coils, then wound the braids loosely around them. "Do you like it, sweetheart?"

"Oh, Lia, I love it! Thank you so much."

"Good. But we're not done yet. Come see." Lia took her back to the sofa and handed her a package of clips she'd bought just for tonight.

"These are for me?" Kimberly asked, her voice high and breathless. "They're so pretty."

Lia opened the package of hairpins, each one studded with a sparkling blue rhinestone. She scattered a bunch throughout Kimberly's hair.

"The blue looks so pretty."

"Yes, it does." Lia stretched. Okay. So far, so good. After hair, she helped Kimberly with makeup and took lots of pictures. "Okay, sweetheart. Ready for your surprise?"

"Another one? I thought the clips were my surprise."

Lia's heart swelled. This child of Gabriel's was sweetness itself.

"Come upstairs to my room."

Kimberly gasped out loud when she saw the large box on Lia's bed. "Is this…oh, wow. It is. It's a new dress, isn't it?" she asked on a squeal.

"Open it."

Lia switched her phone to video mode and recorded Kimberly's face when she undid the ribbon and opened the lid. Nestled inside layers of delicate tissue paper, a dress in navy blue waited for her. Crystals and rhinestones caught the light and the chiffon skirt fluttered softly as she lifted it from the box.

"It's…it's the most amazing dress I've ever seen! I hope it fits. Oh, God. What if it doesn't fit?" Pure torture crossed her face and Lia assured her it would fit.

"Remember when I measured you? This was why. The dress was made just for you. It'll fit."

Kimberly bounced on her toes and kicked off her sneakers. "Can I put it on right now?"

Lia stopped recording and helped Kimberly put on the dress, tying the sash in a large bow in the back. She started recording when the young girl examined herself in Lia's mirror.

"I look like another me," she whispered.

Another me, Lia repeated silently and her heart twisted a little. She remembered that feeling. The glimpse of the woman every little girl can't wait to become. Again, Lia ruthlessly shoved aside sad thoughts and helped Kimberly with her hosiery and finally, accessories.

"These are mine, too?" She ran her fingertips over a small black velvet evening bag and a pair of black velvet pumps with kitten heels. The shoes had little bows on the toes. "Oh my gosh, Lia. This is…is this so awesomely cool and amazing!"

"The little handbag is my gift to you. Everything else is all your dad, Kimberly."

Her lip wobbled and her eyes began to water.

Lia grabbed some tissues. "Don't do that. Your mascara will run. Here. Put some in your bag." She handed her a stack of tissues. "And your lip gloss. Oh, one more thing. Where are you in your cycle? Should we put in a tampon, just in case?"

Kimberly shook her head. "No, I have another week, at least. I've been counting, just like you showed me."

"Good girl."

Lia's phone buzzed. "That's your dad, wondering if you're ready." She texted back. "I told him to come on over now."

"Lia, thank you for watching my sisters tonight. And for all of this. Dad's not going to believe it's me." Kimberly bit her lip for a moment and then rolled her eyes. "He's probably gonna get all tough when he sees me just like he always does. He thinks nobody'll see what he really feels inside."

Wasn't that some keen insight from a girl hardly thirteen years old? "What do you think he really feels inside?"

"Oh, you know. He's proud of me. Of all of us, really. And he wishes my mom were here to see us. And he can't believe how big we're getting. Stuff like that."

A knock sounded on the door downstairs. Kimberly leaped up but Lia held her back. "No, no, no. You wait right here. You have to make a grand entrance."

Giggling, Kimberly agreed.

Downstairs, Lia opened the door and gasped.

Gabriel Ivers was made to wear a suit.

Tall, lean but broad across the shoulders, he stole her breath. He'd shaved, done something to his hair, and smelled absolutely intoxicating. "You…you…oh, wow."

"Yeah, I know. I look hot." He stepped inside and grinned. "Olivia's watching the two wild ones so get over there as soon as you can so I don't have a heart attack before we get to the restaurant."

"I will." She went to the refrigerator, took out the corsage box. "Here you go."

"Thanks. Does she like the dress?"

"Loves it."

"Well? Where is she?"

Smiling, Lia again aimed her phone and started recording. "Okay, Kimberly. Your dad is here!" she called.

She kept the phone focused on Gabe's face while Kimberly slowly walked down the stairs. When his jaw dropped and his eyes went wide, she knew he was pleased. Then he pressed a hand to his mouth and blinked rapidly. That's when she knew he was showing exactly what he felt.

"Cocoa-Pop," he said, his voice choked. "Happy birth-day."

"Thanks, Daddy. Thanks for my dress, too. It's beautiful."

"You're beautiful." He held out the corsage to her, helped her slip it onto her wrist.

A horn honked outside.

"Okay. You better get going before your table is given away." Lia *shooshed* them toward the front door.

When Kimberly took her puffy jacket off Lia's couch, Lia shook her head. "Sweetheart, you cannot wear that jacket with this outfit."

Her expectant face fell. "But it's all I have."

Lia grinned. "Your cloak, my lady." She opened her closet with a flourish and took out a black wool walking coat.

Gabriel took it, held it out for Kimberly. She slipped it on and ran a hand over it. It was a little large for her, but it would work. "It's so warm."

"There are gloves inside the pockets in case you're cold. Have you got your little bag?"

"Yes."

"Okay, away with you both before somebody turns into a pumpkin."

She met Gabriel's eyes as Kimberly joined him at the door. *Thank you,* he mouthed.

Giggling, Kimberly spun around to wrap Lia in a hug. "Thank you, fairy godmother!"

Lia shut the door, tears stinging her eyes. Something inside her went *pop* and she was afraid it just might be her heart.

༼

NEXT DOOR IN Gabriel's apartment, Lia couldn't seem to shake that feeling that everything had just changed.

Permanently.

"Right, Lia? Right?"

With a start, Lia tuned back in to Maddie, who was regaling her with tales of the holidays that had just passed. She smiled when baby Emmy curled up against her with a book and her favorite blanket. And she smiled when Olivia, her harshest critic, kept asking her questions about Supreme Court justices and women in Congress.

"I think I might want to do that. When I grow up, I mean."

"Run for public office?" That completely jerked Lia out of her spiraling thoughts. "Admirable. But I see you in a lab somewhere, studying things under a microscope."

Olivia shrugged. "I'm not into microbiology. I like science at more general levels and I especially like science's impact on our society, like cleaning up the water in Flint, Michigan."

Lia's belly fluttered. "Public health is definitely a worthy endeavor."

"Not just health, though. Safety, too. And technology."

Intrigued, Lia wondered what programs she might find to encourage Olivia's passions. "Technology? What kind?"

"Oh, maybe solar panels and wind farms. That sort of thing."

There it was again. That tiny flutter inside her core. Beside her, Emmy yawned so Lia decided it was time to put

Gabriel's youngest daughter to bed. "Come on, little one. Time for sleep."

"Where Dad-dee?"

"He's out. Is it okay if Lia tucks you in?"

"Eee-uh." Emmy put her head on Lia's shoulder, wriggled her butt and clutched her blanket.

"Night, Emmy! I love you." Maddie waved.

"Good night, Em." Olivia waved, too.

"Kiss." Emmy held out her arms. Lia walked her to her sisters, who dutifully kissed their baby sister good night.

Lia took the toddler into the bedroom she shared with Maddie. The crib and twin bed were gone now. Only the bunk beds remained. She knew Gabriel had made them himself. Across the room, only one of the dressers remained, the one he'd used as a changing table. But Emmy was doing super well with potty training. Lia took out pajamas and training pants from a drawer, changed Emmy and helped her use the bathroom. The baby was uncharacteristically quiet tonight and went down without a fuss. She was asleep before Lia left the room.

Back in the living room, she found Maddie on the sofa, humming to herself. They found a movie to watch while Olivia browsed the internet with Gabriel's tablet. Lia kept an eye on that screen throughout the evening, making sure the little girl wasn't accessing inappropriate sites. She sent Gabriel's in-laws the videos she'd recorded of Kimberly, had Maddie in bed at nine o'clock and Olivia by ten, just like Gabriel always did.

Lia sat in Gabriel's living room by herself, uncomfortable thoughts irritating her, pinching like clothes that were too tight. She got up, considered making coffee, changed her mind and sat down again. Seconds later, she was up, made a peanut butter and jelly sandwich and took it back to the sofa to eat it.

As she ate, she scanned Gabriel's new built-in on the short wall in the living room. It was a work of art. She hadn't yet slept in this bed. Oh, they'd used it a number of times since he'd built it. But she left as soon as he was done.

The man was *fast*.

Not that she had any complaints. He was thorough, too. Talented hands, those full lips—he could—and usually did—have her sweaty and boneless in a matter of minutes. And yet...

She sighed.

She felt restless. There was a buzz of...of what? She couldn't quite name the discomfort deep inside her, that flutter of anxiety or something. Sighing in frustration, she studied the new wall unit.

The deep walnut wood gleamed in the low light. There were four tall cabinets. The two center cabinets hid the bed. They were slightly forward compared to the end units. All four had doors on the bottom and shelves on the top that Gabriel had filled with books, framed photos and albums, figurines and toys. Lia examined the books.

She'd never seen Gabriel read. When did he have the time? But the books on his shelves were as interesting as he was. Repair manuals on everything from his SUV to appliances, novels from best-selling authors to classics including, she noted with a happy smile, Austen, non-fiction titles on potty-training, encouraging gifted children, and...and grief.

That restless flutter of hers became a damn tornado.

She straightened, scanned the rest of the shelves, picked up a photo of Gabriel holding a tiny wrapped bundle with a look of utter astonishment on his face. It had to be Kimberly in that bundle. Similar photos of Gabriel holding more bundles with more children at his side appeared. Olivia, Madison, and then Emerson. His look of astonishment had transformed in each photo until in the last, it was clearly one of pride. She tugged out one of the photo albums, almost fumbling it when she understood what it was.

His wedding album.

She almost put it back. But morbid curiosity stopped her, compelled her to look. She opened it and gasped. The first picture was of Janey in her gown, a grown-up version of Maddie. Snowy white tulle framed her face and all that luxurious dark hair looped and coiled low at the nape of her neck in a style as romantic as the one Lia had just arranged for her oldest daughter. A sob caught in her throat. Linda and Stuart beamed at their daughter in another photo as bouquets were admired, and in another, father and daughter stepped into a limo.

Lia was six pages into the album before she found Gabriel. He stood at the altar beside Mike, of course. They wore tuxedos in classic black, with straight ties rather than bows. His blond hair was short, almost buzzed, and his jaw smooth. He looked like a boy playing dress-up, she decided. The next photo stopped her heart.

Gabriel's first glimpse of his bride.

His face was split by one of those sudden smiles of his, the one that flashed like lightning and heated everything in proximity. His eyes glimmered with hope, with anticipation.

With love.

Oh, God. The buzz, the flutter, the tornado inside her finally broke and she understood what she'd known for some time now at some subconscious level. She wanted *this*. There! She'd admitted it. She wanted more than a few stolen minutes when the mood struck. She wanted more than an afternoon of babysitting. She wanted more than a glimpse of Gabriel as he walked past her window. She wanted to be part of his world, his life, and his future. She wanted to sleep in his bed, beside him. She wanted to be the person he called when he had a problem, the person he thought of when life was rough and when it was easy. She wanted *to matter* just once in her life. She'd never mattered to her father. She certainly hadn't mattered to her former husband. It was all here, right here.

All she had to do was believe him when he said he was in love with her.

Her phone, sitting on the coffee table, vibrated. She glanced at the screen and went still.

Jared.

What could he possibly want?

She should have blocked him, deleted him from her life. She wasn't entirely sure why she hadn't.

With a sigh, she picked up the phone, tapped the text message, and slapped a hand to her mouth.

Jared's baby was here. He…she…they'd had a girl.

A daughter.

Emma Rae, seven pounds, ten ounces. Oh, look. He'd included a picture.

The sob welled in Lia's throat. She was all chubby pink cheeks and a rosebud mouth with delicate tufts of hair Lia knew would grow into the same lush waves her mother had.

They'd named her *Emma.*

Damn it, damn it, damn it. Damn *him.*

Her name. *Hers.* How could he do this to her? How?

She fell to Gabriel's sofa, covering her face and doing her best to stifle her sobs. She couldn't find an explanation, couldn't justify Jared's cruelty to…to rub her face in her loss like this.

Chapter Twenty

KIMBERLY'S HEAD RESTED against his shoulder on the ride home. The blizzard had shut things down Thursday, but today wasn't half bad. Still, Gabe was happy he didn't have to drive.

They'd had a great time. His little girl's eyes shined as she stared out the window at the city sights on their way into Manhattan. They'd gone to The Steak House, one of the best restaurants in New York where Kimberly, to his total shock, ordered a steak and lobster. She'd told him she was growing up so it was time she stopped eating only chicken fingers. She got tons of compliments on her new dress.

Gabe had to admit, it looked amazing on her. When Lia had first suggested ordering a custom-tailored dress, he'd balked. She'd wear it once. But, as usual, Lia was right. You only turn thirteen once so why not? Besides, it hadn't been expensive. Not like this dinner was gonna cost him. Jeez, sixty bucks for one steak? He could have fed his whole family for that price.

He'd ordered cocktails and an appetizer. Wine for him, Shirley Temple for her. She seemed to like the shrimp appetizer they'd presented with a flourish. He made a little toast to her and to her birthday and her pretty blue eyes sparkled. Then, he took a small box out of his pocket and slid it across the table to her. With a little gasp, she opened the box and found the small diamond heart necklace inside. While he fastened it around her neck, he told her it used to be her mom's. He'd given it to her right after she was born, thirteen years ago.

Kimberly's little chin wobbled as she thanked him for the best birthday ever. Their server took pictures of them and even arranged for some music. Gabe had asked Kimberly to dance but she was embarrassed. She didn't know how and he promised to teach her.

After dinner, they'd ordered dessert and Kimberly's arrived at the table with a single candle and a chorus from the wait staff that made her cheeks turn pink.

"This was a pretty great idea, Cocoa-Pop. I think we should do this on every birthday."

She thought about it for a minute and shook her head. "No, 'cause then it's not so special. But once in a while, getting you all to myself like this, yeah. That's special."

His heart twisted. "Sweetheart, you can talk to me any time you want. You don't need a special occasion for that."

She lifted one shoulder. "I know, but…well, you're busy. I don't like to—"

"Kim. Never too busy. Never."

She met his eyes and nodded once, reminding him so much of Emmy, he grinned. "Okay, so let's talk right now. In three more birthdays, you'll be able to drive. In five more birthdays, you'll be starting college. Do you have any ideas what you might want to study?"

"I kind of want to be a teacher."

"Sounds good. Education is always important."

"What about you, Daddy? What do you want to be when we grow up?"

The fork had frozen on the way to his mouth. The question sounded so profound. He'd never thought about it like that. Most of the time, he mourned who he used to be and didn't much care what he would be after Janey died. It didn't matter. Nothing did, except for the young lady sitting in front of him and three more like her at home. But Kimberly was waiting for his answer.

He'd shrugged. "Doesn't matter."

"Sure it does. You should do what makes you happy. You really liked building bridges and tall buildings, didn't you?"

"Yeah but—"

"So you should be able to go back to work if you want. Do you like your part-time thing?"

"Mm-hmm. But I have responsibilities."

"Daddy." Kimberly put down her fork and squeezed his hand. "You don't have to worry about us. I'm old enough now to watch Emmy and Maddie. Mrs. Morgan's really nice and oh, Mrs. Vella told me to tell you she's home all day with Mason. He's just a year older than Emmy. And then there's Lia."

Lia.

"You love her a lot."

Damn it, he did. He lifted his glass, sipped some wine, not at all sure he was a fan of this growing up business.

"You're wasting time again, just like with Mom."

He coughed on his wine, staring at his daughter.

Kimberly rolled her eyes. "Oh, come on. Uncle Mike said you were hopeless."

He'd deal with Mike another time. "I'm sorry."

His daughter swallowed another bite of her chocolate cake and gave him one of those don't-be-an-idiot looks her mother had patented. "Daddy, you don't have to say you're sorry. Olivia and I talked about it and we think Lia would be a great stepmom so you don't have to worry about us at all. You love Lia. You're happy when you're with her. You don't get mad and yell at us. And you try all of her ideas to save time because it makes her happy to help you."

"What about Mom?" he asked after his gut stopped churning.

"Daddy, remember when I didn't want to go to school after Mommy died? Grandma told me she was sure Mommy wouldn't want me to cry every day for the rest of my life and that the only way to stop crying was to do all the things I used to do, like school and stuff."

He remembered. Linda and Stuart had stepped in, consoled his girls when he'd been too numb to get out of bed.

"At first, I was mad but Grandma was right. It got easier every day and now I don't feel guilty when I laugh."

That was a bullet straight through his heart. "Sweetheart, you shouldn't feel guilty for living."

Another don't-be-an-idiot look. "I know. That's what I'm trying to tell *you*. I miss Mommy all the time. I still cry sometimes. But I'm trying to be happy and I think you should try harder, too. You love Lia. Grandma said it and so did Uncle Mike. Olivia could see it too and even though she was kind of mad about it at first, she really likes Lia now.

And everybody knows how Maddie feels."

That made him laugh. Yep, everybody knew. He leaned closer. "Wanna hear a secret?"

He grinned when she nodded.

"I already bought the ring."

Kimberly clapped both hands to her open mouth. "Oh my God! When are you gonna ask her?"

"When the time is right. I have to be sure."

Kimberly wrinkled her nose. "How do you know that?"

Yeah, good question. "It depends on a lot of things. When all of those things line up, I'll know."

Kimberly was quiet on the trip home. The limo slowed to take an exit and he tightened his hold on her, everything she'd said during dinner worming into his brain. How the hell did his kid become so wise?

Marriage.

A shock wave rippled over his body. The last time he'd tried marriage, it hadn't ended well. With a smothered laugh, he shook his head. What a stupid thing to think. Marriages aren't supposed *to end*. That was the damn point.

⌘

GABE UNLOCKED HIS front door and found Lia on the couch. She was sound asleep.

Holding a finger to his lips, he motioned Kimberly inside toward her room. She pecked him on the cheek and obeyed.

Gabe quietly closed and locked the door, not wanting to wake Lia. He crept closer, saw her face streaked with tears and a balled-up napkin clutched in her hand. What the hell happened tonight? He watched her sleep, her misery slicing through him.

Okay. Whatever it was, it could wait until morning. He'd open his bed, tuck her in and hold her all night. He'd fix it. Damn right he would.

He shifted the coffee table out of the way, slid the shelves apart and lowered his bed. Just then, Lia's phone vibrated on the coffee table. He couldn't help but glance at it. It showed a list of text messages from Jared.

Her ex-husband.

Is that why she was crying? Dread took root in Gabriel's heart when he grabbed the phone and scrolled through the list of messages. What the hell…the messages were full of baby pictures. Snap after snap of a newborn. Emma Rae, seven pounds, ten ounces.

Oh, hell. Christ in heaven, the idiot actually gave the name *Lia* picked for a baby they'd lost to the daughter he had with his mistress.

Rage flooded him and it took every ounce of self-control he had not to pitch the phone at the wall. He kept scrolling through the long list of messages.

It was a group message.

Okay.

Maybe, just maybe, there was the slimmest chance Jared didn't actually realize Lia was in the group message.

Whatever. Didn't matter. All that mattered is that it wrecked Lia.

Son of a bitch. He bit off a vocal curse, scrolled through her phone again and blocked Jared's number. He knew he had no damn right, but he couldn't *bear* seeing her like this—mascara smears under her eyes, nose red, tears leaving white tracks through her makeup.

She was so good. Patient, kind, and thoughtful. She deserved to be happy. She deserved to be a mom and have kids of her own.

He could make that happen for her. He could give her that.

He pulled a pair of sweats from one of the drawers around his bed, headed to the bathroom, and changed into them. He checked on Maddie and Emmy, then found Kimberly excitedly relaying their entire evening to Liv in a hushed whisper.

"Are you letting Lia sleep in your bed, Dad?"

"Yes. She's upset about something and I want her to stay here until I know she's okay. Good night, girls."

"Daddy. It was the best birthday ever, even though Mommy wasn't here."

Unable to speak, Gabe nodded and kissed the top of her head. When he walked back to the living room, he found Lia awake and sitting on the edge of the sofa.

"Sounds like you really hit this one out of the park," Lia said softly.

He shrugged. "It was all you, Lia. I just followed orders. The dress, the limo, the restaurant."

"Gabriel." She said nothing else until he met her gaze. "Your daughter didn't want anybody else but *you* with her tonight."

Huh. That was true. "Yeah." He brightened at the thought. "Yeah, that's true." He crouched beside the sofa, ran the back of his hand down Lia's face. "And you? Are you okay?"

"Yeah. Fine. I'd better go. It's late and I'm sure you're exhausted."

"Stay."

"Oh. I don't—"

"Lia. Be with me tonight. Please."

Lia's entire face softened. Slowly, she leaned in and pressed her mouth to his. "There is really nowhere else I'd rather be."

He tucked her into his bed, loved her slowly. Gently. Everything between them was usually rushed, sandwiched between all their other responsibilities. Tonight, he wanted her to feel it, to know it all the way down to her atoms, that she wasn't just loved.

She was treasured.

She was respected.

She was everything.

He opened his eyes, astonished to see it was around six a.m., which meant everyone had slept through the night. All night, he dreamed of how life could be if he and Lia were married. They'd waited long enough. It was time to move forward. He lay there, plotting it all out in his head.

He'd take her out today. He'd buy her flowers, take her someplace fancy, lay it all out for her, tell her what she meant to him, tell her about all the plans and dreams he'd tried to bury with Janey that were still there, hiding in one of the broken pieces of his heart until Lia helped him find them.

Homework was done and the girls had no huge projects due or tests to study for. Chores, though. He needed groceries. Kimberly could watch her sisters after he put Emmy and Maddie to bed tonight. He could take Lia to Il Piacere. The food was great, the atmosphere quiet. In fact, he'd call Sal, the maître d' and arrange things so that the ring he'd already bought could be put in her glass or on her plate.

No, that was boring.

He'd buy a book. Lia loved Austen. He'd buy a hardcover edition, tie the ring onto a ribbon and put it between the pages, like a bookmark.

Okay. He had a lot to do today and a lot riding on what he had to do today, so time to get moving.

He got up, used the bathroom, headed for the coffee maker in the kitchen. Lia, he noted, was a sprawler. The knowledge, the intimacy of it, made him grin. Of all the things he missed about Janey, it was intimacy that he missed the most. Sharing private jokes and secret dreams, even the ridiculous ones not even Mike knew about.

"What are you smiling about in the middle of the night?" she said and he nearly leaped out of his body.

"How long have you been awake?" he demanded, coming to sit beside her on his bed.

"Since you used the bathroom."

"Sorry. Didn't mean to wake you." He leaned down, kissed her full on the mouth.

She squeaked in protest. "I haven't brushed my teeth yet."

"Don't care." He kissed her again.

Her hair spilled over his pillow and he hoped it would smell like lilacs now. Purple and peach—not a typical color pairing he'd ever seen in the clothing stores the girls dragged him into, but they reminded him of Lia. Lilacs in her hair, peaches on her lips.

"Lia. I saw the messages on your phone. I am so sorry."

She froze in his arms and then pulled away. "It is what it is," she said with a shrug and that rage balled up inside him again. What a stupid saying that was. People—friends, even Linda and Stuart—had said that same thing to him after Janey died. As if it helped.

Helplessness replaced his rage. "Talk to me, Lia."

She shook her head. "About what? He has a baby. I never will." She tossed aside the covers and headed for the bathroom. He gave her a couple of minutes and then he followed.

"You done in here?"

"Yes, you can use—"

"Don't need to use it."

He reached out, hauled her against him, and touched his mouth to hers, waited the second it took for her to catch up, and poured himself into the kiss. When it was over, he had to sit on the edge of the tub or he'd have fallen. Lia felt it, too. She sank down to the toilet facing him, head cocked to one side, a tiny frown line between her eyebrows.

"Whoa," she said.

"Good whoa or bad whoa?"

Lia smiled. "Good whoa. Always good. How do you do that?"

"Truth is, I don't do anything. It's all you." He leaned over, took her hand, stroked his thumb over the soft skin and let those words sink in. She loved him. She *had* to. Would she deal with all his chaos if she didn't?

"Lia, what would you say if I told you I've always wanted to open my own engineering firm?" he suddenly blurted.

Lia's eyes popped wide. "I'd say you should totally do it. It would be a ton of work, but luckily, you know a virtual assistant who could provide all sorts of organization tips and help whenever you needed it."

He felt twenty pounds lighter. "What about you? What have you always wanted to do?"

Lia bit her lip and whispered. "I'm already doing it. My little business. I've wanted to expand it for years and it's finally happening." She slid her hands along his thighs but he caught them so he could think straight.

Frowning, he asked, "Why did you say it was little? Your business."

"I don't know," she admitted with a shrug. "It's just what Jared—"

"I'm not Jared," he reminded her for what had to be the hundredth time. "I think your business is awesome. I love that you're expanding it with new clients and soon, a staff of your own. I know all about the work it takes, wearing all those hats, and you impress and inspire me."

Believe me, he begged her silently. "You know, not even Mike knows about my imaginary firm. I can tell *you* all the things nobody else knows about me."

She smiled and he stared at her for a minute or two. Why couldn't she admit they'd crossed a bridge, one he'd been dead sure he'd never travel again? He took a deep breath and dove in.

"Lia, last night was amazing. Kimberly was so happy."

Her smile widened.

"It's because of you," he continued. "I wouldn't have thought of any of those things by myself."

"We make a pretty good team."

A team. Yeah. Yeah, exactly that. Certain now, his smile bloomed as he took the leap. "We do. We really do. Let's get dressed. I've got some chores to do this morning but I want to take you out tonight. Nice dinner. Dress-up clothes." He stood, found his razor and the shaving cream.

"You're gonna put the suit back on?" Her eyebrows rose.

"Women love men in suits," he said, dropping his voice down real low and waggling his eyebrows.

But she didn't laugh. Instead, she shook her head, turned on the faucet, splashed water on her face. "I don't think I'd be very good company," she finally said, grabbing the towel he kept on a hook next to the sink.

Gabe sighed and scratched his neck. So much for all his big plans. Maybe…maybe he should just…ask. No fanfare. No gimmicks. The truth. The whole of it.

"Your ex's news really shook you, didn't it?"

Her eyes snapped to his, her pain clear. "Yes, Gabriel, it did. Of course it did."

"Why?"

Her face changed, exasperation twisting her features. "Why? Oh, I don't know," she said, flinging the towel at the sink. "Maybe because karma is clearly a stupid bitch who keeps punishing *me* instead of him?" She put her hands on her hips, nostrils flaring.

Gabe's eyebrows shot to his hairline at Lia's language.

"First he cheats, then he leaves, and now he gets the baby I wanted? What do *I* get?" she demanded, pulling up her top, revealing her incisions. "Scars. Nothing but scars."

He sank slowly to the toilet and must have made some kind of sound because Lia turned, and pressed both hands to her mouth. The fury that drove her a second before was gone.

"I'm sorry, Gabriel. Like I said, I'm not good company." She reached for the door.

"Wait," he said, his voice rough. She turned back, faced him. "Am I a fling? Is this—are we—am I just sex to you?"

Her eyes narrowed and a distinct flush began to crawl up her neck.

"What, exactly, are you asking me?"

"It's a yes or no question, Lia." His tone curt. "Either I'm…handy or I mean something to you."

She only stared at him, that flush now tinting her cheeks.

Ice ran through his system. He'd sworn he'd never do this again, never risk this kind of hurt again but somehow, she'd sneaked past all his defenses. He'd let himself *believe*, let himself *hope*. He should have just kept his head down. He had his children. Why couldn't that have been enough? And the real irony was that he'd been *so sure*. Well. He supposed that was his answer. He stood up, moved for the bathroom door.

She shot out a hand to stop him. "I…God, Gabriel. I *literally* just realized I was all the way in love with you about eight hours ago. I snooped through your photo albums and I saw your wedding and the look on your face and I wanted that. I want that so badly."

The hope all but exploded out of him. He stepped closer, cupped her cheek in his hand. "Good. Okay," he said, relieved. "Here's the thing. If Jared wasn't such as monumental ass, we'd never have met. So I'm *glad* he's an ass, Lia. I'm *glad* he cheated and *glad* you divorced because that mistake led you right here. To me."

She opened her mouth but he shook his head.

"But I'm *not* glad about your surgery. I know how much you want kids. But, Lia, I have four of them. They're yours. *We're* yours. If you'll have us."

Her face went completely, almost comically, still.

"Lia? Breathe."

She gasped. "What?"

Shit. He was fumbling this. Christ, they were in a bathroom! What the hell was wrong with him? "Lia. Say something, please?"

A breath exploded out of her and then she gasped another one in. "Are you—did you—you want—Did you just *propose?*"

"Yeah," he admitted, kind of sheepishly. "I bought you a ring. It's in the other room. I'm sorry. I had it all planned. Nice dinner, just us. I was gonna buy you a book and put the ring inside it but—" He trailed off when he realized she wasn't happy. "I want you. There's no reason for us to wait. Life is so short—I'm already thirty-seven—and we're just wasting the time we've got."

Her eyes narrowed and she tugged her hands back. "That's not enough for marriage, Gabriel."

"You don't think so? Lia, a few months ago, the only reason I got up in the morning was to take care of my girls. Since I met you, I'm thinking about a future again. A future where I can do the kind of work I love, open my own place, and know with absolute certainty that my girls are loved when they're with you."

"So I'm the babysitter." She tightened her lips.

"No!" Was she deliberately being difficult? Impatience snapped at him but he forced himself to respond calmly. "I'm saying I see you as my partner in this future, as my wife." His breath exploded on that last word in a happy laugh because it all made sense, such perfect fucking sense. He had to make her see that. "I'm not the most patient—"

"Really? I hadn't noticed."

He bit back a curse. "Lia." He ran his hands up her arms, tunneled them through her hair. "I love you, I'm completely in love with you, and I'm pretty sure I've grown on you by now—"

"Jesus, Gabriel. You're not mildew." She moved aside but he blocked her.

"Sweetheart, I'm sorry. I'm doing this all wrong but it makes perfect sense. I love you. I want us to be a team. Always. You don't have to say yes right now, but please, just tell me you'll think about it?"

She didn't answer him. Instead, she took a very definite step back. Frowning, he tried to figure out how he could salvage this. He wanted to marry her, for God's sake. Did she not get how monumental this was for him? How impossible it was to even think about such a thing even a few months earlier? He'd thought she was practical, with her life hacks and tips for working smarter. He'd thought she'd appreciate him laying it all out in a logical way. But he'd missed a step or two.

He needed to show her his whole heart.

"Lia, I've been…" he searched for the right word "…waiting. No. *Wasting*, I think. Just killing time. I didn't care about anything except taking care of my girls and the truth is, I wasn't doing a good job of that. I know I'm not as patient as I should be, especially with Maddie and Emmy. But ever since you came into my life, I'm…Christ, Lia. I think I'm…well, it's like I woke up. I want to make plans. I want us to get married. I want to start that business. I want to find a house, a real home where there's room for dollhouses and…and that fluffy dog Maddie wants…and your office with that big-ass desk. Lia. None of this happens without you. I don't want it without you."

"I…I don't understand. I'm not her, Gabriel. You told me I'm not at all like Janey, so how is it possible that you love *me*? And even if you are, we never talked about us being long-term, being permanent."

Her use of the word *if* burned like acid but he let it go. "Isn't that what being in love means?" he snapped.

She held up a palm. "You're still mourning your wife and then…what? You wake up this morning and decide to *propose*? You've gone from zero to sixty in seconds and I'm—I'm dizzy. I…I need to think. I need time."

Think? Time? They loved each other. She loved him. People in love got married, made a family. There was nothing simpler to his mind. But there was one huge blaring mistake he had to rectify. She still believed she was nothing but a stopgap measure. "Amelia," he whispered, pulling her back. "I'm in love with you. I think I have been since the first day. You didn't just jump-start my car. You re-started *me*. I was half-dead inside. You brought me back to life."

The smile that split her face warmed him down to his bones.

"I was afraid, Lia. So afraid to lose the few pieces of my heart I have left but I'm done with that. I'm not scared anymore. I want us to be together. You, me, the girls. I'd want you to adopt them, if you want, so you could really be their mother."

"You want me to be their mother?" she echoed.

"Yes, if that's what you want. But more than anything, I want you to be my wife. Lia, please. Please say yes."

She sank back down to the toilet. "Gabriel, I…I'm overwhelmed. This is all so…so confusing. I need to think—"

"Lia, do you love me?"

"Yes," she said without hesitation.

"The girls?"

"God, yes."

He lifted a shoulder. "Seems pretty clear."

"Daddy!"

His expression immediately changed to one of concern as he pulled open the door. "Take the time you need. I'll be right here."

Chapter Twenty-One

L IA SAT AT her kitchen table with a cup of coffee and her client to-do lists. She hadn't seen Gabriel in a few days now.

He was giving her time.

She laughed once, shook her head, and put a hand to her heart. Patience was *so* not a virtue of his, but he was giving her time. And he had so many others. Tender, loyal, smart, and insanely hardworking, he didn't rest until he made somebody's dream come true. Kimberly's thirteenth birthday was such a success, he was planning to make the Daddy Birthday Night a tradition with each of the girls, albeit not quite as fancy as that one. Baby Emmy's third birthday was in March and both Olivia's and Madison's birthdays were in the summer.

Maddie wanted a night at the theater. Gabe had revealed he'd prefer to visit the dentist than the theater, but she knew he'd go.

It was what he did.

He provided. He said yes to whatever was in his power to give his daughters. Yet, they weren't *spoiled* to her mind. She'd noted that Kimberly still hadn't received the cell phone she'd been asking for since Christmas.

Her smile faded when she wondered when he got to do the things *he* enjoyed. She knew he liked to fish but he hadn't been out east since she'd met him. Then again, it was winter.

With a start, she wondered when was *his* birthday? His daughter said it was in April, like hers, but when, exactly? God, there was so much about him she *didn't* know. He rarely spoke about his own family. She knew through Mike that they'd grown up near the Putnam Valley house Gabriel's in-laws owned. She knew he adored his work and missed it. He was still working in the city once or twice a week and when he came home, he couldn't seem to stop talking about his day. And she knew he felt guilty about leaving the tenants as well as the girls. That was why he often made his rounds well into the evening after he got off the train.

Her phone buzzed and she lunged for it, pressing the button for video.

Roseann appeared, still in bed by the looks of her. "What in the actual hell?" she demanded. "I just opened my eyes, read your text, and thought I was dreaming. Does Viv know?"

"I texted her, too."

"Well?" Roseann prodded. "If you make me wear a fuchsia bridesmaid's dress, I'm replacing you as my best friend."

"I haven't said yes."

Roseann's head tilted. "What?"

"I didn't say yes."

"You turned the Super Man down?" The note of incredulity in her best friend's voice told her Roseann thought that was a mistake.

"No. I told him I need time to think about it."

"Oh, honey. Your parents have you so screwed up—"

"It's not that!" Lia snapped. "It's just...I can't mess this up, Ro. It's too important. *He* is too important. I can't hurt him. I'd die if that happened."

"And how is he taking that?"

"He's...impatient. He hasn't been over here since he asked. But he's not ignoring me or anything. He's just...doing exactly what I asked."

"Okay, so why do you sound so sad? You're not still hung up on Jerk-Off, are you?"

Lia stared at Roseann. "Actually, I've hardly thought about him since I moved here. You were right about that, Roseann."

She waved a hand. "I usually am." She sat up in her bed, the image shaking until she got herself settled. "Honey, you're crazy about him."

"I am," Lia admitted.

"Then where's the downside?"

Lia sighed and put her chin in her hand. "He's been so hurt, Ro. He told me he planned to just waste time until...until death. He never planned on...on me, but now that he knows he's in love with me, he doesn't want to waste another minute." She squeezed her eyes shut, the honesty of his simple statement just too sad to bear.

"Lia, how do you feel?"

"I'm in love with him, too. With all of them." She spread her hands apart. "Roseann. This is the most important decision of my entire life. If I mess this up, I hurt *five* people I love."

Roseann sighed. "Okay, honey. You want to be logical about this, so let's give that a shot." She sat up, folded her legs and leaned forward. "A, you say no. You hurt five people you love and who love you back. Maybe they get over it. Maybe they don't. B, you say yes. You get married again. Things are great for a while and then, a year or two down the road, he cheats."

Lia's head snapped up.

"Hey, you wanted to be logical about this. You never thought Jared would cheat, did you?"

Lia was forced to shake her head to that.

"Okay, then. So, you get a few good years, it doesn't work out. Oh, no!" She waved her hands. "A bad decision. You win."

"Win?" Lia would hardly call this winning. "That's not what this is about—"

"You're right. That's *not* what this is about." Roseann agreed. "This is about you being afraid."

I fought what was happening between us because I was afraid, he'd said. *I'm done with that.*

Why couldn't she be?

"Or, C. You get married. And it works, because you both *make it work*, every day, for the rest of your lives." When Lia said nothing, Roseann cursed. "Lia, you both were married before, so you know exactly what it means. It's not all white dresses and champagne. You found a guy who's going into this with *none* of those delusions, a guy willing to make that commitment, to do that work. Don't compare him to Jared. It's not fair—to either of you."

"But Jared was—"

"A mistake. Yes. I know." Roseann sighed. "Did you ever think maybe that was a good thing?"

"What?"

"Lia. Jared showed you how to know the real thing when it came along and be smart enough to grab it with both hands."

A little frisson of hope flared in Lia's heart.

OVER THE NEXT week, Lia saw so little of Gabriel, she wondered if he'd left town. When she'd see one of the girls walk by her window with Mrs. Morgan and ask about him, it was always "Oh, he's in Unit Q, fixing a faucet." Or, "He's in the basement, doing the recycling."

On a gray and gloomy Thursday in the beginning of February, she sat facing her kitchen window with her laptop and cell phone and her shoes on. When he walked by, she'd catch him. School started in half an hour. He'd be leaving any minute now, carrying Emmy in his arms, holding Maddie's hand, Kimberly and Olivia behind them.

"Oh my God."

This was what she'd done—exactly what she'd done—after Jared left her. Sat with her nose pressed against the window of the apartment they'd used to share, just so she could get a glimpse of him with his new family. It was like...picking at a scab.

This was ridiculous.

She was ridiculous.

Gabriel was an incredible man. He'd been with one

woman since college. Olivia had told her about all the women who'd tried so hard to impress him. He never accepted a single invitation so why was she so stupidly unable to trust what they both felt?

She shut her laptop with a soft snap, stood up, collected her coat, hat, gloves, and bag. A change of scenery. Some fresh air. Maybe she'd head into the city this weekend, talk Roseann and Vivian into a nice dinner. With one arm tucked into her jacket, she pulled open her front door and stepped out—right into Gabriel, standing a step below her.

"Oh!"

"Hey, Lia."

He grinned that lightning-fast smile of his, the one that always made her think she'd imagined it. A smile mirage. She tripped, would have fallen, but he caught her before she fell.

He caught her.

"You okay?"

"No. Yeah. I'm fine. Just…surprised."

He winced and looked down at his feet. "Yeah. I'm sorry to bother you—"

"You're not. Bothering me. I'm…happy to see you."

"Yeah? I'm happy that makes you happy."

His hands were still on her shoulders. He dropped them abruptly and a shiver crawled down her spine. God, she missed him.

Her mind suddenly re-engaged. "Oh, you must be on your way to school to drop off the girls?"

He shook his head. "I dropped off Kim and Liv but I'm keeping Maddie home. She's running a fever."

"Oh no."

He looked…tired, she decided. Tired. Sad. Frustrated. Here he was, standing at her door, running a hand through his hair that had gotten too long again. His nails were blue today. The happy color made her smile.

He stepped up another step so that they were on the same level. "I miss you."

"I miss you, too."

He waited for her to say something else…something more. But she couldn't get the words out.

He frowned but said, "I have to get back and relieve Mrs. Morgan." He waved a hand toward his door. "I came by to, you know, see how things are going, see if there's any way I can ask you to do something for me."

"Things are good, Gabriel. I've been doing a lot of thinking. I know how you must feel—"

"Do you?"

His usual impatience peeked through the mask of civility he'd worn since she opened her door and rather than make her mad, she found it oddly charming.

"I'm sorry," he said immediately. "You wanted time and I'm trying to give it to you, I swear."

"I know and I love you for it. I know you don't understand this, but I'm trying so hard to make sure I don't hurt you or your girls. I know you hate when I bring up Jared, but it's not that. My parents despise each other and well, it's just so easy to make a mistake. That was fine when it was just me but I can't risk it with your children."

His eyes searched her face and then he sighed. "Okay. I can't fault you for that." He turned to go.

"Wait. You said something about a favor?"

"Right." He pinched the bridge of his nose. "I've had another long night. My brain's foggy. Maddie's fever is about a hundred and three. I've been pumping her up with Children's Tylenol but can't get it lower than a hundred, which is why she's home today. But Jim called and needs me in the city. There's a crisis. I've been going in almost every day for a few hours. Mrs. Morgan's been great about the extra hours, says it's not a problem but...well, she's elderly. I'd feel better knowing you were nearby and able to help, should she need you?"

"Yes. Yes, absolutely."

"You're sure? I remember you said you had some appointments this week?"

For a minute, she was blank. "Oh, right. Interviews. Jessica next door? She gave me some names so yeah, I've already been in contact with them and—" Abruptly, she stopped talking.

"And what?"

She waved a hand. "Sorry. I was babbling about my work when you have your own to get to." Jared had always hated when she did that. "Are you leaving for the train right now?"

He shook his head. "Gonna go kiss my girl good-bye first, make sure she's feeling okay before I do."

"I'll come with you." Lia turned and locked her front door.

Inside Gabriel's living room, Mrs. Morgan was on the sofa while Emmy played with a toy shopping cart and cash register.

"She's asleep, Gabriel," Mrs. Morgan said. "She complained of a bad stomach ache but I gave her that next dose you mentioned."

Gabriel pressed his lips together and sighed. "I hate this. You know how I get when they're sick."

"I know. I'm sorry."

After a minute, he finally said, "Okay." He grabbed his bag, crouched beside Emmy and got a bunch of kisses. "You be good, E-Rex, okay?"

"'Kay, Dad-dee. Love you."

"I love you, too, baby. See you later. Oh, and Lia?" When she looked up at him, he added, "It's not babbling when you talk about your work. I like hearing about it. I like how you get all fired up whenever about it." With one long look at her, he left.

"Lee-uh. Play store!"

"I have to—Emmy! Good girl. You said my name correctly."

Mrs. Morgan laughed. "We've been practicing our L sounds. I've told Mr. Ivers I think her speech will develop just fine at its own pace, but he thinks she might need some fancy speech lessons."

That had been her doing, Lia realized. She'd done more research, given Gabriel a list of speech pathologists.

It warmed her down to her bone marrow that he'd been listening.

After Emmy had filled her toy shopping cart a few dozen times, Mrs. Morgan cleared her throat. "That man is purely in love with you."

"Feelings can change," she replied. Her parents had taught her that too well.

To her shock, Mrs. Morgan slapped her hand. "Of

course feelings can change. What a crock of sewage! Only things sure in this world are death and taxes, missy. You want *sure*, become a mortician."

"Lee-uh. Pee-pee." Emmy wiggled and clasped a hand to her crotch.

Thank God, she thought as she hustled the wiggling toddler to the bathroom.

Chapter Twenty-Two

A LOUD KNOCK on her door that night startled Lia out of sleep. With her heart galloping, she hurried to the back door, peeked out the window and found Kimberly in nothing but her pajamas.

"Kimberly, sweetheart, what's wrong?" she said as soon as she flung open the door.

"Lia, you have to come." She clutched at Lia's hands, pulled hard. "It's Maddie. Something's wrong. She's not just sick. I think she's dying." The girl's voice cracked.

"Where's your dad?" Lia ran for her jacket, the bag with keys and phone, followed Gabriel's daughter out the back door still wearing pajamas and slippers.

"Still at work. I tried calling, but he's not answering. I think his phone might be dead because it's going straight to voice mail."

"Okay, okay. Don't worry, sweetheart. I'll do what I can."

Lia stepped into Gabriel's apartment to find Maddie screaming in the bathroom, hair plastered to her face. Olivia was wild-eyed with fear, trying to hold Emmy, also crying. Mrs. Morgan was in a state.

Lia never should have left her alone but the elderly woman had insisted Lia go home.

"Oh, Miss Blake, I don't know what else I can do for the poor child. Her fever is still up and now she says her stomach hurts so bad, she can't walk."

Oh, God. Lia's heart almost stopped. Think. Think, damn it! *Fever. Pain.*

"Maddie! Maddie, baby, talk to me. What's going on?"

"Lia," she sobbed, wrapping her arms around Lia's neck. "I have to poop, but I can't. My butt hurts and my back and my belly and my legs and everything!"

Lia's blood went cold. She'd once done some research for one of her authors on the signs of appendicitis. This sounded like every one of them.

"Okay, okay, baby. I need to check something. Can you sit up for me?"

"It hurts," she cried.

"I know. I'll be fast." As soon as Maddie let go of her neck, Lia lifted her pajama top. "Show me where it hurts the worst."

"Here. My belly button."

Gently, Lia pressed her hand to Maddie's middle and released. Tears filled Lia's eyes when the child screamed again. "It hurts everywhere, Lia!"

At that, Lia's heart *did* stop. She turned to Olivia. "Liv. Would you please get you and Emmy dressed to go outside?"

"Outside? Why? Where are we going? What's wrong with her, Lia?"

She took a deep breath. She couldn't lie to these children. She just couldn't. "To the hospital." Lia wasn't sure exactly sure if this was appendicitis, but knew one thing. No run-of-the-mill virus ever caused screams like this.

Olivia's face crumbled. "Oh, God. Where's Daddy, Lia? Where?"

"Clothes. Right now. Kimberly, will you help? I need you all to be strong now and keep Emmy calm. Mrs. Morgan, will you please pack snacks and cups of milk into Emmy's bag?"

"Yes. Yes, I can do that."

It took Lia close to fifteen precious minutes to get all four Ivers girls dressed for winter, not to mention Mrs. Morgan. She'd found Gabriel's car keys, put a scared and trembling Emmy into her car seat, and then organized Maddie under some blankets with Mrs. Morgan holding her tight. Kim rode in the front with her and Olivia took the third seat. She started the car, turned the heater to blast, and stepped outside to furiously scrape the frost from the windows, praying the whole time.

At this late hour, there was little traffic and she pulled up to the hospital only fifteen minutes later, her palms sweating. Thirty-five minutes. It had been about thirty-five minutes since Kimberly pounded on her door.

Maddie's cries hadn't stopped.

They'd gotten worse.

Lia didn't bother to park. She drove straight to the emergency room's entrance and leaned on the horn. A security guard rushed to her door. "I have a six-year-old girl with severe abdominal pain and fever. I think it's her appendix."

"Stay here." He disappeared into the sliding doors, returning a minute later with a wheelchair.

"Kim. Can you carry Emmy, please? Liv, take the bag."

Lia jumped from the SUV, carefully lifted Maddie from Mrs. Morgan's arms and put her in the wheelchair, tucking the blankets around her.

"What your name, Miss?"

"Amelia Blake."

"I'll park the vehicle, get your keys to you."

Lia didn't spare a thought to the car. She checked that all four girls plus Mrs. Morgan were accounted for and ran inside.

The next hour was a blur.

Maddie was examined, poked and prodded, an IV inserted into the back of one hand. Her abdominal pain was so bad, she barely noticed the needle in her hand. Lia tried Gabriel's cell number repeatedly. No response. Next, she tried looking for Paradigm itself, found a number, but got an automated answering system. It took ten more minutes to find an emergency number, which got her to their security department. Quickly, she relayed the reason for the call, got a promise from the man who answered that he'd radio the crew who had been working around the clock ever since the crisis—whatever it was—began.

A woman who identified herself as Dr. Kuo stepped toward her, led her outside into a hall. "Okay, Mommy. We got Madison's blood work back and her white count is extremely elevated. We're running antibiotics now but we're gonna want to get her into surgery as soon as we can. I'll have a nurse bring you the consent forms, but meanwhile, can you tell me when she last ate?"

Lia cursed. "She hasn't eaten since breakfast," she relayed what Mrs. Morgan had told her. "But I'm not her mother.

I'm her neighbor."

Dr. Kuo's eyebrows shot up. "Where are her parents?"

"I'm trying to reach her father now. Her mother died two years ago."

"Any other next of kin I can speak to?"

Frantically, Lia tried to think. She could call Mike but only had a cell number for him. It was nearly two a.m. She could try to find Linda and Stuart's number.

"Yes. Let me try to reach her grandparents."

She went back to the girls. Maddie was curled in a ball on her side, sleeping. Mrs. Morgan held Emmy on her lap. "Kimberly, do you know your grandparents' phone number or your uncle Mike's?"

She bit her lip. "I really want my dad, Lia."

"I know, sweetheart. I've got the company's security guards getting word to him. Right now, I need to call your other relatives. Can you call Grandma?"

"Um. I think so." She took Lia's phone, dialed a number. Lia heard Stuart's sleepy voice answer. "Grandpa." And then she burst into tears.

Lia took the phone. "Stuart, this is Lia. I'm at the hospital with the girls. It's Maddie. We suspect appendicitis but we can't reach Gabriel. He's on a job site. I think a structure collapsed so his phone's either dead or has no signal. They need consent for surgery and I can't give it. I didn't know who else to call." She gave them the name of the hospital and location.

"We're on our way. We'll be there in an hour."

"Grandma and Grandpa are coming," Lia told the frightened children.

She sent Mike a text so he'd know what was happening though he probably wouldn't see it until he woke up. There was nothing she could do, not a damn thing more she could do, except wait.

They'd put Maddie in a curtained area that was quiet, relatively speaking. Lia asked for chairs; they were dragged over. Mrs. Morgan looked ready to collapse and Lia wasn't sure she could handle another emergency so she directed her into one while Kim and Liv sat huddled together in the other. Lia paced back and forth, rocking Emmy on her shoulder. From time to time, Maddie whimpered and Lia cringed. She must be in such pain.

Gabriel, where are you?

Finally, close to an hour after they'd arrived, her phone buzzed. "Gabriel!"

Kimberly and Olivia bounced up.

"Christ, Lia. Jesus Christ. What happened? What's wrong? How is she?"

His voice shook and Lia's heart crumbled. "She's in so much pain, Gabe. They want to do surgery."

"Oh, Jesus. It's definitely the appendix?"

"That's what they're saying."

"I never should have left. I *knew* she wasn't feeling well. I never should have left her and then my phone wasn't getting a signal. God, Lia. When the foreman rushed over to me with that radio call, I—"

"Gabriel, listen to me. You are needed here. Maddie is going to be fine as soon as she's through the surgery. Get in a cab and get here."

"Yeah. I'm on my way. One of the crew is driving me.

We're almost to the tunnel. Lia," he said. "Please. Please hold on to my girl. Don't let her die. Please, Lia, I'm begging you. Don't you let her die."

What could she say to that? God, how could she promise him that? "Gabriel, the girls want to talk to you. They need to hear your voice," she said with meaning.

She heard him curse and sniffle and curse again. "Yeah. Okay. I got it. Put them on."

"Daddy!" Kimberly cried. "I went to get Lia. Maddie was screaming so bad and I didn't know what to do. I'm scared, Daddy."

Still rocking Emmy, her arm numb, Lia heard Gabe's deep voice speak in that soft soothing cadence she'd come to love. He was doing it. He was shoving aside his own fear to do what he did best—take care of his daughters.

"Dr. Kuo!" Lia called out. "I've reached her father."

The doctor hurried over, held out her hand for the phone. "Mr. Ivers? I'm the pediatrician on call...yes, yes...she's sleeping now. We're giving her antibiotics and pain medication. Does she have any allergies I should know about? Yes...yes...that's fine. Yes, her white count is extremely high and she's showing some abdominal swelling...no, not yet, but yes, all indications lead me to believe our safest course of action is surgery but we can't do that until you arrive and sign the consent because it's not life-threatening yet...of course. I will not let that happen, Mr. Ivers...yes...yes. Okay."

Dr. Kuo handed the phone back to Lia.

"Gabriel, I love—" she began but heard the dial tone.

He'd ended the call.

❧

IT FELT LIKE hardly any time had passed and at the same time, it felt like an eternity. Gabriel ran into the ER wearing his safety vest and outdoor gear, carrying a hard hat. "Lia!"

Lia opened the curtain, waved. "In here."

"Daddy!" Both Kim and Liv ran to him, wrapped their arms around him as if they'd been parted for a lifetime.

"It's okay. It'll be okay. Let me see Maddie now."

Immediately, they released him and he fell to his knees beside her bed. "Hey, Maddie. Hey, Ducky. Open your eyes, baby."

"Daddy."

Gabriel's face was white, but his hands were gentle as he stroked the sweaty hair from Maddie's face. "You're gonna be fine, Maddie. Just fine."

"I'm really sleepy but it hurts, Daddy."

"I know, Ducky. I know. But Dr. Kuo is going to fix that. Close your eyes. Don't worry about a thing. I got you." His lip quivered and Lia's heart did a long, slow roll. She moved to him then, gave his shoulder a comforting squeeze. His hand immediately lifted to hers.

It was ice cold and still shook.

He stood up slowly, pressed a kiss to Maddie's head. Emmy was dead weight in Lia's arms now and never stirred. "I'll take Emmy."

Lia shook her head. "No. You need to sign forms. I've got her."

"Where's the doctor?" Before she could answer, he strode out of the curtain, raised his voice. "Dr. Kuo? I'm looking for Dr. Kuo."

A curtain down the hall opened with a soft snick. "Right here."

"Gabriel Ivers."

Dr. Kuo walked to him, shook his hand. "Let's talk privately." She turned to Lia. "You all can wait in there." She indicated a waiting area just across the hall from where Maddie rested.

Lia held out her free hand to Mrs. Morgan, helped her to her feet, and headed for the waiting room. Kimberly and Olivia collapsed to a few empty chairs near a TV that played quietly in a corner. The room was empty. Mrs. Morgan sat down and after a minute, so did Lia, her arm screaming in relief when the weight of the sleeping baby in her arms was redistributed.

It was quite a while before Gabriel reappeared. The lines in his face went deep and Lia tried to stand, but he lifted a hand and shook his head. He sank to the chair beside hers, and ran his big hand over his youngest daughter's back. "They're taking her up to surgery now." He scrubbed both hands over his face and jerked in alarm when Olivia jumped up.

"Daddy, I'm sorry! I'm so sorry!"

"It's okay. She'll be fine."

Frantically, Olivia shook her head. "I hate when Maddie talks all the time and won't shut up and then she wakes me up. I get so mad at her, Daddy, and sometimes I wish...I wish she'd never talk again and now—" Her face dissolved just as the horror of what she'd left unsaid registered in Gabriel's brain.

Gabriel scooped her into his arms. "Sweetheart, it's okay. That's just anger. You didn't really mean it."

"I didn't, Daddy, I swear! But now Maddie's—"

"Going to be fine," he finished for her with conviction. "I'm not mad at you. This isn't your fault. It's mine. I should have made arrangements for emergencies like this. I thought my cell phone was good enough. I'm sorry."

A nurse came in, told them they could move up to the sixth floor and wait there for Maddie to come out of surgery. Lia cleared her throat. "The grandparents are on their way. Can you help them find us?"

"Yes, of course."

"You called Linda and Stuart?"

Lia nodded. "And I texted Mike." She shifted to the edge of the seat, tried to get up. Gabe stood first, carefully transferred Emmy to his arms. "I didn't know what else to do. I can't make medical decisions for her. I'm not family."

Gabriel looked at her sharply and then turned away. "Let's go."

The girls were asleep on their feet. The sixth-floor waiting room was carpeted and had comfortable furniture instead of hard plastic chairs. Gabriel directed Mrs. Morgan into a rocking chair and Lia into the center of one of the plush sofas.

"Girls, come lie down." She patted the cushion. Olivia immediately curled in to her. After a minute, Kimberly sat on her other side. Lia covered them both with coats and rubbed their backs. Gabe stood with Emmy on his shoulder.

"Gabriel, let me have her. Sit down."

He ignored her.

"Gabriel?"

"I'm fine, Lia."

She studied him for a minute, saw the tension in those long, lean muscles, the worry lines etched in his face. She knew him so well now. She could tell he was holding it all inside, being the strong comforting father figure he thought everybody needed. *Fine* was the last thing he was.

But she let him be.

"Mrs. Morgan, are you okay? Anything I can get for you?"

Gabe's head shot up at that. "You just can't help yourself, can you?" he asked, his tone biting.

Lia stared at him, bewildered. "What?"

"Helping. You can't help helping, which is funny, because if you really wanted to help me, you'd have given me an answer. Maybe if you had, we could have avoided most of this drama tonight. *You'd* have been able to make the decision they waited almost an hour for *me* to make."

Okay. Lia took a deep breath. Maybe she'd deserved that. She knew he was upset, knew that was his anxiety talking, and she refused to react. His need to blame someone gave him an outlet for all his guilt, so she didn't reply.

But oh, it *stung*.

"Amelia."

Bracing herself, she lifted her eyes to his.

"I'm sorry. That was mean. You asked for time. You have it. I...fuck..." He broke off and shook his head. "I have no excuse."

Before Lia could reply, Linda and Stuart rushed in. Gabriel brought them up to date on Maddie's status. The girls continued to sleep and Gabe continued to pace. Another hour passed.

"Mr. Ivers?"

Dr. Kuo stood in the doorway. Without a backward glance, Gabe followed her, still holding Emmy against his shoulder.

"Gabriel. Give Emmy to me." Linda held out her arms.

He looked at the baby like he'd forgotten she was there, put her carefully in her grandmother's arms before disappearing with the doctor.

"Lia, honey, thank you for calling us."

"I'm so sorry to drag you down here in the middle of the night. I didn't know what else to do when I couldn't reach him." Lia looked down at the two heads resting against her. She smoothed the hair back from Kimberly's face and tucked a jacket higher around Olivia's shoulders.

"How is he, Lia?"

"Scared."

Linda shook her head. "No. It's more than that. He seems unusually tense."

Lia lowered her head. "That's probably my fault. He...he proposed." At Linda's knowing look, Lia shook her head. "You knew?"

"I figured it would be coming soon. I've seen how he looks at you, Lia. I've seen him look that way before and I'm so damn happy he's looking that way again because I love him like he was my own."

Lia's mouth fell open. "I...oh, God, Linda. I think I made a terrible mistake. I told him I needed time. I was married before and I...it was a mistake. I have to be *sure* this time. Not for me, but for *him*. And for four little girls who've been through way too much already."

"Lia." Linda crouched in front of her and took her hand. "I think it's admirable that you're trying to spare them more hurt. But, honey, sometimes you have to go with your heart."

Lia pressed a hand to her heart and knew the answer it wanted so badly to give.

∾

GABE FOLLOWED DR. Kuo through the corridor into a large room sectioned off by curtains hanging from tracks in the ceiling. She flicked one curtain back and he froze in his tracks.

His daughter, his precious Ducky, was so still, so lifeless in a bed that was way too big for her, wrapped in blankets, a tube strapped under her nose, that he had to stop and watch her chest rise a few times. Christ. Jesus Christ, when he thought about what could have happened... Damn it, he had one job.

One job.

Take care of his girls.

That was all. And he'd done nothing but fuck that up since Janey died. Kimberly's first period and Olivia skipping school and Maddie's appendix. This wasn't a pile of construction materials that collapsed, it was his *family*.

He moved slowly to Maddie's bed, took her tiny hand in his. "She's so cold."

"It's the anesthesia. We've got her under some warming

blankets. She'll be fine, Mr. Ivers. The appendix hadn't burst but it sure was ripe. She'll stay here for a few days and be driving you crazy again in no time."

Gabe sank into the chair next to Maddie's bed. He stroked her head, her pale little face, her hand. Good thing Lia knew what to do.

Lia.

Hell, he'd messed that up, too. Allowed her to worm her way into his life, his plans, his heart, where he'd vowed never to let anyone since Janey. He'd *listened* to her. He'd believed her when she told him he owed it to his daughters to make himself happy, believed her when she assured him he could balance everything. Believed her when she told him she loved him.

Not enough, he concluded. Nowhere near enough, or she'd be wearing his ring already.

He watched Maddie's chest rise and fall for a while. He kissed her head. "Ducky, wake up. Daddy's here, sweetheart. Can you wake up for me?"

Her eyelids fluttered but she didn't stir. His wild, impulsive, loud little girl was none of those things and he wanted her back. "Come on, sweetheart. You need to tell me everything that happened while I was at work. I promise I won't tell you to be quiet. I won't tell you that ever again." He swallowed hard. "Lia called me but my phone was broken and it took me a while to get her message but as soon as I did, I came right away, Maddie."

He inched his chair closer to her bed, dropped his head to the mattress and squeezed his eyes shut. He hadn't cried since he'd lost Janey. Yeah, he often had nail polish on his fingers and barrettes in his hair and there was even that one time he'd let Maddie dress him in a skirt and tiara but tears were where he drew the damn line.

They didn't help.

But they burned at the back of his eyes and all down his throat. He was choking on them, choking on the string of mistakes he'd made and as he fought to suck in air, they almost strangled him.

"Oh, God, Maddie. Baby, I'm so sorry. Never again, sweetheart. I'm not leaving you girls ever again."

"Daddy."

His head shot up at that sweet, sweet sound. "Maddie, baby. It's okay. I'm right here."

"I'm thirsty."

Thirsty. Shit, that had to be a good sign, right? "Thirsty. Okay. Okay, hang on, Ducky." He stood up on legs he could barely feel, lurched out to the nurse's station and called for help. A few minutes later, they brought a cup of water with a straw.

"Here, Maddie. Little sip, okay?"

He guided the straw to her pale, cracked lips, held it steady while she sipped.

"How do you feel?"

"Sleepy."

"Okay. You sleep. I'll be right here."

"I want my bear, Daddy."

The laugh burst out of him. Of course she did. "I'll go home and get him for you." He'd go to the damn moon if he had to.

She shook her head weakly. "He's in Lia's bag."

Lia.

His spine straightened. "I'll find Lia and get your bear and come right back."

"No! Stay." She reached out for his hand with both of hers. His gaze shot to the IV needle in that tiny hand. She must have been so scared. And he hadn't been here.

That was when the first tear finally fell.

He sat beside his girl for a long time, thinking, praying, beating himself up. He'd fallen in love with Lia…against all his promises, his better judgment—hell, even against his will. She was amazing. She was all the things he wasn't—patient and kind and so beautiful. He knew he didn't deserve her, but damn it, he wanted her with the kind of bone-deep desire he'd been sure he'd buried with Janey and for a minute, just for a minute, he'd let himself believe he could have it all again—happy kids, work he loved, and a woman who loved him.

He'd believed all those sappy clichés about love conquering all.

He was an idiot. Yeah, that was the only thing that was clear. He was a colossal, card-carrying, grade-A, crackerjack, first-rate, world-class *idiot* and even though Lia may *think* she loved him and his daughters, he knew the truth. Love meant pain and he was fucking done with pain.

He pressed another kiss to Maddie's forehead, slipped his hand from hers, and dragged himself back to the waiting room.

"GABRIEL."

He stopped inside the waiting room door, the image of Amelia covered by three of his girls seared forever into his brain. Kimberly was curled in a ball, her head on Lia's lap. Olivia slept, half-sitting up, tucked against her side and on her lap, Emmy, with her thumb in her mouth.

Slowly, he walked toward her, dread filling his gut, every step killing him.

"How is she, son?"

Linda and Stuart stood up, joined him near the sofa where Lia was trapped. A strong hand clasped his shoulder and he looked around to find Mike there, too. Christ, when had he gotten here?

"Groggy. Thirsty. Not much pain now but she's still working off the anesthesia. She wants her bear."

"Oh! In my bag." Lia's giant purse was on the floor at her feet. He opened it, found the bear and spotted his car keys. He gripped them tight, hating what he now knew he had to do. He sighed heavily. Best for everybody if he just ripped off that bandage.

"I need to talk to you, Lia." He pocketed the keys, put Maddie's bear down and gently transferred Emmy to Mike's arms and Olivia to Linda's where she resettled almost instantly. It was going on four a.m. and he obviously wasn't the only one feeling it.

Lia looked at him with concern. Mike, who knew him better than most, shook his head. "Gabe. Don't."

Gabe spread his arms apart. He had no choice. "Lia. Thank you for all that you did."

"Of course." She reached her hand to take his. He recoiled like it was poisonous. "What can I do? Tell me what you need."

"I need—" The words almost choked him. "I need you to leave. Please."

Mrs. Morgan's mouth opened in an O of shock. Stuart shot him a look of pity that he didn't need or want.

"What?" she asked in a tortured voice, the word a white-hot lash of pain against his already battered heart.

"I can't do this, Lia. I love you so much." His voice cracked and he shook his head. "But it's not enough. I did everything I could to make you believe it. I tried to give you time, but we have to face the truth. Time can't fix this."

"No, Gabriel!" She rushed forward, clutched his hand. "I was scared, I was just scared but I'm not now. My answer is yes because I love you, I love the girls."

He jerked. He'd wished for—*prayed* for her to say those words and now they shot through him like bullets. Why the hell couldn't she say it when he'd asked? Now it was just another kick to the nuts. He pulled his hand free and dropped his head. "I tried, Lia. I tried so hard, but you keep measuring me by mistakes I haven't made and can't fix. You want certainty and you want guarantees and I can't do that. I can't give you that. So I'm asking you to please leave."

"No."

"Move out," he continued as if she hadn't spoken. "Go back home or stay with your friends in the city. Just please, please don't be near me anymore because the only thing I *am* sure about is I'm *not* strong enough for this."

Lia's lip trembled and tears spilled from those beautiful dark eyes. He knew he was hurting her, knew he was being cruel, but it was essential to his survival to get it done.

Sever the limb. Make a clean break.

As if that were possible.

He picked up Maddie's bear, turned to Mike. "Can you take everybody home? Please?"

"I won't go," Lia said.

Gabe turned, looked at her one last time, and managed a small smile. "You will. It's what I need and you're not cruel. This is what you do, Lia. You give people what they need. Do this for me. If you ever cared about me—about us—please do this."

He turned and headed back to Maddie's bedside, her bear clutched in his hand and the look of devastation on Lia's face etched on his heart.

Chapter Twenty-Three

GABE REMAINED AT the hospital, sleeping in Maddie's room, hovering beside her when the nurses came in to rouse her for a walk around the room. The anesthesia should have worn off by the day after surgery, but Maddie was lethargic the next day, and the day after that. Gabe was ready to throttle some answers out of Dr. Kuo, but the woman just patted his shoulder and said every child heals at her own rate.

On the third day after surgery, Dr. Kuo came into Maddie's room where Gabe had been trying—unsuccessfully—to get Maddie to eat breakfast.

"Hello there, Miss Ivers."

"Hi."

"I've come to look at your scars."

Every time she said that, every damn time, Gabe's entire body winced. His precious child, his perfect baby—scarred.

But alive, he reminded himself. He had to be thankful for that and he was. Still...he'd have sold his soul to have avoided this.

Dr. Kuo pressed on Maddie's belly, which was noticeably less distended. The laparoscopic incisions were covered with a simple gauze dressing now. "Okay, Maddie, this looks very good to me. I think we can spring you out of here today.

How does that sound?"

Like a lottery win, Gabe thought. His smile was real and huge when he turned to Maddie. "Home sounds great, doesn't it, Ducky?"

"Ducky?" Dr. Kuo repeated with a laugh. "Now I think I need to hear the story about why your dad calls you Ducky."

Maddie didn't laugh. She didn't smile. She didn't even beg to tell the story about how all the girls got their nicknames, the way she'd always done every time the topic came up. She shoved the hair out of her eyes. It really needed to be washed. It hung in strings around her too-pale face. Lia would have—

Abruptly, Gabe shoved the thought aside and answered the doctor's question. "I call her that because of a dinosaur in a movie called *The Land Before Time*."

"It's silly," she said, listlessly.

Gabe's heart dropped. "Do you want me to stop calling you that?"

She shrugged. "I don't care."

"What about getting to go home today? Isn't that happy news?" he tried again.

Another shrug.

"Maddie, sweetheart." He sat on her bed and took her little face in his hands. "Dr. Kuo says I get to take you home and I'm almost as happy as I was when you were born and I got to take you home and keep you forever. Why aren't you happy?"

Her big brown eyes were flat and unhappy as she looked at him. "I wanted to see Mommy. But she's not here."

"Mommy? Maddie, Mommy's—Oh, Maddie. Did you

think you were going *to die?*"

"I wanted to! I wanted to go to heaven to see Mommy! Ow!" When she began to cry, she curled over her still-sore belly and all Gabe could do was rub her back.

A nurse stepped in when he heard Maddie's cry. Dr. Kuo asked him to page Dr. Vahle, stat. Ten minutes after that, a tall woman with wild hair stepped into Maddie's room.

"Hello. I'm Dr. Vahle, but you can call me Bobby."

Maddie frowned. "I don't want you to look at my belly."

"That's not why I'm here."

Maddie relaxed a little when she heard that. "Bobby's a boy's name."

"Yep. That's why I like it. My name's really Robin, but I like Bobby."

"It's stupid."

Gabe's eyes bulged. "Maddie. Manners?"

"Well, it is."

"You think it's stupid, and I like it. What do you think, Mr. Ivers?"

"Uh, well, I guess it's cool."

"Okay, we've got one vote for stupid, one cool, and one like. I might ask all the other kids to vote."

Confused, Maddie made a face. "Daddy asks us to vote when we have to make family 'cisions. A name isn't a 'cision."

Smiling, Dr. Vahle said, "That's true. A name is a name and you can't really change it. But still, I think I'll take a vote. I like to know what people think."

"About what?"

"About everything. Like right now, I want to know what

you think."

"I think Bobby's a stupid name for a girl."

"Madison!" Gabe barked but Dr. Vahle held up a hand.

"Mr. Ivers, why don't you take a break, maybe go hunt down a treat for Miss Maddie here? Maybe an ice pop?"

Gabe hesitated for a second and finally nodded. He knew what kind of doctor she was; *psychology* was printed on her ID badge. He just didn't like the idea of leaving his six-year-old alone after she'd just revealed she'd hoped to die.

Half an hour later, he came back with a treat and Maddie was chirping like a little bird about how she got her name. He stood in the door, stunned by the transformation.

"Oh, your dad's back. Bye, Maddie. I hope you feel better fast."

"Bye, Bobby. Sorry I said your name was stupid. I didn't really mean it."

"It's okay. Mr. Ivers, can we chat in the hall?"

He nodded. "Maddie, are you hungry?" He opened the bag, handed her a plastic spoon and took the lid off a small carton of Ben & Jerry's.

She gasped and nodded vigorously.

"Be right back."

Outside in the hall, he found Dr. Kuo talking to Dr. Vahle. "Please, I'm begging you, please don't tell me my six-year-old is suicidal."

"Not at all, Mr. Ivers. Maddie simply made an entirely logical conclusion based on limited information. The last time she saw her mother was in a hospital. So when *she* was brought to the hospital, she assumed she'd go wherever it was that her mother went and they'd get to visit. She was in a tremendous amount of pain and focusing on that...that 'happy thought' as she called it, is what helped her cope. When Dr. Kuo said she could leave today, it popped that bubble and your daughter was crushed."

Yeah. He knew the feeling.

"Have you considered any sort of grief counseling?"

"Um, well, I went a couple of times but..."

"Okay, I strongly recommend you set up a few sessions for Madison, and suggest you do some family counseling as well, but I'm not worried and don't think you need to be, either."

F-u-c- "I...Christ...I have no idea where to even begin." And the thought that Lia would know exactly who to call scraped at his wounds with a dull blade.

"I can help with that."

True to her word, Dr. Vahle provided him with a list of resources and later that afternoon, tucked it into the folder of discharge papers he'd had to sign and that was that.

Maddie was sprung.

He drove five miles under the speed limit, determined to keep her safe.

Back at the apartment, he found a spot almost right in front of the courtyard, parked, then jogged around to Maddie's rear seat and scooped her into his arms.

"Yay! I get carried."

"You sure do, Ducky."

He refused to look in the direction of Lia's apartment. He strode up the courtyard steps and to his front door, but it was pulled open before he could find his key.

"Welcome home!" the girls all shouted.

"Easy, easy. No hugging."

Inside, the living room was decorated with large construction paper signs that said, "Welcome Home!" and "Get Well Fast!" and a dozen balloons. Linda had made a cake with Kim and Liv and even Emmy made a card that was all orange circles, but hey—it was the thought that counted. He got Maddie tucked into a corner of the sofa, brought her a piece of cake, and laughed when Liv asked to see Maddie's scars and said they were cool. Mike handed Maddie a wrapped present and when she discovered a rainbow of nail polish colors inside, begged to have a manicure party right now.

The hospital had removed her polish when they'd prepped her for surgery.

While Maddie blew on her wet nails and the fumes threatened to suffocate them all, she asked the question he'd been dreading.

"Where's Lia, Daddy?"

Gabe shifted Emmy to his other knee—she'd surgically attached herself to him since they'd come home—and sighed. He glanced at Mike, eyebrows raised. Mike crossed his arms and shook his head.

"I don't know, Ducky." And that was the truth. "She's leaving soon. She may have already left."

"But I thought—" she began and then bit her lip.

"What?"

"I thought you were gonna get married."

He nodded once. "I thought so too, but she didn't want to."

"Did you break up?" she asked.

"Yeah." It was for the best, he told himself for maybe the hundredth time. So why didn't he believe it?

"Gabe." Linda put a hand on his shoulder, gave it a rub. "Why don't you try to grab some sleep in the other room? She's fine. She's home and she's going to be just fine."

Sleep. He'd forgotten what that was. "Yeah. Maybe." He dragged himself off the sofa, tucked Maddie in, made sure she had her bear, and sternly told all the girls not to play rough, hug, dance, or run around. He used the bathroom, and then collapsed onto the bottom bunk in the girls' bedroom.

It was a long time before sleep finally took him under and his dreams weren't of his daughter. They were of Lia.

"HERE YOU GO, sweetie."

"You're the best, Ro."

"Of course I am." Roseann tucked the blanket around Lia's legs.

Lia didn't laugh this time. She was too raw, too busy beating herself up to appreciate Roseann's wit. She accepted the hot mug of coffee Roseann gave her, but it did little to stop her shivers. She was fairly certain nothing could make her feel warm again. Outside, snow glistened in the fading sunlight, one last blizzard before spring. Lia hated March. Yesterday, it had been too warm for a jacket and today, it was back to Arctic blasts of cold. "I really appreciate you letting me crash on your couch."

Roseann rolled her eyes heavenward. "So you've said

about a hundred times now. Knock it off."

Lia sighed, burrowed deeper into the blanket. "How could he do that, Ro?" she whispered. "He said he loved me, said he was in love with me. How could he send me away like that? He won't answer my calls or texts. He won't even tell me if Maddie is okay!"

Fresh tears clogged her throat and Roseann handed her a tissue from the box on the table by the sofa. Roseann wrapped her arms around Lia while she cried. "Shhh, Lia. Maddie's fine. I talked to Gabe's friend, Mike. She's home and she's fine. Gabe, on the other hand, is miserable."

"Good." Lia clapped a hand over her mouth. "I didn't mean that."

"Yes. You did and it's fine. You're entitled to that much." Roseann brushed unwashed hair out of Lia's face. "Sweetie, listen to me. I'm not defending him and I'm not taking sides, but I need you to listen to me. Gabe has been through hell, more than once. He's reacting to *those* experiences, not to you. The same way you react to Jared and your idiot father, he's reacting to *his* past. That's what this is about. I promise you, when he calms down, when life gets back to normal, he'll call."

"No." Lia lifted her head. "He won't."

She knew him. She knew she'd crushed his heart and he would go back into his cocoon. Maybe in a year or two, he'd find a way to see her, talk to her. But forgive her?

No.

He'd do whatever was necessary to protect himself from more pain.

"Then maybe you should."

"I can't."

"Yes. You can. You can go straight over there, knock on his door, and—and propose to him."

"Propose! Roseann—"

"Lia, you've been glued to this couch for days, crying about how much you love Gabe and didn't mean to hurt him. Go tell *him* that."

"But what if—"

"No! Damn it, Lia. Gabe's right about that part. You don't get guarantees. We don't know if a guy's married with two-point-five kids and a dog. We don't know if he's gonna take off with his golf buddy or fall in love with the airhead upstairs just when we find out we're pregnant with his baby. We don't know, Lia."

Roseann's eyes held pain of her own and Lia looked away. Love shouldn't be this hard. It just shouldn't.

"It's a risk, Lia. A leap of faith. Sometimes, we roll the dice and get the seven. Other times, we crap out. Honey, I don't know Gabe the way you do but even I can see he's as loyal as they come. One woman, Lia. His whole life, he's been with one woman and now he wants to make it two. I'd say your odds don't get any better than that."

Lia couldn't speak. She'd heard every word Roseann said, but fear and doubt were still wrapped around her heart like damn boa constrictors.

"We know something else, too." Roseann handed Lia another tissue. "We know that if you don't take that leap of faith, the odds of you ever being happy again are next to nothing. You gotta be in it to win it, remember?"

Abruptly furious with both of them, Lia kicked off her

blanket. "I'm taking a shower."

"You go ahead, sweetie," Roseann said. "But if you think you're gonna be able to just wash any of this away, you'll be disappointed."

Disappointed? Lia almost laughed. Disappointment would be a step up. "I'll get dressed and get out of *your* hair."

Roseann narrowed her eyes and followed Lia into the bathroom. "Hey, this is me you're talking to. I don't do the ice-cream-and-chick-flicks thing. I do the ass-kicking thing and your ass is the one that needs kicking here. I get why you left. What I don't get is why you haven't been back there, in his face, forcing him to deal with you."

"It's not that simple!" Lia whirled on her best friend. "I didn't trust him, Ro. I didn't believe him when he told me, showed me in a dozen different ways, that he loved me."

"Why the hell not?" Roseann shouted.

"Because!" she yelled right back. "Because I'm…I'm scared! For God's sake, Ro, I'm a train wreck. I can't have kids, I can't for the life of me figure out my own parents, and I can't understand why Jared preferred a vapid child over me." She slapped a hand to her chest. "Don't you get it? There is obviously nothing lovable about me. Nothing."

The pathetic honesty of those words echoed in the small bathroom and ricocheted around Lia's heart. Unable to bear it anymore, she dissolved into another fit of tears and cried until she was empty.

When she lifted her head, Roseann thrust a roll of toilet paper at her.

"You done now?" she asked.

With swollen, red-rimmed eyes, Lia glared back at her.

"Yeah. I am."

"Good. Shower and get dressed. I'll drive you over there."

"Fine."

"Damn right." In the bathroom doorway, she turned, looked Lia right in the eye and said, "I love you. I've loved you since we were in first grade so don't try to feed me that bullshit again."

"Okay."

"And one more thing."

With a long-suffering sigh, Lia put her hands on her hips. "What?"

"If he ever does something like hook up with an upstairs bimbo, *then* I'll kick his ass. Meanwhile, you love him. You love him as much—more than—he loves you. Got it?"

"Yeah."

The door slammed after Roseann.

Lia had to admit, the hot water did wonders to improve her outlook. So did the time alone to reflect on certain mistakes.

Gabriel was a good man. He'd given her no reason to doubt him. She would spend the rest of her life apologizing to him for that. But first, she had to get him to agree to see her.

She dressed in jeans and a sweater, didn't bother with makeup.

"Lia. You might want to see this." Roseann held up Lia's cell phone.

Lia snatched the phone, heart thudding against her ribs. "It's from Gabriel."

"ANYBODY SEEN MY phone?" Gabe asked the girls.

He'd tossed it on to the kitchen counter after he'd spent most of the night shoveling and plowing. Another snowstorm had dropped nearly a foot of snow over Bayside. Since he wasn't sleeping anyway, he'd grabbed the baby monitor, and cleared snow a bit at a time all throughout the night. There was something soothing about snow in the middle of the night. All the quiet and the clean made him…not *content,* exactly. But close to it.

It had been a few weeks since he'd seen Lia. Three, actually. Maddie had returned to school. The grandparents went home. Mike was working in Pennsylvania, on a new property he intended to rehab. Emmy was talking nearly as much as Maddie now. She'd be three this month. He was trying hard to be happy about it. Three years down and just fifteen more to go before he could consider himself *done.* His last child would be an adult—at least so far as the law went.

Fifteen more years.

He could hold out that long. He'd made it almost three years, hadn't he? He waited for the pain, braced for it, as he'd learned to do. But it was different now. Less sharp, with all the jagged edges a bit dull. But when he allowed himself to look inside, it wasn't only Janey he saw. Even though she was gone, he loved her and always would. He loved what they'd made together…their daughters and their life.

But things had changed.

He loved Lia, too. He loved her with a bone-deep intensity that filled him with the kind of hope that he'd been sure had died with Janey. Hope for the future they'd build, hope for the dreams they'd make, the girls they'd raise.

Janey's death left him wounded and bleeding. Lia healed him, showed him what still *could be*.

Though she was gone, too—it wasn't because of death. It was because of *fear*. He wished he could tell her everything would be fine, but he'd be lying. Life, as miraculous as it could be, often sucked. It kicked you around, slit you open, and laughed at you while you tried to regain your balance. You had two choices, to his mind. You either checked out, like he'd done after Janey died, or you moved forward.

He was moving forward this time.

He was doing his best to get through one day at a time. He got up every morning, fixed hair into braids and pony-tails without tangles, now that Lia had taught him that trick with the special brush and spray conditioner. He made breakfast, took kids to school, answered tenants' calls, washed clothes and dishes, put away toys, played with Emmy, got kids from school, supervised homework, made dinner, collapsed into restless sleep and did it all over again the next day. He checked out some pre-schools with Emmy, took Maddie to the acting class Lia had given her for Christmas. If he occasionally barked at the girls, they didn't talk back. They just gave him a sad little look and backed off.

He suspected they'd had a family meeting or two with-out him.

The only thing he hadn't gone back to was work. He'd told Jim that he could consult from time to time, but even part-time, getting to and from the city with four other schedules to manage was just asking for trouble.

No shame in admitting that he wasn't Superman.

He almost laughed. That's what Lia and her friend Roseann called him. The Super Man. Yeah, well, strong he might be and fast, too. But not indestructible.

When he quietly stepped back inside where it was warm, he found Kimberly on the couch.

"Cocoa-Pop. You okay?"

She shrugged. "I heard you go out. I got scared."

"I'm sorry, sweetheart. I was taking care of the snow."

She shrugged again. "It's okay."

Uh-oh. He knew that tone. "It's not okay. Don't say it is when it's not."

Her eyes snapped to his. "What about you, Daddy? You always say you're okay when we all know you miss Lia."

"I'm—" He bit his lip. He was about to say he was *fine*, but that would have made her point. He nodded and shoved his frozen hands into his pockets. "Okay, fine. When did you get this smart?"

"Liv's not the only smart one in the family, you know."

He lifted his hands. "Sorry."

"Daddy, we have to call her. We have to give her another chance. You're so sad and it makes us sad. Even Emmy."

"No, sweetheart. We just need more time to get over it." He walked down the hall to the bathroom because he was done with this conversation. You can't change a mind that was made up. That's why he asked Lia to leave. He could give her all the time in the world, but it wouldn't change how she felt. Nothing would.

She loved him. He was sure of that. And she loved the girls. But her fear eclipsed her love and that's the part he was doing his best to get past. Didn't she get how huge, how colossal *his* fears were? He'd scaled some huge structures during his career—bridges, skyscrapers, and a monument or two—but this? It was a long way down but he'd risked the fall because Mike was right. The risk was the reward. *Lia* was the reward. He could see it, he could see the life they could have built together and—aw, hell.

Move on.

They'd spent the day watching movies in his living room bed. One movie stretched into two. Gabe dozed from time to time while the girls watched, chatted, played, and giggled. When he woke, he could tell by the way all four of them were staring at him that he'd apparently suffered another makeover and hoped he wasn't wearing blue sparkly eye shadow.

Pink fingernails, okay. But he drew the line at blue sparkly eye shadow.

He staggered to the bathroom and grinned. They'd clipped his hair into something that looked like a Mohawk. Maybe he'd let it grow even longer so they could braid *his* hair. He kept the clips and headed to the kitchen, browned the meat for the stew, added some stock, and set it to simmer. He looked around when he heard a buzz.

"You found my cell? Who is it?"

Kimberly held his phone, thumbs blurring over the screen. "Uh, it's Uncle Mike. I'm telling him about our movie." Kim glanced at Maddie, who immediately leaped for the shelf where he stored the board games.

"Daddy, can we play a game?" Maddie asked, holding The Game of Life in her hands.

God, he *hated* this game. "Sure can, Ducky. Are you sure this is the one you want to play? I'd like to play Clue myself."

"Okay! Let's play Clue. I want to be the red lady. Can I be red, Daddy? Can I please? Please?"

He laughed. It was so good to have her back to her normal self.

"You called it first, so yes. You get to be Miss Scarlet. But later, okay? Let's watch our movie."

"Okay. But *I* want to snuggle with you now."

Smiling, he stretched out on the bed and made room for her to curl against his side. There was a little skirmish when Emmy stuck out her lip and said, "My dad-dee." Luckily, he was able to get them to reach a peace accord without involving the UN.

"Your hair looks pretty, Daddy."

"I like it."

"You do?"

"Sure. Hey, Kimmy, where did you put my phone?"

Kimberly got up, ran down the hall. "Bathroom. Be right back."

"Can we do my hair next? I want it up with my tiara. Where is my tiara?" And then Maddie let out a typical Maddie-like gasp. "I know! We can play dress-up, Daddy. I want to wear Kimby's birthday dress. Can I? I can, right? Right?"

Gabe glanced at the clock on the cable box. How could it only be two o'clock? He flung an arm around her, held her in place. "Snuggles first. Then movie. Then, maybe later, dress-up, as long as your sister doesn't mind."

She clutched him tight for about half a second, then took off down the hall to find Kimberly, which meant Emmy needed to follow.

"Quick, Liv! Come here. Seize the moment." He snagged her ankle, dragged her toward him for a hug, making her giggle.

The second movie ended near three o'clock. Gabe checked the stew, told the girls they could squeeze in a game before dinner. But one game became two and Gabe figured, it was stew. You can't really overcook it.

"Daddy, can we make a snowman?" Maddie asked after Kimberly guessed Mr. Plum in the library with the knife.

He considered it and decided they'd been holed up all day, so why not? He turned off the stew. "Okay."

"Yay!"

Maddie ran down the hall for her boots. He followed, managed to get Emmy zippered into her snowsuit, then dragged on his own snow gear.

"I found a scarf, Daddy!" Olivia said.

"And a hat." Kimberly held one up.

Outside, in the center of the courtyard, he directed the girls on how to collect snow and pack it into a large ball. Maddie ran around, looking for appropriate stick arms. The Vellas heard them playing and came out to join them, little Mason encased in a snowsuit just like Emmy. Mrs. Morgan watched from her window, opening it just long enough to hold out a carrot for the snowman's nose.

The bottom ball took a while until the kids figured out how to work together. They got the middle and top balls in place and Maddie had just stuck in the arms when Emmy let out a shriek.

"Leeee-uh!"

Gabe whipped around, not enjoying the sensation of his heart jumping for joy at the same time his stomach fell. Ah, hell. His eyes skimmed her from head to toe, took in the black coat she'd let Kimberly wear for that magical birthday dinner Lia'd helped him arrange. Her hair was down and she wore a bright white hat over it that reminded him of that quiet, clean snow he'd shoveled in the middle of the night. She looked beautiful and sad and excited all at the same time. She stood at the top of the courtyard stairs in a shaft of light from the Vellas' window and he knew he'd never get over her, not if he lived a thousand years.

Emmy took off running for her and Lia scooped her up into her arms. "Hi, Emmy."

Maddie was next.

"Lia! Lia! You're back! I'm so happy! Are you happy, too? Are you?"

"Maddie! Oh, Maddie, how are you feeling, sweetheart? Are you all better?"

"I'm all better. Wanna see my scars?" She began undressing right there in the courtyard.

Gabe was still gaping.

The Vellas exchanged a glance. "Who'd like some hot chocolate?"

"I would," Kimberly said. "Daddy?"

He couldn't tear his eyes off Lia, but managed a nod.

"Me, too!" Emmy wriggled to get free and took off after her sisters through the Vellas' kitchen door.

Gabe glanced at Mrs. Morgan's window. She'd pulled

the shade down.

It was just Lia and him in the snow-covered courtyard.

"What are you doing here, Lia?" he asked.

Her smile faded. "I got your…" She broke off with a gasp that she covered with both gloved hands.

"Lia?"

"I…oh, God, Gabriel. I think I…"

He'd never seen her so…so at a loss for words. She shook her head a few times and then seemed to make a decision. She stood straight, met his gaze and nodded. "I have something I need to fix," she finally said.

He shook his head. "Not sure this can be fixed."

She took a step closer. "It can."

She said it with such confidence, his eyebrows climbed. Where the hell was that conviction when he'd proposed? Annoyed, he clapped the snow from his hands and then waved toward his front door.

"May as well come inside since it's obvious this is gonna take a while."

He opened the door, wiped his feet, stepped aside for her to enter. He didn't invite her to sit. He didn't offer her anything to drink. He just sat on the sofa, still wearing his outdoor gear and waited for her to get to the damn point.

She stood just inside his door, glaring at him. God, she was gorgeous. Why had he made her leave?

"Gabriel, you and I went from barely tolerating each other to *in love* without any of the steps in between. We haven't even been out on a date!"

He sucked in a breath. She'd said no because he hadn't taken her out to eat? He'd tried once and look how well that turned out.

"I had no intentions of getting married again. And you had no intentions of that, either. Janey was your whole world."

Okay, so maybe she had a small point there. Crossing his arms, he let his head fall back against the couch cushion. "I've got four kids next door so would you mind getting to the point?"

Temper sparked in her eyes and she whipped the hat off her head, sending crackles of static through her auburn hair. "Oh, you want the point? Fine. Here's the point. I'm not your first anything—not your first date, your first kiss, your first love, or the mother of your children. I have nothing to offer you except the things that make me who I am, things that—in case you've forgotten—bothered you just a few short months ago. You said I butted in, passed judgment, and interfered when all I was trying to do was help. Then, you have *one* conversation with your best friend and suddenly, we're sleeping together. And then, suddenly you say you're in love with me and want us to get married and become a family and live this life with all these dreams because life is short and then you get pissed off because I don't fall into your arms in a swoon!"

He could only gape at her while she paced back and forth in front of him, punctuating various statements with a finger stabbed in his direction.

"Gabriel, you're a marvel of management, juggling the kids and this building and your job, but you keep rushing your way through life. You rush through the work on your to-do lists, you rush the girls through their day, you rush me through sex—"

"I didn't hear you complain," he shot back.

She whirled on him. "I'm not complaining, you ass! I love sex with you but God, I really love it when it takes all night and we've done that exactly once!" She raised clenched hands, shook them. "You just don't get it. I've been a few steps behind you since we met and then you streak past me to some finish line that exists only in your head while I'm struggling to catch my breath just to keep up with you. I love you and I love your girls, but you never once asked me what *I* wanted in life until the day you proposed—in a bathroom, for God's sake—while I was reeling from my ex-husband's latest betrayal! And when I asked you for time, time to make sure I'm not making another colossal mistake, you say *sure, no problem* and then ignore me for the better part of two weeks!"

He opened his mouth, but she kept right on going, which was fine by him because he hadn't really heard a word since she'd said *I love you.*

Present tense.

"And then, just when I think I've got things all figured out, your daughter gets so sick, *I* have to rush her to the hospital with no power of attorney, no legal means to make a single decision about her care! I spent all night in that hospital reassuring three other children, made sure they were fed and watered and safe, and just when I was ready to say yes—I mean, *literally* at the exact moment when I was positive that loving you, loving all of you can't possibly be a mistake, you kicked me out!"

"Lia, I'm—"

"You didn't even bother to tell me if she was okay." At that, her voice cracked and all that impressive fury dissolved. Gabe's stomach twisted. She was right. He hadn't.

Battling tears, she struggled to hold on. "You asked me *to adopt* those girls and suddenly, I'm forced to send text messages to your best friend just to find out if Maddie was even alive! God, Gabriel. God. I only came here tonight because of your text messages but if I'd known—"

"Wait, wait, wait. My *what*?"

She held out her phone. Messages *from him* lit up the screen. I miss you. The girls miss you. I love you. Come back.

Kimberly.

"It didn't occur to me that one of the girls got hold of your cell phone until I came all the way here. When you saw me, it wasn't *hope* I saw on your face. I thought...well. I guess it doesn't matter."

"What?" It *did* matter, damn it. "What did you think?"

She shook her head. "Gabriel, when I saw these texts, I had such hope we could give this another chance, that you wanted me back, but...I'm sorry. I was wrong." Lia stalked to his door.

His head spun and it wasn't until Lia opened his door that he figured out what to say. "You're not wrong. Not one bit. Close that door and come back. Please."

She didn't close the door. But she didn't walk through it either. So he walked toward her, put a hand on the door, and shut it.

"Amelia. It's not about all the firsts. I'll love Janey until my last heartbeat, but she's gone. Now it's about moving forward. *You* taught me that. For the past two years, I was sure that was impossible and then I met you and everything, every single thing in my life changed. I couldn't stop thinking about you. Wanting you. And feeling guilty for holding two women inside my heart."

Her eyes slipped shut when he admitted that.

"No, no, no. Don't do that, baby, please don't do that." He cupped her face in his hands, waited until she looked at him to say what he knew. "I was a kid when I loved Janey. It was real and it was everything and it gave me four incredible kids. I'm not a kid now, Lia. I *know* what it means to be in love. It's not all heart flutters and skin tingles. Those things are nice but that's just biology. Love is *work*, Lia. It's stomach viruses and midnight hospital runs. It's first periods and science projects. It's bills and jobs and juggling schedules and in the middle of all that, it's *choosing* you to be my partner through it all. I may have fallen in love with you by chance but I swear to God, Lia, I'm *staying* in love with you by choice so don't you ever feel sad you're not my first."

She stared at him, eyes damp, but shook her head. "But...but you said you feel guilty."

Gabe sighed. "I did. It took me a while to get over that, Lia. Mike got me to see the truth. He got me to see that I'm allowed to feel things like hope and happiness again and I did, Lia, I swear to you I did. I *do*." He put his arms around her the way he'd wanted to do since she appeared on the courtyard steps.

"I really love Mike," she said against his chest and his heart took off at a gallop because he knew exactly what she meant.

"Lia, I did bulldoze over you, I did rush you, and I did

skip a bunch of steps in the ritual but not because I was trying to hurt you and not because they don't matter. I just wanted us, Lia. I wanted to be an *us*. I was excited again. I was looking ahead and yeah, I have a problem with patience—"

"You think?"

The laugh exploded out of him at her indignant tone. He couldn't help himself. He kissed her nose. A few seconds later, she laughed, too. She tugged off his hat and that's when her own laughter bubbled up and out.

"Nice hair."

"Yeah, well it's my own fault. I fell asleep. That's risky here." He kissed her once, tender and slow, and it went on for a long, long time. "Lia?"

"Hmm?"

"I love you. I'm done feeling guilty about it."

She giggled. "Oh, the words every girl longs to hear."

He tickled her ribs. She squealed and squirmed and it was another very long time before she spoke again. "I love you, too."

His stomach pitched at the leap of faith she'd finally found the courage to take. He kissed her again.

"Um, Gabriel?"

"Mmm." He pressed a string of kisses to her cheek, her jaw, her neck, smiling to himself when he heard her struggle to talk.

"Would you…please… Will you do something for me?"

"Little busy here."

She tugged on his hair so he finally lifted his head and looked into her eyes, saw all his questions answered in their depths. Slowly, she smiled and crooked a finger. "Ask it again," she whispered.

His smile flashed and another laugh burst free but he lowered to one knee.

"Amelia. I didn't think it would be possible to say this again and mean it, but I love you. Will you marry me?"

"Yes—"

"Not done yet." He took her hands in his. "Will you raise my daughters like they were yours?"

"God, yes—"

"Still not done yet. Will you keep interfering and passing judgment and butting in for the rest of our lives and help me learn patience because I'm a better dad, a better man when you're with me?"

She sucked in her cheeks and studied him through narrowed eyes. "You should have quit while you were ahead. But, because you tacked on that last part, yes." She wrapped her arms around his neck and squeezed.

He lifted her off her feet as he stood, spun her around and kissed her. It wasn't fast or instant this time. It was slow and steady and full of promises, promises it would take them a lifetime to keep.

Epilogue

THE ALARM CLOCK on the table beside the bed rang while it was still dark outside. Lia slapped at it with a groan. It couldn't be morning. It just couldn't be. But it was. With a sigh, she hauled herself to a sitting position, scrubbed the sleep from her eyes, and lifted the covers off.

A strong arm wrapped around her, tugged her back into the warmth.

"Where are you going at this unholy hour?" Gabriel murmured, his voice thick with sleep.

"It's almost six. We've got a long day ahead of us."

He rolled her underneath him, kissed her soundly.

"Mm. Gabriel. Stop. Mmm. The girls will be awake. Mmm. Gabriel."

"We have eight minutes until the alarm rings again."

Loud sigh. "What have we discussed about rushing—"

Gabriel smiled and rolled off her, got up and strode into the bathroom inside their bedroom. "You. Me. Shower."

Giggling, she agreed. In no less than twelve minutes, he had her panting and weak-kneed.

"How do you *do* that?"

He grinned at her while he tugged on his jeans, his skin damp and fragrant. "You know that old saying about necessity being the mother of invention? That." He watched her slather on her favorite body lotion, the one that smelled like lilacs. He'd planted lilacs under their bedroom window when they'd bought this house because he said they reminded him of her. She smiled when he took the bottle and rubbed some into her shoulders.

"Don't take this wrong," he began, his breath ticking the back of her neck. "But I can't wait until you have gray hair and a couple of wrinkles."

Speechless, she spun around to glare at him.

"Okay. You're taking it wrong." He rubbed lotion on her arms. "I mean, I want us to have a long and happy life together, Lia. I want to see laugh lines around your eyes." He kissed the corner of one eye, then the other. "I want to see the proof of that long and happy life on you."

"I am. And we will." She took the lotion bottle from him, gave him a peck.

He stopped her when she opened the bathroom door. "I want time with you today." He kissed her shoulder. "I've got a site visit this morning but I'm free from eleven on. The rest of my day is paperwork. How's your schedule?"

Lia shook her head but smiled. She loved that he made time with her a priority. Now that he'd returned to Paradigm full-time, his hours were unpredictable. Good thing she got to set her own. "I've got a staff meeting at nine, client calls after that, plus I have an appointment at the winery for a tour—that's for a new cookbook one of my clients is writing. After school, Emmy has a pediatrician appointment—you wanted to be there for that, remember? That's at three-thirty. Maddie has rehearsal after school and Liv and

Kim need a ride to the mall."

"Uh…gimme a minute…" He shut his eyes, thinking. "Okay. If you can manage the pediatrician, I can grab Maddie after rehearsal ends, swing by the mall, pick up Kim and Liv at five and then be back here for dinner." He tugged on a shirt that smelled like Downy. "After that, you're mine."

Smiling, she hugged him. "I really like the sound of that."

"Me, too, Lia. Me, too."

"I'd better start breakfast. It's my turn," she said with a grimace.

Gabriel frowned and she hoped he'd take a little pity on her. "Okay, fine. I'll cook if you get the girls dressed."

"Sold!" she said with such enthusiasm, he laughed and was still laughing as he headed downstairs. He laughed a lot these days and Lia took a great deal of personal pride in that.

She dressed quickly, fastened her hair into one of the braids she'd become so adept at weaving, her gaze floating to the portraits on the wall above their bed.

There were snapshots and candids and formal studio poses. There was one of the six of them snapped at a New York City protest. The girls all wore T-shirts that said *Proud Feminist*. Gabriel's said *Men of quality do not fear equality.* There was one from the famous Dad-and-Kim birthday dinner, which was now surrounded by more such dinners.

But her favorite was the one of all of them taken earlier that summer.

Their wedding portrait.

They'd married at Linda and Stuart's home, with Mike

as best man and Roseann, Vivian, and four Ivers girls as bridesmaids. Lia had worn a simple strapless gown and Gabriel had worn a suit. They'd written their own vows and Lia had spent weeks obsessing over how to include her new daughters in the ceremony in a way that would hold special meaning for each of them. In the end, she decided instead of wearing a single wedding band, she'd wear five.

One ring from each Ivers.

They were extremely narrow bands, each just wide enough to engrave the name of one of Gabriel's daughters. The ring he'd given her was slightly wider and studded with tiny diamonds.

It had been a gorgeous summer day. Flowers spilled all over the backyard and the girls had helped their grandfather make a flower-covered arch. To her complete shock, *both* of her parents had walked her down the aisle. In the days leading up to the wedding, Lia spoke to each girl privately. She'd promised good-night kisses and bedtime stories to Emmy, and to always model what a healthy and loving marriage looked like to Kimberly. She'd promised that she'd learn how to cook something besides *Meatloaf Again* to Maddie, and to help Olivia become the kind of woman other little girls might one day read about. During the wedding, when each of Gabriel's daughters stepped up to place their own ring on Lia's finger, it was Olivia who'd broken down first and cried great big happy tears. Of the four girls, it was Olivia who called her Mama-Lia, something she'd started as a joke.

Everybody kind of liked it now.

They'd spent an amazing weekend at Montauk while the

girls stayed with Linda and Stuart. Before picking them up on Sunday, Gabriel took Lia to see a house near Linda and Stuart's that was up for sale. It was a large rambling two-story, with a three-car garage and a swing set in the backyard. They'd bought it and moved in just before school started.

The girls had some emotions to deal with. They were excited about getting new rooms and about Lia living with them but they didn't want to leave their Bayside friends. And when Maddie began begging for a baby brother, Lia told Gabriel about Roseann's selfless and loving offer to carry a child for her.

"If you want a baby, I'll do whatever I have to do to give you one," he'd told her. "But don't do it *for me*. I already have all I could ever want."

It took her a few weeks to do her typical careful and detailed analysis to arrive at a decision. With Gabriel and their girls, Lia decided their family was complete. Together, they explained to the girls that there couldn't be more children. She cried when little Emmy pressed a kiss to her tummy to make the boo-boo all better.

Those girls had become her world now.

Lia poked her head into Emmy's room. The crib was long gone. At four years old, Emmy slept in a bed with her bear and her baby blanket.

"Good morning, Emmy."

Emmy lifted her head from her pillow with a smile. "Hi, Lia. Hi. It's morning?"

"Yes, sweetheart. It's morning. What should we wear today?" She moved to the dresser, found a pair of blue shorts and a matching top. "How's this?"

"Pretty."

Lia helped Emmy brush her teeth and fix her hair. She was still a handful, still Daddy's little E-Rex, and still charming. She gave Lia a sunny smile and said, "Can you put the front up, please?"

That was her favorite hairstyle. Her hair was longer and thicker now, so Lia often scooped the front up and left the back long, where it fell in soft sunny curls to her shoulders.

"Okay, head downstairs. Daddy's making breakfast."

"Yay!"

Lia went to Maddie's room next and repeated the steps in this dance. Maddie was eight years old now, still a chatterbox and still easily distracted. Lia found her reciting lines from the play her theater group would be performing next month.

"Good morning, Dorothy. Time for you and Toto to get ready for school."

"Oh, Auntie Em, must we?"

"You must."

Giggling, Lia helped Maddie find an outfit to wear and pinned up her hair. Lia had this down to a science now. She made a narrow braid down one side of Maddie's head, fastened the rest of her hair into a bun and wrapped the braid around it. Maddie said it was the perfect style to hold her tiara on without it falling off.

When she poked her head into the room Kimberly and Olivia decided to share, she found both girls already awake and getting dressed. "Lia. I need to talk to you," Kimberly said with wide eyes and an urgent tone.

Lia remembered being fifteen. "Sure, Kim. Liv, could you give us a few minutes?"

"It's okay. Liv already knows."

Concerned, Lia sat on the bed next to Kim. "What's up, sweetheart?"

"Um. Well. There's a school dance coming up and this guy…Kaden…he asked me to go with him."

Lia's heart stuttered, then took off flying. Gabriel was going to lose his mind when he heard about this. Good thing she'd be right there to help him hang on to it. "Do you like Kaden?"

Kim shrugged. "I don't know yet. I've only been in school for like, two weeks. He seems pretty nice, but it's too soon to tell. What should I tell him?"

"Well, let me ask you this. Did he ask you to the dance as a date or did he ask you just as a friend?"

Kimberly exchanged a horrified glance with her sister. "I have no idea!"

"Okay, okay. Let's not panic. When's the dance?"

"Like three weeks."

Hoo, boy. A lot could happen in three weeks. "Okay, so there are two ways you can approach this. First, you could just go to the dance as friends. You each pay for your own night. No pressure. No expectations. Or, you could maybe invite him here one day after school to play video games and just hang out without anybody else around, see if you like each other."

Liv jumped on the bed. "Or, you could just blow off the dance, which is a totally archaic tradition that no longer has any basis in today's reality."

"That's a good suggestion, too. Thanks, Professor." Lia smiled at Olivia. "But I think Kimberly wants to go to the dance. Am I right?"

"Yeah, but—" Kimberly bit her lip and shrugged. "I think I like him. Can I invite him over today?"

Lia shook her head, remembering the family's schedule. "No, not today. But tomorrow or any other day this week is fine with me. I can juggle some client work to make sure I'm home to keep your sisters busy. And I'll help you discuss this with your dad."

Kim rolled her eyes. "He's gonna freak out."

"Yep." Olivia jumped up.

"I'll help you," Lia said again, and was rewarded with one of Kimberly's fast hugs.

Downstairs, the morning rush was its typical chaos. Maddie couldn't find the shoes she wanted to wear, Olivia's braces were killing her, Kimberly's hair looked "terrifying!" and Emmy just wanted to stay home and bake brownies. While Gabriel scooped bacon and eggs onto plates, Lia helped tame hair, administer medicine, and locate shoes and backpacks.

As soon as everybody sat down at the table, Lia took a breath and said, "Gabriel, Kim wants to invite a friend from school over one day this week. I said it would be okay on any day except today, because our schedule is so packed. His name is Kaden."

Gabriel's fork froze halfway to his mouth. "*His* name?"

"Yes. He invited Kim to the dance next month. I think we should meet him before then, don't you?"

"Yes. Yes, I absolutely do. Is he one of those guys who wears eyeliner and has tons of piercings?"

"Um. Gabriel. You wear nail polish." Lia took one of his hands. He snatched it back.

"I wear nail polish because it makes my girls smile. I'm

not rebelling against anything or anybody."

"I'm only suggesting you keep an open mind," Lia said, holding up both hands.

"We'll discuss this tonight. Girls, let's go."

He stood up, kissed Lia, and walked down the driveway with the girls. Lia set the dishes into the sink to soak and watched their neighbor, Donna, stop for Emmy. The preschool drop-off was Donna's job. Lia did the pick-ups. Emmy adored playing with Donna's little girl, a quiet child named Jennifer, who loved to draw. Lia adored Donna, who was fast becoming a close friend. Gabriel buckled Emmy into the back seat of Donna's minivan, where a booster just for her waited.

The buses chugged up their street. Maddie's was first. Lia watched from the front window as Olivia ran up the steps to her bus, calling something over her shoulder that made her father smile and wave. The high school bus was last.

She watched Gabriel stand there until all the buses and all the girls were long out of sight. She moved to the front door, stood on the porch, until he turned and noticed her there. He jogged back up the drive. She met him at the bottom of the porch steps, put her arms around him.

"You knew this day would come."

"She's fifteen, Lia."

"Almost the same age you were when you first set eyes on her mother."

He groaned and shut his eyes. "You are so not helping."

"Yes. I am." She wrapped her arms around his waist, rose up on her toes to kiss him. "I'm reminding you that you've raised a whole crop of good kids. She's not going to do anything risky."

"It's not her I'm worried about, it's him. What the hell kind of name is Kaden, anyway?"

"That's what we're going to find out when she invites him over. And one of us will drive him home so we can check out the family, too."

Gabriel stared at her in amazement. "Every once in a while, you show a devious side. I like it. It's kind of a turn-on." He glanced at his watch. "You know, I don't have to be anywhere for fifteen more minutes."

She smiled at him. "We've discussed this. You know how I feel about rushing these things. We have all night, every night."

She saw the cloud pass over his face, the one that told her he was scared that might not be true for them, just like it wasn't true for Janey. But in true Gabriel form, he battled it back and kissed her cheek before heading for his truck. "Okay. See you later."

As she watched him walk away, the way he wore his jeans made her think patience wasn't always a virtue. "On the other hand," she called out. "It is a long, long time until tonight." And then she ran.

It took him a second. Then he was chasing her into their house, shedding clothes as he ran up the stairs to the bedroom where they would make the most of however much time they'd have, knowing even if it was a lifetime, it would still never be long enough.

The End

More by Patty Blount

The Paramedic's Rescue

A Match Made at Christmas

Available now at your favorite online retailer!

About the Author

Powered by chocolate, **Patty Blount** is a hopeless romantic who frequently falls in love with fictional characters, only to suffer repeated broken hearts when the story ends, kicking her back out into the real world. Goodness and Light is her first contemporary romance for adults—to date, three of her novels for teens have been published, with a fourth expected in 2015.

For more from Patty:
Visit her website at PattyBlount.com

Thank you for reading

Nobody Said It'd be Easy

If you enjoyed this book, you can find more from all our great authors at TulePublishing.com, or from your favorite online retailer.

Made in the USA
Middletown, DE
16 January 2019